Southern

Rain

BOOK ONE, TORN ASUNDER SERIES

TARA COWAN

Chapter One

Adeline crossed the bridge and into the Holy City, changing lanes when the car in front of her seemed to be panicking. It was almost evening, and the wind was up. Waves lapped beneath her, and the bridge appeared to be swaying a little. Another time, the swaying might have freaked her out, but she was more concerned right now with finding Battery Street and arriving there by five o'clock. Her new employer had been very firm on that point. And something told her she didn't want to tick him off right from the start. His tone over the phone had been a bit terse.

Of course, that could have something to do with the fact that she had demanded in-house quarters. He had first said he wouldn't be able to accommodate her, obviously not understanding that for a preservationist, housing was key. It was different for her crew: being men, they could pile up in a rent house and split the minimal cost.

Still, the job was the site of a lifetime, and she would've signed and broken a lease when she left if necessary. But she had suspected the owner was playing hardball and that he had really wanted her, too. So Adeline had taken a risk and said that, in that case, she was afraid she wouldn't be able to come. There had been a long silence on the phone. But he had called her the next day to say that he thought they could make arrangements. And she had smelled victory.

She made a left down a tree-lined street full of houses. She wanted to just stare at them for hours. There was so much to restore, too. She mentally gave a mid-nineteenth century a fresh coat of protective paint, shored up the falling balcony, and painted a porch ceiling blue. But she had no time to tarry today.

It had been a long time since she had been to Charleston, and she was in awe of its beauty. She was also a little lost. The drivers weren't pushy like they were in Asheville, but the roads were narrow. And Siri was being a little twit, telling her to make a U-turn, apparently not recognizing roads that had been there for hundreds of years.

She tossed her phone into the passenger seat and drove toward the ocean. She knew of the street, of course: it was every historian's dream. But she hadn't visited since she had toured Edmondston-Alston House with her parents about twelve years ago. She saw a seagull. "Okay, you're a good sign—no, get away!" She swerved to avoid it and heard an oncoming car lay down on its horn. She jerked back into her lane and looked behind her. She bit her lip, seeing the other car right itself.

But she had found Battery Street, with three minutes to spare. She stepped on the gas a little, since there was an old truck tailing her. Apparently not everyone was as mesmerized by the breath-taking scenery as she.

In the few minutes she had left to get there, she went over in her mind everything she knew about the man who owned the house. She glanced at her purse and dug out the card where she had written his name and cell number haphazardly. *Adrian Ravenel.* She hadn't been able to find out his age, but he had sounded relatively young on the phone, or at least under forty. He was apparently a psychiatrist. He had owned his home for a couple of years and was now wanting to restore it to its former glory. And he wanted to do it right.

Somehow, he had known one of her professors from North Carolina and had asked for names of preservationists. Dr. Hadley had given hers, giving her the opportunity of a lifetime. She had finished the job in Raleigh and made preparations to move to Charleston. Not that it was a huge move. Her Rav-4 was loaded down, but it held basically everything she owned.

"Which one are you?" she said, a little on edge. Then she saw it, recognizing it from the pictures the owner had emailed her. It was a grand dame wedged between two slightly larger ladies. It was painted a butter yellow color and had three porches and balconies, one on top of the other. There was an observatory at the top from which the residents of the house had probably watched the Battle of Fort Sumter once upon a time. Her pulse accelerated at the nearness of history. Then she looked at the clock, and excitement dissipated as nerves began. One minute.

She turned into the driveway, which took her around to the back of the house. She felt like she had invaded deeply private family areas which no one in the Victorian Era would've seen just calling for a party. There were wonders all around her, but she reached for her purse and got out quickly. Her legs were a little weak from the drive, but at least her white Loft trousers weren't too wrinkled, and her heels, turquoise blue, were pristine. She looked in her car mirror at her hair, short with springy blonde curls, and checked her make-up. Not exactly fabulous, but it would have to do.

Using her historical instinct, she went around to the front of the house, the wind whipping her hair, and used the big knocker. There was no answer, so she plied it again, louder this time. She looked up. The porch roof was clean but in bad shape. She hoped no one used the balconies above it just now.

Finally, the door opened, and a tall man with a graceful build opened the door. She would put him mid-thirties in reality, but he looked younger, his black hair parted neatly on one side and swooping down a little on his forehead, straight and fine. His face was attractively chiseled, his eyes dark and confident but reserved.

"Dr. Ravenel, I hope," she said.

"Yes, come in," he answered, stepping back to allow her entrance. She crossed the threshold onto ancient battered wood floors. They creaked but held so much promise. She looked around her. There was a turned staircase which graced the end of the room. It seemed to be in good shape, but she would have her crew check it out. The impossibly high ceilings were fabulous, but the crown molding was decayed from its once intricate glory, and the chandelier was too modern, as was the paint color.

"I hope you had a good trip," he said, as though being polite.

She dragged her eyes away from the possibilities around

her and nodded. "I did, thank you. My crew will arrive in three days, after I've been able to scope out what needs to be done."

He nodded, seeming to study her, to take her measure. She felt like he was psychoanalyzing her and cut her eyes away, not wanting to reveal too much. He had a look about him that made her think, uncomfortably, that he knew what made you tick. "Come into the library," he said. "There's some tea." She smiled, following him. It wouldn't be the South without tea.

She was tempted to look around as they walked but knew she needed to talk terms with him. Exploring could wait until tomorrow. Still, she couldn't help but notice the stunning view of the harbor or the white built-ins which gave the room a light, cheerful feeling. He sat across from her in the chairs in front of the fireplace. It wasn't lit, and she would be surprised if it worked.

"You say the job will take about five months," he said, apparently all business.

"Yes, although if we hit snags, as many as seven." She had found it was important to be honest about those things.

He nodded once. "This crew you speak of—have they had background checks?"

She lifted her brows, surprised by the question. "Of course. The foreman has been in this business for twenty years—he knows as much about preservation as I do, or at least about how it works in actual operation."

"Do any of them have a criminal background?" he asked, apparently not impressed.

She was astounded. "Well, yes, Jose had a DUI seven years ago. Will that be a problem?"

"No," he surprised her again by saying. He sat back, long fingers around his sweating glass. It seemed as though air conditioning had been installed in some of the rooms, but that had probably been in the seventies, and it seemed to be struggling. "Your resume said your Ph.D. came from North Carolina?"

She nodded. "Yes, it did," she answered, suddenly wondering whether he was going to ask for her transcript.

"It must be a good school to have held onto Dr. Hadley this long," he said.

She smiled. "The best, in my opinion. How do you know him?"

"He was my dad's college roommate. They've been friends ever since," he said. Apparently ready to move on, he lifted his eyes as though contemplating whether they had gone over everything. She couldn't imagine there would be much more. She had signed his massive contract electronically, and they had discussed terms. He had driven a hard bargain, but he hadn't skimped on the commission. She would give him that. "Jane's not here, but I can show you to your room. She'll want to show you how the house operates—I mean the parts we live in. I can answer any questions you have when I get home from work in the evenings."

"All right," she said chipperly, standing with him.

"Jane was concerned about our living quarters," he said, holding the door for her and letting her pass through. "Is there any chance that you can work on one room at a time?"

"Not if you want to keep to the five-month schedule, I'm afraid," she said. "Often, we have to let certain projects lie for a period before touching them again, and we're generally working on something else during those times."

He grunted, leading her up the splendid staircase.

She winced. "Will she be very upset?"

"It'll just have to be."

"I'll be sure to leave areas for you to live as I go," she said, following him into the upstairs hall.

"The family quarters are that way," he said, nodding to the right. "We'll move out when you get to those rooms. I assume we'll be able to at least move into a different bedroom?"

"Oh, yes, of course. As I said, I'll leave one open at all times," she answered, surprised when they started up another flight of stairs. He didn't seem to be winded at all at the top of them, and she kept her lips shut, breathing quietly but quickly through her nose, pretending she wasn't either.

This part of the house looked like it hadn't been touched since 1862. And not in a good way. He led her all the way to the end of the hall, where he opened a door which squeaked miserably. She followed him into a room which was apparently in the eave of the house. Being tallish, she had to walk bent over in part of it. There was a narrow twin bed which at least appeared to have fresh linens on it. But she bet it squeaked and was hard. The rest of the furniture was sparse: a battered chair here, a barren dresser there.

"Well, I'll leave you to it, then," he said. She studied him, her eyes slightly narrowed. There was an almost imperceptible gleam in his eyes. This was payback; she would bet her life on it. Either that, or an attempt to get her to find her own lodgings. Well, she understood not wanting to take a stranger into your home and not having the ability to watch TV at night without a bra on, or whatever the male equivalent of that was.

But he *had* agreed to it, and dank lodgings were better than spending a third of her commission on rent. And so she said, "Great. This will do nicely."

He looked mildly disappointed.

She spent the whole next day going over the house, armed with her clipboard and the numbers for her usual suppliers. The absolute first thing would have to be stabilizing the balconies. It would cost an arm and a leg, but this house would be nothing without them. And apparently the Ravenels had gotten a historic grant for part of the project, so that would help.

She needed to speak with Dr. Ravenel about a few matters, but he had been gone before she awoke. She jotted notes down (after risking her life on the upper balcony) that she would ask him when he got home.

It was important for her to find the innate character of every house, to get down to its bones, to feel the lives it had led. She went into a large downstairs room that was now being used mostly for storage and looked around. She was unsure what the room had even been used for originally. She bit her lip, gazing at the thick white molding and the battered floors. The green printed wallpaper was expensive and had a certain richness to it, but it had probably been hung in the 1960s. Anything with a 19 in front of it simply wasn't allowed in this house.

Laying the clipboard aside, she turned to one of the corners by the door and flecked the paper up with her nail. "Come on," she gently coaxed, being very careful. She saw a very pale turquoise, a popular color from the Jacksonian Era, and her heart sped. She pulled a little more carefully, expecting a paint. If it appeared to be original, they would have to reproduce it with a good copy. But then she felt it and realized it was a fabric. "Are you silk?" she breathed, pulling up just a bit more and running her fingers over it.

Gasping, she released the wallpaper and backed away, rising with wonder. The family who had lived here, whoever they had been, had been extremely wealthy. And she wouldn't dare touch that for fear of damaging it. She needed Joe and the crew and a thousand supplies. And a guillotine for whoever had papered over it. "Okay. I'll leave you," she said, backing away and hoping to heaven she could save it. She was already picturing a framed scrap of it on the wall and a tour guide saying, "This was what the *original* wallpaper looked like." She shuddered.

Adeline went on to other rooms. When next she looked up, she realized it was late in the afternoon. She heard the front door click open and closed, and she went out onto the second-floor landing to look below. A thin woman in her early sixties with clipped short silver hair entered, holding the hand of a little boy in a posh school uniform. He was a precise miniature of Dr. Ravenel, and a voiceless, "Oh!" left Adeline's lips rather in the way that happened when one saw a box of cute puppies. He didn't look like he felt well, and the woman stroked his hair, letting him lay his head against her as they walked.

They disappeared beyond her sight, and the wheels in her mind turned. Dr. Ravenel hadn't mentioned a child. He couldn't be more than six years old. That would make everything more difficult. He would be bound to get into everything, so they would have to keep it secured, both for his safety and for the protection of the relics and supplies.

Deciding it was time to find out more about the familial situation she would be working around, Adeline brushed her hands off and went downstairs. She found her way to the kitchen, knocking and entering, surprised to find a fully modern room with marble countertops, white cabinets, stone floors, and a sleek island. She sighed. She didn't think it would hurt the character of the house, and they had to eat, after all. She didn't see the Ravenels wanting to cook nineteenth century style, however much she coaxed.

The woman was putting a snack in front of the little boy but looked up, surprised.

"Hi, I'm Adeline Miller," she said, smiling, hands in her back pockets. "Dr. Ravenel probably mentioned the project."

"Oh, yes," the woman said, shoulders easing, smiling back. "He did. Nice to meet you. He says you're from North Carolina."

She nodded. "Are you his mother?"

"No. I *have* known him since he was smaller than this one, though. I retired from my job as a legal secretary, and then my husband died, and I didn't like the silence. The Ravenels needed a nanny, and I needed them," she said, adding a sliced apple to the snack.

The little boy looked up at Adeline with big black eyes, his hair falling this way and that on his forehead. Adeline smiled at him and then at the woman. "I'm glad you found what you needed," she said. "I'll let you get back to it," she added, seeing the woman was pulling a thermometer from a drawer. "I just wanted to ask if you know Dr. Ravenel's schedule?"

"He's lucky if there *is* a schedule," she said, sticking the thermometer beneath the boy's arm. "Hold that down—don't wiggle, child. He's supposed to work from eight until five. He drops this one off at school and then heads over to work. I pick Jude up from school, and he's usually home by six. Oh, and he teaches a night class at the College of Charleston on Thursdays, so it's nine o'clock on those nights."

Adeline lifted her brows. It would be difficult to catch him. "Thank you."

The woman nodded, checking the temperature with her glasses halfway down her nose. "You're welcome dear. Forgive me, I need to call his father," she said, looking up apologetically.

Adeline winced sympathetically. "Yes, of course."

She was almost out the door when the woman called, "I'm Jane Lindsey, by the way."

Adeline stopped, looking at her quickly. "Oh! I thought Mrs. Ravenel was Jane."

Mrs. Lindsey looked at the boy, a little on edge, and shook her head. She was seemingly relieved when he went on licking the peanut butter off his bread, his fever apparently not affecting his appetite. "No, just me," she said, with an attempt at cheerfulness. "I'll send him to you when he gets home." And with that, Adeline left the room, her thoughts in a tangle of confusion.

Chapter Two

It was April, and the evening shadows had not quite begun to fall at six o'clock. Adeline, having taken a shower, put on comfier clothes, and wrapped her curls with her favorite bandeau, went outside to bring in the rest of her things. She crossed the brick pavers to her car and had just opened the back hatch when a black Land Rover turned in. She pulled one of her boxes toward her and attempted to lift it. Okay, it was heavier than she remembered. She would wait until Mr. Ralph Lauren model got in the house before she hefted it in.

She heard his door close and was surprised when he came around behind her car. "Hi!" she said in a friendly manner.

He nodded his greeting. "How did everything go today?"

"Great! So many stories waiting to be told." She pushed the box back. "Speaking of which: do you know any of the history of the house? Oh, wait. Never mind, you can tell me tomorrow. Your son is sick, isn't he?"

He lifted his brows, apparently surprised at her knowledge.

"Yes. But we couldn't get him an appointment today, so I'll be taking him to the doctor tomorrow. What did you say you needed?"

She brushed a corkscrew curl back with her clean hand. "I always like to incorporate the history of the house, find out as much as I can about it before I dig in. Do you know if there are any records? Did it have a name?"

"I think in the twentieth century it was called the Ravenel-Thompson House, after the two previous owners."

Her heart jumped with historical interest. "Oh, you have a connection to the house, then," she said.

He nodded. "An ancestor built it in the early 1830s. I think the Ravenels had it up through the 1890s, when they sold it to the Thompsons. Our parents used to drive us by when we were kids, telling us the family story."

"What is the family story?" she asked.

He lifted a shoulder. "They had a plantation on the Ashley and would come here for the social season in the winter. I'm not really sure about the particulars. We're not really a historical family—except my brother. But it was John Ravenel who built it, if that helps."

"It does: thank you." She turned back to her depressing mound of boxes, surprised when he didn't leave.

"Do you need help with any of that?"

She looked up, raising her brows. "Why... Yes, thank you. If you could take this one inside, I would be appreciative."

He lifted it, despite his perfect white shirt and tie, and took it toward the door. He didn't return, but he did carry it all the way to the top floor, so it was a start.

Not yet provided with the wi-fi password, Adeline sat down on her bed with her phone, running up data but needing to research the Ravenels. The mattress was just as hard as she had thought it would be.

Apparently *Ravenel* was a big name in these parts, as her grandfather would've said. They were some of the first settlers and had been at the very highest rung of society, comparable with names like Middleton and Alston. They were French Huguenots. Persecuted for their religious beliefs in France, many families had fled to South Carolina. Despite their oppressed history, many had become owners of slaves.

Adeline hoped to incorporate the history of all who had lived here, slave and free. Though how she was to do so when she was having difficulty tracking down the right John Ravenel, she couldn't say.

She thought a good place to start was to look for their plantation among the Ashley River Road plantations. She searched "Ravenel" and "Ashley River plantation" but found nothing. It could've been burned or auctioned off so long ago that the connection was tenuous. Still, she would've thought there was something. It didn't sound like it was mere familial puffery. (Adeline didn't think she was really a descendant of Queen Elizabeth's hypothetical illegitimate child, as her Uncle Dave asserted, for instance.) The Ravenels were certainly a well-connected family, historically speaking, and most people who had owned homes on this street had indeed been planters.

Frustrated, she decided she would need her laptop. Her

contact lenses were annoying her, and the small print seemed to be getting smaller.

Almost ready to go to bed, she decided to Google "Adrian Ravenel, psychiatrist." She found his office's website immediately and then read a few reviews. It seemed most were well-pleased, raving about his knowledge and intuition and his caring manner. She checked the particular doctor's name again. Yep, the same one. Hmm. She raised and lowered her brows.

She scrolled on down the returned search list, seeing his page on the college's website about his psychology course. There also seemed to be an article about when he bought the house, one of those local history spotlights.

She wondered about his wife. After figuring out her earlier mistake, she wondered whether he might be divorced, since she hadn't seen the woman. Dr. Ravenel seemed to have primary custody of the child if that was the case. Maybe she just hadn't yet made an appearance; maybe she was high-society in that way. But there was no doubt that the Jane he had spoken of was the nanny.

Her heart jumped in her throat. She saw a link to a newspaper article, the title: "Local Psychiatrist's Wife Killed in Car Accident." She hoped that had nothing to do with him, but why would a search of his name turn it up unless it was one of those annoying flukes? She clicked on it, moistening her lips when she read the first line. "Lauren Ravenel, Charleston socialite and wife of renowned local psychiatrist, Adrian Ravenel, was killed yesterday in an I-95 collision. A native of Savannah, Georgia, Mrs. Ravenel—" It cut off, offering to let her purchase a subscription.

Adeline swallowed, her heart beating fast, stomach twisting with the sick feeling that things like that really did happen. One could almost pretend they didn't, that people didn't die young. There was no good reason it should be so shocking when, of course, she had known people who were in similar situations. Dr. Ravenel could probably tell her that it was the mind trying to shut off reality to cope, or something. It sounded like something he would say.

Her mind whirled with the new development. She bit her lip, thinking of the little boy she had seen in the kitchen, and the man who, while he seemed cold, must have loved his wife. She was glad she had looked now, so she wouldn't say anything else. The nanny seemed to have been ordered not to talk about it in front of the child.

Still, she felt guilty, invading someone's personal life, and she clicked out of all of it quickly. Gosh, what if he found out she had done that? It was unprofessional. She wouldn't do it again.

Adeline descended the stairs the next morning, reflecting that she really needed to go get some groceries. She had done a couple of trips for fast food yesterday, but she couldn't do that forever. For now, she wondered if she would be allowed any fridge or pantry space.

She went into the kitchen to be brought up short by Dr. Ravenel. He was standing behind the counter in more casual clothes than he wore to work—jeans and a faded blue long sleeve T-shirt. It looked like what people who sailed wore on the boat. He was sliding a plate toward his son, who wore cute little sweatpants and a Charleston T-shirt. Dr. Ravenel looked up, dark eyes meeting hers.

She kind of caught up short, biting her cheek and thinking she should have known not to come down dressed in her sister's old exercise shorts and her brother's old Asheville High track shirt. She should've remembered that they were going to the doctor.

Oh, well. She smiled. "Headed to the doctor?"

"We've already been," he answered, passing her under scrutiny, for what purpose and with what result she didn't know.

"Oh, that was early," she said, glancing toward the fridge, wondering if he would sacrifice a bottle of water.

"There's water in the fridge."

Crap. He was a mind-reader. "Oh, thanks," she said, color unaccountably high. She walked forward and opened the industrial fridge and looked around, snagging a Nestle from the door. There were other water bottles in there, but they scared her. As she turned back around, Dr. Ravenel was saying quietly to his son, "If I took away eight of your grapes, how many would you have left?"

"Four," the boy said without even looking up.

Dr. Ravenel studied him, then looked up at her. "I hope everything went okay this morning?" she said, smiling.

"Just allergies, but he gets a day off school for it, and I get a day off work." The little boy grinned up at him, popping a grape into his mouth. Dr. Ravenel tucked the corners of his mouth in a smile. She knew that a day off work in his kind of job wasn't a treat. He would be slammed with work tomorrow. But she liked that he didn't let the little boy know.

"Oh, good," she said, wondering where Jane was. She had thought she was a live-in nanny, but—

"We gave Jane the day off. She's gone to visit some friends."

"Oh, good for her," Adeline said.

Suddenly all she could think about was her legs, which were quite visible in her shorts. They were a little bit chicken-like, and her knees were knobby, but they were pretty long, and someone—she couldn't remember whom—had once told her they were pretty. Or maybe that was her feet. They were long and bony—not that one could see them in her old Toms. Oh, great, the left shoe had a stain on the top.

Realizing that she had been staring at her legs longer than was probably socially appropriate, she looked up and saw that he was watching her. Okay, embarrassment complete. Maybe she should make it look like she had been looking at a bug bite or something. Not that she really cared that much. He probably thought she was weird, but he might as well know that now, she thought.

The silence really was dragging out, though. So, she said, "I think I'll start on sanding the stain off the cabinets in the library today. I don't need the crew for that, and I'm pretty much finished with the planning process."

He didn't respond. He seemed to know she was using it as a conversation filler, and apparently, he didn't like those. "Why do you feel uncomfortable around me?" he enquired cordially.

She blinked. Okay, so much for not letting things get awkward. "Umm... That's an odd question," she said, giving him a confused look.

"I can tell you do," he said, seemingly not uncomfortable at all. "And also that you don't normally feel that way."

She lifted her brows. "How do you know that?"

"Because you're comfortable, confident," he said, still regarding her like a specimen. Well, wasn't this a fun little experiment for him. Good grief, how did his family bear it, if he did this all day? And how was he so flipping accurate?

She studied him, not knowing what to say. Nothing but candor was apparently acceptable to him. The truth was, she didn't know why she felt thrown off around him. Maybe it was because he kept surprising her, or rather, his personal life did. But if she was just doing her job, not really concerned about her host except insofar as she had to follow his requests, she wouldn't care. She usually didn't care. *The truth is, you've been interested ever since you saw him looking like a tall drink of water, Adeline Miller.*

Okay. Attraction. She wasn't used to it, but she could deal with it. She usually attracted the Jack Johnson or Jason Mraz type, but they weren't really boyfriend material. So she didn't date that much. And she was rarely attracted at all. And certainly not by this type. He was...Martha's Vineyard. Pristine, and...gorgeous. That was probably why she thought about it more than in passing. It was like her mind was afraid she had been missing out on a whole new type.

"Sorry if I've given you that impression," she said, giving a reasonable go at genuine surprise. "I'll try to notice in the future. I guess I have been a little distracted by the house."

"Never mind," he said, looking at his son, who was watching them intently. "Finished, Jude?"

"Nope," he said, still looking between them.

"Eat the rest of your toast, and we'll get you dressed."

"'Kay," he said, nibbling on his bread.

Adeline pressed her lips together for a moment before saying, "Is it... Would it be possible for you to give me your brother's number?"

He lifted his head. And his eyebrows.

She bit her lip, flushing. She almost never did so. She was basically fourteen again. "No, I'm not looking for a date. You said he was interested in history. I thought he might know something about the house. I'm having a difficult time tracking down your family's plantation, and if I could just go there, I could get a good sense of their style and tastes."

"Oh." He glanced at his watch. "He'll be in court right now, I think. But he'll be finished by the afternoon."

Now she sent him a look of enquiry.

"He's an attorney," he said flatly, giving her a level look. He turned, got a pen and paper, and wrote it down. He handed it to her. "I'll text him to let him know you'll be calling."

"Thanks!" she said. "I'll be off, then. I have a bit more inspection to do, and then I'll be in the library all day." Thank goodness she was making her escape. It would take her a couple of hours to recover.

He nodded.

"Hope you feel better, Jude," she said as she was leaving.

"Law Office of Hartman and Joyce, how may I help you?"

Adeline pressed her lips together. Great. He hadn't given her his private cell. "Hello," she said, after a pause. "May I speak with Mr. Ravenel please?"

"Just a minute, let me check... Yes, he's in. I'll transfer you."

"Thanks." She walked across her little room, glancing out the narrow dormer window, watching as a cross-over SUV parked and a woman got out, going to the trunk and pulling out what looked to be cleaning supplies.

"Hello, this is Harris Ravenel."

"Hi, this is Adeline Miller. I think Adrian told you I would be calling?"

"Oh, he probably texted me. Let me look." There was a rustling. "Oh!" he said with recognition. "Yeah, I'll be happy to help if I can, but I'll be forthcoming and admit my concentration was Modern Britain."

"Oh, that's fine," she said, smiling. "I'm mostly curious about your family's history. I take it the rest of them are more of a scientific inclination?"

He laughed. "I guess you could say that. I've never done as much research as I would like, but I always listened when my grandmother told me the family stories."

Her heart sped. "Is your grandmother still with you?"

"No," he said with a smiling wistfulness. "I'd refer you to her immediately if she were. What are you looking for?"

"At another time, any tidbits you have. But for now, I was wondering if you have any information about the plantation your family owned. I can't seem to find it. Or if I find one, it's owned by the wrong Ravenels."

"Dad always said it was on the Ashley River. That was what his grandpa told him. But I'll admit I've driven through there several times and I can't quite figure it out. Most of those houses are open for tours now with a strong family story. And it's not our family story."

That's what she had found. "Hmm." She thought for a moment. "Is it possible it was burned during the Civil War?"

"Of course it's possible. There's a reason there is only a flanker at Middleton Place."

"Yeah. But wouldn't there still be some record of the house, some mention of it in one of the other plantations' archives? If I'm correct, your family moved in the first circles. There are records of them: they just haven't made it onto the internet yet."

There was a silence, but she could picture him sitting back in his chair in deep thought. Finally, he said, "Yeah, it just doesn't fit. I'll call my dad tonight, but he isn't very interested in his family lineage," he said with a smile in his voice. "He's a chemistry professor."

"Oh, right," she said, smiling. She sat at her computer and pulled up a map of Charleston, zooming in on the river. Well, it was a fairly long river. Maybe it just hadn't been on the plantation row. "Thanks for your help."

"No problem. I'll get back with you."

"Thanks."

"All right, talk to you later."

She was about to say goodbye, when, still looking at the map, she said, "Oh, Harris?"

"Yeah?"

"Do you have any idea what it might have been called?"

"Oh. Yeah—I guess that would be helpful, actually," he said with a laugh. "Santarella. It was called Santarella."

Chapter Three

The rice plants tossed in the early autumn breeze. It was the threshing season, as the wealth of vibrant green attested while the lady cut up through the narrow path on her chestnut mare. The day was darkening before its time, and clouds were rolling in.

Slaves dotted the fields near Miss Ravenel's path as she cantered by. They were working with urgency, sweat glistening and running down their faces, even though there was a gentle breeze, the kind that stirred just before a storm. But most of them paused as she neared in the next field, watching.

The ribbons on her hat fluttered as she made her progress. Her speed was not strictly proper for a tenderly protected young lady. But there was no one about for miles; very few were even on the island. And then, reaching her destination, she halted with experienced hands.

She patted Eliza Lucas's neck as she caught her breath, blue eyes scanning the slaves absently, and then, in the distance, the Big House, brick and Palladian in style, with two flankers.

Her eyes again strayed to the fields, taking stock as the Negros would bend, scythe, and load. The low hum of their songs reached her ears. A breeze fluttered the sleeves of her riding habit. The temperature was extraordinary, and she ought to have been perfectly content. And yet a restlessness stole over her. Perhaps it was the months stretching out in front of her before the social season began after Christmas.

She jerked her head up. The dinner bell was ringng, obviously calling her to the house, though not for dinner. It wasn't yet three o'clock.

"Alright, Eliza," she said, giving the horse her head again and covering the open field in mere moments. She rode into the stable yard before continuing to the porch, where her father was standing in his gray suit and burgundy waistcoat, his arms crossed, waiting for her. "Is something wrong, Papa?" she asked, holding tightly to the gray's reins.

His silver hair and beard were striking. His eyes were deep set and contemplative, almost unknowable. He was not a tall man. But he had a presence none could deny. Neither child nor slave ever dared to cross him. "I've just received word from your brother that they'll be returning around two o'clock. It's close on two now," he said, eyes running over her horse's points with the knowledge of a connoisseur, as though checking that all was in order. He had spared no expense on Eliza when he had purchased her last year and presented her as a gift for Shannon's nineteenth birthday. "I thought you might want to be here to greet him," he added, looking back up.

"Yes, though whether he deserves it is another question."

"We have discussed this, Shannon," he said, in his thick, cultured drawl. "Young ladies do not take tours abroad."

"They might if their fathers would take them," she returned provocatively.

"And their fathers might do so if they did not have business affairs to attend to." He glanced at her new green riding habit, which was becoming against her pale skin and rusty red hair. "And wardrobes to purchase," he added grimly.

She twinkled. "Dear Papa. Very well, I shall take Eliza to the stables."

"I'll tell your mother," he said, going back inside.

Miss Ravenel, accepting a groom's help in dismounting, left Eliza in the hands of their head groom, Harry Tilman, and caught the train of her skirt over her arm for the walk to the house. She crossed the checkered porch and went into the great hall. The butler, John Tilman, said, "Mrs. Ravenel's in your room, Miss Shannon."

"Thank you, John," she said, handing her riding whip to him. She went up the left side of the double staircase, which, having been built in colonial days, reflected that era. "Yes, Miss Shannon. You run along now. Mrs. Ravenel's been asking for you."

"Yes, John," she said, continuing in an unhurried fashion to the turn at the stairs and then up the next flight. The upstairs consisted of four bedchambers, hers and Frederick's on one side, her mother's and father's adjoining on the other. There was a great drawing room between, which was used as a ballroom as well. Off this large room was a large portico.

When she topped the staircase, she turned left and went toward her chamber, which was the smallest above stairs but commanded an excellent view of the front lawn. From her door, she saw her mother waiting for her, her maid, Phoebe, also present with a cream-colored dress draped over her arms. Her mammy, too, stood in the wings.

"You stayed out late, Shannon," her mother said in a chiding voice which nonetheless flowed like honey. "Frederick and young Mr. Haley will arrive at any moment."

She rolled her eyes discreetly and turned to let Phoebe unlace her.

"I saw that, Shannon," she said. "But you wouldn't wish to look discomposed when Mr. Haley first sees you. You were visiting your aunt when they left for Europe, but indeed, my dear, you would not have known him."

"Very likely not. I was at school when he last visited Charleston, I think." She had only seen him once. She had a vague image of a too-thin boy with hair that could use a brush taken to it.

"Yes, I believe so." Mrs. Ravenel's eyes were narrowed on Phoebe's handiwork with her hair, her lips pursed slightly. "Release a few more wisps, Phoebe." Mammy placed her hands on Shannon's shoulders to correct her posture. Shannon sat up taller.

"Yes, ma'am," Phoebe said.

Shannon cast a look over her shoulder at her mother. "Good heavens, must we impress Massachusetts?"

"Naturally not, but you have a reputation to uphold. If you think the gentleman won't be looking to see if what he has heard is true, you are mistaken, Shannon."

Shannon was more striking than beautiful, with red hair which waved gently, sometimes with a hint of blonde. She had dark blue eyes, extremely pale skin, and eyelashes and eyebrows which were so light as to be almost invisible. A long face, a nose which tilted slightly downwards in an attractive manner, lips which were full enough to be enticing, and a very slightly cleft chin. She was very willowy, but with a passably sized décolletage, her waist narrow, her height medium. Her family name and fortune were enough to give her a perhaps undeserved reputation as an exotic beauty. She was, however, very unusual, and she had quite a following in Charleston.

At twenty years old, she was sought-after, and there were several matches which her mother and father had hinted would please them. But she was biding her time. Her mother often chided her for behaving as though her options would always be as broad as they were now, reminding her darkly of several beauties' reigns which had ended abruptly in her day.

Finally, once Phoebe had puffed a delicate measure of expensive perfume onto Shannon's wrist, her mother smiled at her and said gently, "There. You look lovely, my dear."

"Thank you," Shannon said, torn between exasperation and amusement. She picked up her fan and brushed her skirts to the side to leave the room, her mother following behind. The two women were of a height, but there the similarities ended. Her mother was a dark beauty of forty-five years, every edge and corner gently and femininely rounded. Shannon was not without curves, but bony childhood had long since given way to thin womanhood. Her chest was not flat, but it would never be described as full, like her mother's. While Shannon's best features were her collarbones and the way every bone in her chest could be seen before the swell of her breasts, her mother's were her eyes, large and dark, slanting downward just slightly, and full lips. Shannon's neck was very long, while her mother's was short, giving way to a lady-like round chin, with nothing so masculine as a slight cleft in sight. The two ladies were simply not to be contrasted.

Mrs. Ravenel, however lovely she had been in her day, never sought to push her beauty forward. She knew her day had passed and that her daughter's had come. She dressed fashionably and expensively but not in a vulgarly flashy manner. If her figure was a bit fuller than it had been upon her marriage, that was the consequence of the bearing of two children and the passage of twenty-four years, but this she carried with the grace for which she was renowned.

They descended the stairs together, Shannon two steps ahead of her mother so that both skirts could fit. They met Mr. Ravenel in the foyer. He was looking at his watch and, after glancing up at them, said, "They are late. We cannot be expected to await their pleasure."

"I'm sure they will be here soon, Mr. Ravenel," Mrs. Ravenel said in a calm voice. "And for my part, I'm glad they are a little behind schedule, for it gave us the opportunity to dress Shannon. Doesn't she look lovely, my dear sir?"

Her father turned from his perusal of the sweeping lawn to cast his eyes over his daughter. "Very lovely," he said, shifting his eyes, which were now a bit narrowed, to his wife. Her mother held his eyes, and some sort of tension passed between them which Shannon did not understand.

Clearing her throat, Shannon said, "I daresay the tides were against them. They have been so treacherous the past few days."

"Indeed, my dear," her mother said. "Mr. Haley will think our ways quite different from his, I don't doubt. I only hope they do not hinder him from his travels home in two weeks."

"As to that," Mr. Ravenel said, "he is welcome to stay as long as he wishes. He has always been a pleasant boy, for a Northerner."

"Yes, of course," her mother said. "I only meant that his mother will be missing him after a year of being parted from him."

"Hardly," her father said. "Aren't there a dozen of them?"

"Eight, I believe," her mother answered somewhat stiffly.

Shannon looked between them. But there was no time for further conversation: they heard hoofbeats.

John Thomas Haley cast his eyes over the fields which sprawled out in front of him. Negros dotted the landscape, the women dressed in simple homespun with rags on their heads, the men in white shirts and tan trousers, none of them with any shoes. It had been some time since he had been to South Carolina.

He glanced at his friend and saw only tender affection as his eyes rested on his ancestral home. His conviction that Frederick Ravenel was the best friend a man could have could not be shaken. But for a moment, he wondered how they had ever become friends. Their worlds were as divergent as though they had been raised in different countries.

"Haley! What the devil's gotten into you? Writing sonnets to the French beauty still?"

"I never wrote a sonnet to her," he said, a little shortly, mind elsewhere, as he gently spurred his horse into motion. He might not be the high stickler his father was, but an entire raising could not be thrown off entirely. Even if he had wanted it to, and he didn't.

When Frederick was again beside him, he felt his friend's study. "You know I was only joking you," Frederick said.

John Thomas's lips lifted. "Yes, of course," he answered.

"*Your* behavior is always impeccable. You didn't give her encouragement, if that is what troubles you."

"It doesn't," he answered. "And nothing troubles me. Will your mother be angry that we are late?"

"Likely not. It will be my father who is tapping his foot in the great room, I imagine. He loves a schedule, and we have let three o'clock slip by."

He looked at him, brows drawn together. "Three o'clock?"

Frederick lifted his brows, and then, with recognition, laughed. "Oh, don't you know how sacred three o'clock is in the Lowcountry? Have I never told you? It is when we take our dinner, John Thomas!"

He blinked, startled.

"You think us unfashionable," young Mr. Ravenel said mournfully.

He laughed. "It is too unusual even to be unfashionable. I merely think you are strange."

"Thank you," his friend said, taking this in good part as they rode up the oak-lined drive.

When they arrived in front of the austere house, two boys of perhaps twelve or thirteen ran out, staying back as they had been trained until the gentlemen had their powerful thorough-breds under control. Frederick, a slight young man, both in stature and build, leapt down, removing his hat, and running a smoothing hand over his dark hair before handing his reins off to one of the boys.

John Thomas got down equally athletically, although with less flair, he thought, a little smile hovering. He glanced at the slave boys and then walked beside Frederick up one side of the tall steps. Eventually, they were on the porch. The door opened, and the family came out onto the checkered portico, looking, somehow, excessively wealthy, which they were. Mr. Ravenel was redoubtable, Mrs. Ravenel all that was charming in Southern ladies, and of course, the daughter of the house, of whom Frederick was so fond, though he would never say so.

"My boy," the elder Mr. Ravenel said, smiling and extending his hand. "We had thought you might stay in Europe."

"No, even Maryland was too far away for me, Father," he said, smiling and kissing his mother's cheek. "You look well, Mother."

"I am, my dear," she answered, smiling gracefully and fondly upon him. "You have changed since I saw you last," she added, scanning his face.

"A man changes a great deal from twenty-two to twenty-three," young Mr. Ravenel said, laughing. "Haley can attest: he has a year on me." Turning to his sister, Frederick said, taking the hands she was extending, "Well, old girl, how have you been?"

"Oh, Frederick! I *have* missed you. I was thinking last night that perhaps I had not, but I see now that I have."

"If only a little," her brother supplied for her, anticipating her next words.

"How are you, young man?" Mr. Ravenel was saying to John Thomas at the end of this exchange.

"Well, sir," he answered, giving a smile which Mrs. Ravenel found to be charming. He was an exceedingly handsome young man, in her opinion. Young ladies might not notice it, but there was something in him that more experienced ladies noticed almost immediately. One's eyes might scan over his straight, sandy hair and eyes of a blue which might be found in any person one happened to meet on the street. But one took a second look at his firm jawline, his thin upper lip which could quirk into a humorous smile, and the sparkle of intelligence in those common eyes. His cheekbones, too, were high, and his aquiline nose made a pleasing picture. "Mrs. Ravenel, Miss Ravenel," he said, nodding to them. "Thank you for welcoming me to your home."

"My dear boy, you are more than welcome to stay as long as you wish," Mrs. Ravenel said in her honey-voice, truly meaning it. "I'll tell Cook to set dinner back thirty minutes so you will have time to change out of your travel clothes," she said to the young men.

"Yes, ma'am," Frederick said, knowing when they had been commanded even if his friend did not yet. "Come along, Haley," he said, preceding him through the door onto the wooden floor. "I daresay you'll take the downstairs chamber, unless they have you in one of the flankers—no, here is John Tilman waiting to show you. How are you, John?" he asked the man who was waiting with regal patience.

John Thomas followed him through the doorway but just then caught sight, for the first time, of Miss Ravenel's face. He had turned toward the great room but stopped, looking over his shoulder, lips parting. Miss Ravenel was looking directly at him, a smile in her eyes.

Chapter Four

The dining room at Santarella was colonial in style with blue paneling all around. There were matching fireplaces on either end of the room. Above one of them was the Ravenel family coat of arms, which had been commissioned by an ancestor.

It was not in the dining room that the family and their guest dined, however. Instead, they were in the formal parlor, where a large, round table provided for more intimate conversation. Elegance still abounded. The room was hexagonal in shape with the same blue paneling. Portraits of Ravenels past hung suspended from long chains and ribbons.

They were served by two footmen, who brought dishes through the access door from the kitchen. Shannon's father sat on her right and her mother on her left. She glanced up from time to time, but she was rather quiet. She had decided to heed her mother's advice to hold her tongue, for purposes of her own.

"How is the economy in Massachusetts, Mr. Haley?" Mr. Ravenel asked.

Mr. Haley was polite and respectful, but the older gentleman's voice and cool smile did not seem to daunt him. "I could not say, sir," he said, long fingers around the stem of his wine glass. "My father never talks business in his letters, and my elder brother rarely writes. I believe there has been a little trouble with the tariffs, or so my sister tells me."

"How old is your brother?" Mr. Ravenel asked him, studying him with cool interest and a slight smile. A rice king, surveying a guest at his leisure. Two footmen entered, bearing pitchers with which they replenished the glasses.

"Twenty-seven, sir," Mr. Haley said, glancing at the Negro as he filled his glass before restoring his attention to the older gentleman.

"Your father intends him for the family business, then."

"Yes, he does."

Frederick had begun to grow a little flushed, perhaps embarrassed at the interrogation. And something in the set of Mr. Haley's shoulders suggested he preferred the family business to remain just that.

"But he is only three years your senior. Why not join in their ventures yourself?"

"My father has four sons, Mr. Ravenel, and only one business. I will join the Navy, as my education has prepared me. I believe that was my father's purpose in sending me to the Naval Academy." He looked mildly amused, as well as baffled.

Shannon's eyes flew to Frederick. He was wiping his mouth carefully, eyes on his plate.

"As to that, a man may wish his son to have a military education for many reasons," Mr. Ravenel said. Frederick did not respond.

Shannon shifted her gaze and noticed Mr. Haley looking at her. He turned his head, his color rising slightly. Her mother turned the conversation to the young gentlemen's travels. Their adventures were fascinating, some of them so humorous they were all in stitches. When dessert was brought, Mr. Haley finished answering a question about Vienna, where they had seen the young Empress Sisi at the theater. After this, he said, looking up at Shannon with a slight smile, "You have scarcely said a word, ma'am."

Her father smiled upon her with pride. "Our Shannon keeps her own counsel. But when she chooses to speak, all within distance would be well-warned to prepare for the blast."

Shannon laughed. "What a picture you paint of me, Papa. I am neither so quiet nor so effective." She smiled at Mr. Haley. "I am merely Elizabeth Bennett. Are you acquainted with her, Mr. Haley?"

"Quite personally," he said, holding her eyes with a sparkle in his own.

"Then you will understand that I am of 'an unsocial, taciturn disposition, unwilling to speak unless I expect to say something that will amaze the room, and be handed down to posterity with the éclat of a proverb.'"

Her mother, unbeknownst to any of the other diners, slipped her eyes closed. It was a true trial to have a daughter who not only ensured every man in the room knew that she had a brain, but who also was not embarrassed to quip with them, as though she were their equal. That she was their equal, her mother had no doubt. That it behooved a young lady in search of a husband to behave as though she were not, she was equally certain.

But Mr. Haley was smiling, not quite with as much diversion as he was in truth feeling, for there was something else in his expression, an arrested look, which Mrs. Ravenel had no qualm in assigning to shock.

"Don't tell me you read romances, Haley," Frederick broke in. "We shall part ways here and now, if that is the case."

Mr. Haley broke his gaze with Shannon, flushing slightly as he looked away, and responding to Frederick's banter in kind.

Once conversation had shifted and another subject had died down, Mr. Ravenel said, "Ah, Frederick. Your uncle has agreed to allow Marie to visit next week."

"Yes, she will arrive on Tuesday," Mrs. Ravenel added, smiling serenely.

A high red stole into Frederick's cheeks. There was a pause. He pressed his lips together and then said, "I am glad to hear it. Marie is dear to us all, of course."

Mr. Ravenel narrowed his eyes at his son. "Indeed," he said. "Indeed."

Birds were singing outside the windows of the room where the visitor from Massachusetts was writing a letter to his mother to inform her of his safe return. The countryside was a welcome change after the cities of the Continent, though a valet tending him who was not allowed to meet his eyes was not. He had sat with Frederick and his father in the library the night before and watched as they talked about the harvest and, in truth, the best way to exploit Negro labor. There had been a maid standing in their presence, serving them, and they didn't seem to notice. The affront to human dignity sat ill with him. But it was a way of life, handed down through generations. There was no more respected man in Charleston than John Ravenel. And his family might say he ought not, but John Thomas would cover his revulsion to keep from insulting Frederick's family.

He looked up suddenly, hearing a noise, and was pulled from his thoughts by the sight, just inside the doorway, of Miss Ravenel. She was wearing a dove gray dress, which made her dark blue eyes shine, and she was looking a bit uncertain. He stood out of deference and bit the inside of his cheek. That she was the most beautiful woman he had ever seen he had by now accepted, however unworthy a friend that made him. It was an unaccustomed feeling, the strong attraction he felt. He swallowed. Frederick would murder him.

"Forgive me for interrupting you, Mr. Haley," she said. There was something about a South Carolinian accent which was pleasing to the ears. Soft and flowing, like honey—why had he never noticed it?

"Have I invaded your domain?"

She smiled, still looking distracted as she came forward. "As my domain is every acre of Santarella, you could hardly fail to do so." She lifted her head to look up at him when she was quite close. She regarded him without embarrassment or hurry, in a way vaguely, disconcertingly, reminiscent of her father. "I need to speak with you about my brother," she said.

Surprised, he lifted his brows.

She moistened her lips, making his blood flash hot, then cold. He hated himself. He cleared his throat. "About Frederick?" he asked, forcing himself to meet her eyes.

She nodded once, looking away finally. "You know him better, now, I think, than I do." She had walked a little distance away, but she looked back at him. "Is he happy in the understanding between him and Marie?"

He held her eyes for a moment, and she seemed to know that she needed to say something more to gain his confidences. She held his gaze levelly; intelligence seemed to emanate from her eyes. "Only, I am very fond of Frederick, and of my cousin, and I couldn't bear for either of them to be made unhappy."

"Miss Ravenel, you must know that your brother would never speak ill of the lady he is to wed. I can hardly see how I am to help you."

"No," she said, nibbling her lip and looking contemplatively at the expensive candlesticks on the mantle.

"He told me once that the understanding is of long-standing date?" he said kindly.

"Oh, yes. It has been recognized between our families for years and years," she said, looking back up at him. "But they are not engaged, and nothing is settled until they are, in my view. But I think the purpose of her coming next week is just that, and I want to be sure that they are not being forced to this. I do not know the private conversations between Frederick and my father, or Marie and hers. When he speaks of her, is it with bitterness?" she asked.

John Thomas shook his head. "No, he speaks of her very rarely at all."

She pressed her lips together, looking at him shrewdly. "I think of my cousin's happiness, too, you know. Will he be faithful to her?"

"He already is," he answered. She lifted her brows, a little surprised, and waited. "You could not think he would embarrass her, when half the country knows she is to be his wife. Or that he could possibly desert her now. Don't you know him at all?" he asked mildly.

She sat down slowly, looking truly shocked. She shook her head in wonder and was silent for some time, assimilating this. She looked up slowly, her eyes landing on him. "This is your influence," she said. "When Frederick entered the Naval Academy, he was as wild as anything."

John Thomas flushed slightly, looking away. "It is no such thing," he said.

"I think it is," she said argumentatively.

He looked up, surprised. "Whatever my influence, you may be certain I would never encourage him to marry a woman he does not love." He caught himself up and pressed his lips together.

The fight seemed to go out of her. She hesitated a moment and then said softly, "Do you think they will be happy, despite that?"

He was silent, his lips still pressed together.

"Well?"

"I should not have said that," he said.

"Well, you have, so you may as well answer my question."

This surprised a slight smile out of him. After a moment, he said, "I think he cares for her. It is only that they have been separated for the better part of four years and do not know one another. And he does not love anyone else."

She held his eyes. "Yes, I suppose that is important," she said, looking away with a flush.

He studied her for a long moment before he said softly, "They will marry, Miss Ravenel, and I think, perhaps, that they will be happy."

She swallowed. "Thank you," she almost whispered. "My great flaw is that I seek to impose my beliefs on everyone around me," she said with a fleeting smile. "Arrangements are natural in our circle in Charleston, and I must someday accept that, too. But I have always thought that I could not marry where I did not love."

There was a long silence. "No," he finally answered, meeting her eyes. "Nor I."

Shannon was no fool. She was well aware that she was the product of an arranged marriage. That her mother and father had built a strong dynasty together, and that doing what they ought had likely been the right thing. But she was equally aware that they did not linger in one another's company or share little looks.

And Shannon probably never would have wanted anything else had she not had a teacher at her select school who had imbued her with notions which her mother would be the first to deprecate. For John and Louisa Ravenel had very decided notions of their own about what was expected from their only son and only daughter.

With this in mind, Shannon decided to see what she could ferret out about Frederick's current state of mind when he joined her in the withdrawing room, where she was reading one day. She closed her book, looking up with a smile. "Hello, dear brother," she said, extending her hand.

Shaking his head, he took it and returned it to her with an iris. She smiled, for they were her favorite. "I found it, lingering for you," he said, sitting next to her.

"Thank you," she said, laying it in the folds of her voluminous lavender skirt. "Have you deserted Mr. Haley?"

"He likes to be alone sometimes, I think. Very Quakerish, you know. I showed him the best riding paths."

She studied him. "I do not think he is quite so Quakerish as all of that. He drank the bourbon you poured for him last night."

"Yes, and if his father knew, that would put an end to his existence," he answered, laughing. "Modesty in all things, and some such. Makes me glad we're Presbyterian."

"What *is* a Congregationalist?" she enquired. "I know I ought to know that, for they populate the entire Northeast."

"He's explained it, but I am all in a tangle in three minutes. But I don't joke him for it: he takes it seriously. But he is *not* a stick."

She tucked the corners of her mouth. "Isn't he?" she said.

"No." He smiled. "I dared him to swim across the Thames. Well, I was a little drunk," he confided. "I never thought he would do it, but he did, in record time. Never been so close to being arrested in my life."

"Good heavens! If you had been, and in a foreign country, you would've quickly seen how Puritanical *our* father could become!" she said.

His eyes twinkled.

"But I wonder why *his* father allowed him to go on a grand tour," she mused.

"Oh, he thinks culture beneficial for young men," Frederick said, waving a hand. He studied her. "Well, come, Shannon, out with it: you're dying to ask me about my impending nuptials."

She smiled, not at all embarrassed. "Well, she hasn't said she would have you yet," she quipped.

He smiled a little.

"Will you be happy, not entering the Navy as you always wanted?" she asked softly.

There was some hesitation. "Well, it doesn't matter. If you had seen the poverty I did on the Continent and in England, Shannon... Who am I to complain because my father wants to bestow thousands of acres upon me and all of his business interests?"

"Not complain," she said. "Make your own path."

He shook his head, looking at her. "That has never been an option, Shannon. For either of us. I won't drop the torch. And it isn't a bad life, you know."

"I won't drop the torch either," she said, stiffening. "But I *will* make my own way."

"Well, I'll back you, if you wish me to. But you are a female, and it will be easier. So I will do as he wishes and someday take over Santarella and Ravenel House, and all of it. I would do it even if Father weren't pushing me to. It's our heritage, Shannon."

She smiled, reaching to cover his hand. "You know you are his pride," she said.

"Or his pawn?" he enquired, with a bit of a sour look.

She shook her head. She couldn't allow that. "You know he loves you, Frederick."

"*You* are his favorite," he said, lips tipping up in a smile.

"Oh, no," she said, getting up. "We are not playing that old game." She extended her hand. "Come, let us find your friend before he decides Southern hospitality is a mere hoax."

He tugged her hand, pulling her back a little. "You know you've given him a leveler, Shannon."

She lifted her brows. "Did he say so?"

"Good Lord, no. I caught him gazing at you at dinner one night. I hadn't noticed it until he did, but indeed, you've turned into a very pretty woman, Shannon."

"Thank you," she said drily, her pulse nevertheless speeding for reasons she could not explain.

He smiled. "Ah, you've noticed him, too."

She jerked her hand away and turned on her heel. "You might've stayed in Europe if you only meant to torment me."

Chapter Five

"John Thomas, do you remember..?"

At Frederick's words, John Thomas, atop a sleek thoroughbred, looked around to see what had caught his friend's attention. As he saw a pretty little dapple mare being led into one of the corrals by a Negro boy of perhaps twelve, the enquiring look on his face died a gray death into a level look of scorching grimness.

"If you—"

"'I upon my dapple ride/to catch a glimpse of him before the tide. Eyes so blue and locks so fair/I die for my next breath of air,'" Frederick chanted gleefully, upon his own neat chestnut, reins held loosely in his hand.

Leaping at him, it did not take Mr. Haley long to catch him roughly in a headlock.

Undeterred, Frederick said, doing his utmost to free himself, "'*Mon chéri, mon chéri,* come back, come back, come back to me!' Ow! Haley, I say! Don't make me teach you a lesson!"

He could hear his friend laughing, as well as feel it, being caught just then in a deathly grip. Frederick managed to struggle free, offering by way of truce as he did so, "They *are* rather blue, aren't they? One doesn't notice upon first glance!"

"Ravenel..." John Thomas said warningly.

"What? If I should've had sonnets composed to me by a French beauty, I should— But I never did have, travelling with *you!*" he finished bitterly.

"Frederick, if you don't stop talking nonsense—"

"Am I?" Frederick asked quizzically. "Even my sister can't seem to drag her eyes from you, and she, you know, is not generally susceptible to men."

It had been a shot at random, but Frederick was not ill-pleased with the results. Haley looked at him quickly and colored up. Then he looked down, brushing something off the sleeve of his brown riding coat. He was quiet for a moment before saying with more violence than usual, "You shouldn't speak of your sister that way," and riding off in the direction they had meant to go.

Frederick, following him with twinkling eyes, kept further thoughts to himself, instinct warning him it was the best form of self-preservation.

Shannon stood upstairs in front of the long window, which overlooked the field below. She smiled softly, watching her brother and Mr. Haley on their horses. Words must have been spoken, for they were now laughing, trying to wrestle one another off their horses, like boys. Once, Mr. Haley had Frederick in a headlock, which she imagined he must have voluntarily given up, since he had size on Frederick. Then again, Frederick was a South Carolinian. He could fight a man twice his weight.

When he released him, Frederick backed his horse away, lifting a hand in the air as he uttered some warning. Mr. Haley kept his hands on his reins, eyes glittering as he smiled, apparently promising nothing.

How different he was with Frederick! She watched him, a faint smile on her lips. She saw his jawline, the way he held himself, and his elegant structure, and she began to realize the appeal her mother had noticed right off.

She wondered what it took to penetrate his reserve and suddenly wanted to penetrate it. What a privilege it must feel for him to laugh with one in such a way, and how wasted it was on Frederick. She smiled.

She heard a whisper of skirts behind her and looked over her shoulder. Her mother was standing beneath the high doorway.

"Shannon," she said, her hand resting on the skirt of her expensive green gown.

"Yes, Mother?"

"Marie has arrived, my dear. You'll want to come greet her."

"Yes, of course," she said. "Does Frederick know? He wouldn't wish to insult her."

"Your father has sent Coffey for him. Come, my love," her mother said, lifting her skirts and starting down the stairs.

Shannon followed and was soon in the great hall. They waited with her father, hearing sounds of the horses on the pebbles and the carriage steps being let down. In moments, Marie was ushered in.

Marie Ravenel was neither pretty nor plain. She was on the small side of average, with dark auburn curls which wisped about her face. She had very pale skin, though with a slight pink tinge. She had the same slight cleft as her cousin, Shannon, but her face was sweeter and less striking. The down-turned nose, too, was similar, but Marie's was sharper, and her lips were thinner. Her eyes were not framed with ethereal blonde lashes and brows but, rather, made do with plain brown. There were lines about her mouth which suggested fragility; yet, as soon as she opened her mouth and one heard her deep, sure little voice, that image was somehow dispelled. Finally, as Mrs. Ravenel catalogued, her figure was not as good as Shannon's. She was thin, but her waist was not as narrow. She had some décolletage, but Mrs. Ravenel thought Shannon had more, and in any event, Marie's was not set off by that fortunate bony chest and those collarbones.

"Marie, how lovely to have you here!" Shannon said, going forward to kiss her cheek, extending her hands.

Marie took them, seeming to squeeze them a little too tightly, and to search her face. "Shannon. You are in great beauty, as always. I have missed you in Charleston."

"And I you, sweet Cousin."

Her mother smiled gracefully upon them. "My dear Marie, you are welcome here." Meeting her eyes, she said, with something like reassurance, "Very welcome."

Some of the tension seemed to ease from Marie's shoulders, and she said, "Thank you for having me, Aunt Louisa."

"I hope you left your mother and father well, my dear," Shannon's father said, kissing Marie's cheek.

"Yes, Uncle," she answered. "They send their love to all of you."

The door beneath the stairs opened suddenly from outside, and Frederick strode in, still in his riding wear, of course. "My dear Cousin," he said, going forward, extending his hands. "I did not mean to slight you. You are early!"

"Yes, indeed," she said, laughing softly. "But it is of little consequence. I am glad you are home, safe, Frederick."

"As am I," he said, and Shannon noticed that he pressed her hands slightly. Marie seemed to search him. "I have a friend staying here," he said, "but he would not meet you in his sweat, so I showed him the back stairs."

This caused Marie to flush, for there was little doubt of Frederick's intentions now. She smiled, some worry in her eyes, and said, "I shall look forward to meeting him at supper."

"Shannon, take Marie up to her room, my dear, so that she may rest and refresh herself before the meal," Mrs. Ravenel said gently.

"Yes, Mother," Shannon answered, lacing her arm through her cousin's and starting up the stairs. "Come, Marie, you look worn to the bone. It must have been a tedious journey, however short."

"I have had a great deal on my mind," Marie said. Her brows drew together when they reached the landing upstairs. "I suppose Mr. Haley is staying in the downstairs chamber," she said. "Oh, but Shannon, please tell me they have not relegated Frederick to the flanker."

"I do not know why everyone always speaks of the flanker so distastefully. There are perfectly elegant rooms there. But no, of course they would not embarrass you by putting you in his room. You are to stay in my mother's, and she is to share Father's."

"Oh, Shannon! Move me to one of your elegant flanker rooms. I would not invade your mother's domain for the world."

"My dear, the fault is ours, for not remembering that we would have you and Mr. Haley here at the same time. My father would not allow his niece to sleep in a separate building from the rest of us. Now, it is all settled, and no one is put out. Go rest, Marie: you are fidgety, and it isn't like you."

She pressed her lips together, meeting Shannon's eyes with her own dark ones. "Very well. Wait for me before supper. I want to walk down with you."

"Your wish is my command," Shannon said, smiling.

Shannon sat at her vanity as Phoebe put the finishing touches on her hair. It was parted down the middle and caught back smoothly at the base of her head in a large, loose twist. They were engaged in this endeavor when there was a knock at her door. Marie cracked the door, and Shannon said, "Do come in, Cousin. Phoebe is just finishing with me."

Marie nodded once and went to open Shannon's jewelry box. "Your pearls?"

Shannon regarded her cream gown. "Yes, I think so—unless you want them."

She shook her head, coming forward to clasp them for Shannon.

"Thank you, Phoebe, I shan't need you until time for bed."

Phoebe gathered Shannon's discarded day dress and left, eyes properly averted, saying, "Yes, ma'am."

Shannon met her cousin's eyes in the mirror and said, "Something is troubling you, Marie. Tell me."

Her task finished, Marie walked to the window, steepling her hands and resting her chin on them. Somehow, one could tell she was from two old families by looking at her in profile. She was silent for some time as Shannon watched her. "I have to know, Shannon... Is this what Frederick wants? What he *truly* wants? I'll not have a man on sufferance, and I do not want him to be unhappy either."

Shannon studied her for a long moment, not knowing what to say. "Marie, this match has been planned from your childhood. He has always known that it would be."

"That concerns me little," she said. "If he wished, I might release him."

Shannon lifted her brows. "Do you wish to release him? Marie, *you* must be certain and happy in your choice."

"I am... I do not want to say *resigned*: that does Frederick a disservice, for truly, he is lovely, and you know how much I love both of you," she said. She bit her bottom lip, looking again out the window. "I mean that I will be content." She met Shannon's eyes. "I am my father's only daughter, and he is a very wealthy man. Family means something to him. My marrying Frederick means something to him—it meant something to our grandfather. I wish... I wish to see the happiness and success of this family, and marrying Frederick is not a burden. I believe he means to propose tonight, and I need to know. I do not expect you to tell me that he loves me, or even that he is giddy with happiness. Just tell me if he feels the same, if you think he has a chance at happiness—if *we* do, I mean, together."

Shannon rose and went to take her cousin's hands, feeling a bit overwhelmed by Marie's nobility, and somehow shamed by it. *You are more than this, Shannon.* She swallowed around the tightness in her throat, saying, "Yes, I did not know how to say it, but you have said it so very eloquently. Frederick feels precisely the same, my dear cousin, for I had these same fears and asked him, busybody that I am. And I believe, moreover, that he will concern himself very much with your happiness."

Marie smiled slightly, a little emotionally, and pressed Shannon's hands tightly. Shannon laughed around her emotion, saying, "What a pair we are! I shall be so delighted to welcome you to our family." She thought of all the times when they had been little girls playing together, and the seriousness of adulthood, the poignancy of this rite of passage, tumbled down on her.

Marie embraced her for a long moment before saying, "We ought to go down. We mustn't keep your father waiting."

Shannon laughed. "No, we must not."

Shannon sat in the window seat in the long room, underlining sentences in an old volume of Shakespeare, writing a note to ask her father later. She had never yet baffled him with a foreign old word. But in the end, she lay it aside, for she could not concentrate.

Frederick had taken Marie for a walk in the gardens, and the family had gone to bed before they had returned. The two of them had not offered any interesting information at breakfast, though Frederick had taken the chair next to his cousin's. Her mother had warned her not to pry, which had instantly set up Shannon's hackles, but she had obeyed, trying not to show her interest.

They had gone for a long ride today, and Shannon wasn't invited, when she always had been before. Interestingly, Mr. Haley had not gone with them either. In fact, she had found him, apparently absorbed, reading in the library and had retreated before she could disturb him. That he had looked quite the Southern gentleman she did not dwell upon.

Frederick and Marie announced their engagement before dinner, standing together at the massive doorway of the long withdrawing room, Marie a little flushed. Shannon noticed, inconsequentially, that Frederick wasn't much taller than his bride, though he was still a bit larger, so that they were proportional. They looked well together, but they were a bit of a mismatch, Marie with her old-world fragility, Frederick with youth and vitality, handsome in a dashing sort of way. But they were to be husband and wife, and Shannon must remember that.

The thought that Frederick would pay first homage to a young lady other than herself made her unaccountably petulant, though she laughed at herself for it. But no longer could she tell him when Marie had annoyed her or tell Marie when she wished she could have hit Frederick. She was the superfluous cousin now, as Marie must have felt her whole life. She was deposed. Her hand squeezed on the arm of her chair, and for a moment, her heart sped unworthily. Could it be that not to be married could be more unpleasant than being married to one of her mother's choices? To have her own wedding, her own groom, her own house in Charleston—that was something. She would not, in any case, be left behind. But she looked around the room, her heart slowing, and saw the faces of her family. She could never be replaced in this family. She was the daughter of Santarella.

Her father had smiled almost instantly at the news, going forward to Marie and kissing her cheek. "This makes me very happy, my dear, my son," he said, turning to Frederick and shaking his hand.

Frederick smiled, looking down at Marie, and saying, "Me, too, Father."

"Well, shall we host a grand engagement party at Santarella?" Mr. Ravenel asked.

"Certainly, we shall," Mrs. Ravenel answered, sitting on one of their antique needlepoint chairs, her skirts pooling elegantly at her feet. Seeing her, Marie seemed to remember her duty. She went forward and charmingly kissed her future mother-in-law's cheek, saying, "I am very glad to join your family, Aunt."

Mrs. Ravenel smiled. "And I shall be very happy to hand Ravenel House and Santarella over to the care of a new mistress, when that day comes. I can think of no worthier young lady."

"I can: you, ma'am," Marie said. "So we shall pray that day does not come for a long time." She looked toward Shannon, who got up, going to her and saying simply, "Dear cousin!"

Marie embraced her, studying her when they pulled apart. Shannon smiled, pressing her hand. "But we have monopolized you: Mr. Haley will want to offer his felicitations."

He had been standing rather in the background, but at that, he came forward, offering his hand to Marie. She lay hers in it. "Certainly, I do," he said, in a quiet, friendly manner which seemed to calm Marie's nerves. Really, for a New Englander, he was such a gentleman, Shannon thought, smiling in a pleased way at him. "I don't know how you shall put up with Frederick for a lifetime; a year was quite enough for me," he added.

This caused everyone to laugh and Frederick to utter a protest, but it severed any tension in the room, and they were all much more comfortable after.

Chapter Six

Adeline sanded to her heart's content. It was therapeutic to her. She pictured these shelves with the same white paint as the rest of the built-ins and knew that was the way they were supposed to be. She had even found remnants of paint on the back of one of the doors. "You're going to be so pretty," she said distractedly, tongue coming to rest between her teeth as she worked on a challenging corner.

Her eyes strayed up now and then, behind the desk to the diplomas there. Undergraduate degree in biochemistry, minor in psychology, from Georgia Southern. M.D. at LSU School of Medicine in New Orleans. Residency at the USC hospital in Charleston. She had gone to the same school for everything. Sometimes she wished she had branched out a little. But she loved Chapel Hill, and their Ph.D. program was stellar. And she'd been accepted when a lot of her friends from undergrad hadn't.

Why didn't he hang those at his office? Maybe he thought they intimidated his clients. *Okay, Adeline, you're twenty-eight.*

Get over your little crush and move on with your life. She didn't even like him personally, which was even more annoying. It was like being infatuated with the football player in high school who was a total jerk to you. He looked more like the polo type, but the metaphor was sound.

She wiped a springy curl back from her forehead and sat back, surveying her work and thinking that she needed to finish it before the crew arrived tomorrow. Thomas didn't have a deft hand and always over-sanded. She didn't have the heart to tell him he was bad at it. She went back to it, and she was starting to get hungry by the time she looked at her watch. It was already noon.

She was wondering whether she should go pick something up when she caught sight of a movement by the door. Looking that way, she saw little Jude standing shyly in the archway, his feet crossed at the ankles. She smiled. "Hi, Jude. Have you had lunch?"

He nodded, biting his lip. His big black eyes were full of life, however.

"I'm jealous," she said. "What did you have?"

"Daddy made fish and 'sparagus."

She lifted her brows. "Do you like that?"

He nodded, giggling at the silly question. Poor kid. Probably wouldn't know a chicken nugget if he saw one. "How old are you, Jude?" she asked in a friendly manner.

"Six."

He looked a little smaller, though his eyes looked older. "Wow, first grade?" she asked, thinking it was better to over-class him than under.

"Kindergarten," he said, confirming her suspicions. "Jus' for 'nother month."

"Practically an upperclassman," she agreed. She noticed, for the first time, a long scar running from the top of his neck and disappearing down into his shirt. A nasty wound for such a little boy. The front door opened, and Adeline saw through the doorway Dr. Ravenel come in, carrying the mail.

He frowned, seeing his son. "Jude, what are you doing? You're supposed to be taking a nap."

"I did," he said, craning his neck to look up. "Short one."

Dr. Ravenel put his hand on his head, not precisely a loving gesture, but rather, as though he were preventing him from running off. He sent Adeline a narrowed look. She held up her hands. He pressed his lips together, looking from Jude back to her. She realized, suddenly, from the tightness of his mouth, that he didn't want her near him. Having always been perfectly respectable, she was shocked for a moment. But then again, she thought, shoulders relaxing, he was probably just over-protective. That would certainly explain his searching questions about her crew. And she hadn't known him long enough to be offended by his lack of trust. Or rather, that was what she told herself. The sting was just now slowly fading.

She turned back to her sanding. She felt his eyes upon her in the doorway, almost as though he were hesitating. Finally, he said, "Come on, Jude. Let's let Ms. Miller work."

"Can I have some ice cream?" she heard him ask as he skipped away at his father's side.

"I think I have some vanilla," he said.

Her stomach rumbled. Yes, she needed to get her keys.

The next day was spent in its entirety explaining the schedule of work to the crew, who had arrived fresh from the job they had finished in Charlotte. The commission should be checking into her bank account soon, which was good since she lived job to job, with no paycheck between. The architect she always worked with had flown down for the day to discuss the porch with them, and three hours were spent out there with his drawings and a tape measure.

Her loose white linen sleeveless top was practically soaked when they finally came in. Note to self: do not wear white in South Carolina again.

That finished, she put the two indoor guys onto pulling wallpaper from the dining room, watching carefully for the color that would materialize beneath it when they got down to it. Unfortunately, it was a 1980s pink, so she pulled out her scraper and carefully flicked up that layer and then another, which seemed to be a weird yellow. She hesitated at a green, thinking it could be the original color. It wasn't terribly off, but some instinct told her to go further. She flicked it up and found beneath the green a soft yellow, just like butter, and her heart sang. That felt right.

"Jake?" she said.

"Yeah," he said, leaving what he was doing and coming to her. He was only thirty or so, but he looked much older. She had a feeling he had probably lived pretty hard, but he was great at his job.

"Can you get me a three-foot square down to this yellow?"

He whistled, running his hand over what she'd uncovered

with a carpenter's appreciation. "Think we can match it?"

"I'm going to match it," she said with determination. "Okay, I'll leave you to that."

She went down the hall, intending to work on her bookshelves some more. But she decided instead to go have a look at how they were coming along on the balcony. Joe, the foreman, was yelling some remonstrance down to Thomas and Jose. She winced and stepped back in the house. Probably better to let them work it out.

She didn't know the crew intimately—they were usually all business and didn't discuss personal lives very much—but she did know after two years that construction workers argued like middle schoolers.

It was about four o'clock when her phone rang. Adeline looked down and saw a number she didn't know. She answered, thinking it could be one of her suppliers. "Hello? This is Adeline."

"Hey, Adeline, this is Harris Ravenel."

"Oh, hi!" she said, glad and surprised that he had actually returned her call. "Hope you found something good."

"Well, I talked to my dad. They're off in Wisconsin or some place for a conference this week, but they'll be back Tuesday. He couldn't shed much light on the situation, but he said there's a box of old family documents. It's in the basement at their house if Adrian wants to drive you to get it."

Her heart sped. "That sounds absolutely perfect," she said, thoughts jumping with the possibilities of what might be in that box.

"But it'll have to be next week," he said. "Listen, I'm coming to Charleston to see Jude—my nephew—this weekend. I have a folder full of stuff here that might be helpful. Something I kept when we were going through my grandparents' estate."

"Oh, wow. That would be awesome. I thought you were local..?"

"No, we're Georgia folks," he said, humor in his voice. "Adrian's the strange one."

She pursed her lips, trying not to smile. She didn't think his brother would thank him for that.

"I live in Savannah," he explained.

"Oh. Are your parents there, too, then?" That was about a two-hour drive. That would be super-fun with Sir Ravenel.

"No, they're over in Statesboro," he said. Perfect. She didn't know where that was, but it was bound to be a longer drive than Savannah.

"Okay, great," she said, trying to infuse enthusiasm into her voice.

"I was going to be there around two. Want to meet at Kudu around 12:30? Or I could just bring it to you there if you can't get away..."

"No, I need to get out. That'll be perfect." She was pretty sure Kudu (Coodoo?) was a coffee shop. She was more into juicing herself, but she wasn't going to complain. There was a folder heading her way.

Adeline drove back through Charleston, her car loaded with groceries. It had taken her a while to get to the store. It was tough having to pull off every three seconds to see a house and maybe snap a few pictures. She regretted even more that she hadn't been able to explore the city, but surely she would be able to sometime? She was like a kid at a fair as she turned back onto Battery Street, the houses rolling by grandly, the smell of salt thick in the air.

"Okay, let's see if I can turn in without hitting anything," she said softly to herself as the narrow driveway rose in her future. She really hoped she could have some fridge space. And a little pantry space. She would be more likely to be granted it by Jane, she thought. That was why she had gone shopping while Dr. Ravenel was at work.

She opened the hatch and looped as many bags as she could over her arms and walked up the brick stairs and onto the little side porch, smelling the smell of old brick. She was really wishing she had thought to bring her eco-friendly cloth bags by the time she got to the kitchen. The plastic was leaving marks on her arms.

She found Jane at the counter, filling bags with Cheerios, presumably for future lunches. "Hi, hon," she said, glancing at the grocery bags. "Need some help, there?"

"No, I got it," she said. "Do you mind if I..." She nodded toward the fridge.

"*I* don't," she said, eyes twinkling a little. "And I don't see how you're to live here if you don't have some food. So expensive buying all your meals." She went to open the fridge and freezer for her, looking around. Both were surprisingly full for an industrial size. She saw baggies of carefully washed fruit, fresh vegetables awaiting his pleasure, tons of water, and a crisper full of fresh fish. Almond milk—gross. Avocados—hey, she could live with that. Corn so fresh it hadn't been shucked, and every kind of juice imaginable. Okay, she'd just put her slab of meat for tacos here, her two percent milk there, and the butter up in that little tray. The green tea could sit next to his austere water bottles.

"The pantry's over there, hon," Jane said with a tilt of her head. Adeline laid down her baggies and walked over. "Let's see if we can make you some space..." She shifted some pasta and whole grain tortilla chips, saying, "He won't mind, I think, giving you a little space. There—is that enough?"

Adeline looked at her box of cereal, her pasta sides, the taco shells, and everything else. "Yeah," she said affirmatively, quickly realizing she was still living like a college student. Oh, well. "Was Jude feeling better today?" she asked, placing her items.

"He was a little fussy this morning. I expect a phone call any minute," she said. "You're from North Carolina?"

"Yep," she answered, wondering if there was a bandage around. Her Birkenstocks weren't broken in yet. She'd realized it as she was walking by the 'sparagus.

"Your mama and daddy are there now?"

She nodded. "And my brother and sister."

"Oh!" She smiled. "Are you close?"

"Oh, you know...we live here and there now, lead different lives. We were really close as kids, though."

"Oh, that's nice," she said. "Jude's too much of a loner. I wish he could've had a brother or sister before..."

"Poor little guy," she said.

Jane pressed her lips together, silent for a moment. "Adrian never talks about it, poor boy. But Jude has a good family, on both sides, although I don't think the Thomases come around enough. It's probably too hard for them. That's her family," she explained.

"He has you, too," Adeline said, realizing the woman assumed she knew by now, but touched by the tender affection she saw for the father and son duo.

"Yes," she said, laughing slightly. "Wrapped me around his finger completely from day one." She looked up. "I know you won't see them much, but don't mention Mrs. Ravenel when you're around the little one. He used to have bad dreams, and his father thinks he has them less when he isn't reminded of her. Which may sound a little cold, but I have to admit it's true." She smiled. "And I let him deal with matters of the head—that's his business. Even if he's rather less adept with matters of the heart…" Adeline thought she heard her mumble.

"Got it," she said, studying her. "Well, I'm going to go back to work. Have a nice afternoon."

"You, too, hon."

Adrian opened the pantry, immediately sensing the difference. He was just trying to figure out dinner, but new items snagged his attention. He looked them over, his lip curling, and said over his shoulder, "Jude?"

"Yup?" he said from the barstool where he was sucking his juice box.

"Don't eat anything on this shelf," he said, pointing.

Jude leaned up, looking. "Why, Daddy?"

"Just don't." He was considering take out for supper. He could feel weariness from the day in his shoulders, and he was drained. Two of his most difficult clients had had two-hour sessions, and that was just the start. He glanced up at the windows, the rain pelting them, the palms blowing, and sighed. "What do you want for supper, Jude?"

"Ice cream."

Okay, so much for that. He pulled some spinach noodles out and started on a tomato sauce. Jude hovered, glancing at the window from time to time. He eventually got up and attached himself to Adrian's leg. Adrian brushed his hair back. "It's not a bad storm, Jude. It's nothing to be afraid of."

"I think it's a hurricane."

"No, we'd know way in advance," he said, moving to get a new spoon, which was difficult with a forty-pound attachment to his left leg.

There was a bolt of lightning and a clap of thunder. Jude pressed harder. Adrian sighed, putting the spoon down, kneeling, and detaching him with a little difficulty. He cradled him close and kissed the top of his hair. He went over in his mind methods of calming children during storms, starting with the root of the problem, which was usually them picking up on a parent's anxiety. In that case, it was best to communicate with them about the exact nature of the storm and keep calm. It was something else with Jude, so that left only physical contact. Jude pressed his face into his shirt.

Another thunder roll sounded, this one rattling the shutters, and Ms. Miller materialized in the door. "Whoa, it's really coming down out..." She caught herself up, catching his quelling glance. She winced apologetically, and he stood, bringing Jude with him. He picked up the spoon and gave the sauce a stir, and she glanced out the window. After a hesitation, she went to the table and sat, laying her phone in front of her. It was hard to remember she lived here now, that she had a right to do that. He studied her for a long moment before refocusing his attention on Jude and the sauce.

But she kept distracting him. She glanced out the windows from time to time, obviously a little skittish in storms herself. And she would look at him periodically, as though assessing whether he knew the serious nature of the weather.

She picked up her phone and looked at the screen, sliding her thumb. She pressed her lips together and looked back up at him, and then at Jude. After a moment, she walked over to him softly, holding the phone out. Jude had his back to her and likely didn't even know she was there. His face was buried in Adrian's neck. He met her eyes and then took her phone. She had a radar map of Charleston pulled up. "Tornado Watch" was splayed across the top in bold red.

He raised and lowered his brows. It must've gotten worse than predicted. But probably still nothing to worry about. He nodded, handing it back to her. She went back to the table and sat, asking, "Need help with anything?"

Great. Now she was going to be attached to him, too. He knew he should say something to soothe her, but he didn't want Jude to know she was scared. Best to give her a job.

"You could get plates."

"Sure," she said cheerfully. She stood and found them almost instantly. Either she'd been snooping or it was a woman's intuition. Probably would've taken him five minutes in a strange kitchen. "Do you, uh, have a S-A-F-E room?"

"I can spell."

"He can spell," Adrian affirmed. "Might as well get three plates."

Pressing her lips together in a way he personally thought a little cattish, she shrugged and got another plate down. After filling the plates, she opened the refrigerator. He watched her for a moment. She was obviously looking for a canister of parmesan. He didn't know whether to tell her there was a block of fresh waiting to be grated or that he thought cheese that would last for two years in a canister was gross. But she located the block and held it up, looking at him, and saying levelly, "Really?"

He shrugged. He wasn't going to argue with her. She located the grater and made a fine dash on all of their plates after he had filled them. "I'll get the plates," she said softly, looking with sympathy at the ball of tension in his arms. She walked across the stone floor, balancing the plates on her arm like the waitress she must have been in college. "Here you go, Jude, it smells so good," she said, setting two plates in front of Adrian.

"Don't want to eat, Daddy," Jude mumbled miserably. Adrian kissed his head and pried him off his chest. "You have to eat a little. Don't be rude: we have a guest."

Jude looked measuringly at Ms. Miller and then took the bite Adrian was offering.

"Good boy," he said, forcing a few bites down him while he could, but not too many. He wouldn't put it past his son to throw up during a storm.

The wind seemed to pick up, and he looked up at the preservationist, who was again on her phone. "I think we've been upgraded," she said cryptically, trying to sound light-hearted.

Jude looked between them, trying to figure out what that meant.

Crap. He sighed, just as the electricity went off. Food abandoned, Jude pressed himself into him again. "Come on," he said, standing, glancing over his shoulder. "Will you grab some water?"

"Sure," she said.

He waited at the door until she caught up and then took them to the closet beneath the stairs. They sat across from one another, her legs tucked to the side to make room for his longer ones. She was looking a little pale and pressing her hand against her stomach. Great. Maybe Jude would pick up on her energy and have a full-blown panic attack.

"At least we got to eat a little," she said, looking like she wished she'd done anything but.

"It should pass soon," he answered.

She met his eyes, shaking her head. She handed him her phone. They were under warning until 11:30. He glanced at Ms. Miller. They were going to be stuck here for a while.

Chapter Seven

Two hours had passed, and Jude had long since gone to sleep against his father's chest. It had been a real mind-blower when Adeline had walked into the kitchen and seen the man holding his son like that. She'd never seen anything so hot in her life. She'd figured the poor little guy had to get all of his affection from Jane, and maybe his uncle, who sounded a lot warmer.

Now, Dr. Ravenel was leaning his head against the wall, the boy resting comfortably against him, his head on his chest. They hadn't talked much: it was a little hard to think of anything but the driving rain and hail, which was loud even in here. They were still under a warning, but it seemed to have slacked a little.

The closet was kind of cozy—wood floors, the bottom of the stairs visible, a pipe running along the wall... She felt a little like Harry Potter, but she wasn't too claustrophobic. She wondered vaguely about the engineering of the house, whether any of it was original. She would bet it was: they'd been built tough back then. It would be interesting to dig into.

She looked at her phone, but it had long since gone dead, probably a good thing since her grandma was sending her panicked texts about the tornado in Charleston. She looked again at the two across from her. "He's out," she said.

"Hopefully for the night," he agreed, turning his head. "It's getting late."

She looked at her watch. 10:15. She quirked a brow.

"Late for a six-year-old," he amended. He seemed about to say something else and then didn't. After a minute, he finally said, "My wife—his mother—was killed in a car accident about two years ago. It was storming like this. He was in the car."

It was said coldly, almost with clinical detachment. Adeline studied him carefully. He looked younger than his thirty-four years (yeah, she'd looked at the date on his undergrad diploma). He changed into exercise clothes when he got home. He looked good in them. Jane, apparently having a house of her own, usually stayed long enough for him to go for a run. His face was a blank slate. But she'd be a fool not to see how carefully he was concealing any emotions his words might bring. A muscle in his jaw had hardened. She thought of the scar on the boy's neck and the way his father, not the cuddly type, had held him so protectively. She wondered what it would be like to have lost the love of your life, the mother of your child, like that, the agony, the soul-searching it would bring. Had it thrown his life completely off balance and sucked him down into a vortex of grief? He seemed to be well-adjusted, but she was catching him two years after the fact.

"I'm so sorry," she said softly. "No wonder he's so scared."

There was a long pause. "He'll eventually not be afraid," he said. "I had hoped he would be there by now, but it may take a few more years." He studied her. "Why are *you* afraid of storms?"

"I'm not," she said, straightening. No one knew that, not even her family.

"All of the signs are there," he said calmly, eyes searching her face. "Almost nothing ever comes of a storm, so there's no rational reason to be afraid. Your fear, therefore, is rooted in something emotional."

She swallowed. "Oh, you know... My mom and grandma were always panickers about it. I guess they'd get me worked up."

"That's a perfectly reasonable explanation for a childhood fear. But I'd put you at thirty now—"

"Twenty-eight," she said, narrowing her eyes.

"All right, twenty-eight. And the justification for childhood fear has long since passed. Either you need to turn that switch off in your brain or talk with someone about something that happened, which caused this later in life."

She pressed her lips together, looking at her Toms. She drew her finger along the seam of her shoe. Okay, he was freaky. She was silent for a long time, not wanting to talk about it really, about the shame and fear that had come from one of her few irresponsible moments. There had been a party in college. A stupid boating party. There was drinking and a storm, and one of the boys had died. Everyone at school and in that half of the state knew. They were all devastated. She knew she wasn't at fault for his death—none of them were—but it had taken a while to recover. And they had barely made it back themselves.

"Yeah, I guess it was this really scary boating party."

He studied her. He knew, obviously, that there was more to the story.

"Remember that you're able to take precautions now, as you weren't then. One situation has nothing to do with the other. And simultaneously that you're not in control at all, that doing all you can is enough."

She swallowed, holding his eyes. She looked away, a little thrown off. Moistening her lips, she sat quietly for a few moments, surprised. She brushed back a ringlet. "Will that be for your usual rate, or..?"

He cracked a slight smile for the first time she had seen. "Free of charge. But don't count on it next time."

Adeline bolted out of bed the next morning at six o'clock. She'd had a nightmarish night, surprisingly indifferent to the continuing storm but terrified about her balconies. Dr. Ravenel had seemed completely unconcerned, as if he hadn't even thought of it, when he had asked her why she was twittery now as they had finally gone up the stairs. It was enough to induce an apoplexy, worrying that the balconies would give.

She ran down the stairs, into the foyer, where she smelled Jane's breakfast cooking, and out onto the porch. She rant to the front yard. They were still there, but she couldn't tell if there was any damage. If there was, she needed to know before Joe got there and started doing that jaw-clenching, silent fuming thing. She crossed the road in her hastily shoved on Keds, skirting small tree limbs, and climbed up onto the parapet, the roiling bay right behind her.

Shielding her eyes, she gave it a good looking over. It seemed like everything was okay. She stared for several minutes, trying to get the feel of it, to make sure the angle was right. Yes, it looked the same. She scanned her eyes across the row of houses, her heart catching. She looked at the house for the first time as someone who stood here or boated out in the sea would. Aw, it was so pretty.

It was easy to get lost in the details, the deliveries, the insane schedule. But she had a pretty awesome job. She leaned off the railing. Okay, onto the fireplace in the dining room.

On Saturday morning, Adeline was still scraping atrocious white paint off a fireplace that was supposed to be stained to bring out its beautiful grains. It was massive and several hundred years old, probably imported from Europe. Her desire to learn more about the Ravenel family intensified. Few had had that kind of wealth. What was their story?

She dropped her scraper. Kudu. Folder. Harris Ravenel.

She looked at watch. Eleven-thirty. Okay, that gave her an hour to get there. And she smelled like a monkey. The organic deodorant was not working out. Not in Charleston. She shoved her hair back with her arm because her hands were too dirty, collected her thoughts for just a moment, and then hurried out of the room and up the stairs. She got into her impossibly small shower, which seemed to have been installed in the 20's, and took the world's fastest shower.

She didn't have a closet, so she had put her clothes in drawers, which slowed her down considerably. At least, it did because she unaccustomedly couldn't decide what to wear. She ended up in a pair of close-fitting robin's egg blue pants, nude flats, and a long white top. Now for her hair. *Grr*, why was the pressure on to look good? She'd never even met the guy. Professor Jung downstairs would probably tell her it was because she had built up a fantasy about him through their amiable phone chats, imagining what he must look like. And he'd probably be right, freak that he was.

Okay, maybe she was the freak. She looked in the mirror, adjusting the blue and pink floral bandeau around her curls and clipping in her feather earrings. Yeah, she'd just go have coffee and get her folder.

She grabbed her tribal weaved purse and set out. She checked her watch. Twelve o'clock. She was sweating, but she had put on the good stuff this time.

She got in her Rav-4 and was soon heading toward downtown. She found the little coffee shop pretty easily and parked, looking around and suddenly realizing she hadn't asked Harris for a car or shirt color to look for. If he looked anything like his brother, though, she'd know him, she thought wryly. She put her purse on her shoulder and walked toward the door.

As she stepped in, her phone started ringing.

"Hello?"

"Adeline? I just wanted to let you know I'm here."

"Oh, great, I am, too—at the door."

She looked around and saw a man standing, phone against his ear, looking toward the door. He smiled, removing his phone and remaining standing while she walked toward him.

"Nice to finally meet you," he said, extending his hand with a smile.

He was cute. He had a good body. But he was no Adrian Ravenel. His hair was a shade lighter and slightly waving, his nose shorter, jawline not quite as razor sharp. He looked much more amiable, however. "You, too. Thanks so much for meeting me."

"Not a problem," he said, taking his chair again. "You want to me to go order for you?" he asked.

Gentlemanly. Her job would be a lot easier if his brother was. "Yeah, thanks. A coffee—whatever is good."

She handed him some cash, but he waved it off, going away and returning in a few minutes with a delicious-smelling concoction. Maybe she *could* get into coffee. "Thanks again," she said, opening the lid to let it cool.

"My pleasure. I know Adrian's forking out the cash for this house. He wants it to be right." He sat back with a casual air of confidence, studying her like he found her interesting. She had a feeling he did it to everybody, and it made him likeable. "Were you there during the storm the other night?"

"Yeah, it was pretty intense. We had to go to the closet for several hours."

"I thought about calling you," he said, laughing. "Mom couldn't reach Adrian, and she called me, panicking."

"Oh, wow, that sounds like my mom," she said. "But it wouldn't have done you any good: my phone went dead, and I doubt we had any service anyway."

They talked for a few minutes about the damage, and then she said, "Don't let me keep you too long. I know you wanted to see your nephew."

"We're taking Jude to Fort Sumter," he said.

"Oh, how fun!" she said, perking up.

"Why don't you come with us? We could use some female company."

She loosened her spine. "No, don't be ridiculous. I wasn't asking for an invitation."

"It would be fun…" he said. "Think of all that history… It might even help with the house."

It was a low carrot to dangle in front of her. But she sighed. "No, I couldn't."

"Come on: Adrian practically insists we bring a woman with us after Nantucket." His eyes twinkled, faraway in remembrance.

"What?" she asked, watching him, anticipating a story.

"We went—all of us—to Nantucket last summer. Adrian, Jude, and I took a sailing excursion… This old lady on the boat told me that she thought our relationship was wonderful. I didn't grasp what she meant at first." he said.

"Oh, no."

"She asked me if we had used Adrian's sperm for Jude, and I answered that we had—"

"You didn't!"

"Well, technically it's true!" he defended. He'd obviously used that line multiple times, probably after facing the wrath of his entire family. "I'd only just realized her mistaken impression at that point, and I didn't know how to correct her. She said we'd made a good choice." His eyes narrowed. "Which is insulting, when you think of it."

Adeline shook her head. "It was no more than you deserved."

She sighed. "All right, I'll go, if only to prevent a domestic dispute. If you're sure your brother won't mind."

"Of course he won't." He sounded much more certain than Adeline felt. "All right, that's settled." He reached for the folder. "These are some family letters and random documents. I'm not sure if it's from the time period you want, but I thought it might lead us to Santarella somehow." He pulled out an old letter. He should probably be wearing gloves (there was no doubt he should), but they were his, and if they'd survived this long, they must be pretty hardy. "This one seems the most promising. I was looking at it last night."

It was from 1860, just on the brink of war, although they probably didn't know it yet. It seemed to be from a mother to a daughter, but she couldn't be sure, for they had different last names. The mother discussed a dinner they had hosted, after which the tides were unfavorable, and their guests were trapped for three days. Adeline straightened, her mind spinning with possibilities.

"Tides…" she said.

"Doesn't sound like the Ashley, does it?"

She thought for several more seconds, holding his eyes, in a vague reverie, the light bulb finally going on. "The Sea Islands," she said.

He nodded, smiling. "The Sea Islands."

Chapter Eight

The Ravenels were invited, as they often were during the autumn months, to dine at the home of the Middletons, which could be reached best from Santarella by the Ashley River. Mrs. Middleton included a note that there would be dancing for the young people, for she had also invited the Christians.

"And I must say, Shannon," her mother said, readjusting a pin in her own hair that she did not consider her maid had gotten quite right, "that this is an excellent opportunity for you."

Shannon, standing in her mother's doorway and watching Abigail's ministrations, said with her chin in the air, "And why is that, Mother?"

"Pertness is unbecoming in a young lady, Shannon. Either of Arthur Middleton or Seymour Christian would make you a fine husband. What is more, I believe either is yours for the taking, if you will only bestir yourself a little."

Shannon looked contemplatively at her mother in the

mirror, crossing her arms within her elegant wrap. "I grant you that it would not be unpleasant to live among the Middletons. But do you not think Arthur a bit...effeminate?" she asked, lifting her brows at her mother.

Her mother met her eyes. "His look is a bit so. But that is because he lacks whiskers. I will grant you that he is almost... femininely beautiful. But he is one of your brother's oldest friends, and, indeed, my dear, I am certain he doesn't lack... manly attributes." Shannon flushed slightly, and her mother gave her a displeased look. "I mean that I know him to have often been out shooting with Frederick and Harry Drayton, and he may not be a sportsman, but he handles himself well enough on a horse. Have Seymour Christian if you prefer, but for heaven's sakes have *somebody* before you are twenty-one, Daughter."

Her not much chastened daughter thought little of these things as she found herself, not long after, being rowed on her family's yacht by her father's slaves. And she was her charming self to their host and hostess when they were shown to the door at the colonial mansion.

Mr. Middleton and his lady were the parents of four children, Arthur and Elizabeth, who were precisely Frederick and Shannon's ages, and Lillian and Henry, who were ages ten and eight, respectively. They were all pretty children, with dark hair and handsome eyes.

Elizabeth was one of Shannon's closest friends. She was on the tall side of average with a pleasing figure and a pair of laughing blue eyes. She and Shannon shared the distinction of being granddaughters of governors of South Carolina and of being two of the most eligible young ladies in the state.

As soon as supper was finished, Miss Middleton lost no time in pulling Shannon to the side while Marie was taking her turn at the piano to say, "My dear, what do you mean by never mentioning Mr. Haley in your letters?"

Shannon lifted her brows. "I mention him often, as I recall."

"Not everything," Elizabeth said, looking appreciatively across the room, where he sat with Frederick, young Mr. Middleton, and Seymour Christian at a card table, laughing over something Arthur had said. There had been a slight stiffness among the young men when he had first entered with Frederick which had evaporated, inexplicably, almost immediately.

Shannon's eyes twinkled in response. "Indeed, I am given to understand that he has three brothers. It makes one very curious, does it not, to meet the Haley family of Massachusetts?"

Elizabeth agreed to it, clapping as Marie finished the first piece and Mrs. Middleton entreated her to honor them with a second. Elizabeth, looking lovely in a gown of ice blue, its tightly fitting bodice and extremely wide skirts accentuating her lovely figure, watched Marie for a moment. "You will be very happy to gain her as a sister-in-law, I daresay," she said, abandoning her levity, as she always did, so gracefully.

"Indeed, I love her very dearly," Shannon said. "She has been almost a sister to me since we were mere infants." They paused as a footman brought coffee for the ladies and port for the gentlemen.

"She will make a good wife for him—your brother, I mean," Elizabeth said, looking at Shannon quickly.

Shannon lifted her brows slightly. "There is no question of that. She would make any man an ideal wife, as would you, my friend. Won't you marry Seymour Christian and silence my mother on that head?"

"And have him pining for you within a month? No, I thank you very much."

"For me?" Shannon asked, surprised.

Elizabeth lay her blue fan aside. "Can it be that you don't know?"

"No, Elizabeth, he doesn't love me," Shannon said, shaking her head. She didn't want to shock her friend, unsure how much she knew of the ways of the world. "He is intrigued by... other things."

"Lust for you, you mean," Elizabeth said, leaving no question as to her intelligence. "Well, if it is all the same to you, Shannon, if one's husband must lust, it ought to be after oneself, I think."

She saw Mr. Haley glance up at her. How on earth had he heard that far across the room? Shannon's eyes twinkled in response to the slightly embarrassed smile she saw in his. Shannon pretended to ignore him and said, "Perhaps we ought to turn the subject. We might be overheard."

They did, talking of more mundane matters, but Shannon could not quite still the voice in her head that warned her that Mr. Haley had heard every word they had yet spoken. Irreverent commentary on his beauty had not interested him, then? He hadn't looked up *then*.

"Well then, shall we have dancing?" Mr. Middleton, ever the gracious host, asked.

His children encouraged it, and soon the governess, Miss Richardson, who had been invited to join the party once the younger children were put to bed, was warming her fingers in preparation for a reel. Arthur, with a smile, asked Shannon to partner with him. "It ought to be Miss Marie Ravenel by seniority," he said, offering his hand, "but I should not dare."

Marie smiled, surrendering the piano stool. "You have gotten yourself a much prettier partner, Mr. Middleton. Your true motives are not hidden to us."

"Well, I shall ask Miss Middleton, then," young Mr. Christian said. "There is beauty and to spare in this room tonight." The adults laughed at this show of gallantry.

Mr. Haley stood, though Shannon knew he did not dance. "Miss Christian, will you do me the honor?" he asked, extending his hand. "I fear your Southern reels, but you won't criticize me too harshly, I hope."

"Indeed, no!" the young lady said, taking his hand and allowing herself to be led to the dance floor.

Shannon's eyes narrowed, unaccustomed jealousy searing her.

The reel started, and Arthur, apparently noticing more than she, said, "I ought to have asked her. You wouldn't have minded it, I know. I didn't think of it, but I ought to have."

Shannon realized suddenly that Mr. Haley had acted to prevent Miss Christian from being the only young lady without a partner. "You are too severe upon yourself," Shannon assured Mr. Middleton. Her eyes rested on Mr. Haley's face for a long moment. Then she transferred her gaze to Arthur. She studied him. He was of a passably good stature, enough taller than the ladies that he might be accounted a handsome match in a dance. His eyes were the same chocolate color as his hair, and his features were indeed almost too beautiful for a young man of twenty-three years.

"Nonetheless, Haley is a good man. I couldn't think at first what Frederick was about, bringing a Northerner among us, but I see now. I shall endeavor to call our esteemed neighbor off of him."

Shannon lifted her brows. "Shall you? The elder Mr. Christian? Pray, what is he saying?"

"That there is no hope for it but secession."

"There is nothing wrong in that," Shannon said, shoulders relaxing. "Your own father says it, and even my father is unwilling to discount the possibility."

"Yes, and if we were all of one mind, it would be a perfectly natural conversation. But as it is, Haley disagrees, and Mr. Christian says all manner of things to spike his guns, subtle jabs at Northerners, Negro-lovers especially. Frederick doesn't know where to look, he is so embarrassed, and Haley turns the other cheek time and again—just sitting silently, I mean."

Shannon lifted her brows, glancing down to find that Mr. Haley was, in fact, a capable dancer. She couldn't quite fathom his way of life. What was it like in Boston, she wondered? "We have no notion of that in Charleston," she said.

"Of turning the other cheek?" Arthur asked.

She looked back at him, pulling herself out of her abstraction with a slight smile. "I believe we find it morally repugnant to do so. Which cannot be as it should, when one considers it."

"Well, unless Haley is spiritless, if he spends very long in the man's company, he will very like throttle him, which cannot be right either."

"No, indeed, what a shocking thing in a common parlor," she answered, eyes dancing. And when she looked down the row of dancers, she caught Mr. Haley looking away from her.

Shannon's aunt and uncle arrived the next week upon invitation, bringing with them a valet and a lady's maid. Frederick was finally relegated to the flanker, and the ladies took Mrs. Richard Ravenel up to her chamber to rest. She was a rather retiring lady, always an interesting contrast to her husband. Uncle Richard was several years younger than his brother, and, though they favored very nearly, he was not nearly so elegant. He had a booming voice, which echoed off the walls of Santarella and amused Shannon for a few minutes before making her flee to the gardens.

She was feeling low and a bit lonely. She wished she were back in Charleston and wished herself nowhere but Santarella simultaneously. She tried to fill her time: she walked often in the gardens, took long rides, and read for hours. She thought the cause was that Frederick and Marie were spending all of their time with one another. She thought it odd for a couple that was the product of an arrangement and asked Mr. Haley if he agreed one day when she happened upon him in the library. She had almost feared Frederick's guest would think him neglectful, but he seemed to like solitude of country life. She sometimes saw him out riding and found him often reading.

He shrugged, his eyes upon her. "I think perhaps they wish to get their marriage off to a good start."

Standing by the wing chair, she said, eyes dancing a little, "And you think I ought to leave them alone."

Laughter leapt to his eyes. "Yes," he said bluntly.

"Very well, I shall. But, unlike you, I need human society. Will you ride with me?"

She had wanted to test him, to see if he would ride alone with a young lady. But she flushed when she realized he was looking at her knowingly, his eyes twinkling. His lips quirked into a smile, a little wry. "You think I'm prudish, don't you Miss Ravenel?" he said in his charming voice.

Her flush deepened. "Indeed, I do not. I honor you for your principles. Truly, they are refreshing in this...lackadaisical day in which we live."

His eyes twinkled. "That was very inventive," he approved.

"I thought so," she agreed, finally smiling.

His smile held for a moment and then slowly slipped away, his expression arrested. He was still holding her eyes, only a faint smile there now. "Yes, I'll ride with you, Miss Ravenel."

Her heart was flying like a thoroughbred at the derby. She couldn't have torn her eyes away even if she had tried. She moistened her lips. His distracted eyes trailed there, and then back up. Suddenly she couldn't breathe. The moment lengthened.

A shot sounded outside, jolting them. He looked away toward the window, and Shannon closed her eyes for a moment, taking a breath. By the time he turned around, she was composed. "What on earth—?" she asked, masking her breathlessness.

"I believe I heard your uncle mention something about shooting birds this morning," he answered.

"Oh. Heavens, we had all better take cover."

"Ought we?"

She moistened her lips, still recovering. "We'll go to the west field, which will be miles away from him." She smiled, the teasing light returning to her eyes. "That is...if you're certain you wish to."

"I'm certain," he said, lips tucked in gentle amusement, eyes twinkling. Looking at him, her mouth went dry, and she lost all of the arts of which she was so capable, every method she had used to bring men to their knees. He left her feeling ruffled, unsure.

He looked away, this time running his fingers through his fair hair. He reached to snatch his hat from a nearby table and then extended his hand to take her riding whip. "After you, Miss Ravenel," he said, clearing his throat.

She did so, holding her train, and he tucked the whips under his arm as he drew on his gloves. They walked in silence, and he was thoughtful enough to walk slowly. They made it to the stables, and her horse and his borrowed gray were brought out. He lifted her into the saddle gently, as if she weighed nothing. His hands lingered for a moment around the smallest part of her waist to give her time to arrange her skirts and secure herself. She met his eyes, her hands still on his shoulders, and he searched her face without embarrassment or hesitation.

He looked away finally, and she watched as he took his horse, saying softly, "Thank you."

Henry stepped away, answering, "Yes, sir." Then they set off toward the west field, which was being rotated out of crops this year and was, therefore, suitable for riding. Shannon narrowed her eyes surreptitiously, watching for signs of weakness in his horsemanship; she had often been disappointed by young men who had been raised in the city. But there was nothing to disappoint in Mr. Haley's handling of the powerful chestnut. Then she remembered that there was a country estate in Massachusetts. She conjured images of hunting parties on gray, cold days, of gentlemen returning from shooting with braces of pigeons over their shoulders.

"Is Boston your home, Mr. Haley?"

He glanced over at her and answered after a moment, "For half of the year, yes." He let her precede him through a gate. Once he had closed it, handing her his reins, and remounted, he added, "My family lives the rest of the year at Harmony Grove."

"Is there farming there?" she asked.

"Yes, we have a few tenants. And some hired men."

She smiled. "Then you must feel quite at home at Santarella."

He glanced at her, taking her measure for a moment. "Santarella is very different from Harmony Grove, Miss Ravenel. As I'm sure you know."

She studied him closely. She had not missed his meaning. "You think us very sinful, don't you, Mr. Haley. With our slaves and gambling and largesse."

This had been said in a quipping tone, but he looked at her seriously. There was a long moment, in which he hesitated. Finally, fingering his reins, he said, as though compelled, "I think slavery is a sin, yes."

He was a strange specimen. She had been taught all the strongest arguments for slavery, from the practical to the religious, and she could have argued the subject with him as well as any Southern Congressman. Instead, she asked, "Do you find the institution of slavery sinful, or the owners?"

He glanced at her. He took his time in answering, the horses walking along at a plodding, pleasant pace, the grass padding their way. "Certainly, the institution," he finally said. "As for the men... I like to think that had I been raised in...in this part of country—"

"No, what *were* you going to say?" she asked, quick to note his very slight hesitation. The militant sparkle in her eyes evaporated as they began to dance.

"I don't know what you mean," he said shortly. A little too shortly.

"A name for the South," she pursued, casting the blowing ribbons from her hat over her shoulder, glancing out at the sprawling green fields as she thought. "One of your common derogatory terms that you realized just now is not quite proper."

He tried very valiantly to keep his jaw rigid, but he gave a reluctant smile and said wryly, "Very well—the belly of the beast."

She gasped. "No!"

"I assure you it is a very common expression in Northern congregations and parlors," he said, giving an unexpected ripple of laughter.

Shannon was wiping her streaming eyes, saying as she caught her breath, "Very well: had you been raised in the belly of the beast, as were Frederick and I—what then?"

He had been watching her while she laughed, a faint, distracted smile in his eyes. He sobered, however, as her question registered. "I would like to think I would still have the same principles," he said softly, seriously, "but I suppose that is impossible, or at least unlikely." He looked at her, that look, the one thus far only Frederick had been privileged to see during his visit, entering his eyes, and said, "And I think I shall leave it at that, Miss Ravenel."

She pressed her lips together, imperfectly concealing a smile, and said, a challenge in her eyes, "Afraid, Mr. Haley?"

"Merely unwilling," he answered firmly.

She held his eyes, her smile slowly fading. She swallowed as the moment stretched out and studied him slowly. She said quietly after a time, "Forgive me, Mr. Haley. I shouldn't have pressed you. It was...inhospitable." She looked up at him penitently, biting her lip.

His lips parted. "No," he said. "You had a perfect right to curiosity." He made a survey of her beautiful, vulnerable features, and time seemed to lengthen or perhaps stand still. "You're too sweet by half, Shannon, in your heart. Someone will hurt you someday." His eyes scanned her face.

Shannon swallowed. "H...Heavens, no," she said, trying to keep her hands from trembling. "If I am penitent, it is because I am a shrew," she said, feigning lightness.

He smiled, and her heart clenched for reasons unknown. His gloved hand covered hers on the reins, hesitantly. He looked at her for a long moment. "Well, I suppose we went down an alley where we had no business."

"I rather forced you there at gunpoint," she interjected.

He laughed, removing his hand and taking both of his reins as they set off. "In any event, Frederick and I agreed to let that subject lie a long time ago."

Chapter Nine

With one thing and another, Mr. Haley stayed longer at Santarella than he had originally intended. In large part, this was due to Frederick's desire of his support during the engagement party that was to be hosted at Santarella. There were to be upwards of two hundred select guests from the finest South Carolinian families at this soirée. Another factor was that the tides were against him, making it almost impossible to leave. And so the autumn unfolded.

Shannon was sitting in the window seat in the blue paneled library reading *A Complete Guide to New England* when Frederick came in, sweating from his ride, dashing off his hat and wiping his forehead.

"Good heavens," she said, looking at him in awe, "is it still so warm?"

"Haley and I raced."

"On foot? I can't think you would win that, dearest," she said, biting her lip.

He gave her a sour look, going to the desk and picking up a piece of paper. "On horses. I had thought the humidity would kill him, but he's holding up well enough. And I have recently made a Will. I can cut you out of it easily enough."

She laughed. "I do not live in much terror, Brother, knowing I play second to Marie in *that* instrument. Is that what you are reading?"

He nodded, eyes still skimming it. "The lawyer mailed it from Charleston. Apparently, they sent the mail boat and now it's trapped. The crew is staying in a cabin at Ridgecrest," he said, frowning over one piece.

"Very unfortunate," she said. "Where is Mr. Haley now?"

"Changing."

"Did you take him to the beaches?"

He nodded, laying the paper aside. Then he walked forward, sitting with her in the window seat. "He says they're prettier than the beaches of Massachusetts, but perhaps he was being polite." He reached for her hand. "Shannon, you must help me."

She lifted her brows. "Of course, but what are you talking about?"

"Marie is nervous—what on earth is the cause? I know how females talk. Surely she's told you?"

"She has told me very little, I am afraid," Shannon answered, studying his dark eyes.

He looked away in thought. "I've racked my brains."

"Perhaps it is her father, agitating her out of all reason."

He shook his head. "She never lets him trouble her." He fingered the cuff of his coat, a habit from childhood. "Do you think it is all of the details, the...the hurly-burly?"

"I doubt it."

"The wedding night?"

"Frederick Shannon Ravenel!"

He scowled at her, giving her a revolted look. "Mary Shannon Ravenel!" he mocked.

"You are not supposed to speak of such things with your sister," she chided piously, lifting her chin.

"Well, with whom am I supposed to speak?" he demanded, put off by her virtue.

"Well, I don't know—but not me!"

"Will you tell her not to worry?"

"No, I most certainly will not," she said, equally revolted. "Besides which I don't think that is what is troubling her. I think perhaps she is merely overwhelmed with it all and desperately eager to make you happy."

"I am happy."

She smiled, pressing his hand. "I am glad to hear it." After he had returned her smile, she said, "Have you spoken of religion yet?" His brows drew together. She enlightened him. "If you remember, my dear, Uncle Richard let Aunt Coraline raise her Catholic."

"Oh, God," he said, laying his head in his hand. "Maybe we won't have any children."

Shannon laughed, but admonished, "Frederick! You do not mean that."

"Well, I wouldn't want Catholic children."

"Very well, raise them Presbyterian."

He looked up. "She's pretty devout, isn't she?"

Shannon nodded.

He sighed. "We'll have to discuss it, I suppose."

She said, "May I offer you a piece of advice, dear brother?"

"Well, if that isn't just like you!" he protested. "I asked for it ten minutes ago, and you ate me up!"

"Pertaining to something different," she said, her nose in the air.

"All right," he said, sighing.

She moistened her lips, studying him. Finally, she took his hand between both of hers. He had a gentleman's hands. She wondered if Marie had noticed it. "Don't...attempt to shelter Marie. Remember that she is a Ravenel. She has a strong mind. Discuss things with her; treat her as your equal. She may *seem* demure, but she won't be happy otherwise."

He studied her a moment before nodding once, and then again, thinking on it.

Chapter Ten

S hannon stood at the doors of the upstairs ballroom, watching the dancing in progress, hearing the sweet strains of the cello and wishing, discordantly, for a moment of peace. There was nothing like watching a ball from the safety of another room. But the wish to escape was a bit foreign to her. It was not an exaggeration to say that she was the most sought-after young lady in Charleston. She had nothing from which to shrink and everything to enjoy.

She watched Frederick and Marie dance a waltz, her mind trailing to a week previous when she and Marie had sat in the withdrawing room. They were penning the last of the invitations, their skirts arranged elegantly so that they pooled on the floor and did not wrinkle. Matilde, the housekeeper, took the letters from them and sealed them, creating neat stacks on the table.

"Have you discussed when the wedding will take place?" Shannon asked, wincing over the necessity of inviting a man she did not care for. She glanced at her cousin, a little surprised she had been forced to ask this question.

"Frederick says he will leave it all to me," Marie answered, pressing her lips together as she ruined a letter with a large blot.

"How very like a man," Shannon responded dryly.

Marie looked up quickly. "No, I believe he truly meant it for my benefit, wishing me to be perfectly comfortable, you see. I should like to be married in the spring, but that is the planting season."

Shannon surveyed her, finding her indecision odd. It was not her way. "Would you like to be married at Santarella, or..?"

"No, in Charleston," Marie answered, nodding once. "In my father's house. That is what makes it difficult, you see."

"Well, then, be married in February," Shannon suggested. "That will give you enough time for preparations but will leave time enough before planting."

Marie's shoulders loosened. "Yes, I suppose that will be best. Only, your mother does not think that will leave enough time for the gown to arrive from Paris."

"Marie, you must cease taking orders from my mother at once," Shannon said firmly. "She will control everything from the beads in your hair to the timing of the birth of your children if you allow it, and allow it you must *not*."

"Oh, Shannon, hush," Marie hissed. "What if she should hear you?"

"She is making a morning call at Ridgecrest," Shannon said, brows lifted. "Besides, I don't mean it to her derogation. I am very managing, too. If it was in your nature to follow, I should let you, but it is not, and if you continue in this way, I believe you will explode in the most untimely fashion. And *why* do you keep looking toward that door?"

Marie took a breath and pressed her lips together. After a moment, she said, "The gentlemen—our fathers and Frederick—are talking about settlements, and dowries, and wills... It seems so very...uncomfortable and..."

"Distasteful?" Shannon suggested. She pretended that she had known this meeting was taking place today. Pretended that it did not wound her that she felt herself to be left out of family business more and more each day. "But there is money involved, my dear cousin—a great deal of it. It must always have been the case had you married any man of wealth—or any man at all, considering your own family's fortune."

"Well, you will feel it should all be foregone someday, Shannon, when it serves only to make your betrothed feel trapped."

Shannon glanced up at Matilde at Marie's sharp tone. The slave woman was studiously surveying her wax, not looking up. "I rather doubt Frederick has said as much," Shannon said quietly, almost tartly.

Marie's eyes flew to hers. "No, of course he has not. But it is very treacherous, Shannon, such an arrangement. One feels as though one is balancing on a rope, and..." She glanced at Matilde, flushing a little when she realized her openness. She closed her lips.

Feeling a rush of sympathy, Shannon pressed Marie's hand on the table, giving her a look of compassion and commiseration. Marie smiled gratefully, returning the pressure. "He doesn't feel that way, Marie." She pressed her hand again, holding her eyes. "I promise you. I am his sister. I would know it if he did."

Marie held her eyes for a moment and then glanced up at Matilde. She again closed her lips. Shannon, following this, said, "Matilde, take these to Mr. Turnbull, if you will, for posting. We are already far too late in doing so."

"Yes, Miss Shannon," she said, glancing between the two girls, obviously knowing precisely why she was being dismissed.

As soon as she left, Shannon said, "Come, what is it?"

Marie sighed. "Have you ever thought that Frederick and I are very different, Shannon? He has led an exciting life, has that certain dash..."

"Dearest, do stop," Shannon said earnestly. "You are worrying yourself for naught and must believe that Frederick is perfectly content until he gives you reason to believe otherwise."

Shannon thought of it now, as she stood watching them dance. They seemed to be perfectly comfortable, even with easiness between them. She thought that was always the case when they were together. And perhaps Marie's imagination got the better of her in the dark of night as she lay in her bed, far away from Frederick.

In any event, Shannon knew she needed to return to the ballroom. Her father was standing with Seymour Christian and his father, attempting to catch her eye. She had been summoned.

"She is pensive," Shannon's dance partner said, "and yet so pretty."

Shannon glanced up at Mr. Christian with his dark, reckless

eyes and rakish smirk. "Oh, Seymour, not tonight," she said, using his given name since they had been children together, he slightly older, albeit. But they were close enough in age for him to have once given her braid a firm yank she hadn't forgotten.

"You disappoint me," he said.

"I was given to understand that I couldn't?"

He smiled. He did have a rather attractive smile, although not just to her taste. It was the kind of smile to ensnare a girl, and then leave her in a wasteland of misery. "Naturally, but where shall I be without your sparring? You know I came only for your sake."

Her eyes flitted up to his. "I know that we could make our families very happy, Seymour. But I am not certain that we should suit. Or that I should like your keeping a mistress."

His eyes widened. "You little shrew. Do you call yourself a lady and say such things to a man in the middle of your father's ballroom?" He was, perhaps, justifiably angry, but his hand was digging into her dress, gripping the fabric at her back.

"That's enough, Mr. Christian," she said sharply, and his grip loosened. "Now, I am sorry, but you cannot pretend it would be otherwise."

"It could be," he said, the tension draining out of him. "If I happened to love someone able to keep my attention."

"Thank you, but that sounds a rather exhausting proposition, sir."

"I might make you another proposition," he responded, a dancing demon in his eyes.

She ought to have been outraged, but instead she choked on a laugh. "To think they allow you in decent society."

His eyes scanned her face, more serious now. "I must have you, Shannon. And I will one day."

Her lips parted. She might have interpreted that in several ways, but her brain heard the undertone in his voice. And she was eager for the dance to end.

Shannon escaped the ballroom, lifting her wide skirts slightly, surreptitiously opening one of the glass doors which gave onto the balcony. She had danced with enough gentlemen to appease her mother, beginning with the sainted son of Ridgecrest. She had talked endlessly with the select of South Carolina. The air in the ballroom was thick with heat, the smell of perfumes, and talk of politics.

But on the balcony, the night was cool, and the stars were clear overhead. She placed her wrap around her arms, picking up where her short lace sleeves came to a point and ended. She touched her forehead. The pins and the weight of her hair were beginning to cause a headache.

Her mood was somber, and she tracked it easily enough to the changes within her family, to a few weeks in which she had not been perfectly happy. *He is leaving in three days.*

She swallowed, her eyes almost blinded with moisture. She pulled her wrap tight, crossing her arms.

The door opened, creaking, and she looked quickly over her shoulder, her heart dropping when she recognized that elegant stature. It was strange how Seymour Christian fell abysmally flat in comparison. She had always thought her tastes ran to men with dark hair. She had been mistaken.

She met his eyes, and Mr. Haley merely studied her. There was a sweetness in him, not noticeable at first, that his eyes occasionally gave away. And there was trouble there and, she thought, worry, which made her knees rather weak. Frederick's friend was not to be troubled with his sister's emotions. "Are you well?" he asked.

She forced a smile as he stopped before her. "Indeed, I am, Mr. Haley. I do not believe we have danced tonight, though I saw you were the second to whom Marie gave her hand."

He smiled briefly, placing his hand along the rail. He had removed his gloves and discarded them somewhere, it seemed. He looked extremely elegant in formal dress wear. "Your cousin is charming," he said. "Frederick is very lucky."

"Yes, indeed, he is. I have other cousins, from my mother's family. But Marie has always been my favorite." She studied him with curiosity. After a moment, she asked tentatively, "What do you think of Frederick's Charleston friends?"

He lifted a shoulder. "They have been friendly enough."

"And our neighbor, Seymour Christian?" He could not see the fiend in her eye, but it was there, nonetheless.

He stiffened, almost imperceptibly, turning his face away. "I saw you dancing with him."

Shannon looked at his profile, assessing. Her heart began pounding rapidly, her headache dissipating on a heady wave of—something. "My father is rather keen for me to marry him." She watched him closely.

His jaw hardened. Heavens. "I noticed," he said.

She let a heartbeat of silence pass and then said, "Do you think I ought to marry him, Mr. Haley?"

"No." The word was firm and unhesitating. His blue eyes, which could laugh beautifully but were just now steadily holding hers, as though taking her measure, were dark with desire. He swallowed, and her mouth went entirely dry. Good heavens, one would think swallowing a simple enough performance. "He would not make you happy," he said, barely above a whisper.

She managed to swallow, her throat feeling raw. "How do you know what would make me happy, sir?" she asked, tilting her chin up.

"I don't know," he said softly. "But I know you have not been these past weeks." There was a long pause. He soaked in her features. "And that you deserve to be, Miss Ravenel."

A tear rolled down her cheek. His lips parted. "Do not cry," he said, lifting his hand and then hesitating.

She met his eyes, biting her lip as another tear tracked down her cheek. And then his hands were on her waist, tugging her gently against him. She slowly lifted her eyes to his, content to rest there, her gaze searching, but not hurriedly. His body against hers made her feel weak and feminine. His lips brushed hers, sweetly at first, and then, after the first taste, hungrily. Her eyes slipped closed.

It was not long before they were moving in rhythm with one another, want and need which had been carefully restrained for weeks spilling over. Frederick's friend, this gentleman who was supposed to make a pleasant visit with them and then walk as nonchalantly out of their lives. Only there was nothing nonchalant about him. Her fingers touched his face, finally exploring his interesting jawline, feeling the very slight stubble as they progressed. His fingers were pressing into her back, pulling her closer, closer, and their lips worked in perfect harmony.

Just when she started to realize that they needed to cease, that it was dangerous to tread any further, he broke the kiss. He looked at her as though she had just performed a miracle, or perhaps witchcraft, startled and shaken, his breaths coming heavily. The desire, if anything, was only heightened in his eyes. He was still holding her waist. "I shouldn't have done that," he whispered, looking remorseful. "To use you in such a manner... I'm not even courting you."

She studied his face. "Only because you have not asked, Mr. Haley," she said, her lips lifting in a slight, shy smile.

There was a heartbeat of silence. "Do you want me to?" he asked, eyes never wavering from hers, looking entirely stunned.

She laughed, eyes glittering. "What you must think of me. I promise you I do not kiss every gentleman I happen to encounter on a balcony in such a manner."

He touched her arm. "No, of course n— I thought it was impossible," he said, making a rapid survey of her face.

She lay her hand on his. "We may learn one another better, if you like, before truly courting."

"No, I do not like," he said firmly.

"Are you perfectly sure you wish to entangle yourself with a Southern girl?"

His lips lifted as he exhaled. "I think, and have been thinking for some time, that a Southern girl is all that will do for me."

Her lips parted. She said shakily, "Very well, talk to Papa in the morning."

His smile faded. "Yes, I will..." His brows were troubled. "But he isn't going to allow it!"

"You don't know that," she responded. "Your family is well-respected in Massachusetts, is it not?" At his single, distracted nod, she said, "Well, then. What more can he want? He has been attempting to arrange my marriage since I was seven years old."

He smiled briefly but again looked distracted. "He will want a Southerner for you. From an old planting family. I have heard him say as much."

"Oh, what is that, but a mere aspiration?" she asked. "Jane Bell married a man from New York last year, and you would have thought he was the heir to a European throne." Her cheeks flooded crimson. She bit her lip.

He finally gave his smile, which she felt to her toes, and there was such a twinkling look in his eyes that a bubble of laughter escaped her. Releasing her unwillingly, as though he knew he must not touch her again tonight, he said, "I will speak with him in the morning." She thought he almost took a step toward her, but he refrained. He stood away from her, dragging a hand through his hair as though attempting to gather his wits. With a few feet between them, she felt shy. He was suddenly the handsome friend who had walked in with Frederick the first day, unknown to her and terribly enticing. She felt wholly unlike herself, weak and vulnerable and dependent. But though he had caused it, she could not bring herself in that moment to blame him.

Chapter Eleven

There were a hundred freaking sea islands off the coast of South Carolina. Adeline had found that out before she ever drove toward Fort Sumter. She was going to have to decide whether looking for Santarella was a waste of time, or if it was worth it to learn about the family history.

In point of fact, she wasn't precisely driving to Fort Sumter. She was riding with Harris in his little Infiniti, which he explained by way of student debt. She laughed, liking his sense of humor, and said, "Don't I know it. I'll be paying until I'm sixty."

"Adrian's a lucky devil," he said with masculine envy. "Full ride to med school."

She lifted her brows. "Is he that smart?"

"He's a wizard. Jude's just like him. The kid was reading at three. Which was lucky, since the Thomases are all kind of ditzy. I roomed with Jude's uncle in college. No common sense—just money."

Adeline was silent for a moment. "He...told me what happened. It was an awful thing."

He looked at her, lifting a brow. She kind of wished he'd look at the road, but no biggie. There was another silence. "Adrian talked to you about that?" he said finally.

"He told me his wife had died in a car wreck," she affirmed.

"He doesn't talk with *anybody* about that. Not with me, and I was there, for crying out loud. How long have you known him?" he demanded.

"About a week," she said, wishing she hadn't said anything. If Harris said something to him, it would sound like she had been gossiping. "Jude was terrified in the storm, and I think he thought he should explain. That's literally all he said, though: 'My wife was killed in a car wreck, and he was in the car.'"

"Hmm." He left the topic, and they were soon talking about Santarella and the possibilities. He turned into the parking lot next to the departure point and paid the fee. They walked toward the wharf where the large white boat was waiting to take them. There was a nice warm breeze, and seagulls stood here and there on posts. She liked living by the sea.

They were nearly to the boardwalk when they heard, "Uncle Harris!" Jude started running toward them. Adeline saw Dr. Ravenel leaning against the boardwalk. He had been looking at his phone but at that looked up. His eyes narrowed.

Harris laughed when Jude caught up to them, catching him and tossing him in the air once before putting him on his hip. "Let's go see your daddy," he said.

When they made it to him, the elder brother was still leaning casually, arms crossed, eyes still narrowed. "Harris," he said. "Miss Miller." He seemed to be confused and a little suspicious.

"You knew we were meeting today to talk about the house," his brother said pleasantly.

"No," he answered, looking at Adeline. "I didn't."

"Well, we did," Harris said, obviously carefully concealing his exasperation. "And I commanded her to come. Thought we could use the company of a lady, eh Jude?"

Jude smiled shyly at Adeline. She had never seen him as exuberant as he had been upon seeing his uncle. He looked impossibly cute in his little bowtie and boat shoes.

There was an ominous silence from the dock. "Oh. Well, we had better board."

Harris halfway rolled his eyes and then said, "Sure. Lead on, Nephew!" Jude did, dragging Harris behind him. Adeline fell into step beside Dr. Ravenel, which was awkward.

Several seconds of silence passed as she walked on the boardwalk, wondering if she had worn the right shoes. Surely, they wouldn't get wet on a historical tour.

"Did you learn anything about the house?" he finally said.

"We think it—Santarella, I mean— may have been in the Sea Islands. I'm not sure how far I'm going to pursue that. It could take months to figure out where it is...or used to be."

He seemed to be thinking. "I think it's worth pursuing," he said finally. "Even if it puts us a little off schedule."

Well, that was easy. "I think it's a good decision. I could make it time-period-appropriate easily. But I'd far prefer to know how it was when they lived here."

"What were you wanting the precise date to be?" he asked.

He wasn't a true history-lover, but at least he cared.

"Well, that's up to you, but I was thinking 1860. It'll bring in the history of Fort Sumter, just across the way, and it should've been at the height of your family's wealth." The boardwalk sort of popped beneath her. It sounded a bit ominous, but hundreds of people had to pass over it every day.

"I assume it was my family. We could've been cousins and the entire thing was blown out of proportion, you know," he said.

"Is there any chance you know whether you're descended from Frederick Ravenel?"

He looked at her, expression arrested. "Yes. That was my grandfather's name. He was named after his...great-grandfather, I think."

"Then you're it. The original Ravenels," she said, smiling. "I have a friend who's a title abstractor. We ran Ravenel-Thompson House back to when it was built."

"What is his wife's name, my many-times grandmother?" he asked, brushing a fly off his temple. "I knew that once, I think."

She thought for a minute. "Mary, or Marie? Something like that."

He shook his head. "I don't think that's..." He narrowed his eyes, distracted by his son boarding. Harris held his hand securely, though, and he was soon safely aboard. When they got to the steps, he said, "You go on," giving her his hand for stability while she climbed the steps. It was like lightening. It made her hand feel like it was on fire, and her arm felt weak. Good heavenly days, he had nice hands. She just needed to get on the boat and sit down.

She did, sitting next to Jude and Harris, lifting her pamphlet to fan herself.

He sat on the other side of Harris, for which she was thankful. She'd just focus on the history for the rest of the tour.

"Glad to see you found your manners," Harris hissed once they were heading toward the island. Jude sat between Harris and Ms. Miller, holding the railing as the two looked for dolphins and chatted about them.

"I don't know what you mean."

"You were rude to her!" Harris exclaimed in an under voice. "What the heck, Adrian? It's not like you."

"I didn't realize you'd be bringing your girlfriend," Adrian said, raising and lowering his eyebrows.

Harris sent him a level look. "Dude. What's up with you?"

"Shh. I don't want Jude to think we're arguing."

"He can't hear over the narration." There was no need for either of them to listen: their grandparents had taken them countless times on their summer visits to Charleston. "You know we just met today. I'm just trying to be friendly."

"Just take care you're not too friendly."

Harris looked at him like he'd grown another head. "And so what if I am? She's pretty, smart, well-educated, owns her own business..."

"She's not your type."

"She's more my type than yours."

A pause. "True," Adrian said, conceding that point.

A slow, small smile began on Harris's face. It was like a

lightbulb went on in his head, though what it was, Adrian was at a loss to know. "You're jealous."

"What? No, don't be ridiculous." It felt like he had been playing dodgeball since he'd boarded. He should've sat next to Ms. Miller.

Harris's dark eyes sparkled. "It's fine! It's about time you showed some interest in women."

"I have *always* shown interest in women. And I have no interest in Ms. Miller. As you said, we couldn't be more different."

"Oh, I don't know. Opposites attract, and all that. This could really work," he said, twitching his brows.

"Opposites don't really attract: it's a myth. And she eats tacos and wears shoes without socks."

"Yeah, well, so does ninety percent of America, Adrian."

"I'm not interested, all right? Date her if you want," he said roughly. "I'm not dating anyone."

Harris studied him. "What do you mean?"

"I'm not going to bring woman after woman traipsing through Jude's life. Children don't need that kind of instability, especially ones with traumatic childhoods."

"It wouldn't be woman after woman. And Jude needs a mother, you know."

"He had one: she died. There's nothing I can do about that."

Harris's features softened in a way he hadn't meant for them to. "I know. Sorry. It's none of my business." The boat was now nearing the island, and Jude and the preservationist were enthralled. Jude was attracting the attention of all the old ladies on the boat. He was a beautiful child.

Harris turned back to him. "You may as well be nice to

her, though. I think you're still miffed she bested you on nego-
tiating live-in status. But she did, so move on. She's going to
be there for months."

"I'm perfectly nice. Even cordial."

"All right. Whatever." Harris turned as the boat came to a
halt and extended his hand toward Jude.

"D'ya see the dolphins, Uncle Harris?"

"Sure did," he said. "Are you sure they weren't sharks?"

"Ms. Miller said they were dolphins. She said they're
friendly. They like following boats."

Harris smiled at Ms. Miller and then led Jude off the boat.
"I'm sure she's right."

Adrian followed her off. He offered his hand, but she said,
"I'm good—thanks!"

They toured the premises for an hour. It seemed like a long
hour to Adrian, but Jude was having the time of his life, as was
the preservationist. She explained several things to him, in
much greater detail than the guides could. It was while they
were standing up on the battlements trying to pick out his
house that Harris dropped the bombshell.

"You're going to have to drive her to Statesboro to get the
box from Mom and Dad."

"What? No. It was your idea. You drive her."

"I live in Savannah, Adrian. I can't drive to Charleston to
pick her up and then back to Georgia. And I'm just trying to
help with the house."

"I know. But I don't have time. I can't take a day off work,
and Jane can't be there this Saturday for Jude."

"So take him with you."

"I'm not taking a six-year-old on a two-and-a-half-hour drive, picking up a box, and turning around and coming home. He'd be miserable, and then he'd beg to stay with Mom and Dad, and I wouldn't get him out of there until six o'clock, if I got him out at all. He'd end up staying the night, and I'd have to pick him up on Sunday."

Harris laughed. "True."

"Why can't she just go herself? I'll give her directions, and—"

"Oh, come on, Adrian. She'd feel awkward, knocking on someone's door she'd never met and asking for family documents. And mom would make her feel uncomfortable, but she won't if you're there. Just to warn you: Mom thinks you're coming, and she mentioned that you hadn't been in three months. She'll think you don't want to see her if you don't."

Adrian sighed, rubbing his forehead. "All right, but it'll have to be next Saturday. We talk on the phone twice a week. I don't know why I'm suddenly the prodigal."

"Yeah, well, you don't have supper with them every Sunday night," Harris said bitterly. "It's enough to make me think about getting a cat."

Adrian laughed. "You chose Savannah. What is she doing now? I don't think she's supposed to be touching that." Harris followed his eyes to where Ms. Miller was giving the patient Jude a history lesson. It reminded him a little of his grandma, breaking the rules and then asking the security officer whether he wanted the boys to learn or not. He smiled a little.

They wrapped things up, and Adrian put Jude on his shoulders for the long boardwalk back to the boat. Jude gripped his hair, making him wince, untangle his little fingers, and give him his hands instead. "Look Daddy, there's the bridge. They said it's the Ravenel bridge. Is it named after us?"

"I don't think so. Probably some kin." He sat him down inside the boat once they were there, not trusting it to someone else this time. He followed him in, letting Harris be Ms. Miller's escort this time. He'd brought her, after all.

It was late by the time they got home. They had gone out to eat at a cute seafood shack. Then, to celebrate Jude's impending kindergarten graduation, which Harris would be unable to attend, they had gotten ice cream, which was, as Jude had whispered to Adeline, his favorite.

Then Harris had driven her to Kudu to get her car. It was already dark, and it felt strangely date-like. Probably because she had caught him looking at her legs earlier. Not in an inappropriate way, but male attention always made a girl hyperaware. He stopped right next to her door. "I'll wait to protect you from any lurking creatures," he said.

"Are you trying to freak me out?" she demanded, reaching for her purse.

He laughed. "Thanks for going. It was fun."

"I enjoyed it, too," she answered, reaching for the door handle.

"Oh, wait," he said, reaching into the back. "The folder."

She looked at it, and then back up at him. "Harris, are you sure? I'm not sure I should take it."

"Just to borrow. I trust you—if you can't take care of old documents, who can?"

She smiled, finally taking it. "I'll guard it with my life."

He smiled, and she got out, going to her SUV. She waved and drove off toward the Battery. Charleston was grand at night. Masterful house after house rolled past. Lights and fountains, hidden worlds behind every expensive window.

She went in the back way, locking the door behind her, and climbed the stairs. She saw a light beneath Jude's door and heard the two of them in there talking, Jude giggling now and then. She smiled, inexplicably lingering, before starting up the next flight of stairs.

She took another shower and put on her old pajamas. She yawned and looked at the folder, which was beckoning. But she was too tired to make any sense of it, so it would have to wait until tomorrow.

Chapter Twelve

Adeline spent the next few days chipping paint and sanding the dining room fireplace. When her stain arrived, she commandeered the can before the crew could and spent the next four hours oh-so-carefully rubbing it on.

When she finally stood, rolling her neck, she was pleased with her masterpiece. She quickly took a picture of it to send to her secretary in North Carolina. She could pair it with the "before" picture on the website of Miller Restorations. She stepped back and admired its breath-taking beauty. But not for long.

Moving on to the library, she suspected the fireplace in there of hiding an older coal-burning fireplace behind it. Two hours later, she had two men in the room with her, prying off the wooden mantle, while she stood behind, her hands templed against her lips as she prayed there would be something behind it. And that, if there wasn't, they wouldn't damage the 1880s mantle in their hands.

"There's something here," Jake said, reaching in bravely, sitting on his knees on the hearth.

Adeline hovered over them, finally deciding to sit on the desk facing them. She didn't notice at first that there were obviously signs that the desk was being used currently. But while the guys worked on a particularly treacherous nailing near the base of the mantle for about thirty minutes, she had more leisure to look around her. There were huge tomes of psychological philosophers, old and new, some of them with sticky notes in them. A neat stack of bills which hadn't been opened. A file organizer with tabs which read, "Work," "Jude," "Lauren," "Taxes," and "Preserv." She'd really like to take a long gander at two of those. There was an expensive wooden pencil holder, a black and white picture of him and Jude, and a sticky note that said, "Call N." To have so much stuff on it, it was the neatest desk she had ever seen. She didn't think she could make it look like that even after an hour. No wonder he had been a little touchy about having the entire house turned upside down at the same time.

She had just, thankfully, returned her attention to the men when she saw the man himself materialize in the door. She first noticed that he must have just gotten home from work. He wore a suit as well as James Bond. She second remembered that she was sitting on his desk.

He was looking in the room, taking note of the men at the fireplace, and then looking at Adeline again. She jumped up. "Sorry. I was kind of enthralled. We think there may be an older fireplace behind it." He nodded, entering. The men said polite greetings. He answered them, perfectly politely, but with loads of reserve. He watched what they were doing with mild interest for about three minutes before coming over to the desk and picking up the bills from it. He hesitated, but, glancing over his shoulder and seeing the men fully engaged in their work, he took his keys out of his pocket and locked one of the drawers.

She lifted her brows. They had talked about this. He studied her for a moment before taking one of the notepads and writing, "Client files." He slid it toward her.

Oh, well, she guessed that was different. She just wondered why they were here. Then again, sometimes he shut the door and had long phone conversations. She had thought they might be to a girlfriend, but now she wondered if he did phone consultations. She nodded, and he ripped the top note off and distractedly crushed it in his hand, looking around for what else he could save from destruction.

"I'm pretty sure Jane's in the kitchen with Jude."

"Yeah, I'm going," he said slightly dryly, and with alarming perception. "Hope you find the fireplace."

She did, too.

In about another hour, once the other had been safely removed and the brick behind it demolished, she stood as dramatically as though she were at the opening of Tut's tomb, awaiting treasures.

"There it is, ma'am," Thomas said with satisfaction. "Mantle and grate. It's missing the cover, and it looks like it hasn't operated in centuries."

She got up, running her hands over the exquisite mantle and the insides, which were cast iron and cool to the touch. Had it been worth it? It would cost a lot of money to fix. "I think... Of course, we won't actually use it. I can find a cover easily enough."

"I think you can fix it," Thomas said. "I've seen you fix worse."

She appreciated the vote of confidence. But the materials were going to be really expensive. She'd have to talk to Dr. Ravenel about what he was willing to do. Just then, she felt something up above the mantle. The object was between the mantle and the wall above. She could've sworn it was the same wood carving. Heart pounding, she took Thomas's tool from him and, though they probably thought she was mad, pulled the wall away.

"Yes," she whispered, seeing that she had been right. "Thomas, remove this whole wall."

He swallowed, looking nervous. But he obeyed. The longer he worked, the more the men's jaws hung open, and she covered her mouth, tears starting to her eyes. The mantle continued all the way to the ceiling with exquisite carving, sometimes painted cream, sometimes showing little inlays of wood. At the top, it ended in molding that flowed into the ceiling without skipping a beat.

She shook her head as they all stared in silence. There was not a doubt in her mind that it had come out of a European castle. Until she looked in the center and saw, very demurely, a coat of arms painted the same color. One almost missed it, for the rest was so detailed. There was an eagle and a lion and a shield with a star and a palm. And the words, "*Que sursum volo videri.*" She swallowed.

"What does it say?" Jake asked. "Want me to google it?"

"'I would see what is above,'" she said. It was rather lofty.

"A religious thing?" Thomas asked.

"I think so," she said. "The family who lived here, if Ancestry.com is right, were French Huguenots. I think it speaks to their commitment to their faith, despite persecution."

She could stare at the fireplace for hours. Good heavens, and to think it was hiding just behind this desk all the while, and that she could've missed it. It lit a fire in her to find out about the lives of the family. And to be able to reproduce this beautiful house.

There was no question: She would be restoring the fireplace. And she was finding Santarella.

Adeline discussed the necessary changes to the original plan with her employer. He, looking at the fireplace, whose worth he seemed to understand, even if it was badly in need of repair, had said, "Yeah, do whatever it takes."

She had felt a rush of gratitude for him. So many people couldn't afford it when they ran into things like this or weren't willing to extend the time it would take. But he seemed to be all in, even though this would prolong the project by a month and cost figures which had caused her to wince while she was telling him. She wondered how he had gotten his money, besides his probably exorbitant salary. She hoped he wasn't a drug dealer, or something.

Okay, she needed Harris to buy her another one of those coffees. She was loopy and talking to the silk wallpaper again as she coaxed the layers over it away very carefully. She looked at her watch: ten o'clock. Officially a workaholic with no life. It was time for bed. She would have to remember to live tomorrow.

She went upstairs and spent fifteen minutes on the phone with her mom, who not-so-subtly asked if Adeline had found a church in Charleston. She wrote *Find Church* in her calendar for Sunday. Her mom told her all about her sister's 5th grade class's cute production, choreographed and costumed one-hundred percent by Annie, and about her brother's C in Biology, which Adeline assured her mom wouldn't harm Austen's chances of getting into a good MBA program. She'd have to text that kid, though. He was a fifth-year senior: he should've gotten that out of the way ages ago.

That finished, she took a shower in the refrigerator-sized shower and put on a big T-shirt. She was tired, but the folder, long-neglected, beckoned her. She reached for it on the tiny nightstand and opened it.

Skimming through the letters, she was at first confused by the constant references to Massachusetts. It seemed like these had been pulled and separated because they were from the war era. At least, that was what she assumed. There were references, standing out to her in the letters, to Union lines, Naval bases, and "difficulties." She couldn't see the whole picture, though. And, obviously, they hadn't been writing so that someone would later read them and know every aspect of their lives. In fact, they seemed to be writing almost cryptically, she thought, in some of the letters.

There were names—Frederick, Marie—yes, she knew who they were! Her heart sped. But Shannon and Rose were new to her. She had no idea how they were connected to the house or family. And she had a feeling it would take the box in Mr. and Mrs. Ravenel's basement to find out.

The next day, Adeline was microwaving her breakfast turnover, bold and feminist and everything, but still too skittish to use his actual stove, when Dr. Ravenel came in, dressed for work, a cute little lunch box and backpack in his left hand.

"Hi," she said. "I think he spilled something on his uniform. Jane took him that way." She nodded toward a little hall which led to a bathroom.

Dr. Ravenel was in a gray suit, a white shirt which showed his trim waist, and a blue tie. "What is that?" he asked, eyes on the microwave.

"Breakfast," she said.

"It stinks."

"Do you think so?" she asked, looking at the microwave. He stared at her for a long time, his temper seeming a little short. "I'll...light a candle, or something," she conceded.

"No, whatever, I'm going. The whole house is a wreck anyway."

"The joys of restoration," she said. Really. Not. A Morning Person.

He nodded once, turning to go. He turned back. "Oh, I forgot to mention: I'll drive you to Statesboro next Saturday if you still want me to."

Her heart sped. "That would be awesome."

There was some noise in the foyer, Jude and Jane talking. He glanced that way and then back at her. "We'll leave at one o'clock, if you want. Jane's free that afternoon, so she can keep Jude."

"Sounds good to me."

Chapter Thirteen

John Thomas stood outside the door of Mr. Ravenel's library the next morning, more nervous than ever in his life. That Frederick was going to murder him was by now accepted. He would be shocked and probably horrified. But Frederick would have to wait.

He again looked at the closed wooden door. There was no question that John Ravenel was an intimidating man. He had stayed up until three o'clock in the morning and had risen at six. His children were wary of crossing him. But that had never troubled John Thomas until he had wanted his daughter.

And there was equally no question that Shannon was the jewel of Santarella. She might feel neglected just now, but it had not taken him two hours in company of the family to see the pride they felt in her. And to know that expectations for her were every bit as high as they were for Frederick.

Shannon Ravenel was not just a belle of South Carolina, but *the* belle. If that hadn't been perfectly obvious before, it had become so last night at the ball. He was quite out of his depth with her. No unattached man could refrain from soliciting her hand, no mama anxious to marry a daughter off could cease to mourn her existence, and the other young ladies either loved or hated her strongly. The thought of her with a low-ranking Naval officer was laughable, when her father seemed to have either a Middleton or a Christian in his sights. The thought briefly entered his mind that her mother might not feel the same, that she might be an ally. But there was no denying that her father would have the final say.

A negative answer was more than he could bear to think of. Was that mad? They hardly knew one another. He knew almost nothing about Shannon, although every tidbit Frederick had ever let fall had been carefully called up as he had lain sleepless in his bed last night. She had been brought up at Santarella and Ravenel House, had attended a select school in Charleston before being presented to society. That was all he could recollect. There was no question that she was different from any woman with whom he had ever, in his vague imaginings, pictured himself.

He thought of riding onto Santarella lands that day with Frederick and seeing the human bondage around him. He dwelled briefly on the vast differences between him and Miss Ravenel before feeling frustrated with himself. Shannon may have been raised in the heart of slave country, but she could no more help that than he could help his feelings for her. And surely love was enough to overcome any differences between them.

He had fruitlessly tried to remember whether any previous courtships had been mentioned. Her kiss had perhaps been borne of passion, but it was not that of a novice. This hadn't particularly disturbed him, except that to learn he was capable of swift and blinding jealousy had been disturbing.

He lifted his hand to knock, waiting.

"Come in," Mr. Ravenel called in a pleasant voice, so different from his father's sharp, "Enter!"

It was fortunate that he had this thought, for he walked in with a smile flitting across his features. "Ah, Mr. Haley," the man said. "I'm glad to know there are two of us not sleeping the day away."

"I cannot pretend to your stamina, sir," he said, giving a charming smile. "I did not rest well."

"I hope you find your chamber comfortable enough," the man said, the look in his deep-set eyes perfectly pleasant. But one always had the feeling that he was measuring, measuring. Not unlike his daughter.

"Oh, yes. Santarella is a very comfortable house," he said.

Mr. Ravenel indicated with his hand for him to sit in front of his desk. "We will be sorry for you to leave. And my son will be sorry not to have you stand up with him at his wedding."

John Thomas nodded, not certain how to open the negotiations. Especially not when he thought that the man would be entirely taken aback. He cleared his throat and tried to gather his thoughts.

"Is something troubling you, young man?"

He looked up quickly. "I... Yes." Summoning military confidence, he said, "I wish to speak with you about Miss Ravenel, sir."

Mr. Ravenel lifted his silver brows. "About Shannon," he

said with surprise. "What is it about my daughter that you wish to say, Mr. Haley?"

His hands, clasped in his lap, clenched. "I wish to ask your permission to court her, sir."

Dead silence. The wind could be heard outside. The dishes from the kitchen in the nearby flanker were heard clanging. Mr. Ravenel's eyes never left him, and his face gave away nothing. "Does Shannon share this desire?" he asked.

"Yes, sir."

His sharp eyes narrowed, and he made a deep study of John Thomas's face. "I confess myself to be rather surprised, Mr. Haley. I thought you came to us merely as Frederick's friend."

"I did," John Thomas answered.

The man sat back, surveying him. "And then you met Shannon."

John Thomas slowly nodded, holding his eyes.

"Well, I am certain it has been a very romantic setting and that Shannon has been feeling herself a little left out. She has been spoiled. But you will go back to Massachusetts, Mr. Haley, and Shannon will stay in South Carolina." He gestured pleasantly. "A few months will pass, and you will never think of one another again."

"*No,*" John Thomas said. The word had been torn out of him, much to his own surprise, and, if he wasn't mistaken, Mr. Ravenel's. "I am deadly in earnest, sir," he said, seriously and firmly.

Another long silence followed, during which Mr. Ravenel again regarded him. After a minute or two had passed, he said, "I see. You may not know, Mr. Haley, that I have been in talks with George Christian regarding an alliance between my daughter and his son."

John Thomas was shaking his head. "He is not worthy of her."

"And you think you are?" the man questioned, a little less pleasantly and almost before John Thomas had finished speaking.

"No, I... I don't think anyone could be—"

"Then there is one thing, it seems, upon which we agree, Mr. Haley."

"—but I will be faithful to her, and he will not. I love her, and he—"

"Are we speaking of courtship, Mr. Haley, or marriage?" Shannon's father interjected in a strident tone.

John Thomas halted the back and forth, hesitating, but saying after a moment, "Whatever you are willing to allow, sir."

This surprised a laugh out of Mr. Ravenel, who remembered suddenly how much he liked the young man. And how steadying his influence had been upon a boy he had worried about more hours of the day than he cared to think of. He thought of that wild gleam in Seymour Christian's eyes and realized that young Haley had taken his measure almost instantly. He had carried those thoughts to their natural conclusion when he himself had overlooked them, though he was no stranger to the ways of his peers.

"I like you, John Thomas. My family likes you. But Shannon is the only daughter I have. You cannot expect me to give her away without second thought to any man who asks for her hand. I ask that you give me some time to think and to speak with her mother."

"Yes, of *course*," John Thomas said softly, rising. The air was thick in the room, and he was eager to leave it.

"We'll be speaking soon," Mr. Ravenel said, picking up a paper from his desk.

"Yes, sir," John Thomas answered, inclining his head and turning to walk toward the door. When he opened it, he startled Frederick and Shannon, who had both, to his surprise, been standing outside. There were also several slaves, all of whom seemed to be busying themselves in the foyer. Frederick's jaw was hanging open, and he surveyed his friend in real astonishment. Shannon was standing with her arms crossed, glancing at him, looking as though she might burst into tears. No one said anything for a heavy moment.

And then, without warning, Shannon started for the front door, which the butler opened for her, and fled, all but running. John Thomas's eyes followed her. He opened his lips, looked at Frederick, and closed them. He looked back at the door. "We'll... talk later," he said, starting after Shannon.

When he arrived on the porch, he looked past the columns to the sweeping view ahead and saw her running away from the house. She was wearing a green dress with the widest hoops possible and seemed to float gracefully down the hill, her skirt caught up just slightly in her hands. His breath caught, from her beauty and from the possibility of chasing after Shannon the rest of his life. It was as though he almost saw into the future, and he felt a heady rush of longing and pain and the knowledge that anything else would be second best.

He set out after her and overtook her at the base of the hill beneath an ancient live oak tree, many of its branches touching the ground. He caught her arm gently, not touching her otherwise, and said softly, "What is it?" She was not looking at him, her countenance still turned, a storm of emotions present. He said, "Is it because I spoke to him of marriage?"

She laughed softly, not pleasantly. "No." She looked at him finally. He made a study of her features. "He will not allow it, John Thomas. I should've known that. I was...deceiving myself. And I cannot bear the way he spoke to you."

He continued to hold her arm, partly for comfort, and partly because he knew she was struggling for air in her corset. He smiled softly, his thumb stroking the fabric of her pagoda sleeve. "I have been spoken to ten thousand times more harshly without wilting. And he said he would consider it."

"You do not know him," she said, looking away across the gray November day. "He must and shall make an alliance for me of his own choosing."

"Only if you allow it, Shannon," he said firmly, looking at her, unwilling to allow her to give in.

She met his eyes, seeming to calm at his words. Her eyes were deep blue and seeking, the set of her lips vulnerable. "Are we mad?" she whispered.

"Perhaps," he said, reaching up to brush a strand of her red hair back, still amazed that he was allowed to do so. Although her father might feel differently. He smiled. "Was I mad to speak of marriage?"

"No," she answered. She bit her lip, looking afraid of what he would say. His lips parted at her words, and she whispered,

"Ask me, John Thomas."

"Your father…" he said softly. He searched her face rapidly.

"I want his blessing," she said. She moistened her lips. "But I do not have to have it."

He took a breath, his lips lifting in a smile. He sank to one knee, taking her hand into his. He met her eyes and saw tears. "Then will you marry me, Mary Shannon Ravenel?"

Her lip trembled, and she nodded. "Yes," she whispered, a smile blooming on her beautiful lips.

He met her smile, holding her eyes for a long moment before bringing her hand to his lips and kissing the place where his ring would sit. When next he looked up, she was biting her lip, trying to hold back fresh tears. "You must get up," she said, attempting a note of levity. "You will be spending most of your life at my feet, you know." He laughed, getting up and bringing her to him in an embrace beneath the tree. She lifted her head and met his smile.

He lifted her off the ground, spinning her around and around as she squealed, alternately protesting and laughing like a child.

Mr. Ravenel exited his library and climbed the staircase, his hand sliding up the banister as he looked ahead of him, eyes unseeing as his mind worked. He came to his chamber and knocked, waiting to hear, "Come in," before he opened the door.

His wife was sitting in front of a mirror as Abigail pinned her hair. He closed the door behind him and stood off to the side, crossing his arms, waiting. Glancing at him, Mrs. Ravenel waited until Abigail was finished and then said, "That will be all. You might see if Miss Marie is in need of your services."

"Yes, ma'am," Abigail said, eyes on the floor as she gathered her mistress's night garments and left.

Mrs. Ravenel looked up at her husband again before reaching for her first earring. "Tell me there hasn't been another squabble in the kitchen," she said long-sufferingly, with a soft sigh.

"No," he answered seriously.

She turned around in her chair, hand on its back. Searching his face, she said, "John, you're frightening me."

He sighed, drawing a hand through his silver hair. "Young Haley came in to see me this morning. He wants Shannon's hand in marriage."

Her lips parted slowly. She searched his face. After a stunned moment of silence, she said in a voice of shock, "And Shannon wants to marry him?"

He nodded once, leaning against the mantle, his arms still crossed. His look was contemplative, measuring her response.

"What did you say?" she asked incredulously.

"I tried to wave him off, but he wasn't having any of it. I told him he must give me some time. But I am opposed to the match, Louisa. Entirely opposed."

She lifted her brows and measured her words before saying in an equitable voice, "She could do worse."

"Could she?" he asked, shaking his head and saying bitterly, "I question our wisdom in allowing Frederick to bring young men into the house, if this is the result."

"Nonsense, we must welcome our son's friends," she said.

"And she *certainly* could do worse. He is a young man of character and breeding. And he has prospects. It isn't what I would've chosen for her, but—"

"Do you truly entertain the notion?" he asked, looking at her in surprised horror. "He may be from a good family—what do we know of Massachusetts? He may be a young man of character—I do not deny it. But it is *not* what we have planned for her."

"And what have we planned for her?" she asked, brows lifted.

He shook his head in frustration. "We have discussed their futures, both of the children, Louisa. You cannot pretend we have not. We wanted a Southern man for her, a man of property and of her own standing. Preferably one who moves in her circles and will give her the life she has always had, and protection. I should not have to say any of this to you."

"Indeed, but have you considered, my dear sir, that Shannon is past twenty and has evaded us at every turn, that she intends to marry precisely as she chooses—"

"She will do no such thing. She will listen to her father."

She looked at him, her back stiffening at the interruption. "Then I warn you that you will be the father of an old maid, for all it has ever taken to give that headstrong child a disgust of a man is for you to approve of him. What is it in particular that you have against Mr. Haley? I have seen them together and have often wondered whether there may be a connection there."

Lips tight, he answered, "Nothing in particular, until he decided he wanted to marry my daughter. Do you like the notion of her living in Massachusetts?" he asked austerely.

"We have no notion where he will live, since it will be wherever he is sent by the Navy."

"Very well, do you like that idea any better?" he demanded.

"We always knew we must steel ourselves if a young man from Virginia offered for her," she said.

"Well, he is not from Virginia," he countered. "He is a Northerner, an abolitionist, and he is not good enough for a Ravenel. A Massachusetts Puritan—can you imagine it? Shannon's children lecturing us about morality and modesty and wearing linen bonnets. A Southern man is what she must and shall have. He would not be so presumptuous, he would not counter her father's decisions as to whom she ought to marry—"

"No, he would keep a Negro whore on Queen Street," Mrs. Ravenel pronounced slowly and coldly. Silence followed. There was a bit of a standoff between them, their eyes locked, her chin lifted high. He broke the stalemate finally, sighing and pacing toward the fireplace. He lifted the poker and stoked it. When he looked back at her, her gaze was not so hard.

"Forgive me," she said, returning to her ladylike tone. She sat back down, laying her forehead in her hand briefly. She sighed. "I merely want what is best for Shannon. I think we *both* want a good man for her."

"Agreed," he said firmly.

"Why, then, what is to be done? If she loves Mr. Haley, she'll not have another. She is too much of a Ravenel to be swayed," she said, looking at him significantly.

"I collect the Shannons are an easy-tempered family," he said.

"I do not deny that the men in my family are resolute. The ladies, however, are known for their gentility," she said austerely. This was entirely unanswerable, and Mr. Ravenel did not attempt it.

"Nonetheless," he said, regaining his footing, "I should be a very poor father if I allowed her to marry the first young man whom she happened to think she loved."

At this moment, further conversation was interrupted by a knock at the door. Mr. Ravenel glanced at it with a look of strong annoyance. "Return later," he said.

A muffled voice said, "It's me, Father."

Mr. Ravenel released a sigh and went forward. He opened the door and was confronted with his son. "May I come in?"

Mr. Ravenel stepped back, ensuring his displeasure was evident from the set of his mouth. "What is it, Frederick?"

"I have something to say. I know you are talking about Shannon." He looked between them as Mr. Ravenel closed the door behind him.

"Yes," his father said, looking him over with suspicion. "How much did you know, son?"

Frederick held up his hands. "I knew nothing! Oh, that there was some attraction between them—yes, I should think anybody could have seen that. But marriage—no, he said nothing to me, and he still hasn't. I'm as shocked as can be. Well, I'll trim his ears for it, but I must say that it ought to do him credit that he spoke to no one before you, Father."

"How long has there been an understanding between them?" his mother asked.

Frederick glanced at her. "As I said, I wouldn't know, for he hasn't mentioned it, and neither has she."

"The person we need is Marie," his father said, eyes narrowed in calculation. "Perhaps she'll know. If that damned Negro-lover has been courting her the whole of the autumn, he'll answer to me."

Frederick's eyes kindled. "We'll leave Marie out of it, if you please. If you think either Shannon or Haley would ever speak of what is in their hearts to anyone, you're mistaken, Father. And if you imagine that John Thomas would act even for a moment in a way that was base or ungentlemanly—well, you don't know him," he said, looking between them. "He is the best man who ever lived, and I'm mad enough to shove him off the dock just now, but if a man ever could be worthy of Shannon, it is he."

His mother smiled and said softly, "This is quite a recommendation you give him."

"It is the truth, and I could say more. Shannon won't meet many men like him in her lifetime," he said, looking back at his father.

His father, leaning against the wall by the window, said in a large-minded spirit, "Well, well, you are fond of your friend, and I'm sure we all are. I've nothing to say against the boy, but I know nothing of him or his family, after all."

"Oh, his family is excellent," Frederick said. "He doesn't puff it off, but they're comfortably circumstanced. The name Haley goes back to the colonial days in shipping."

This surprised Mr. Ravenel. "But from all he says—"

"Oh, don't mistake their piety for poverty, or a sort of middle-class gentility. Everyone up there is like that—well, think of the Puritans, landing on the shore, and you'll have a pretty good notion of his ancestry."

"But what is any of this, my dear?" his mother questioned. "What does Massachusetts society mean to us?"

This was too much for Frederick, whose eyes widened.

"Well… But…if you are looking for society, tell me where you may find an older one, at least in this country?"

Mrs. Ravenel summarily depressed the notion that she had ever cared for society—why would she, a Shannon, married to a Ravenel, have the need to do so?

"Never mind that," Mr. Ravenel said, frustration growing. "What of his family name?"

"I told you it is an old family, a well-respected one," Frederick said.

"Yes, but who ever heard of a Haley?"

"Perhaps no one in South Carolina," his son answered. "But—"

"And what of his other relations? If she married a man from the South, we would know these to the last degree—"

"His mother is an Adams!" Frederick delivered finally, conclusively. "And yes, directly descended!"

A silence fell over the room as, indeed, such a pronouncement could only be expected to produce. Mr. Ravenel's eyes slowly met his wife's. She opened her lips and then closed them, pressing them together as though, for once, at a loss for words. Mr. Ravenel was similarly discomposed. There was a triumphant gleam in Frederick's eyes, but he was wise enough to keep his counsel.

A minute passed, and finally the master of Santarella cleared his throat. "I have a notion, Louisa, which, if it is agreeable to you, I will present to the boy."

Frederick, blinking, was too much astonished at hearing his father, for the first time, say "Louisa" to listen to his mother's reply to this. She must have been agreeable, however, for the next thing he heard his father say was, "We will invite him to stay on at Santarella, and if they are still of the same mind, say in a month or two, and I like what I see, I will give my consent."

"It seems reasonable," she said, inclining her head regally. "He will have to remove with us to Ravenel House and linger much longer than he intended, but if he indeed loves Shannon, that will not weigh with him."

Chapter Fourteen

W ith what her brother informed her was a gross lack of proper feeling, Shannon shrugged her shoulder at his demand to be told why he had not been informed of the blooming romance. She informed him in the library, with Mr. Haley present, that she could not see what business it was of his whom she chose to have a romance with.

Her affianced, catching the dangerous spark in Frederick's eye, and the clenching of his jaw, intervened, asking her if she wouldn't let her brother and him have some private conversation. He also reminded her that Marie was waiting to talk to her upstairs. She did not like this dismissal, but she bestowed a smile upon him as brilliant as her glare upon Frederick was scathing and gracefully left.

He closed the door behind her, drawing a hand through his hair, and turned to face Frederick. His friend was appearing a perfect stone, his fists clenched at his sides, his proud jaw jutted in the air. John Thomas swallowed.

"If you imagine, Frederick, that anything has been done in a secret manner... Shannon—"

"Shannon, is it? For how long has it been Shannon?"

"Since last night," John Thomas said in a calm voice, undaunted. "We never spoke of this until then. I give you my word, if that still means anything to you," he added.

Frederick met his eyes, and there was a slight loosening in his shoulders. "Of course it—John, why didn't you *say*?"

"I just told you—"

"No, I mean, how could you have fallen in love with my sister and never spoken a word? I grant you that it would've been an awkward business, but..."

There was a brief silence during which John Thomas sought about for the answer. He shook his head. "I've never... been in love before, Frederick," he said, so softly that his friend knew he had trod in a very private spot. He sought about desperately for a retreat. "Not like this," John Thomas added, not looking at him, but walking to the bookshelves and glancing unseeingly over the old tomes. "It is difficult to talk about." He looked back over his shoulder, his features slightly more open. "But mostly, I never thought she would have me, Frederick! I never imagined that she would possibly—"

"Oh, pooh, why shouldn't she?" said Shannon's fond brother. "I'm certain you're a catch, and too good for her."

John Thomas smiled, shaking his head. "That isn't true, and you know it, I imagine. But we won't talk any more of that. She did accept me—"

"Do you mean to tell me that the two of you have become engaged?" Frederick demanded, looking thunderstruck. When

Mr. Haley merely held his eyes, he burst out laughing. "And to think, I've been trying to convince my father and mother merely to *consider* it."

John Thomas was touched and met his eyes. "Have you?"

"Of course, you scoundrel. Do you imagine there's anyone else I'd prefer as a brother-in-law?"

This brought out Mr. Haley's smile, and soon, Frederick was proposing a toast to the marriage and making his friend feel acutely uncomfortable by pouring out an ungodly amount of bourbon.

Meanwhile, the conversation above stairs had a different, more feminine flavor, and it had certainly begun less violently. Marie, sitting on Shannon's bed, her checked skirts belling around her, studied her cousin, who was restively rearranging the flowers which the maid Venus had brought up. Shannon was never an open book, and this momentous day was no different.

"Certainly, Frederick mentioned to me that he thought you sometimes flirted with Mr. Haley and that he could not drag his eyes from you," Marie said by way of opening conversation after an overloud silence. At least, it was overloud to her. Shannon seemed to be lost in a dream.

She looked over her shoulder, a sparkle in her eyes, and said, "Did he?"

"Yes, but he thought it nothing more than attraction," Marie said.

Shannon would only tuck the corners of her mouth and turn back around to her arranging.

"Do you think your father will consent?"

"I mean to ride out the storm until he does. And if he doesn't, I mean to do as I please anyway. No one shall tell me whom I will marry."

Marie stiffened a bit but then decided that Shannon had no thought of insulting her, lost as she was in her own affairs. She sighed. "Shannon, do you *truly* love him?"

Shannon slowly turned, her elegant skirts rustling, her eyes brilliant in the sunlight. She smiled, and Marie was startled with what she saw in her face. So far from not being in earnest or seeking to throw dust in her parents' faces, she was lovesick. "Oh, my dear cousin. He is... Oh, I cannot explain it to you. There, you've made me act a fool," she said, swiping at her eyes.

"*Dearest*," Marie cried, reaching for her hands. Shannon gave them, smiling lovingly, and laughed, sinking down beside Marie. The bed ropes groaned as their skirts plumed. "Oh, it is the most wonderful thing," she said, blinking away her own tears and knowing, as she hugged Shannon tightly, the slightest pang of jealousy. "He will be a wonderful husband to you, and, oh, such pretty children you shall have!"

"Yes, but it will be different," Shannon said, pulling back, "when we are in Ravenel House."

Marie reached up, frowning, to touch her cheek. "How could it?"

Shannon looked away and got up. "Oh, I don't know. Charleston's elite... It is such a fierce society. I was bred among them, but he was not."

Marie levelled a look at her and said, "Shannon, I do believe you're afraid of happiness. Or that you doubt him or your power over him."

There was a pause until Shannon moved away, saying, "Nonsense. Come, help me pack, Marie."

Shannon's father had built Ravenel House upon coming into his inheritance as a young man. He had thereby made himself the most eligible bachelor in Charleston. Louisa Shannon, a distant cousin, an heiress, and a beauty, had long since been chosen for him, however. Upon their marriage, she brought with her a wealth of skill and had set about putting a woman's touch on the house and sealing it as the Battery's greatest entertaining gem.

Shannon remembered balls at Ravenel House as a little girl. She would escape her nursery at midnight while her mammy slept and look through the banister at the dancing ladies and gentlemen below. Then, when she was eight years old, she had been sent away to school for so very long. She would come home for Christmas and during the summers, usually to Ravenel House, because that was where her family was during those seasons. During the winters, she remembered musicales, salons with cards, dinners, and Mammy tucking her in saying, "Don't slip down to the party, now, Miss Shannon. You know your papa will be mad if you do that again."

In the summers there were garden teas and sailing parties. Her mother would allow Shannon to come out on the balcony with the ladies in her pretty new dresses and watch the gentlemen below.

The house contained three levels of balconies and commanded an incomparable view. The foyer was at once elegant and impressive. When Shannon had been brought out here upon her eighteenth birthday, there was no question that she had dethroned the reigning beauty, and that the era of Shannon Ravenel had begun. She might have had anyone she chose, and her choice now made society think that one of their circle never would've been considered at all.

Of course, her choice was not *officially* known. It all seemed very secretive and high-aristocratic. And of course, there had been an almost hysteria to catch a glimpse of the young man, some saying they had once seen him when he had been in Charleston a few years ago.

Naturally, Mr. and Mrs. Ravenel, aware of all this and eager to keep Shannon's glory at its peak, sent out invitations to a ball, which was certain to be the crush of the season.

John Thomas had glanced at Shannon when they had announced the plan at the dinner table. But her eyes had remained downcast, and conversation had soon turned between Frederick and his father to the Illinois Congressman, Abraham Lincoln, who seemed to be gaining popularity for the presidency.

John Thomas went looking for Shannon the night before the ball. He found her in the library, where a few candles were lit here and there. She was looking out the window, hands clasped against her green gown, eyes fixed on the great expanse of water. She was so lovely. He hesitated, unsure, not wanting to disturb her.

She looked over her shoulder. "Oh, John Thomas," she said softly.

He went forward a few steps. "I wanted to check on you. You weren't ill?"

"Ill? Oh, no," she said, shaking her head. "Why do you ask?"

"You were quiet," he answered. He studied her, beautiful and remote.

"Are you fearing that I am cross with you?" she asked, eyes smiling a bit.

His shoulders eased, and he walked her way, coming to stand before her. "You are cross whenever you choose to be. I have no say in the matter."

She laughed, giving her hand. He brought it to his lips and then met her eyes. He brushed his thumb over her knuckles and said almost in a whisper, "You're sure?" There was tender concern in his eyes, and she pressed his hand, looking away. She laughed very softly. "Yes, of course I'm sure." She looked back at him. "I was thinking that I hope you will not be angry."

"Angry?" he said. "With you?"

She looked back at him. The candlelight flickered off her features. "Tomorrow night. You do have a temper from time to time, you know."

His brows lifted. "Do I? Never with you, I hope."

"Not yet," she said, smiling a bit. "But our love is very new, after all."

He squeezed her hand. "Shannon, if I've ever given you reason to suppose—"

"No, you silly man." She laughed, touching his face briefly and then taking her hand away, as though embarrassed. "I mean that there will be several young men there."

The tension eased from his shoulders. "If you are hinting that this is your mother and father's last hope for you to meet someone else—that doesn't trouble me. If you imagine that it will be easy to watch other men try to stake their claim—you are fair and far off, Miss Ravenel."

She gave him a saucy smile. "Would you prefer I didn't flirt with them?"

The thought vaguely dashed into his mind that his mother would be horrified at the thought of her daughter-in-law flirting with other men, not that he was overly concerned with that fact, except as it might wound Shannon. He knew that it sprang from a raising in a different culture. There was more flirting than eating at a common Charleston dinner table. It was very subtle, hidden with innuendo and honey-polite words. These people even coaxed their horses out of an ill temper with a certain tone. "Of course, I would prefer you didn't," he said lightly, hoping he didn't sound stiff.

She looked like a mischievous child. "Well, I can't promise you that." She tipped up on her toes and kissed his cheek, sending a rush of adrenaline through him. "But I *can* promise you the last waltz."

"You must, or I shall unleash my temper on you," he said, eyes twinkling.

On the night of the ball, Miss Ravenel danced with many men. Mr. Haley seemed unconcerned with her partners, casually talking with Frederick Ravenel's Charlestonian friends or dancing with the young belles. They might almost have stilled tongues completely. Mrs. Templeton, for instance, remarked to Miss Davis, her sister, that the boy was mighty cool about the Gregorson boy's blatant adoration if matters truly stood as they had been told. The slaves surely did talk, but hardly ever any truth in anything they circulated, she added, taking a glass from a Negro waiter.

Such doubts were laid waste to, however, when the final waltz came. There was never anything like the way he looked at her as he had her in his arms. And as for Miss Ravenel, Mrs. Foley was certain no one had ever seen the arch creature wear *her* heart on her sleeve, but she was certainly looking up into his face with a smile just for him, just as though they had been alone in the room.

Mr. and Mrs. Ravenel relented the next morning. In the library surrounded by books and a flood of sunshine, they gave Shannon their blessing and even entered the spirit of planning.

Shannon was almost tearful when her father kissed her. While her mother, for once entirely pleased with her, stood with both of Shannon's hands in hers, Mr. Ravenel extended his hand to John Thomas.

John Thomas took it. He met Mr. Ravenel's eyes, and the man said, "You're a good boy. I spoke to you as I do these rascals of mine. I hope I didn't offend you."

"No, sir. You take her future seriously, and I am glad of that."

Mr. Ravenel studied him. "I believe you do, too."

"Yes," John Thomas said seriously.

After another of his long surveys, this one much kindlier, Mr. Ravenel pressed his arm. "You need to invite your mother and father to Ravenel House, John Thomas. They need to meet her." They looked toward the window where Shannon stood talking with her mother, in greater beauty than ever, their skirts belling for a pretty picture. "You'll have some trials, the two of you. You can make her way much smoother if your family feels included."

John Thomas nodded, his eyes still on Shannon.

"When do you report?" Mr. Ravenel asked, dragging him out of his thoughts.

"In May—in Washington," John Thomas answered softly.

"No, Shannon, you cannot possibly be married in December," her mother was heard saying long-sufferingly.

Shannon was looking mulish. "I do not see why we cannot be. It will give us plenty of time to return for Frederick and Marie's wedding." She looked over at John Thomas, her color rising slightly. "That is...if you agree, John Thomas," she said, meeting his eyes.

"You know I do."

"You must not humor her in this fashion, Mr. Haley," her mother said. "You will soon learn that she is headstrong. There is not by any means enough time to order a dress and plan the wedding a daughter of Santarella ought to have."

"I believe in this case she may be right," Mrs. Ravenel's husband said in his genteel drawl. "We are not without connections in Charleston, I trust. Shannon will have what she needs. If John Thomas's mother and father are to come to us, they may as well be wed while they are here."

Shannon eyes lifted to John Thomas's. "Oh, are they indeed coming?" she breathed.

He smiled. "I hope so. I'll wire them this afternoon."

What Mr. and Mrs. Haley's feelings were upon being informed that their second son was to marry a Southern belle, no one could know, for no one had been privy to the conversation in their neatly appointed chamber in Boston the night Mr. Haley had received his son's telegram. Nor did their emotions become much plainer when they stepped off the train in Charleston on the first day of December. Mrs. Haley's love for her son was evident in the way she looked at him, forgetting the shocking news for a moment. But Mr. Ravenel, who had accompanied his son and prospective son-in-law to the train station, could discern nothing else, beyond the fact that they were slightly taken aback by their surroundings. Certainly, it was unfortunate that a slave auction was that day taking place in the Holy City, the poor souls being displayed in chains. It was also regrettable that a slightly wild-eyed man was repudiating abolitionists from a platform nearby with a large crowd gathering.

Frederick was the soul of Southern grace. He exerted himself to the fullest to ensure their comfort, and they liked him, having been previously acquainted with and charmed by him. And they were curious to see King Ravenel, as he was sometimes called in the South.

Mrs. Ravenel, upon greeting them in her expensively furnished home, observed that Mrs. Haley was a plain woman, dressed tastefully but not strikingly. One of her contributions to her son was her plain blue eyes. She was, more or less, what Mrs. Ravenel had predicted a Puritan would look like. And though her husband was nineteen years her senior and nearing seventy, it was easy to see that John Thomas's strong features had been passed from his father.

Mrs. Haley had not known what she would say to the daughter of a plantation or what to expect in her future daughter-in-law. She was even more bereft of words when she first entered the parlor at Ravenel House and beheld a beautiful creature with flaming hair and eyes, breathtaking in an emerald evening gown. John Thomas, taking one of the girl's hands, smiled down at her with such pride that she was moved. Certainly, she had never seen her son look just so. "Shannon, my mother and father," he said.

Shannon, releasing John Thomas's hand, moved forward with both of hers extended toward Mrs. Haley and said, "My dear ma'am, how honored I am to make your acquaintance. We are forever indebted to you, you know, for John Thomas. But there is time enough for all of that. How tired you must be after *such* a journey."

Mrs. Haley, a quiet presence with no nervous tendencies, smiled softly and answered unhurriedly, studying Shannon, "Indeed, but not an uncomfortable one. We are pleased to make your acquaintance, Miss Ravenel."

Mrs. Ravenel, on the watch for any slight mistreatment of Shannon, was not precisely overwhelmed by the warmth of this speech, but it would do. She moved in gracefully, allowed herself to be introduced by John Thomas, and said what was proper with charm and magnanimity. She then suggested that Mrs. Haley allow her to show her to her chamber so that she might rest and be refreshed before supper, a suggestion that the woman seemed to find odd.

The dinner was one of the more interesting ones hosted by the Ravenel family. There was a bit of awkwardness between the two heads of household, the elder Mr. Haley more imperfectly concealing his discomfort at being served by enslaved men and women than did his son. A look had passed between husband and wife, fleeting and not very expressive but telling nonetheless. An endeavor by Mr. Ravenel to engage his guest on the topic of horse racing fell wide of the mark. They could not speak of their respective businesses without stumbling over the inevitable topic and the perilous debate of whether slavery was a poison on the economy (it was, in Mr. Haley's opinion). Even the ladies were experiencing difficulties, their ways of life so divergent as to be almost foreign. When the bourbon was brought out, Frederick exchanged a look with Marie, who had been invited by Shannon for support.

But after a sip and a frowning moment, Mr. Haley interrupted the conversation to say, "I say, Ravenel. A tolerable drink. Very tolerable."

Conversation ceased for a moment, during which his pardonably surprised son stared. Mr. Ravenel, however, the perfect host said, "Frederick and I are very partial to it. My father preferred it older, but I believe this is only five years old."

This started an excellent conversation on the best ways to preserve wine, which varieties aged the most felicitously, the drinks their fathers had acquired, and the old way of doing things.

Shannon, smiling with twinkling eyes at John Thomas, went much more serenely back to her meal. A happy notion struck Mrs. Ravenel to ask Mrs. Haley about the winters in

New England and the troubles they caused with the running of her household. Mrs. Haley, at length, allowed herself to be charmed by the Southern ladies around her.

John Thomas, kissing Shannon before bed, told her with twinkling eyes that he thought it had gone as tolerably as could be expected. "Yes, but it is only the first hurdle of the race, my dear sir," she answered. "There is no use in being too optimistic."

He smiled, his eyes crinkling at the corners. "One of us must be."

"Have you told them yet?"

He shook his head. "I'm going to now." Hand on her narrow waist, he leaned in and kissed her cheek. "Go to bed. You look worn to the bone."

"Well, I am," she admitted, studying his face.

He studied her. "You're sure?"

"Entirely," she said, kissing his cheek and fluttering off, light as a fairy.

He watched after her for a moment and then knocked on his parents' door to tell them that he and Shannon had decided to make their home in Massachusetts until they left for Washington. They were delighted, for they had feared Shannon's influence would keep him tied to the South. In this they wronged her: it had been her suggestion that they do so. Now the only question was how the girl would manage in their world.

Chapter Fifteen

The engagement party far surpassed Frederick and Marie's, with all of the aristocracy of Charleston in attendance and large dancing sets that lasted long into the morning. Neighbors were agog for a glimpse of Miss Ravenel's Northern beau and his New Englander parents. The elder Mr. Haley, who had been more charmed by his son's choice than had his wife, was in an agreeable mood. He had been treated with so much polite courtesy that he told his wife, as he lay down, that they were human, and they would do well to remember it. His conviction that slavery must and shall come to an end was unchanged, however, and he was willing to go almost any lengths to accomplish it, so his wife was unsure what he meant.

In the week that followed, such a flood of presents, from the simple to extravagant, flowed in from far and wide that Frederick declared it his belief that they would all be squeezed out of the house if Shannon did not soon remove herself from the vicinity.

"It isn't every day the belle of Charleston chooses a husband for herself, Frederick," Marie said, helping Shannon to arrange flowers for their bouquets in the morning room.

Frederick, reclining against the sofa, smiled. "You are both belles."

Shannon smiled over her shoulder at him. "Flatterer. I must find Matilde and ask whether these will keep until morning if we put them in the cellar in water."

As she was walking out, her beau, as he was known in Charleston, was entering. His eyes rested on Shannon with a tender smile.

"You are beneath the mistletoe," Marie said, seeing the way Shannon smiled up at him.

He met Shannon's smile, put a hand on her waist on the side that faced the door as though he thought it wouldn't be seen, and kissed her chastely. This greatly disturbed Frederick, as did the thought that it did not appear at all unnatural for them, and that John Thomas changed his mind and went with Shannon.

"For the love of—"

"You cannot mind that he kisses her, Frederick," Marie said once they had left, arranging the large centerpiece. "They are to be married tomorrow, and they are in love."

To this, Frederick did not respond. But he was, however, on the following day, the perfect groomsman and happy for two people very dear to his heart.

Shannon's gown may have been hastily prepared, but it was an exquisite creation, at the very height of fashion. Of cream silk, it fit snugly at the bodice and flowed into a long train, tiny buttons marching all the way from the back of the neck to the waistline. It was given an extra flare of extreme fashion by long sleeves that fit tightly rather than loosely and a collar which was made high to her long throat. The impression was softened by her hair, which was pinned up and woven with pearls and tiny white flowers.

The ladies and slaves attended her in her bedchamber, and Marie said tearfully, "Shannon! I cannot imagine any princess looking finer."

"Yes, thank *goodness* she is going to Massachusetts," Elizabeth Middleton agreed, eyes twinkling.

Shannon wore her fine gown like a second skin, handling the train comfortably, smiling and talking calmly as she was ministered to. She and her friends and maids walked slowly down the masterful, floating stairs into the white hall, flowers all around them.

Shannon and John Thomas were married in the long parlor, with fifty or so persons in attendance and Marie and Elizabeth Middleton as her bridesmaids. Her mother was tearful, her father stoically miserable. The groom looked quite overpowered when he saw his bride, and she looked up at him with blue eyes made so brilliant by the sunlight beaming through the long windows that she appeared other-worldly. She seemed to be fighting tears, never more so than when her father kissed her cheek and took John Thomas's hand, placing hers in it.

Chapter Sixteen

Adeline, not usually a punctual person, presented herself at the passenger door of the Land Rover at one-o'clock sharp on Saturday. It was a little chilly and rainy out, so she wore her white sweater and blue pants which rolled up at the cuffs. It seemed too advanced in the spring to wear her booties, but she did nonetheless. It couldn't be more than fifty-five degrees outside. The weather this year was atrocious.

She watched Sir Ravenel exit the house, locking up behind him, looking sharp in jeans and a linen button down. She was glad to see that he wore chukka boots, too. His fashion was always on point; she'd give him that.

"Ready?" he said, clicking the doors unlocked as he went down the steps.

"Yep," she returned in a friendly manner. In a few moments, she was buckling her seatbelt, and they were heading away from the Battery.

There was an uncomfortable silence, so she said after a couple of minutes, "So, you grew up in Georgia?"

"Yeah." She thought for a minute he'd leave it there, but he added, "My dad's originally from Charleston but he's taught chemistry at Georgia Southern for thirty-seven years now. He met my mom in Statesboro—she's from near there."

"How'd you land in Charleston?" she asked.

"I did my residency here," he said, changing lanes to go to the interstate and not, she noticed, adjusting the heat. It was an iceberg in here. Didn't he know that? "Then I got offered a job at the same hospital. My grandfather was still living here then. And my wife—well, she was my fiancée then—wanted to live here."

She turned her head toward him, interest unreasonably awakened. "She was from here?" she asked casually.

"No, Savannah. She wanted to live close to her family, but not too close."

"So you took the job, and the rest is history," she said.

"Yeah." He pressed his lips together as if feeling that he'd revealed more than he wished. That line of conversation was officially closed. She glanced at the knobs on the dash. Literally, could he not feel the chill?

"You can turn the heat on if you want."

Okay, she was going to have to stop thinking things in front of him. "If you're sure," she said casually, reaching for the knob almost immediately. "How does Jane fit into all of this?" she asked as another long silence developed. They were on the interstate now, the marsh lands flying past them. He was driving a little fast.

"She's an old family friend. She was my uncle's secretary in Statesboro forever. My mom suggested her—she was afraid she was lonely and bored. So I called her, and she said yes."

"After...your wife passed?" she asked. "That must've been a huge relief."

There was a slight hesitation. "No, before."

She could smell his cologne. It was teasing her senses, distracting her from the question of why his stay-at-home wife would've needed a nanny. His arm was really close—okay, like a foot away, but his hand, his excellent, sculpted, veined hand, lay on the console. *Look. Away.*

She refocused her attention outside to the gray skies. It started to rain when they had been driving fifteen minutes.

"Looks like another beautiful day," he said.

Offering conversation, were we? "Maybe everyone won't freak out on the interstate."

"There's no need to be nervous," he said in a voice that, without trying to be, was somehow soothing.

"I'm not."

"You've just never ridden with me before," he suggested, looking over at her, smiling just a bit.

She met his eyes, flushing a little. But if he was going to be a freaking mind-reader, he needed to expect to be offended from time to time. "I trust you to be safe. At least, I do now."

He smiled again. He was pretty free and easy with his smiles today, by his standards. He must feel bad about the microwaved-breakfast commentary.

"So, how did you choose your job?" she asked. *Gah, what is this, twenty questions, Adeline?*

He lifted a shoulder. "I always had a knack for it, I guess." That was an understatement.

"I'm not sure I could do it," she said.

"Listen to people's problems all day?" he asked, glancing at her.

"Yeah."

He was silent for a moment. "There are some days I'd rather talk to wallpaper," he said, after putting the matter to consideration. Great. He'd seen it. "But we all have needs. Some have many needs. And it isn't long before you couldn't imagine letting them down."

She looked at him, at the planes of his face, studying him. She was touched. He had already struck her as a man who took his responsibilities very seriously. If he was a little methodical and clinical about it all, she was beginning to think that hid deep feelings beneath. She hadn't seen evidence of them yet, but the thought was tantalizing, almost as much as the fireplace in the library. "I'm sure many need you desperately."

"The goal is for them not to, eventually. Some won't ever get better, but many will."

"Do most of your clients have clinical disorders?" she asked.

"No, not all," he said. "There are all kinds of people who struggle with mental health. We all do, in our own ways. It takes a lot of bravery to try to fix it."

She looked at him again, studying him. He seemed really serious about it. And when he spoke about the people he helped, it was with compassion. She would imagine there were days when it wasn't easy, when the stress levels were high. Maybe he was just able to compartmentalize it all.

After another long silence, he apparently remembered that she was spending her Saturday working for his sake and said, "So your home is Asheville?"

"Yep," she said, nodding once. "My parents are still there, and my older sister."

He looked toward her. "You're not the oldest?"

She lifted her brows. "How old do you think I am?" Thirty. He thought she was thirty.

"I just mean that I had pegged you for an oldest child. Over-achiever academically—"

"That's not fair: Harris is an over-achiever, and he's not the oldest."

He studied her for a moment. Finally, he said, "We were pushed to get the highest degree in our fields that we could."

"Oh." She thought for a minute. "Well, I guess you mean that the middle child is usually a little bit of a rebel. But believe it or not, getting a Ph.D. was actually a little rebellious in my family. My parents wanted us to have good, stable, dependable jobs: my sister's a teacher, and my brother's going to be an accountant. They're proud of me, of course, but they worry about me."

"They obviously fail to see the doors that have been opened to you by the letters behind your name."

"Oh, they do. I think it was the starting my own business thing that freaked them out."

He glanced at her. "It seems to be going well, though."

"Well, it's lasted for two years, so we'll see," she said, also feeling like she'd dumped too much of her history. Confiding two pieces of information always made her feel like she'd spilled as much of her soul as if she'd broken down in tears in front of somebody. She wasn't as reserved as the man sitting next to her; she was just used to fending for herself.

There was a long silence. He seemed to be chewing on something (figuratively), and Adeline sat in silence. She thought he knew she wasn't comfortable talking about herself anymore. Which made car-ride talk difficult, since he didn't either. She had a feeling that they were both more comfortable with a chatty person who spilled her guts next to them. Or at least, she was. On second thought, that was the kind of thing that would probably make him jump off a cliff.

"I just thought: I should've been calling you Dr. Miller." She made a face, starting to shake her head, but he said, "No, you do for me: I should extend the same courtesy."

She smiled at him. "It's fine, really. I'm not a professor, so it's a little clunky in everyday use."

He smiled, a real one this time. His black eyes glimmered. "All right, then."

The air in the Land Rover was much lighter after that, so much so that the silences weren't awkward anymore. When they'd gone for a few more miles, he turned on the radio. He put it on the Frank Sinatra station. "Is that okay?"

She would've chosen Fleetwood Mac or John Mayer, but hey, it could be worse. At least it was historical. "Sure." And as the miles rolled past, some Michael Bublé came on, too, which was good.

They made it in good time, and soon they were driving through old residential streets near, she thought, campus. The area kind of had that feel. The houses were really pretty, an amalgamation of different historical eras. It was a cozy town;

she imagined it would've been a good place to grow up.

He turned into the driveway of a meticulously neat white Victorian with three stories. There was a small SUV sitting in the drive and a car in the garage. It felt very "mom and dad" and cozy. It made her want to go home for a Saturday night grill-out.

He opened his door, and she did, too, deciding to leave her purse in the car. It looked like the kind of place you could do that. He preceded her up the path, and they went around to the back door, where a tabby was sitting, awaiting her moment. Instead of knocking, Dr. Ravenel opened the door and went in. She followed him, as did the cat.

"Mom? Dad?"

A tall woman with dark blonde hair and a lean figure came into the room. She had her oldest son's features in a more feminine way—clear lines and pleasing bone structure—and an elegant style. Her face was deeply pleasant to look at until you saw that pair of hawkish light blue eyes that saw your soul. And maybe ate it.

"Adrian," she said, coming forward. Her voice was calm, self-assured, and pleasing to the ear. She reached up and gave him a kiss and said almost privately, "How are you, honey? I've missed you."

He leaned into her hug and then away. "Fine. Where's Dad?"

"Upstairs, I think." She had refocused her attention to Adeline, raising her brows and smiling pleasantly as though expecting an introduction.

"Mom, this is Adeline Miller," he said. "Adeline, my mother, Virginia Ravenel."

Adeline smiled. "Nice to meet you, Mrs. Ravenel. Thanks for loaning your box. We're excited to see what's in it."

"It's James's," she said. She studied Adeline's face, taking her measure. That gaze was really creepily penetrating. "I hope it can help." *Veeerrry* dignified. She made Adeline feel like a hippie in comparison.

Luckily, a man strode through the kitchen door. He, too, was tall and lean, and his hair was silver and waving, but she had a feeling, from the odd hair here and there, that it had once been black, like his oldest son's. His features, though, were more like Harris's. He had the distant look of a scholar in his eyes and a bit of the non-functional sciency way about him. But he did smile upon seeing them and say, "There you are. You were caught in the rain, I imagine." He smiled with pride upon his son. Adeline didn't blame him; she would, too, if she'd created that specimen.

"Yeah, a little," Adrian said, stepping back to introduce her to him.

The older gentleman was polite and not quite as daunting as his wife. After the introductions were made, he said, "Why haven't you brought Jude?"

"I was just coming to that," Mrs. Ravenel said, levelling a look at her son.

He held up his hands. "It's too long of a drive just to turn around and go back. He's not a great rider. You know that."

"He could've stayed the night," his dad said, hands in the deep pockets of his scholarly khakis.

"Yes," his mother said. "He could have."

Dr. Ravenel looked at the ceiling for a split second. "I didn't have time to come get him tomorrow."

"I would've brought him," his mother said.

His father seemed to catch his mother's eye then. Lifting her brows she said, "What, James?"

"Well, he can take his own son wherever he chooses," he said. Brave man. Brave, stupid man.

If the woman had been a cat, her ears would've lain back. She said nothing further on the matter. Merely, with a dignified voice, she said, "You'll want to show them where the box is."

"Oh, it's in the basement. I should've brought it up."

"That's okay," Dr. Ravenel said, looking relieved at the change in topic. And like he wanted to bolt from the room. "I'll carry it up."

"I'll come, too," Adeline said. He was not leaving her here with the ice queen. Before they left, Mrs. Ravenel was sitting on one of the bar stools, Adrian's phone in her hand, looking through it.

"Mom." He stopped, his hand on the door. "What are you doing?" he demanded.

She lifted her brows as though in surprise. "Going through your pictures to get the recent ones of Jude. You haven't sent me any in two weeks." She smiled at one she was looking at, her whole countenance changing.

He released a long-suffering sigh.

"Will you send them to my phone?" the elder Dr. Ravenel said, opening the door to let them pass.

"Of course," Mrs. Ravenel said. She saw Dr. Ravenel—the younger—take a deep, silent breath through his nose, and she tried to keep from laughing.

Soon, they were passing through a living room straight out

of *Southern Living*, except for the large Chemistry tomes lying here and there. The basement was a little more questionable, as basements in old houses often were. Adeline held to the rail and tried not to fall going down the steps.

Adrian pulled a string to turn a light on, and his dad roamed around aimlessly for about five minutes, trying to find the box. Eventually, his son joined in, but he didn't seem any better at it. Not wanting to be pushy, Adeline stood back. Until, out of the corner of her eye, she saw a box labelled "Old Family Documents." She cut her eyes to the side, lips pursed. Men.

"I think this may be it," she said.

"Oh, yes, it is. You have a good eye," the father said. She liked him.

Adrian knelt beside it and swiped the dust off the top in that no-nonsense way men had, not really worrying about where it went. But it was efficient. He lifted it. It seemed surprisingly heavy.

"Got it?" his dad said.

"Yeah, it's fine." He carried it upstairs to the coffee table in the living room.

His dad went to it and opened it, saying, "Let's see here..." Adeline was torn between telling him not to touch anything and refraining. She knew that he could probably tell her a lot about it if his mother had been interested in history. As the older gentleman scrounged around in the box amidst folders and smaller boxes, Dr. Ravenel seemed to think he was no longer needed and disappeared into the kitchen, presumably to retrieve his phone.

He could see behind the half-closed door his dad and the preservationist leaning over the box, his dad with scholarly interest, Ms. Miller with the glee of Jude in an ice cream shop. Leaning against the counter, crossing his arms, he said, "You're coming to the graduation, right?"

"Of course, honey," she said, having surrendered his phone. She was making tea now. "I can't believe he'll be in first grade. It seems like just yesterday he was a baby."

It sure did. Time was racing by.

"You'll want him to stay little forever so you can protect him," she said, turning off the stove. "But it won't be long until he won't even want to hold your hand."

"Thanks, Mom," he said.

"Well, it's only the truth. I suppose the Thomases will be there, too?"

Here we go. "Of course, I invited them."

She sighed.

He clenched his jaw for a split second. It didn't give him any patience, as he had hoped. "What do you want me to do, Mom? They're Jude's family. I won't keep them out of his life: it's not healthy, and they love him."

"I know. I think you had to invite them. It's only that Theresa is so insufferable."

"Yeah, well, she's Lauren's mother."

She handed him a glass of tea and said softly, "I know. I'll be nice. For your sake."

He looked down at her, suddenly a little amused. "Thank you," he said, acknowledging her magnanimity.

She squeezed his arm, and the door opened, revealing the two from the living room. The preservationist looked pretty excited.

"Find something?" he asked.

"I hope so. We'll take the whole box and get it back to you as soon as we can," she said, taking in his parents.

"That's fine," his dad said. "Keep it as long as you need."

"Thanks," Adeline answered, smiling. The two of them had obviously hit it off. "I'll go get it."

Adrian set his tea down. "I will," he said.

She looked a little surprised and then shrugged. She'd obviously been single too long. He wondered why. Not that he cared. He went into the living room and picked it up, carrying it through the kitchen and kissing his mom's cheek on the way out. His dad followed them out and patted his shoulder once he had closed the back door. "Be careful."

"All right," Adrian said, smiling a little. "See you in two weeks."

He patted his arm. "Send your mother more pictures. She's feeling her empty nest."

Adrian's brows drew together. "Harris is thirty-two," he protested.

"I know, but these things come and go for women," he said vaguely. "She worries about all of you."

"We're fine, Dad," he said soothingly.

"I know," he said. "I'll let you go."

He nodded, feeling a little relieved. Sometimes, his dad took one down rambling conversations that lasted for thirty minutes. "See you in two weeks."

Chapter Seventeen

The carriage travelled through acre upon acre of gently rolling countryside. The land glowed with health and prosperity and looked so different from South Carolina that Shannon might think herself transported into a different world. Massachusetts, with its neat little painted houses, meticulously constructed yet primitive fences, farmers and their sons tilling the land, ladies inside laboring over supper and scrubbing their floors, might as well have been a separate country. The fields were open as far as the eye could see, and the very soil looked different.

Shannon watched John Thomas as he looked out the window and realized, suddenly, that he was at home. He did not bat an eye at the pristine beauty all around them; he merely watched it, nodding back to a farmer who gave a brusque nod, which she was coming to realize passed for a friendly wave in these parts.

The air was clean and pure but briskly cold. John Thomas

had wrapped a blanket around her shoulders when they had first boarded the carriage after the train, but it was scarcely enough to stop the chill from seeping into her bones. He did not seem similarly affected.

Shannon gripped the strap of her valise but was momentarily distracted from her nerves when they made the turn, and Harmony Grove rose in the distance. John Thomas had been modest when he spoke of *home*. Therefore, she was not prepared for the large, symmetrical white house with neat dormers and uniform windows, sitting on a hill like a beacon of purity.

"*Oh*," she breathed. She realized he had been watching her, rather than his home, and that the smile in his eyes attested to his pleasure with her response.

He reached across the carriage and took her hand in both of his. "Welcome to my home, Shannon," he said softly.

She swallowed the lump in her throat, holding his eyes.

He got down in front of the door and reached to take her by the waist and lift her down. Servants in neat dress came to take care of the horses, and she could see tenants in white shirt sleeves working the fields nearby. John Thomas let her grow steady on her feet and then walked with her to the door.

They crossed the threshold and were ushered into the foyer, and suddenly, there were members of the Haley family all around them, spilling forth from various rooms. Shannon caught glimpses of pale hair and blue eyes, of unadorned dress and the occasional cast of countenance that looked familiar but wasn't. There was the master of the house at the bottom of the stairs with Mrs. Haley. Off to the side was a young gentleman, perhaps a few years older than John Thomas, with spectacles and a distant expression, as though he had been interrupted in his work or reading.

A young woman in a dove gray dress with a plain face was standing quietly, furtively taking Shannon in, while another, a little younger, was openly staring at her with bright eyes. Her pale hair was parted down the middle and caught up very simply, and her dark gray gown with pagoda sleeves was plain but elegant. There was a young man who must be Charles, who was smiling, and then there were the two children, who obviously felt this was the most exciting thing to have happened in their household.

Mrs. Haley was not demonstrative, but came forward, one hand taking Shannon's and the other reaching up briefly to touch her son's face. "Welcome to Harmony Grove, dear children. We had hoped to welcome you in sunshine."

Shannon said pleasantly, "It makes no difference: Harmony Grove is enchanting. My dear ma'am, I do hope your train ride was more comfortable than ours, but I daresay it was not. And so very cold, too!"

"New England winters are not for the faint of heart," she said. She seemed to unbend as she added, "But I daresay you will grow accustomed in time. My dear, you are looking well. It is good to see. We feared your travels might fatigue you."

She smiled. "Indeed, they did. I only managed to survive because we broke the journey at Santarella."

"Oh, John Thomas, introduce us!" said the girl with the bright eyes.

He opened his arms, smiling, and she and the youngest

member of the family, the Sarah he always spoke of with a sparkle, rushed forward. He laughed, kissing their heads. They were looking at Shannon with shy smiles. She felt a little out of place in her exquisite travel gown. "This is Shannon, my wife," he said, his eyes not leaving hers. They knew that, of course, but his lips seemed to savor the word, nonetheless. "I shall introduce all of you properly once Shannon has rested."

"Your brother has told me so much about you that I feel I know you already," Shannon said in an accent which they found fascinating. She became distracted when she noticed the bespectacled older brother had removed his glasses and was staring at her.

Her father-in-law said with kind cheer, "I hope you left your mother and father well, Shannon."

Shannon inclined her head with a smile. "Indeed, quite well, and triumphant as a result of marrying both of their children off within three months."

"Your brother is married, then?" Mrs. Haley asked, eyes softening further.

"Yes, and on his honeymoon in Richmond," Shannon answered.

"A good boy. I believe he is fortunate in his choice of wife," Mr. Haley said. He was in a benevolent mood. Perhaps he liked the patriarchy he was growing around him. And he had left Charleston in charity with his son's father-in-law and charmed by his choice of bride.

"And he married your cousin?" the oldest girl asked. No, she was only the oldest present. She was Lizzie, and there was

Patience, a year older than John Thomas, married to a minister, and living nearby in Weymouth.

"Yes, our dear Marie," Shannon affirmed, smiling softly. "We always marry cousins in my family—that was why I was determined to break tradition," she added lightly, smiling slightly over her shoulder at John Thomas, who gave her a smile but seemed preoccupied with watching his thunderstruck older brother in amusement.

"And you are from a true plantation?" Sarah said, eyes wide. "With slaves and everything?"

"Hush, Sarah," Mrs. Haley said.

John Thomas's attention snapped back, eyes travelling between the actors, wary.

Shannon's eyes looked vulnerable, even as her chin lifted. "Yes. I am. It is a beautiful place called Santarella," she said softly.

A silence fell over the room. The air was suddenly sizzling with tension, various actors looking uncomfortable, the occasional one on his or her dignity. "Come, you'll tire Shannon," John Thomas said. "I can attest to her suffering during her travels, for there was no end to her complaining," he said, reaching for her hand.

She was distant and stiff for a moment, but she finally gave her hand, her smile not quite her own. "How unhandsome of you to say so!" she said in her soft sing-song voice.

Miriam was brimming with a smile. "Oh, you are in love! I can see it by your eyes! How lovely!"

"Miriam!" Mrs. Haley softly chided. "You must not speak of such things." Naturally, if there had been anything warm in

Miriam's words, their effect was only heightened by her mother's reprimand. Another slight silence fell over the room. Mrs. Haley cleared her throat softly. "Shannon, you will wish to rest before supper. John Thomas will show you to his room, I am sure."

The words had barely left her mouth when a young man in a white shirt and sleeve protectors emerged, looking offended. "Pardon me, Mrs. Haley. But there is a Negro woman in the kitchen."

Utter silence descended, as every member of the family looked entirely stunned. The silent ticking of the clock could be heard, the rustle of the wind outside.

"*John Thomas,*" Mr. Haley said almost in a whisper, pronouncing each of the names separately. He looked shocked and shaken as he held his son's eyes.

Shannon flushed deeply. The subject of Phoebe had been the closest the newlyweds had come to quarrelling during their short marriage. Shannon's father had gifted Phoebe to her, a traditional present which Southern planters bestowed upon their daughters. John Thomas, when they were alone, had been stiff. "*Shannon, you must know I cannot keep a slave.*" Before she could interject, he had said, "*I don't think we could take her into Massachusetts a slave, in any event. There have been Supreme Court cases... I am unsure of the law.*"

"*Well, I am not. A Southerner is protected if he wishes to take his slave on his travels to the North.*" Her chin had been in the air. "*And if the slave runs, the Northern state has the responsibility, the Constitutional duty to return it to him.*"

He had dragged his hand through his hair. "*Well, I will not do it, Shannon,"* he said quietly but firmly. And then he had said nothing more, only watched her. There had been a long silence during which she had stared at him, taken aback. Finally, he had added in a gentler tone, *"I will speak to your father in the morning and explain my feelings to him. If Phoebe goes north with us, she goes free."* He had changed the subject soon, the discomfort leaving his expression to be replaced by a look of sincere affection.

Now, though, she saw it again in the hard line of his jaw, in his shoulders. He did not like the taint of slavery which followed her any more than his family did. "Phoebe is Shannon's free servant. We will discuss it later if you wish, Father."

There was a cold silence. "Very well," his father said finally.

"Where shall I put her, Mrs. Haley?" the outraged servant intervened.

Anna Adams Haley looked at a loss for a moment before saying with an ounce of frustration, "In the women's quarters, of course, Peter."

"With the *other* women, ma'am?"

"Yes, with the other women," she almost snapped, though perhaps her anger was directed inwardly.

Another silence descended, and Shannon waited, her thin shoulders stiff. She felt John Thomas's hand on the small of her back. "I will show Shannon upstairs."

She was relieved, although this was checked by the knowledge that she must descend the stairs again for supper. She barely saw the halls and rooms as they made their way to the back of the house and crossed the threshold into a bedchamber. John Thomas closed the door quietly behind them, remaining silent for a moment while her back was to him. She pretended to look out the window, but she saw nothing. She could feel his eyes on her, and she flushed with awareness of the scene below. Awkward silence descended for a time, thick and aware, until Shannon said softly, clearing her throat, "Will you unlace my stays?" She would not for worlds send for Phoebe just then.

"Yes, of course," he said in an extremely accommodating voice, stepping toward her. Her back was to him, so she could not see his eyes, though she wished desperately to do so. His fingers worked their way down the buttons slowly, leaving a searing tingle everywhere they touched, despite everything. She lifted her cold hands to her cheeks. Then he came to her stays. He lingered over the last one, finally letting it fall from his hands. They stayed frozen. She closed her eyes for a moment, and when she could no longer stand it, she turned, struggling to keep the moisture from rushing to her eyes as she met his.

He looked horrified. "Shannon!" He seemed to search for what to say. "Do not cry!"

"I'm not," she said, swiping at her eyes.

He touched her arm, appearing unable to bear the thought that he had brought her away from home only for her to be unhappy.

"I shouldn't have brought Phoebe," she said softly. "You tried to tell me, and I—"

"No," he said, equally softly. "Of course you wanted your maid with you."

She swallowed, taking a breath with her eyes closed. "Your father is angry."

"If he assigns blame, it will be with me since it was my

choice to bring her. But he cannot be angry when he knows she is free." He stroked her arm with gentleness.

After a moment, she walked away slowly, reaching up to remove her earrings once she was by a vanity. She looked at him for a moment and then held her tongue.

"What?" he said.

"They do not *want* her in this house, John Thomas—"

He was shaking his head, holding her eyes. "That is not true, Shannon," he said softly, firmly.

"Perhaps your mother was merely unaccustomed. But you cannot convince me every servant below stairs is not reeling."

He was silent for a moment. "Perhaps. Perhaps not. But you mustn't attribute faults to them before you know them," he said.

Her eyes flamed momentarily before she said, not thinking to watch her tongue, "I regret to inform you that you have married a shrew, John Thomas. I will do perfectly as I please."

No response was forthcoming behind her. She waited in silence. "Then in that case, I will see you at supper," he said quietly, stepping toward the door.

She swallowed a lump in her throat. "S...Send Phoebe to me at six o'clock."

"Yes, I will," he said, and left.

Shannon, awakening from her nap, looked around to find that the sun had receded considerably, leaving just the slightest vestiges of light. Arising in her bloomers and corset, she looked around her. She had fallen asleep on the verge of weeping because she had been forced to say such a thing to him. She had then had no interest in anything but the quarrel. But now, looking around her at the neat, primitive furniture, the somehow appealing emptiness and plainness, she thought of John Thomas here in his boyhood. She smiled softly, if a little sadly, smoothing her hand over the simple white coverlet, taking in the pale gray walls and the large armoire.

She looked at the clock above the mantle and saw it lacked ten minutes to six o'clock. While she waited on Phoebe, she walked to one of the windows and looked out. Land, mostly flat with a gentle roll here and there, stretched out seemingly for miles, though it couldn't be that much, for John Thomas had told her the farm was much smaller than Santarella. She saw sheep in a pasture, nuzzling their lambs and grazing. She reached for the curtain and held it tightly in her hand.

The door opened softly, and she looked over her shoulder as Phoebe entered. Draped over her arms was a dinner gown of cream satin; it had a modest neckline which bowed widely but came within a few inches of her collarbones. There was a bit of lace at the bodice and sleeves, and the craftsmanship could not be hidden, but it was the plainest gown she owned. Phoebe's instincts had never led her astray.

Shannon walked forward rather wearily and then lifted her arms while Phoebe secured her hoops. "Have you settled in, Phoebe?" Shannon asked.

"Yes, ma'am," she said softly. "Mrs. Haley come down and showed me where I could keep your dresses. She asked me how many there were, and when I told her, she said they'd never fit in Mr. Haley's armoire."

"That was kind of her. I'm glad that is settled. I believe I will likely retire early tonight, so I shan't keep you waiting long."

When Shannon was in her dress, Phoebe did up the buttons. Then, at the simple vanity, the maid fastened her necklace and began to brush her hair.

"You want braids, ma'am, looped at the ear?"

"No, you know they give me the appearance of a Roman emperor. Just parted and in a simple twist—you may tie some braids up in it, if you wish."

"Yes, ma'am."

When she was dressed, she went out into the hall, trying to remember her way to the stairs. The floorboards creaked beneath her slippers, and the hall was almost too narrow to accommodate her hoops. She pressed her hand against her middle in a vain attempt to still her nerves—and was surprised to find they had nothing to do with the Haleys and everything to do with John Thomas.

John Thomas waited for Shannon in the foyer and moved closer to the stairs when he saw her appear at the top. She looked too dainty and fragile for a Northern winter. And a Northern family. He regretted almost everything since her arrival, from his family's reception to the scene between them upstairs. He was uncomfortably aware of his own judgment, and that she must have felt ostracized simply for breathing.

There were many things he loved about South Carolina, but Shannon had not been wholly happy there, a little on the outside of her family for reasons too complicated for him to comprehend fully. He had wanted it to be different here. It would be if he had anything to say in the matter.

She reached for the banister and came down, the stairwell lit with a sconce here and there. When she came to where he waited, she stayed on the bottom step, searching his face, her blue eyes stealing his breath. So exquisite. He could still scarcely believe she was his. And that they were here together.

"I hope you rested well," he said softly. His eyes scanned her face. It was so much less than he had meant to say.

"Yes, quite well," she answered. There was a stiffness in her shoulders, which had never masked her fragility from him.

He was hesitant, unsure how to proceed after the scene above stairs. "I checked on you once, and you were sleeping like a baby."

She seemed to thaw a little, a little smile playing at her lips. "No, no, I never slept as a baby."

Smiling softly, he held her eyes. He was surprised to find fear in them. He wanted to wrap her in his arms and tell her he would shield her from everything. But Shannon rejected physical contact when she most needed it and was difficult to reach even with words. He merely covered her hand solidly and said calmly, "I thought I might properly introduce you to them while they're all in the parlor."

"Yes, very well," she said. He helped her down the bottom step and threaded her arm through his.

They walked to a long, rectangular room to find the ladies sewing and the gentlemen chatting. All conversation ceased upon their entrance until Lizzie, regal and elegant, said softly, "I hope you rested well, Shannon."

"Yes, indeed. Your home is very peaceful," Shannon said in her loveliest voice, including Mr. and Mrs. Haley in her reserved smile.

Mr. Haley inclined his head. "Your room will have a view of the pastures, I believe."

"Yes, the lambs are very charming," she said, looking up at John Thomas. "Properly introduce me, then," she said with a smile, a little shy.

Touching the small of her back, he said, indicating him, "My brother Adams. He is the eldest of us, and far more scholarly than I."

She smiled at the young gentleman. He was built on slightly smaller lines than her husband and was plainer, favoring his mother more. When he came before her, she offered her hand, and he took it. He covered it with his other hand rather than kissing it, which she thought rather respectful. "I had not thought it possible," she teased gently. "Are you above Shakespeare, too?"

He looked startled. "Certainly not. Is my brother?"

John Thomas looked down at her, eyes twinkling. "I merely said I preferred—"

"You see? As if anyone could truly prefer anybody. We shall have Shakespearian chats, Mr. Haley, and leave my husband to his miserable Homer."

He agreed to it distractedly, polite and dignified.

Lizzie, when they were introduced, said she was glad to have another sister and that Shannon's pearls were very pretty. She was a year younger than Shannon at nineteen, but she and John Thomas had kept up a steady correspondence during his travels. Lizzie was reserved and perhaps carefully concealing the mourning any sibling must feel upon the marriage of another sibling. She always flushed when she began talking to Shannon, perhaps shy due to her exoticism (to her) and social standing.

There seemed to be an easy friendship between John Thomas and Charles, who had, as John Thomas put it, shared the cradle with him. It was easy to see, though, that Charles was more given to levity, his tone of mind not quite so refined. Adams was refined but did not share John Thomas's spirit. Shannon saw in a glance why John Thomas had formed a close friendship with her brother.

Charles said everything that was proper, welcoming her to the family and asking well-chosen questions about South Carolina and the Sea Islands, gently joking that he could not see why such a beauty had chosen his brother, which made everyone smile.

Miriam, the prettiest of the girls, was seventeen. She had a sweet smile that reminded Shannon of her husband. This earned the girl a lovely twinkle from her fascinating sister-in-law.

Vincent was fourteen and uncommonly well-behaved. Sarah, the youngest, was obviously the delight of the family and equally the despair.

"Oh, Sister, where did you get your gown?" she asked, eyes sparkling.

Shannon smiled, thinking her adorable in her linen bonnet and drooping sash. John Thomas's eyes were tender as they rested on her. "Madame Persaud made it for me in Charleston. She is a lady who pretends to be French but is instead from New Orleans," Shannon said, smiling when the girl's eyes lighted.

"Oh, but how can she be so very bad when she makes such lovely gowns?" she said, almost reaching to touch it. She lifted her eyes to Shannon with rapt admiration. "Are *all* of your gowns so lovely, Sister?"

"Yes, all of them," John Thomas said, eyes warm.

Shannon flushed slightly. "My father spoils me." It wasn't precisely the truth. Shannon, always accompanied by her mother or her mammy, bought whatever she wanted. The shopkeepers presented her father with a bill, which generally caused a great deal of grumbling, but he always paid them. Her mother had always bought as she chose, so perhaps he knew it was a lost cause.

"I noticed that he dotes on you," Mrs. Haley said, rising and saying in brisk Northern style, "Supper is waiting."

They adjourned to the dining room and took their seats. The senior Mr. Haley said a lengthy prayer, during which John Thomas took her hand. She turned her head toward him, but his eyes were closed, head bowed. He was very serious during the more locally concerned entreaties, prayers for the family, for Patience as she awaited her husband's return from Harvard, for a sick neighbor, and the poor children of the parish, for all of their charities, and that their church might shine a light in the dark world. When his theme became more universal, John Thomas's thumb stroked her hand tenderly a couple of times. After three more minutes, he loosened his hold and drew a heart on the inside of her hand. She glanced at him to see his lips turned slightly in a smile. She turned his hand over and drew an X to reprimand him. She felt his hand tremble slightly from an inward laugh, but, thankfully, before he could lose control, the prayer ended.

The conversation bored her for several minutes, the men discussing something political, tariffs and taxes that impacted the shipping business. Shannon ate, or tried to. She was shocked at the quantity of food they consumed at the late hour. And she had no idea what many of the foul-smelling dishes were. She would lose ten pounds by May.

"How did you come by your name? It is most unusual." Shannon looked up when she realized the table had quieted, that the question had been directed at her. "Oh, I..." Who had asked it? Her father-in-law. "Shannon is my mother's maiden name. It was given to both my brother and me as a middle name. Mary is my given name."

"Why on earth would your mother call you Shannon when you have a fine name like Mary?" Mr. Haley demanded.

Really, Northerners could be so direct! "I imagine for the same reason that you call your firstborn Adams, sir. Family pride."

The interrogation complete, the men talked about steel mills the rest of the dinner. The ladies withdrew to the parlor first, where everyone picked up their sewing. Shannon hadn't the least notion how to sew, other than crocheting for aesthetic and mourning purposes. The Haley women were, Lizzie informed her, sewing stockings, scarves, and mittens for the poor. "Oh, how kind!" Shannon said, thinking of the seamstresses at Santarella, who did all of the more mundane work

The men did not linger over their spirits, because there were very little of them, and when they entered, John Thomas searched the room for her, smiled slightly, and sat down to talk with Charles. Another thing that surprised Shannon was that the children were allowed to dine with the adults and even to retire with them after. They seemed drawn to John Thomas, both of them, like flies to sugar water. Sarah soon planted herself on his knee and Vincent sat on the rug before him, peppering him with questions about his adventures and the Navy.

The family did indeed retire early, and Phoebe was waiting to minister to Shannon when they returned to their bedchamber. Shannon's eyes trailed John Thomas as he went into the small dressing room without a word after nodding distractedly to Phoebe. After twenty minutes, Phoebe left, taking all of Shannon's undergarments and trappings with her, leaving her in her nightgown and draping her dressing gown over a chair.

She slipped into bed, her heart beating wildly. She felt prim in the nightgown that Phoebe had suggested she wear to keep off the cold, her hair in a long braid over her shoulder. Would he be angry for her earlier words? Would he even want to touch her? It seemed to have been some time, though it was only their travelling which had caused it.

When John Thomas came out, he stopped for a moment, meeting her eyes and holding them. Then he walked slowly toward the bed and finally sat hesitantly beside her. He lifted his eyes and studied her face with remorse and then stroked a hand down her arm gently, whispering, "I'm so sorry."

Shannon moistened her lips. "For..."

"For the way I spoke to you earlier, and then left. You were upset, and I should've stayed. What was I thinking?"

"Oh, no, why would you stay, after I said such a shrewish thing to you?"

He studied her with his brows drawn together. "Because you are my wife," he said after a moment. "And I love you."

Shannon looked away, swallowing. She responded light-heartedly. "Well, you must, or you would have sent me packing after *such* a day."

"Don't joke about such things," he murmured, eyes roaming her features. And then, as if his mind turned to a new avenue, he said, "Shannon, I'm sorry that my father should have questioned you over your name! Imagine, having a fine name like Mary..."

Her laughter bubbled over. "No, no, that was not so bad. You ought to have been present in the parlor for your mother's discussion with me over a woman's place."

He grinned. "Which you have no notion of."

"What a thing to say! I consider myself a dutiful wife to you. You have no notion of the sacrifices—"

"If you had seen the bills the manager handed me at the hotel in New Orleans, you would not speak to me of sacrifice!" he said, eyes dancing.

She was horrified. "Oh, no, John Thomas, was it so very bad?"

"Yes," he said.

"Oh! I wasn't thinking... I shall never purchase anything again—"

"Shannon Ravenel—Haley—in shabby clothes? I wish I may never see it."

"Charlatan. As if I cared only for fine clothes," she said, picking at the coverlet, pretending unconcern.

His expression changed. "You know I don't think so. Especially when there has been no end to your sacrifices." He smiled, but his eyes were earnest. His hand covered hers, tentatively, and then lovingly.

She met his eyes, smiling, and he kissed her once, gently, and then again, lingeringly. The fireplace crackled and cast a gentle glow over the room. Shy at first, the kiss deepened and lengthened. Shannon, her eyes closed and her fingers trailing down his chest, lost all sense of time and space, the miserable train ride and night forgotten.

Chapter Eighteen

The day was sunny when morning broke through the curtains. Shannon, blinking away the fog, saw on the clock above the mantle that it was nearly nine o'clock. John Thomas was already awake and in the little room next door as she lay in bed, letting herself grow accustomed to the light.

He returned once she had rung the bell and was sitting in her dressing gown. She met his eyes, flushing softly. His smile was slightly roguish, but she had to look away from the deep tenderness in his eyes.

She was sitting with a tray of fruit and bread before her, like a queen, and she said, "Oh, John Thomas, would you like a biscuit? They are not very good."

He laughed. "Smother them in honey—it helps," he said, doing it for her and then feeding it to her. He took a bite himself but ate nothing more. She had only known him for five months, but it was long enough to know he had to be tempted to his meals.

There was a knock at the door, and he went to answer it, wiping the honey onto his handkerchief and carefully positioning himself to cover her state of undress. He took something in his hand and returned with two letters. One was addressed to her, from Marie, the other to him, from Frederick. "Oh, how dear they are!" she said, reaching for hers hungrily. "They must have put a great deal of effort into timing them for our first morning here!"

"Yes, I could kiss them both, for making you smile just so."

"Well, Frederick would think it very odd, but I appreciate the sentiment."

He smiled. Solicitously, he took her glass, putting it on the side table before looking back at her. She became distracted by his eyes, by the way his fair hair fell on his forehead when he looked down.

And then, in the still of the quiet, awareness began to grow between them. He came to sit next to her, and his thumb feathered across her lips. Then his lips brushed hers once, lingering. "Go riding with me," he said softly.

"Yes, I will. Will they mind?"

"No, I think they mean to give us today as a holiday to rest."

"Very well," she said, wishing for the first time since entering the state that it were cooler. Her cheeks were flaming, and her veins felt heated. Her gaze lingered on his face. "I'll join you."

After a time, he left, looking dapper in his riding wear. She watched him leave before finishing a strawberry and picking up the letter.

March 1860, Richmond, Virginia

The Berkeley Hotel

My Dear Shannon,

My sweet sister, I hope this letter finds you already ensconced in your husband's home and surrounded by comfort and love. I wish very much that I could see you there, out of your natural habitat. I worry that you will be cold—is it very nasty?

We are well and settling into married life. Frederick is everything that is kind, and we have enjoyed Richmond very much. We will stay another week and then go directly to Santarella for the planting. Frederick and your father wish very much to have a good crop this year because of the volatility of the markets and the language being tossed around in Washington. Shannon, what are these men about? If only we could talk sense into all of them!

I know I do not have to ask if you like being married to John Thomas. Dear Shannon, the way he looks at you! But likely I am embarrassing you. Well, then, write to me and tell me of Massachusetts and the Haleys. Give John Thomas my love, and his mother my greetings.

Marie

Shannon left the house in her deep blue riding habit, the train looped over her arm and a whip in her hand. The morning was gray and cold as she stepped onto the cobblestone drive. She had received a hastily scrawled note from John Thomas telling her that they would not be alone, which made her smile. She had not expected that they would be since there were siblings in the vicinity.

Charles, Lizzie, and Miriam were to join them, apparently enjoying a holiday themselves. John Thomas had already lifted Miriam onto her horse, and Charles went to lift Lizzie, teasing, "We brought out the tamest old nag we had. Lizzie is afraid of horses, Shannon!"

"Do not tease her until you've ridden perched on the side of one of the creatures!" Shannon bantered.

John Thomas said, "You will always find Shannon's solidarity with the ladies, Charles. You mustn't try to befriend her."

"Oh, I am glad to hear it!" Miriam said merrily.

Shannon laughed, taking her husband's gloved hand lightly as he led her to a spirited little mare. He lifted her up, his hands lingering on her waist as she secured herself. She met his eyes, and she saw desire written in his features. His hands were searing on her waist, and she flushed, looking away before he could see. "Is...Is there a good pasture?" she asked, looking out over the fields. "I have not truly ridden since we left Santarella in November."

"Yes, there is always a good field for riding here," Charles explained.

"It won't be anything to Santarella, from what John Thomas writes," Lizzie said, not quite looking up.

"Well, the Masons wouldn't mind us spilling over into their field, if only there wasn't that fence there," Charles said as John Thomas swung onto his horse.

"It doesn't matter a bit," Shannon said. "Doesn't your elder brother ride?"

"Yes, if you can bring him out of his reverie," Charles said. John Thomas exchanged a glance with him, smiling a little.

As they made their way to the field, they rode the perimeter and to the highest point, where Shannon could see the surrounding farms, encased in charming, primitive fences.

"Is it anything like Santarella?" Charles asked.

"If Santarella had a point this high, you would be able to see the ocean," John Thomas said.

Shannon nodded, "Yes, and the surrounding farms would not be nearly so neat or quaint. It is enchanting!"

"Never mind that," Miriam said. "Shannon, is your habit French-made?"

"Oh, Miriam, this is vanity," Lizzie said. "What does it matter?"

"It is only that I have never seen such a military style, or a hat so masculine!"

Shannon smiled. "No, it is British. No one understands a riding habit so much as they, Miriam. And, indeed, it is vanity, for my father once chided me upon it!"

Lizzie flushed. "Oh, no, I didn't mean—"

"Of course not," John Thomas said. "Shannon tells me she never means to spend another penny upon clothes, in any event."

She gave him a twinkling look. "Did I? I recall nothing of

the sort. May I let her fly?" she asked, patting her horse's neck. "She wants to very much."

"Of course," he answered, smiling. "We'll stay with Lizzie and wait for you."

Shannon rode off, tamely at first, and then like the wind, her posture and technique perfectly trained, and they all watched her without removing their eyes from her.

"A good little rider," Charles said.

"She was trained by a Spaniard hired by her father," John Thomas said. "Well, I assume so, in any event. Her brother was." His eyes did not leave her as she rode, jumping the Masons' fence and then taking it a second time, coming back toward them. The tension in his shoulders eased slightly once she was over.

Shannon joined them, receiving Charles's compliments. "A Spaniard trained you?" he asked.

"Yes, Señor Gonzales," she said. "An excellent teacher, though he always favored Frederick tremendously."

"Does your family raise horses, Shannon, for racing?" Miriam asked.

"No, well, not wholesale. We always enter a horse in the races, if that is what you mean."

"Are the purses very heavy for winning?" she asked, eyes glittering.

Shannon paused a moment. "Yes, I believe they are." She also believed Frederick's entire education had been funded by the purse they had won in '54, but she did not say so. She waited only for Miriam to ask for specific details on the gambling involved. John Thomas had already grown quiet, looking at his hands.

Happily, Charles changed the subject, asking how they had liked New Orleans. John Thomas and he were talking about the differences in the shipping industry there when Lizzie bethought herself of something she simply must attend to for her mother and commanded Miriam to come with her, too.

Miriam looked at her strangely but obeyed, glancing back at Shannon and then casting her eyes down quickly.

"Then I suppose our party breaks here," Charles said, reaching for Shannon's gloved hand and kissing the air above it, which made her laugh. "I am off to Boston for the day and night to see about Aunt Agatha's finances."

"Give her our love," John Thomas said.

"I will," he agreed, riding off.

Shannon's eyes followed him.

"What?" John Thomas asked.

"Do you imagine tending to Aunt Agatha is *all* he will find to do in Boston?"

He smiled slowly. "I couldn't say." His eyes followed Shannon's to where the girls were retreating, and then he looked at Shannon, studying her.

She didn't comment, however, so he said, sidling his horse and leaning toward her as though to kiss her, "Race me?"

She laughed, skittering away from him. "Oh, no, John Thomas, I shall be so sore tomorrow! Remember that I haven't ridden in weeks!"

His eyes twinkled. "Very well. If you are afraid."

She lifted her brows, her eyes sparking with the challenge. And then she took off, leaving him behind. He laughed and set off, quickly coming up beside her.

Shannon did not descend the stairs until ten o'clock the next morning, having dressed in one of her plainer day gowns, of a demure mint green with pagoda sleeves and cream cording. She had walked to the dining room where the shocked servants had, after a long and heated discussion, decided to leave breakfast out for the young bride.

The room was deserted, but Shannon had just poured herself some tea when her mother-in-law opened the door softly and entered. "I hope you were not ill, Shannon. We were beginning to worry."

Shannon smiled. "I am sorry for missing breakfast, ma'am. I found myself very tired from the journey. I shall try to do better." She did not mention that at home, she would likely be in bed even now, new husband or no. "What time do you rise?"

"Five o'clock," the woman answered briskly.

Shannon blinked, gripping the ladder-back chair. "Good gracious! What could one possibly do at five o'clock?"

"Pray," she said.

Shannon's lips parted. "Oh!" She could not think what else to say.

The woman held her eyes for a long moment before finally saying with astounding bluntness, "Well, you are a newlywed, after all. If you are not hungry, you may come with me."

Shannon followed her, a little shocked. She was surprised when Mrs. Haley took her into the kitchen. She was also taken aback by the scene she found there. Lizzie, Miriam, and Sarah were all standing at the long wooden slab in bonnets and aprons amongst the kitchen servants. One could scarcely tell which were which.

"We are baking for the poor," Mrs. Haley said, tying on her apron. "There is always a distribution at church on the second and fourth Sundays."

Shannon looked around her in awe. Lizzie was kneading bread with her own hands, laughing with the kitchen maid who stood beside her. Miriam was adding ingredients to a bowl, chattering to the cook, and Sarah was using a cutter to fashion biscuits without any assistance.

They all looked up when Mrs. Haley closed the door and paused, taking in Shannon's gown.

"Oh, Sister!" Sarah breathed. "Is *this* one of Madame Persaud's creations, too?"

Shannon resisted the urge to brush her skirts self-consciously. "Oh, this? No, I asked my brother and his wicked friend to purchase me silk of this very color in Paris, and what do you think they sent me?"

"Wool!" Miriam said, laughing.

"Yes, but I forgave them because they sent me some exquisite lace, which was ultimately used for my veil."

"Oh, how romantic! John Thomas *couldn't* have known he was purchasing it for his own bride!"

For a brief moment, she saw blind jealously in Lizzie's eyes, but it quickly receded, and the girl lowered her head. "Who made it for you then?" Miriam asked, coming around from behind the counter. Her dark gray skirts were full, but it was obvious she was wearing no hoops. Her eyes were sharp as she surveyed the intricacies.

"I gave it to the seamstresses at Santarella to see if they could do anything with it," Shannon answered, lifting a shoulder.

Miriam touched the sleeve. "Oh, Shannon! Such beautiful material!"

"Well, it did turn out rather well."

"Yes, how talented they must be!"

"Miriam, help Shannon with her apron," Mrs. Haley said in a tone of light censure.

Miriam flushed. "Oh, Mother, Shannon doesn't know how to bake!" she said.

Lizzie and Sarah looked up, appearing thunderstruck. Apparently not as worldly-wise as Miriam, Sarah said, "Is it true, Shannon? What did you learn as a little girl?"

"There is no need to be rude, Sarah," Mrs. Haley said calmly.

"Oh, no, ma'am, don't scold her," Shannon said. "It is only a difference in culture. The same things you were taught, I imagine: reading, writing, mathematics, and French. And then, when I was older, how to be a lady and the mistress of a plantation. But I have no objection to learning to bake," she said.

"Yes, we will teach you," Lizzie said softly. "Come and stand by me, Shannon."

"Sarah, help Agnes with the butter," Mrs. Haley said, taking her daughter's place. Shannon watched as the girl went and began fashioning butter, which had been made fresh that morning at Harmony Grove, into molds.

Lizzie helped Shannon tie on an apron and began teaching her how to knead. Shannon quickly realized the Haley women far outstripped her in knowledge and technique, and, as the morning wore on, endurance. Still, it was a rather happy feeling when the first loaves were removed from the oven, and the kitchen was filled with a pleasing aroma. Taking a momentary rest, Shannon tore off the edge of one the pieces they had been trying and nibbled it, leaning against the large washing sink. There were large slits for windows around the kitchen, and through one of them, she saw John Thomas and Charles riding out behind wagons in their mere shirtsleeves.

"What are they doing?" she asked.

"Planting," Mrs. Haley said.

Shannon looked at her elegant husband, who moved with ease in the highest of society, and said faintly, "Why? Why, when you have everything?"

"The attainment of wealth is so that we can help others, my dear, not so that we may sit about all day. Idleness is not good for the soul, no matter how much we have been blessed."

Shannon blinked, looking back out to where neat rows were even now being plowed. She said nothing more.

Later, when Mrs. Haley, Lizzie, and Miriam had left to place flowers on the altar at the church, Shannon caught a moment to sit in the sunny parlor and compose a letter to Marie. Sweet strains from Sarah's piano practicing drifted in from the music room. The house was otherwise quiet, Vincent having finished his morning Latin lessons with Adams and left to visit the minister. This gentleman, apparently a notable scholar, would be taking over the care of Vincent's lessons for the next five years, his time at the little school in the parish having come to an end.

Shannon felt exhausted, for the day's labor had not ended with wrapping the loaves and packing them in baskets. The ladies had proceeded to sew for two hours. All were tasks which Shannon had only ever loosely supervised, which she never would have undertaken at home. She supposed many Southern women had, but her life was very different from most Southern women. And now, she scarcely had the energy to lift her pen.

March 1860, Harmony Grove

Weymouth, Massachusetts

My Dear Cousin,

Or may I call you sister now? How it pleases me to hear of your happiness and Frederick's. By now you will be at Santarella and bored to tears by incessant conversation on the topic of planting, unless I miss my mark. My mother will not last three weeks before returning to Charleston, and I advise you, dear one, to go with her.

It suddenly struck Shannon that her mother and father had traded a daughter for a daughter-in-law, that all of the positions she had once taken would be filled by another. Jealousy flamed, and she wondered if they were pleased with the exchange, or whether she was missed. She shook her head, finding herself unworthy once more. She didn't know what to say to Marie. She wanted to know everything but didn't wish to admit she was terribly homesick. She didn't know how to explain how the Haleys lived, for they couldn't understand it.

All is well here. Their ways are very different, of course, but it is a peaceful household, never a voice raised or a loud noise to disturb one's thoughts. There is a pretty little pasture for riding, and there is always something to occupy one's time.

John Thomas sends his love. We talk of the two of you so often, and we long for the days when we may again be with you. I think of our picnics and carriage rides with pleasure. In any event, at least I shall not perish out of doors from heat in Massachusetts if I wish to take part in an excursion.

Give my love to all of my family and to your mother and father. Tell my mother that Phoebe is indeed making me wear that very ugly nightgown, and that I shall bundle up like a child if I can summon the courage to step outside the house again.

Your own Shannon

Shannon had just sealed the letter when she heard a noise behind her and looked over her shoulder. John Thomas was standing in the doorway. She would never have imagined that there could be appeal in a man in a state of considerable dishevel, looking tired after a long day's work, but that was only because she had never seen it.

He was smiling gently at her, but he didn't say anything. Her heart leapt.

She looked up at him, smiling a little shyly. "We saw you," she said. "If I had realized I had married a true farmer, I should've learned to milk a cow," she teased.

His smiled, coming into the room, bending to kiss her cheek only, perhaps because of his sweat. He sat down beside her. She marveled at the difference that allowed him to sit in a parlor in his shirtsleeves. How much more was Harmony

Grove truly their home, their retreat from the fashionable world. "Have you had a pleasant day?" he asked, studying her as though she were a wonderful, fascinating creature.

She averted her eyes. "Oh...yes."

He studied her closely. "Come, tell me."

"We baked and sewed for the poor," she said in a light tone. "I confess, I rather felt useless."

He leaned up and took her hands in his and opened them, examining them. Then he studied her face, saw the exhaustion in her eyes, and said, "Shannon, I am a fool. I will speak with my mother."

She pulled her hands away. "I am not afraid of a little work, John Thomas." She stood. "I know it must seem as though my life has always been given over to idleness, but..." Her fingers gripped the chair until they turned white. "Well, I suppose it has. But one cannot last until the small hours of the morning in a ballroom, indeed one cannot be a *woman,* without having a constitution strong enough to withstand a little baking." She swallowed with difficulty.

His brows drew together. "Why are you upset?" he asked.

"Don't you see? I can't sit idly all day long when your mother and sisters are being...industrious. They will have contempt for me, and I won't allow that. And I won't sleep past five o'clock either," she said, trying to cover her agitation, standing and striding toward the door. She stopped with her hand on the knob, looking back at him for a long, searching moment. "You made becoming a part of my family look as easy as breathing, John Thomas. How did you do it?"

He lifted a shoulder, meeting her eyes, slightly at a loss.

After a hesitation, he said, "It was not always easy. But I loved them. Perhaps that made it easier."

She flushed deeply. Opening the door, she fled quickly through it, too rapidly to see him come quickly to his feet and stand, looking after her.

Chapter Nineteen

The series of events which occurred next were never able to be fully recalled by Adeline. There seemed to be one catastrophe/omen/curse after another of the sort which usually only happened in comedies.

The trip home started out well enough. They left Statesboro around five o'clock, on schedule to be home by eight (Adeline was glad she had brought her pretzels). There wasn't much chatting, but the Frank Sinatra in the background was kind of growing on her.

It started to rain when they crossed over into South Carolina, which wasn't far into their journey. "Did you check the weather for today?" she asked.

He lifted a shoulder. "It was supposed to rain a little. Nothing serious."

As he said it, water started to dump out of the sky, and Adeline stiffened in the seat. He glanced over at her. "I'll pull over if it gets dangerous."

"That's not going to protect us from a tornado," she said pessimistically. Did he see that wind? It was bending the trees and shoving the rain off the road.

"Well, look it up," he said.

She picked up her phone. There was no service, it seemed, in Middle of Nowhere, South Carolina. They drove on for fifteen minutes. He was probably thinking it would slacken; it didn't. It wasn't her normal fear of storms that was scaring her: this was a bad storm. It was a lot like being on that boat, with no control whatsoever. "There's an exit," she said, noticing all of the cars creeping onto it.

He didn't argue; he took the exit and followed the line of cars. They turned in at a gas station, pulling the car into the last available spot that wasn't being taken up by other freeloaders sheltering, and he reached for his door handle.

"I don't think you should get out," she said.

He looked at her. "I'm going to see if I can find out how long this is supposed to last."

She bit her lip. She sat back, and he left. He was in the gas station for about ten minutes while she wondered what force of nature had made the weather so bad this spring. He came out, getting wet even though his walk was covered, and getting back into the car.

He glanced at her, seeming to hesitate.

"Bad news?" she asked.

"It's supposed to do this all night—now."

"You mean, like, this bad?" she demanded, shocked.

He nodded. "I talked to the man at the counter, and they had the weather on. I'm thinking we need to get hotel rooms.

He said there's only one decent hotel in town and that we need to get over there before all these other people do."

"Oh, gosh," she said, taking a breath. She blinked, shocked at how easily a freak occurrence could throw all your plans away. "Okay. Yeah, if you think that's what we should do." Her stomach rumbled from starvation, but hopefully they would have a vending machine, or something.

"He said they have a restaurant."

"Oh, good," she breathed, not even caring that he had read her mind again.

He drove about two miles. Then she saw a historic-looking brick building that probably had twenty rooms. It seemed to be a boutique hotel/place of historic interest, and she liked what she saw. It was called the General Longstreet Hotel. At least it didn't look like they would be reliving the Bed Bug Disaster of '14. At least, she hoped not.

It started hailing, and she felt sorry for the Land Rover. But there didn't seem to be anything they could do about it. "I think we should make a run for it," he said, looking ominously at two couples who were making a dash toward the door.

"Yeah." After only a slight hesitation, she opened her door and dashed toward the entrance, stopping too soon and making him slam into her. "Sorry," she said as he opened the door. He didn't answer. Well, she'd made no guarantees about her gracefulness. She didn't know why she pictured his wife as a gazelle. But Adeline never pretended to be.

She swallowed when she saw the line in front of them in the high-ceilinged, historic room. She glanced at him, and he pressed his lips together, obviously noticing it, too. It took twenty minutes for them to get to the counter. Once there, he said to the middle-aged woman with faded blonde hair, "Two rooms, please."

She winced. "We just have one more," she said, kind of under her breath. She looked at the line behind them as though dreading their reactions. Adeline glanced over her shoulder, seeing people barely wedged in the door from the high winds outside. She looked back at the woman, opening her lips to speak, but before she could, Dr. Ravenel said, "We'll take it," very firmly.

Adeline glanced at him, drawing a breath. Okay, she got it. They didn't have a choice. But, really? She hadn't been able to be adult about touching his hand on the freaking boat. How was she supposed to do this? Best case scenario, there would be two beds, or at the very least, a king.

He paid, and the woman gave him the keys. "4A," he said to Adeline once they were walking away. "At least we're on the top floor."

She didn't see how it was an advantage in this monsoon, but why quibble? It was better shelter than the Land Rover. She followed him toward the wooden staircase, where a bellhop was waiting to take bags they didn't have. They told him thanks, but no thanks. As they started up the stairs, she said, "I'll pay you back when I get back to my checkbook."

"I always pay when I take a woman to a hotel," he said, looking super-annoyed and pinching the bridge of his nose briefly.

That surprised a laugh out of her. "Yeah, it would probably be best if we keep this to ourselves."

"You read my mind," he said. He glanced at her. "Would you rather take the elevator?"

"I'm fairly fit," she said. At least...sort of.

"I know."

She looked at him, lifting her brows. Pressing his lips together and looking like he'd like to crush something in his hand, he swung back the door for the next stairway and gave her a look as he held it for her. Okay, so did that mean he was attracted to her, too? Or was she reading too much into the two words, like she always had with guy friends in college? Or maybe she had completely lost her mind altogether. She didn't know why she cared, anyway.

She was wishing she'd opted in on the elevator by the time they reached the fourth floor, and she had to do that quick nose-breathing thing to hide her breathless state. He put the cute skeleton key in the door and opened it.

They stepped in, a clean smell along with the smell of cookies teasing her senses.

She stopped, looking in front of her. There was one bed. One full-sized bed. She swallowed.

She knew the moment he saw, too. He stilled. There was a long silence before he finally said, "I'll sleep on the floor if you want."

She hesitated, checking out the floor. It was an old-style patterned carpet. If it had been hardwood, she might have made him do it. But there was no telling what was living in that. She had a feeling it would make him die inside. "Don't be ridiculous. We're adults." In a tiny, tiny bed. One of them a freaking model. The whole problem was that they were adults.

"Yeah, okay," he said.

They checked out the situation: a clawfoot bathtub with a spray-thingy in the bathroom. It looked clean, but she wasn't sitting in it. The spray-thingy would have to do. And it would take about an hour.

There were long windows, where lights from the street below illuminated the raindrops sliding down. They both stood around a little aimlessly, obviously not wanting to sit on the bed. She'd never been more relieved than when he said, "Why don't we go get dinner?"

"Good idea," she said. She was halfway to the bathroom when she stopped. "Oh, wait. I bet it's fancy. We're not dressed for it."

"It'll just have to be. Everyone down there will be like this. And we'll be paying, so it won't matter too much to them."

She hesitated. "All right. Let me freshen up a little."

She closed the door behind her, looking at her hair. The good thing about springy curls was that the rain couldn't make them much springier. She brushed her fingers over them to smooth them a little and took her compact from her purse, touching up her makeup just a little. She glanced down in her purse, seeing her bottle of perfume. She was never sure why she sprayed it.

"Ready?" she said, coming out.

"Yeah." He followed her out the door.

The dining room was indeed of the white tablecloth variety, with servers in black attire. But there were a lot of bedraggled people in jeans, so she wasn't too worried about it. They got a table and were brought a splendid menu. She ordered a lemonade and fettucine. He ordered wine and salmon. Long drive he didn't want to make, accosted by parents, hijacked into an overnighter by a downpour—he deserved the wine. And it seemed to help his disposition a lot. He never lashed out or said anything when he was moody, she noticed. But the silence was usually pretty ominous.

Now, he leaned back in his chair a little, hand around the stem of his glass, studying her. "Is it lonely?" he asked.

She lifted her brows, pushing her breadstick around in the sauce. "What I do?"

He nodded, eyes on her face.

"Why, does it seem lonely to you?"

He lifted a shoulder. "Going to cities where you know no one, with a crew you're on professional terms with..."

"I've been on my own for a long time. You get used to it." She took a drink. "You get kind of used to doing things your way." She bit her lip, wondering if that was insensitive, if he was still in the stage of wondering how to fill the void, how to bear the loneliness, the loss.

"Yeah." He surveyed her a moment more. "You don't have a significant other?"

She shook her head. "I don't date much."

His brows drew together. "Really? Why?"

Shrugging, she took a small bite of bread and chewed it, covering for time. It was a good question, really. "I don't know. All the guys who are interested in me aren't really husband material. And all the guys I've liked would be friends, you know. I would wait to see whether it would work into something, and then they'd come tell me about a date they had Friday night. *That* was a fun phase." She rolled her eyes.

He studied her. "You shouldn't have let them treat you that way."

"They never knew I even liked them. We were friends, you know?"

"They always know," he said grimly. "They were using you. All the perks of a relationship with none of the responsibilities."

She blinked, thinking about it. Of course, it had happened several times in college, and since then, she'd been on a couple of dates, but she hadn't really thought about it in a while. She guessed he might be right. "That's probably true," she said after their salads had been brought. "But it's ancient history now." She'd had a serious relationship a long time ago, but it wasn't meant to be, and she never thought of him anymore. Meanwhile, she was, it seemed, doomed to spinsterhood while Annie had a local firefighter fiancé. And the funny thing was, it never bothered her. She never even thought about her singleness. Sure, she was lonely now and then, but who wasn't?

She took a bite of the salad. It was good, but it needed more cheese and tomatoes. She looked at him, scrutinizing. "So, do you ever date?"

He looked up. Deer in the headlights. Well, what was good for the goose was good for the gander.

"Uh, no," he said, sitting up and becoming deeply interested in his salad.

"Why not?"

A slight pause. "At first, it was for myself. Now it's for Jude."

She nodded once. She could understand that. "He wouldn't want someone to replace his mom."

He chewed for a moment. "Well... It's not that so much as...

He was pretty messed up after... I think it was a combination of PTSD and depression. He saw a child psychologist for a year, and he's so much better. But he needs my full attention."

"Poor little guy," she said softly. "He was injured, too, wasn't he," she said. It was more a statement than a question.

The rain continued, the fireplace snapped, and the lights were low. The food had been brought, and it was delicious. It created an intimate atmosphere. She never would've asked, and he never would've responded otherwise. His fingers curled in on the table, and his hand maybe clenched.

"Yeah," Adrian answered.

His thoughts swept him up.

He remembered the phone call, the almost overwhelming sick feeling.

"What happened?" she asked softly. Not in a nosy way, but in a compassionate one.

He shook his head, sniffing. It was a stalling mechanism, and he knew that, and hated himself for pointing it out to himself. He sat back in the chair. "Lauren was...difficult sometimes. She'd be perfectly rational in public and then at home... I don't know if it was bad behavior, or—I suspected Bipolar Disorder, but she would never order an exam." He felt her watching him closely. He shook his head, eyes narrowed on nothing in particular in the distance. "It began to be all I could do to stand it—the fights, the cold shoulders, the mind games... I thought about a divorce, but... If I could've gotten full custody—but even still, I couldn't stand the thought of her taking care of him just one day. And it didn't feel right. To divorce the mother of my child. We'd...had good times, too. And she'd come around just enough that I thought maybe it was just a phase. Maybe she was unhappy for some reason."

She nodded, eyes gentle and sad. He studied her for a moment. "So I hired Jane. I told Lauren it was to help her out. She was fine with that," he said almost bitterly. "She always complained about how I didn't know how much she did for Jude." He fingered his napkin. "That day... We'd had a huge argument. I don't know if it sent her over the edge, or what possessed her to drive at that speed in the rain." He had driven at an unreasonable speed himself to get to Savannah, where Jude had been taken by Air Ambulance. Harris had gotten there long before he did.

He had met him at the doors of the hospital while Jude was in surgery and wrapped him in a smothering embrace while Adrian trembled like he had a severe fever. He didn't know how long they had stood there, Harris crying, too, and whispering over and over, "I'm sorry. I'm so sorry, Adrian." All he had wanted was news of his son. It wasn't comforting. He had gone into shock on the helicopter and had possibly flatlined for a moment once they'd gotten him to the hospital. Adrian had always been grateful to Harris for living those moments for him, instead of him. He wasn't sure he could've stood it.

His parents had arrived and had sat on either side of him all night, each of them clasping one of his hands. And then he'd had to go make the phone call to her family... But when they'd let him go back to see Jude, sleeping on the hospital bed, his face unharmed and as sweet as ever, his world had righted.

"I think she was leaving me," he said. "To go to her parents in Savannah." His jaw clenched, and even he knew his voice sounded cold. "But in the end, I don't really care because she almost killed my son."

As Adeline went up the stairs, she mulled over all he had said and hadn't. She could see him over there reliving it, but his words to her had been few. But whew! Just when you thought you had someone figured out. She had apologized for bringing it up, suddenly remembering that his brother had told her he never talked about it. She didn't think Jude was the only one who had been traumatized by the events of that night. But he did seem to be in remarkably good mental health now, considering. He didn't even smother Jude, which she would if he was her baby.

The conversation had turned, though not to lighter topics. Okay, almost anything was lighter than that. But the mood seemed to be set, and they had gone into several surprisingly deep things, although she didn't think she knew him much better at all. It was remarkable how she knew so many facts about his life and almost nothing about *him* at all.

He stuck the key in the door and then stood back for her to enter first. She crossed the threshold, seeing a good fairy had lit the fireplace. Not good, fairy. Not good at all. She swallowed.

He locked up behind them, and she said, "I...think I'm going to take a shower."

"Good luck," he said, somewhat wryly.

She smiled and went into the bathroom, bringing her purse with her as if that could make up for a lack of an overnight bag. It would be super-fun to go right back into the exact same clothes. But at least she wouldn't have that travel-worn feeling that made her feel like she'd been to Woodstock. If she was going to feel that way, it better be actual Woodstock.

Eons later, she emerged, feeling like she'd touched everything in the bathroom, and said, "Your turn. At least there's plenty of hot water, and I didn't get struck by lightning." Thunder rumbled in the distance.

He was sitting on the bed with his phone in his hand, but he looked up. His eyes roved her face in what felt like an extremely intimate way. She felt it all the way to her toes. She would've thought the wet hair and the lack of makeup was shocking him, but he didn't look that way. He didn't look that way at all. She bit her lip.

He stood finally. "Great." He cleared his throat, going into the bathroom.

She sat on the bed, closing her eyes. What was *wrong* with her. It wasn't like her to be such an idiot. She saw his phone lying there. She assumed he'd called to ask Jane if Jude could stay with her. He must be pretty decent: creeps didn't leave their phones lying around or hand them over to their moms.

It was good that he was decent, since there would be about a centimeter between them in this bed.

When he finally emerged, she wasn't prepared. Not for Ralph Lauren model with wet hair, or for the white T-shirt which must've been beneath his button down all day. What was wrong with her? And why didn't she think Jason Mraz was sexy anymore? She stood. She needed to get off the bed.

But that was a mistake, too. He was still standing, his eyes following her. How she ended up right in front of him, she never was sure. She thought she had been going to her purse to get her phone as a distraction.

They were incredibly close. He was looking down at her, eyes dipping from her lips back up to her eyes. There was a steamy, serious look in his. In her mind, she knew the rain was still pelting the windows. But her mind wasn't working very well. She couldn't hear anything. Couldn't see anything but him.

He kissed her. Just a slight brush of the lips, but oh so much more. She slipped her eyes closed, tasting the wine on his lips, feeling the warmth of his body. Her hand touched his chest. Her mind was lost, intoxicated. It was as though she were in someone else's body.

He kissed her again, this time putting a hand on her back and pulling her gently, easily, against him. She had forgotten what it was like. His lips were heaven, tantalizing. He obviously knew what he was doing. The kiss deepened, and she, tipping up on her toes to get closer, to kiss more deeply, wondered if she were in a silly romance novel where the man kissed and touched you just as you wanted, just as a man should, the way that could bring you to your knees. And it was *him*, this mysterious stranger, this man who kept everything bottled up until you wondered if he had any passion. But you always knew it was there, shimmering beneath the surface, and like a treasure hunter, you wanted to find it before anyone else did.

And it wasn't long until romance gave way to unfettered passion. Somewhere in the back of her mind she knew she needed to slow it down. But doing so would've caused physical pain. Breaking away completely would've killed her.

And when they somehow ended up on the bed, and she felt her shirt slipping over her head, and realized her fingers were on his, she didn't even break the kiss.

Chapter Twenty

P rovidence Church was a clean white chapel, though not a small one. It seemed that most of the county attended the church, servant and master alike. Miss Sarah Haley insisted that her new sister-in-law ride with her and her sisters in their carriage, and so they were taken first. Shannon was permitted to sit next to John Thomas during the service, however. They sat on one of the pews of dark mahogany, crafted with clean lines and a door so old it creaked when opened.

Things were rather strained between them. They had been since yesterday. She could no more read her husband's thoughts than understand why the woman in front of her had chosen to wear such a garish plaid.

There was a pretty girl with dimples sitting across the aisle near the front. She kept looking back at them and smiling. There was a great deal of interest, it seemed, in the Southern belle.

Apparently talking was not encouraged, even before the service began. Vincent, sitting on the other side of John

Thomas, began bouncing his feet in boredom not long into the reading. A hand on his knee from John Thomas was all it took to still him, however. When one of the many times for them to rise came, John Thomas whispered to her during the noise, while he was helping her to her feet, "That is Patience." He inclined his head in the direction of the pretty girl.

Patience was married to the Reverend Whitcomb's eldest son, and she sat with his family in the honored pew. Shannon's own father-in-law was a deacon, which apparently meant far more to the congregation than the fact that he was a business-man of sharp acumen. She had been surprised to hear him called Deacon John several different times walking in. The Haleys were apparently held in high regard, as they should be. John Thomas and Adams seemed to be the darlings of the com-munity, likely the conversation of every romantical busybody.

As was Shannon, who was different from any woman there. Her clothes had come under the hand of an extremely modish seamstress. Not a hair was out of place in her deceptively sim-ple twist. But it was more than that. She was a young woman with a stately yet exquisitely feminine manner. With a flavor of beauty which had not quite ever come in their midst, with an air of fragility and a magnetic pull.

Perhaps it was this combination which, once the ser-vice had ended, prompted one girl to say, "She has an oddly sloping nose!"

It had been whispered to the girl's friend, but Shannon's hear-ing was sharp. She did not deign to look over her shoulder, and she could tell John Thomas hadn't heard. Well, she had heard far worse in Charleston, she thought, with a cat-like curl to her lip.

Patience walked her way, and soon she was standing before Shannon, smiling in a glowing way. She spoke softly but sweetly. "Finally, I am able to meet you! How jealous I have been of all of them! Dear brother, introduce me!"

"Yes—Shannon, my sister, Patience—Mrs. Whitcomb, I should say," he added with a slight smile, taking her hand and pressing it. "Are you well, Patience?"

She kissed his cheek. "I am well now you have returned. Only think how lonely with you *and* Jonathan away." She turned her attention to Shannon. "Jonathan is my husband, and in his final term at Harvard. He had finished school, you see, but needed only a very little more to be trained as a minister."

Shannon smiled. "I am sure you must miss him. Is he able to visit you?"

"Not much, with the snows this winter. Oh, Sister, you are cold! What are we thinking, John Thomas? She isn't accustomed."

"I am quite well," Shannon said, laughing.

Hand on the small of her back, John Thomas said, "I'll take you home. Visit us, Patience—the roads shouldn't be too bad in another week or two."

"Yes, and you come to us. The Whitcombs would be delighted to have you. Goodbye, Shannon!"

John Thomas led her to a carriage and told the driver to take them home. Mrs. Haley was still talking with the other ladies, most of whom were her social inferiors, and Mr. Haley seemed to be in a meeting. The children were talking with their friends. None of them had looked remotely chilled.

The young couple returned to an empty house, more or less, since they had returned long before the household of family and servants had any intention of leaving the meeting place. John Thomas unlocked the door and took her fur tippet once they were across the threshold. He looked her over, noting that she looked tired.

"I'll help with your coat," he said, glancing at her face.

She had walked in, her skirts rustling gently, and she stopped near the center of the foyer. "I ought to go up and take off my hat," she said softly, looking at him for a brief moment, the piercing blue of her eyes meeting his vulnerability before she looked away.

He took a step toward her, chest tightening. "Phoebe will still be at church," he said gently. "All of them are."

"Oh." She blinked, surprised. "Yes, I hadn't thought."

He lay her tippet aside, watching her. "Where are the pins?" He moved forward until he was just in front of her, though he still didn't touch her.

She motioned. "Just there. Please don't rip my hair out."

"Very well. If you wish to deny all of my pleasure."

This sally earned a faint smile, and he set about pulling the pins gently, laying them on the side table in the foyer when he had finished. He reached for the top button of her coat.

"Please don't," she said, her hand on his arm. "I am still cold."

Her belled skirt was against his trousers, his hands sliding down her arms. She glanced up at him, so reserved and distant, and then looked away, her color high. He guided her chin back, and she met his eyes. "Forgive me, Shannon," he said, voice scratching.

She held his eyes, her features softening. "I will love them, John Thomas. I promise."

"It was a terrible thing to say."

"Indeed, but true enough. I shall depend upon you to keep me in check."

"I can't think how I came to be such a cad," he said penitently.

"You are cruel always," she said, eyes twinkling slightly. "And heartless."

A smile touched his lips. Her hand came up briefly to touch his face, causing his heart to leap. He drew her even closer, kissing her slowly, lingeringly. Shannon stepped closer, giving her permission, whispering something in his ear that made him long for their little townhouse in Washington.

"Thank you, Shannon," Lizzie said, making the final tuck in the bodice of her gown. Shannon had shown her a deft stitch which would give the gown a Parisian flair, currently all the rage in Charleston. It was for the open ball which would be held at the Weymouth assembly room at the end of May.

"So charming to make it a V," Miriam said, sitting nearby in the small sitting room, working on her own gown. The Haley girls might have sent them to the dressmaker ten times over, but they preferred and were encouraged by their mother to make their own. And they were deft needlewomen. Shannon had been taught nothing so useful as they, but she did know fine stitches, and her sisters-in-law were happy to learn from her. Sarah sat nearby, quietly cross-stitching a sampler but watching raptly.

"Did you have many beaux in Charleston, Shannon?" Miriam asked.

"Miriam!" her elder sister chided, eyes widening.

Shannon laughed. "Yes, I did."

Lizzie looked up, a slightly shocked expression on her face.

"Oh, forgive me," Shannon said, lifting a new spool of thread from the basket at her feet but pausing. "Your brother knows. He jokes me for it."

Lizzie paused for a moment. "Does he? You and John Thomas led such different lives in South Carolina that I'm sure we can scarcely understand."

Shannon studied her. After a moment she said, "Yes, our ways are very different. But John Thomas is the same wherever he is." And she hoped she was, too, although she was uncomfortably uncertain of the truth of it.

Lizzie shook her head. "You don't have to tell *me* that, my dear sister. I didn't mean to imply otherwise."

"Indeed, John Thomas is the best and dearest of brothers," Miriam said. "Oh! No, I don't mean that!"

Sarah fired up. "Well, he doesn't read dusty old books all of the time, or ride off to heaven knows where, or tug on my braids!"

"That is quite enough, Sarah," Lizzie said with amused reproof.

Shannon smiled, looking up to see Patience peeking in the door. The eldest sister was smiling. "What a charming company you make!" she said, cheeks rosy from the chill. She had already discarded her coat and gloves and was wearing a simple gray wool gown with wide sleeves.

"Dearest," Lizzie said, getting up and kissing her cheek. "You've only just missed Mother: she went to take stockings to the tenants."

"Oh, I shall stay until she returns," Patience said, kissing Sarah and Miriam and extending her hand to Shannon, covering Shannon's when she gave hers. "You are such a welcome addition to us, Sister!" she said. "What a pity you should be leaving us for Washington!"

Shannon smiled, realizing suddenly that Patience was the addition the sisters had lacked. She did not have sisters, but she knew the feeling nonetheless. She enjoyed watching them and found that Patience smoothed all of the little troubled moments.

"Oh! Can you imagine?" Patience said. "Jonathan is to visit us next Saturday, and then it will just be a few weeks until the end of the term."

"How wonderful!" Lizzie said.

"And then he shall be yours forevermore!" Miriam, ever the romantic, exclaimed.

"Well, I shall have to share him with his parishioners, but, yes!" Patience answered, laughing. "And Shannon shall have to share her beloved with the tiresome Navy!"

Shannon's eyes danced. "Come, you must have more patriotism than that. I am willing to share him, so long as they return him to me."

"I still cannot picture John Thomas as a sea captain!" Miriam said, her eyes full of wonder.

Shannon sometimes had difficulty herself, but he usually diverted her when she attempted to broach the subject.

She imagined that his father had planned his life as surely as her father had Frederick's. And for the first time, she considered that being a man might be nearly as full of troubles as being a woman.

Shannon and John Thomas had not been in Massachusetts long when the older children in the Haley household began to talk of going to a lecture in Quincy. Shannon would've liked to have gone, for she loved attending lectures, but she quickly came to realize she wasn't being included in the plans, even though Lizzie was going with her brothers.

"May I not go to the lecture?" she asked, sitting in a chair in their bedchamber by the light of the fireplace one night. She wore her dressing gown, which didn't conceal the form of her long legs.

John Thomas had been removing his cufflinks over by the dresser, stealing glances at her now and then. He was pulled from his abstraction by her question, however, and he walked to her, kneeling in front of her. His eyes smiled as he took her hands in his. "I do not think you would like it," he said in his quiet way. "It is an abolitionist lecture."

"What?" she breathed.

He nodded.

"I did not think they had much of a voice, even here," she said, studying his face.

"The abolitionist movement is growing, Shannon. Everywhere."

She slowly removed her hands. "You would go sit down with

radicals who spew nonsense with every breath?" she asked in a shocked voice.

"You know my beliefs, Shannon."

She turned her face away.

"What?" he asked, studying her closely.

"Believing is one thing." She pressed her lips together. "Advocating for the utter destruction of everything I love is another. How can you call yourself Frederick's friend, knowing what it must mean to him?"

"I would never advocate for destruction, whatever others may be doing. Merely for freedom of souls created in God's image, just as I was."

She pressed her lips together. "You mustn't pretend as though even a tenth of the Northern population feels as you do."

"No, not the morality of slavery, perhaps. But every aspect of it. It's poisoning everything. Every conversation. Every political topic. I don't see how they go on in Congress, with all the animosity and tension."

"What are you saying?" she asked, staring at him, disconcerted.

He hesitated. "We need a decisive leader to settle this matter without war. And we haven't one in President Buchanan."

Shannon wished they had stayed away from the subject altogether, but she could not restrain herself from saying, "It isn't a matter merely of political arguments, John Thomas. It is the very way of life for an entire people we are discussing. And your precious Mr. Lincoln—I assume you intend to vote for him?—appeases and appeases, but what shall he do as soon as he is enthroned? Take my father's lands away from him and give them to the slaves—"

"Shannon, this is hysteria," he interrupted, his tone still soft as he took her hand again for comfort. "I believe Mr. Lincoln intends to try to reach a peaceful resolution, and yes, that is why I intend to vote for him."

Her jaw clenched briefly. "If only *I* were a man," she said, ripping her hand away and turning her head, swallowing with difficulty. "I should cancel your vote, and you would not speak for us."

His lips parted, and he looked away, getting up. Keeping his back to her, he finished with his cufflinks and watch and fob over by the dresser, not lifting his head. Shannon watched him for a few moments before exclaiming, "Oh!" She stood and hurried to him, touching his arm. "Forgive me!"

He turned and wrapped his arms around her. "No, no," he said, holding her tightly. "We'll forget this silly lecture if it upsets you."

She shook her head, more upset now by the argument, their first true one, even if they *had* ventured into several uncomfortable moments. "No, I'll go with you. And I'll view it as scholarly, learning what I can. Will that please you?"

He smiled with aching tenderness. "Yes. That would please me." He lay his cheek on her head. "Forgive me. Truly, I didn't mean to upset you, my darling."

"Nor I, you."

"You didn't." He tilted her face up, his fingers trailing from her neck to her chin. Slowly, his lips touched hers, and he pulled her closer. The kiss deepened between them, and she soon felt his fingers on the buttons on her dress. She stopped, breaking the kiss. He paused, looking down at her, flushing slightly, then averting his eyes.

She said softly, a shy little smile on her lips, "You always look disconsolate, but indeed, it isn't my fault!"

He looked up, flushing in earnest. "Oh!" He held her eyes, opening his lips as though to speak, and finally managing faintly, "No! Are you feeling well?"

"As well as ever. It is a terrible thing to be a woman."

"That is twice you have said that tonight. But where would I be if you weren't a woman?" he asked.

She lifted her head to meet his eyes. "Here," she said. "But alone."

April 1, Charleston

Dear Shannon,

You will have seen by my heading that I have left your father on the island and retreated to Charleston. I could not convince Marie to join me. I daresay she feels her duties as a wife keenly at this early date.

Your sister-in-law sounds a very odd girl—the eldest there at home, I mean. It must be jealousy. I daresay she used to think herself a very pretty sort of girl before you trod on her ground. Likely, she cannot comprehend what it means to have the belle of South Carolina with her. You and she might as well be different species.

I am glad to hear that the other girls are kind, but why are mere children permitted such a degree of association with the adults? I cannot understand their ways, Shannon. I had hoped the family would go to Boston, so that you might be better appreciated, but I daresay they will wish to oversee their own planting.

Remember to protect your complexion if there are any outdoor parties, and guard your waistline. I daresay the latter will not be difficult in New England. You must tell me more about their meals in your next letter.

Remind Phoebe that crushed strawberries are an excellent regimen, and that she must not dress your hair in loops over the ears or in any way which makes girls look dowdy. I cannot understand why it has become the fashion. It does not become Marie either. I gave her a hint, but as yet there has been no change.

Remember that a woman's first duty is to her husband, Shannon. I have always abided by this maxim. Give my love to John Thomas and my greetings to your mother and father-in-law.

Your Mother

The abolitionist party consisted of Adams, Lizzie, John Thomas, and his bride. They departed in a single carriage on a chilly spring night and covered the distance with no trouble along the roads. An easy journey was always such a welcome relief, Lizzie said, after the long winter. "Are you cold, Shannon? John Thomas, do remove the blanket from the box."

He reached beneath his feet and did so, leaning forward to tuck it around the girls. As for Adams, sitting across from them with John Thomas, he was rather distracted, staring out the window. "I hope there won't be a riot," he murmured.

John Thomas looked at him, and Shannon looked between them. "We'll leave if we get the feeling," John Thomas said.

"I know. But I would hate for them to be silenced," he answered.

They arrived at a large, white schoolhouse to find many others securing their conveyances. Shannon recognized some of them from the Haleys' church congregation, but most were unknown to her. However, there were very few people whom the Haleys did not know. It was tight-knit, Massachusetts, bound together by a common faith and history.

The cobblestone path was lit by two torches, and two door greeters met them with bulletins on the threshold. There was a crush of people in attendance, and they just managed to find seats before there was standing room only. Yet, despite all of the bodies, it was extremely chilly, and both Shannon and Lizzie left their wool capes on.

Most in the room seemed to be supporters of the abolition, but there was a group near the back which might be dissenters.

John Thomas glanced down at Shannon, while, on the

other side of them, Adams and Lizzie talked with some distant cousins. She had been quiet the past few days, perhaps dreading tonight, but she had never withdrawn her offer to come. He watched as she read the bulletin, and her face paled as she slowly looked up at him. "William Lloyd Garrison?" she breathed. "*Frederick Douglass*?" she whispered faintly.

He nodded once, holding her eyes. She took a shaky breath, touching her bodice as though she could not get enough air. He laid a hand on her arm, but she hissed, "Don't *touch* me."

He withdrew his hand, stunned. He looked forward, trying not to cause a scene. He knew from whence her feelings arose. Garrison was the man who had had a bounty on his head in the South for some twenty years. The man who was wanted dead or alive, the man who had been dragged through the streets of Boston by an anti-abolitionist mob, who in moments would stand before them without any fear. Garrison had achieved a notoriety in the South greater than Satan, stronger than death, and more violent than hatred. And Douglass was more despised than that. "Who did you think it would be?" he said quietly.

She did not answer immediately. "I do not know—a professor from Harvard, a prominent minister. Dear God, what would my father think?"

She had paled more, if possible. John Thomas was becoming alarmed but was unsure how to act. Lizzie noticed then, too. "Shannon?" she asked in concern. "Are you well?"

Shannon looked at her, unseeing and unable to speak, it seemed. Suddenly, realization dawned in Lizzie's eyes, and she met John Thomas's. He held them for a long moment, sending what message, he didn't know. Lizzie swallowed. "Shannon?"

she asked, holding John Thomas's eyes for another moment before looking at her. "Would you like for Adams to take you outside? It is stuffy, though it is so cold."

Shannon blinked, seeming to come to herself. "Oh, I... No. No, thank you." She swallowed.

John Thomas watched her for another moment until he did not think she would faint, and then he looked onto the stage as the mayor came out and made opening remarks. Then Mr. Garrison walked onto stage to a splitting round of applause.

He waited for it to die down, looking scholarly with his high forehead, noble features, and inescapable elegance. He let a hush fall and then began, "I am aware that many object to the severity of my language; but is there not cause for severity? I will be as harsh as truth, and as uncompromising as justice. On this subject, I do not wish to think, or speak, or write, with moderation. No! No! Tell a man whose house is on fire to give a moderate alarm; tell him to moderately rescue his wife from the hands of the ravisher; tell the mother to gradually extricate her babe from the fire into which it has fallen;—but urge me not to use moderation in a cause like the present. I am in earnest—I will not equivocate—I will not excuse—I will not retreat a single inch—*and I will be heard*. The apathy of the people is enough to make every statue leap from its pedestal, and to hasten the resurrection of the dead."

Shannon sucked in her breath, and mouths were hanging open, the attention of the room fully in his hands. She sat silently, seemingly in numb horror.

"I founded *The Liberator* now nearly thirty years ago with one purpose in mind: the extermination of chattel slavery."

And so his story began. He held the audience spellbound until the slightest noise would've been deafening.

"And now," he said at length, "I would like to introduce to you my friend and fellow abolitionist, a man with whom I am honored to share this stage, Mr. Frederick Douglass."

Thundering applause sounded, and the man came out. Shannon stiffened perceptibly. He knew to be lectured by a Negro was unimaginable in her world. Mr. Douglass's eyes were brilliant, encasing intelligence and fervor, and his demeanor was confident. Shannon glanced at John Thomas and whispered fragilely, still pale, "His features are very white."

John Thomas held her eyes, and she looked away, flushing.

He opened, with a booming, electrifying voice, by welcoming them and thanking them for their support of their glorious cause. "And I am especially glad to be here, in the town where he would have often visited, perhaps the very school where he taught: our founding father and that great advocate for freedom of *every* man: John Adams." Once again, there was sweeping applause. "And I am told," he continued in his deep voice, "that we have among us tonight, three of that great abolitionist's descendants." A screeching applause arose, and Lizzie took Adams's hand, tears in her eyes. John Thomas inclined his head at Douglass after a time. Shannon looked up at him, swelling with pride, despite everything.

"And here my story begins: a plantation in Maryland," he began once the clapping had died down.

They listened as he told of his childhood, of being snatched away from his mother and then his grandmother when he was moved to another of his owner's plantations. Of never knowing his family, of never questioning slavery until he learned to read, and knowledge unlocked the pathway to freedom. Of teaching others to read and being clubbed for it, of being hired out to a poor white farmer, who whipped him and others daily, of meeting, finally, the woman who would become his wife, a free black woman who gave him the courage to flee. He spoke with grace and proper grammar, with eloquence and depth, and his audience sat raptly. None more so than Shannon's husband, who was obviously deeply moved.

"I have often been asked, how I felt when first I found myself on free soil. And you here tonight may share the same curiosity. There is scarcely anything in my experience about which I could not give a more satisfactory answer. A new world had opened upon me. If life is more than breath, and the 'quick round of blood,' I lived more in one day than in a year of my slave life. It was a time of joyous excitement which words can but tamely describe. In a letter written to a friend soon after reaching New York, I said: 'I felt as one might feel upon escape from a den of hungry lions.' Anguish and grief, like darkness and rain, may be depicted; but gladness and joy, like the rainbow, defy the skill of pen or pencil."

Shannon sat, stiff and pale. The knowledge of how detrimental his testimony was to the institution of slavery, to the argument that slaves were not intelligent enough to be freed and fend for themselves, was not lost on her. She could not remove her attention from him: she was as captive as the rest of them.

The man at length closed with an entreaty for their support of the cause, thanking them again. The Haleys did not wait to talk with the others, for there were some hecklers outside grow-ing obnoxious. And Shannon walked out in a daze, feeling ill.

Chapter Twenty-One

S hannon had fallen asleep almost as soon as she had changed into her nightgown the night before. John Thomas, sitting in the chair in his chamber long past the time she had been rising the last few weeks, watched her while she slept.

When she began to stir, he sat up, remembering her intense anger the night before and then her shock. He had not known her long, but he knew very well her passion, how it quivered within her, and he knew she had exhausted herself to the point of being ill.

She looked up at him, and he stood, walking to her. He slowly sat beside her, unsure whether she would even speak to him, much less let him touch her. She swallowed, looking fragile to him. "Good heavens." She moistened her lips. "Did I sleep late?"

"Yes." His eyes swept her features. "Are you well?"

"Yes," she whispered, flushing. Her eyes filled. "I'm sorry."

He gripped her hand. "I should have warned you. I ought to have thought..."

She shook her head. "No. Yes. That is, I think I never realized until last night how...how much divides us."

He went entirely still. "Us?"

She turned her blue eyes upon him. "No. That is, the North and South. I had...never heard anyone who disagreed with me. Except you. I thought it was only a religious qualm."

He studied her for a long moment. The sunlight streaked through the windows, casting her beautiful features into fine relief, but his mind was faraway. He hesitated. "Shannon, I... My faith is more than that. By it, I see everything else. It tells me that slavery is wrong. We can argue what is between the covers of the Bible, but I can't deny the way I feel. If you were thinking it was a silly qualm, you were hoping to change me. I'm sorry. We don't have ever to mention this again, but I did need to clarify that. I won't change."

She swallowed, nodding once and turning her head on the pillow, looking away. A tear escaped and rolled into her hair.

"Shannon," he whispered, his voice faltering. "I'm so very sorry if I hurt you, my darling. We ought to have discussed it before—"

She looked back at him quickly.

"Before it came to this," he rushed to say.

Elegant tears began to fall down her face. "Shannon!"

He put his hands on her arms, drawing her up and holding her there. "You know I didn't mean that. It wasn't what I was going to say!"

She shook her head. "I know," she said softly. "I know."

He held her against him, her head on his chest. "Ah, Shannon, then why are you crying?" he asked.

"I'm very sorry for my behavior last night," she said, not answering. "It was unbecoming. It won't happen again, John Thomas. I promise."

"Shannon, if you say that just one more time—"

She laughed softly. "Very well. But I do mean that."

He held her for a moment in silence. "There is something else, isn't there?" he said, holding her out from him, worry in every line of his face.

She held his eyes, confirming his belief, but she didn't say anything more than, "I cannot explain it..."

He studied her for a time before realization dawned. Taking her chin in his hand and tilting her face up, he said, "Shannon, I know what it is to feel disloyal to your family, to yourself."

She met his eyes. "I know you do." Looking away, she added, "It is only... They speak of Southerners, think of them, as though they are evil. And they are not," she said with unshakeable belief. "Not all."

"Oh, Shannon," he said, sighing. "I know. I chose my wife right from the belly of the beast, remember?" She smiled faintly. "My family does not feel that way. Only the foolish do," he said, stroking her hair back.

Shannon swallowed.

He kissed her temple and then laid her back against the pillows, covering her once more.

"What are you doing? Your mother will think I am a fancy lady."

A faint smile flickered. "I will tell her you have one of your headaches. Come, rest. It isn't every day a proper Southern girl is forced to hear an abolitionist lecture."

She smiled, reaching for his hand. He gave it willingly, holding her blue eyes, in no hurry to leave. "You really are a very decent man," she said, tired eyes smiling.

He smiled. "I'm glad to hear you still think so."

She reached up, brushing her fingers through his hair and drawing his head down. Their lips met, and one of his hands gripped the coverlet. The hand that was holding hers left and trembled up into her hair. Shannon's fingers trailed from his jaw down his neck, and he groaned. "I know," she whispered. "But it is daylight."

"Who cares for that?" he said, finding her lips once more. He stopped, lifting his head and meeting her eyes. "Are you feeling better?"

"*Quite* better."

Shannon spent all of the afternoon knitting stockings with the Haley ladies for another distribution to the poor until her fingers were quite stiff. None of them said anything about her failing to come below stairs until long past the midday meal, nor did they ask the reason. John Thomas had told them she had a headache, but Lizzie had already described her as being "very upset" the night before.

Mrs. Haley had nodded quietly, saying after Sarah had left, "She will have to learn that she is in a different world now. She must accustom herself even in Washington. Best she learns it now."

Mr. Haley was the only one inclined to question his son as to why *he* had not come down to assist his brothers. Mrs. Haley had informed him, straightening his cravat, that John Thomas doted upon his wife, to which Mr. Haley had said somewhat explosively, "A man who dotes upon his wife to the point of hanging upon her every whim—" A lifted eyebrow had suggested to him that this line of speech was not fortuitous, and, clearing his throat, he said, "Well, well, they are newlyweds, after all. Send him to me, please, when you see him."

John Thomas had gone into his father's study, saying softly, "You wanted me, Father?"

He looked up beneath his bushy, white brows. John Thomas's breath caught. When had his father become an old man? He was nearing seventy, and there was no denying it.

"Yes, I have something to discuss with you, if you have a moment of your time to give to me."

John Thomas leaned against his desk, saying docilely, "I am always at your disposal, Father."

"Ha!" His father looked at him admiringly. "You are a handsome lad. Much like myself when I was young, though it seems a lifetime ago. You won't tell your brothers that."

"No."

"Now, listen, my boy. You've gotten yourself a beautiful wife, and you have your career laid out before you with boundless opportunity. I will tell you the same thing I told Adams: you must seize every opportunity for advancement. You have the world at your fingertips as my son, but I don't choose to give it to you. I choose to let you find it. It is the Haley way and purifying for the soul. In whatever you do, build a name for yourself, and make your mother and me proud."

John Thomas smiled unhurriedly, briefly covering his hand. "Don't worry about me, Father."

There was a slight pause. "No, I don't," he said finally. "In whatever you do, you must prosper, because of your devotion to the One who created you."

John Thomas was silent for a moment before parting his lips to speak. "I shouldn't worry about Charles, Father. He will find his way."

"He is at loose ends since returning from Harvard," he said gruffly. He never talked about one of his children to another, and that he had strayed into such territory let his son know how seriously his mind was disturbed. John Thomas cast his mind back through his talks with Charles, seeking about for the source. He could think of none but then remembered Shannon's remark about Boston and felt an unwelcome apprehension. She had spotted a restless young man in an instant, something her society was far from lacking.

John Thomas sat silently for a time. But, catching his father in this fortuitous mood, he said, "And Adams?"

"I do not worry for Adams. Saints preserve us from his distraction, but he is a rock. He will always do what is right."

"I know." He gentled his tone. "But you must let him marry, Father."

"Adams knows he must establish his name in the business before he does so," he said gruffly, his mood changing swiftly away from the confiding.

John Thomas studied him, choosing to say no more. It would've been useless.

The library was a short walk from the study and was a much larger and grander room. John Thomas stopped in the doorway, looking at Adams where he sat on the gray pillow of the window seat, writing something. John Thomas studied him for a moment, his heart twisting with affection.

He walked forward. At the noise, his brother looked up. "John Thomas. I hope Shannon's headache is better?"

John Thomas smiled. "Yes, she is with the other ladies now." He went and stood near him, leaning against the window encasement. "Are you courting any lady?"

Adams glanced up at him fleetingly and then away, out the window and over the rolling field. "I want to wait until I am at least thirty to marry."

"Do you ever...see Emma?" he prompted. Emma Rawlins was a young woman in the community whom Adams had wished to marry some six years before. Their father had swiftly put an end to the affair, citing high expectations for his first-born and the youth of both parties.

Adams looked back slowly, holding his eyes, and then away again. "She's married, John Thomas."

His lips parted. "Oh," he said, releasing a breath.

"To Elisha Moore," he said, getting up, glancing back at him. "I...must collect Vincent at Reverend Whitcomb's." John Thomas knew well that a servant was usually sent to collect the young scholar but did not mention it. "Do you wish to come?"

"Yes, I will," he answered, walking out with his brother.

Chapter Twenty-Two

Shannon, spending the morning above stairs, sat at the little writing desk in their bedchamber, reading and returning letters from South Carolina. Since it was Saturday and a rare day in which work was not expected, John Thomas also sat behind her leisurely in a striped chair, reading the newspaper.

Her eyes skimming over the words of the letter in her hand, she gasped. "Oh!" She turned, holding the letter. When he lifted his brows, she said, "Marie is with child!"

John Thomas smiled. "Is she? Frederick writes nothing of it," he said.

"I daresay they don't want it known, since it is early days, but of course, she must tell *me*."

He laughed. "Of course. I shall be an excellent uncle, wouldn't you agree?"

She smiled at him. "Indeed," she said fondly. "It will look, I daresay, like its Aunt Shannon."

"Naturally. Frederick a father!"

She smiled. "The mind revolts, does it not?"

He laughed but shook his head. "You underestimate him."

"If a sister is not allowed to do so, who may? I imagine he will be absently devoted and not set his foot over the threshold of the nursery above twice a year," she said.

He looked surprised. "Truly? We saw my father daily as children. We were with him often, especially here."

"I believe our upbringings were quite different. I was sent to school at the age of eight."

"Yes, I believe I was, too."

She shook her head. "I don't mean in the way that Vincent goes to school. I was sent," she said.

His brows drew together. "You only were with your family during holidays?" he asked.

"Yes," she said, looking away. "Otherwise I was at Ingersoll's Select Seminary for Females."

He studied her from behind. "I didn't know that," he said at length.

"Didn't you? They called me Mary, at the insistence of the headmistress." She moistened her lips. "Never mind. It doesn't matter, except that I believe I will tell Marie not to send her daughter there. She would know nothing of it, having been taught by a governess at home."

He continued to study her, and her cheeks began to grow red. She sought about for something, anything to change the subject and said softly, "She must have conceived right away." She flushed even deeper, until she remembered that he was a New Englander. "Yes," he said absently, elbows on his knees, blue eyes searching her face. Somehow, she did not think he was thinking of Marie at all.

She cleared her throat softly. "Well, I suppose I had better return her letter."

"You will send them our felicitations," he said.

"Yes, I shall—where are you going?"

He had gotten up and was walking toward her, extending his hand so that she might give hers. He rarely touched her unless she gave some sort of permission. She knew it was her own fault and felt vaguely disturbed by the notion, but she was helpless to correct it. "I must go meet with Charles to make the preparations for our trip," he said. "We are leaving Monday, you know."

All of the men in the family were going to a friend's hunting lodge somewhere in Connecticut for a party of hunting or shooting; Shannon hadn't particularly been listening. From there, John Thomas and Charles were journeying on to Washington to make arrangements for their home there and so that he might sign all of the formal papers necessary to joining the military.

She smiled. "Yes, because you must never travel on the Sabbath," she teased.

He smiled, pressing her hand, eyes scanning her face. "Ride with me later?"

"Yes, I shall." She turned back to her writing, averting her face.

He waited in silence and then bent and kissed her cheek tenderly. He left before she could again meet his eyes, and her heart squeezed within her chest, aching with the thought of him, with something else, too.

Supper on Sunday nights was generally a more formal affair in the Haley household. Shannon, having worn each of her more modest options, decided upon a gown at the very edge of fashion. This was a red silk creation with the widest possible skirts, which made her waist appear tiny. The neckline scooped to show to best advantage her thin chest and the tops of her breasts, and it hugged just below her shoulders, displaying her collarbones. The effect was stunning, just as Louisa Ravenel had intended. Shannon had worn it once to dinner and a play in Charleston.

She sat at her vanity in her undergarments as Phoebe did her hair. Her maid parted her red tresses down the middle, streaming sections and braids in and out until it was a work of art.

Shannon glanced at her maid in the mirror.

"Is that pulling, Miss Shannon?"

"No," she said softly, still studying her. There was a pause. "What will you do, now you are free?" she asked.

"I'll stay right here, ma'am."

"Yes. But should Mr. Haley and I ever return to the South?" she asked, almost hesitantly.

Phoebe met her eyes in the mirror and quickly dropped them. After a long time, she said softly, almost fearfully, "I couldn't say, ma'am. That would take some prayer."

"Have we ever been unkind to you, Phoebe?"

"No, ma'am," she said quickly.

"Do you believe all of this that these abolitionists say up here?"

"I don't think they can understand how it is down South, ma'am. Not really," she said softly. Shannon studied her, unsure of her meaning.

"Be honest with me, Phoebe: do you believe all of the slaves should be freed?"

"I'm already free in God, ma'am, and whatever he sees fit for me to be is just fine."

"Very well, but remember that you are no longer a slave, thanks to Mr. Haley: you may speak freely."

There was a long hesitation. "I want my family to be free. I want my people to know a better life. But it's my home. It's our home. I'd be most afraid of what was to come, ma'am."

Shannon swallowed, hitherto unaware of how deeply the slaves had thought on the subject and feeling as though she were being enclosed, suffocated. "Perhaps things will continue as they are," she said softly. Phoebe did not respond; she merely brought Shannon's gown to her.

Phoebe assisted with her diamond earrings and bracelet and then helped with the slippers which had been dyed, at great expense, to match the gown.

Phoebe regarded her. "You look very fine, ma'am." She looked as though she would say something else but refrained.

"Thank you, Phoebe. We shall hope my mother-in-law feels the same."

What her mother-in-law's thoughts were when she entered the dining room, Shannon did not know. Her husband however, looking up from his conversation with his sister, flushed, meeting her eyes. Shannon hesitated at the door, looking around uncertainly. The room had gone silent, and the family seemed to be astounded. No one commented upon it, but Shannon, sitting with a slight blush rising, knew their thoughts completely.

After the blessing was said, she glanced at John Thomas, but he did not look at her, although his eyes had followed her as she walked to her seat. Conversation was stilted for a time until Adams asked his father whether he had seen the article about the difficulties the fishermen were experiencing in the weather. It was not consciously done, but it served as a distraction nonetheless, and Shannon risked another glance at her husband. He was looking particularly handsome in his evening clothes, handsome and healthy, his hair glowing almost golden under the gas lamps. But his eyes were carefully averted.

She caught Lizzie looking at her, but her sister-in-law quickly cast her eyes down.

The plates had scarcely been taken away and dessert had not yet been lain when Shannon, rising, said quietly, "You will excuse me, I trust. I seem to have taken a headache." The men stood, and Mrs. Haley said, overcoming her censure momentarily, "Certainly, Shannon. You must send Phoebe to fetch some of our powders."

Shannon inclined her head and withdrew. She entered her chamber to find the fire lit and Phoebe waiting in the chair. The door had scarcely shut behind her when it opened again, and John Thomas entered, his brows drawn together in concern. "You are unwell?"

Shannon glanced at her maid. "Phoebe, leave us," she said softly.

"Yes, ma'am," the maid said, slipping behind John Thomas, the door clicking quietly closed behind her.

"I do have a headache," she said.

She turned towards her vanity mirror, fiddling with the clasp of her bracelet. He had come farther in, and his hand touched her back. She took a shaky breath and released it. "Can I do anything?" he asked softly. "Forgive me, I didn't know you were unwell."

She moistened her lips and then swallowed. "It is only a headache." She was surprised to find she was fighting tears. Moments before, her only emotion had been anger. She bit her lip hard. "You did not like my dress," she said, hating herself. She unclasped the bracelet, let it fall into her hand, and then put it in her jewelry dish with a soft clink.

There was a long silence behind her, and Shannon turned, looking at him. She saw that he was hesitating. He was at a loss for words, and the realization that he hadn't intended to mention it made her angry again, for reasons even she couldn't understand.

She took a shaky breath. "They...looked at me as though I were a strumpet, and I..." Tears rose again. "Can you imagine how it feels to a woman when her husband refuses even to look at her?"

Startled pain in his features, he lifted a hand toward her arm. "Shannon..."

She turned away to hide her tears, and his hand fell. "I was not seeking to...to make a statement," she said. "I thought nothing of it. They... I was mortified!" She lifted a hand to her aching temple.

"Shannon! Oh, my darling. I can see that you must have felt that way." He touched her arm. "Please don't cry," he pleaded softly. He reached as though to take her into his arms, but she turned from him again.

"I'm not crying. And I don't care for my feelings. I merely wish to know why I was received in such a way!"

There was a long pause, during which he studied her with brows drawn together as though uncertain what to say. Finally, he said softly, "You are the most beautiful woman I have ever seen." He looked away. "When I first met you, Shannon, I..." His voice faded away, and he swallowed. Her eyes burned, and he looked at her again, meeting her eyes. "I know you were not made for this society, but Shannon, that gown is extremely inappropriate."

She glanced back at herself in the mirror, flushing, truly seeing for the first time how much the bodice dipped, how it hugged her curves sensuously. She looked back at him, her color high with mortification. "John Thomas, you have been to Paris. You know—"

"Yes," he said, holding her eyes.

She swallowed, turning, reaching for her wrap, and sitting slowly, keeping her head down.

"Do not cover yourself in front of me, Shannon," he pleaded, voice rasping a little.

"It offends you," she said, voice trembling. "Though why, I cannot think. My mother did not think it inappropriate."

"You were no different than bait to a fish, Shannon," he said, eyes sparking angrily. "A lure to catch an eligible husband. You are more to me than that!"

"I cannot see how I am *bait* or a *lure* now," she said. "You are merely afraid I will wear it in public and that another man might look at me."

"I am doomed to endure men looking at my wife, wherever I go!" he exclaimed. "Had I been unable to withstand it, you may believe we would've had this conversation long since."

"I have never heard you be so prudish! It *must* be jealousy."

"Yes, there is jealousy in me when other men look at you, very well. But that is not the reason I chose to wade into these extremely unpleasant waters with you. I do not like to see you defile your body. And that is precisely what you are doing when you are wearing dresses chosen to please men! Please God, or please yourself, but do not please men!"

Shannon blinked and looked down, fighting emotion. She lost her battle, and, to her mortification, tears began flowing quietly down her cheeks. She wiped them with her hands as quickly as she could, but it never seemed enough.

He touched her back and took her hand. She heard his whispers. *No... My darling... Too harsh... Doesn't matter...* But she scarcely listened. She felt as though she were once again facing overly harsh discipline at Ingersoll's. She knew she was grown. She knew John Thomas would not make her do any of those horrible things. But she could not bear his censure or displeasure, all the same.

"Please," she whispered. "Leave me."

"No."

"*Please*," she said passionately.

She saw, briefly, pain flare in his eyes, but she could do nothing to correct it. Slowly, he stood, and, glancing at her once more, began walking toward the door.

May 1860, Harmony Grove

My Dear Mother,

In response to your question, May is a warmer than its predecessor, but only very little. Yes, we still dine upon a heavy dinner at eight o'clock—it is enough to kill you.

During the days, we ladies keep busy. You would be charmed, I daresay, by the image of your daughter lifting bread from an oven. In addition, we sew almost endlessly. I have no particular objection to sewing. What I cannot understand is why the poor need so many scarves. I cannot decide whether it is guilt of the rich or a penitent conscience which compels such exhausting endeavors.

Last week, we graced the coming out ball of a neighbor and cousin, an Emily Strotham, who is a lovely young lady. In addition, we attended a lecture at Providence Church and a little dance at the home of John Thomas's sister, who is delighted to welcome her husband home from university once and for all...

Here, Shannon was interrupted by Miriam early on Monday morning, who dropped by to ask whether she had seen Charles's riding whip. The men were almost ready to leave, and he could not find it.

"No, but I will help you look," she said, getting up, her hands tightening on the skirt of her wool dress momentarily.

There was a long search, which yielded a semi-destroyed article in the music room and some near tears from Vincent as he explained that he had merely been playing with it and hadn't intended to break it. Vincent's father was inclined to be angry, but Shannon, stepping into the brink, said, "No, of course you didn't! Indeed, I feel as though I am always breaking something and then heartily regretting it afterward. I believe John Thomas has a spare. I will see if I can't find it for Charles." Vincent was thereafter her loyal servant, his eyes following her out of the room in adoration.

Shannon slipped up the stairs and down the hall to their chamber, stopping on the threshold when she saw John Thomas. He was standing at her writing table in his riding clothes, looking toward the door and standing still. She traced back in her mind for the contents of the letter, and, as she remembered them, heat suffused her cheeks, and her heart stuttered.

"Forgive me. I thought you had left a note for me," he said softly. She saw the briefest glimpse in his eyes of how much he had been hoping she had done so. "I see I was mistaken."

"John Thomas," she whispered, the color draining from her face as she cursed her sharp and bitter tongue. She crossed her arms over her chest, biting her lip mercilessly.

He met her eyes, and his jaw tensed. She could see that he was very angry.

She touched to collar of her gown. "Forgive me. I ought not to have said such things."

His eyes were hard—she had never seen them so—and finally, he looked away.

"Allow me to explain," she said softly.

"It doesn't seem that there is anything to explain."

She felt weak and knew she was pale. "Please, I... Last night, I—"

"Never mind," he said, remote from her, it seemed. "It doesn't matter."

Shannon walked quickly toward the writing table, snatching the letter up and tossing it on the coals of the fireplace. He looked up. "Shannon—" But it was soon burned past repair. A long stillness stretched out. She bit her lip, crossing her arms, feeling chilled and light-headed. She wanted to tell him so, but he was immovable.

"I didn't mean for you to do that. You have a perfect right to write whatever you choose to your mother," he finally said. Shannon swallowed. He started for the door. "Just...not at the expense of mine."

Minutes later, Shannon stood in the upstairs window, tucking her wrap about her. The view was gray and cold, and she had a slight sore throat. She stared below her as Mr. Haley and his three eldest sons mounted, staying only to say a few words to the girls in the doorway before riding away.

Chapter Twenty-Three

Her eyes fluttered open. Why hadn't she closed the curtains? It was really bright.

The instant she saw the white sheets (hers at Ravenel-Thompson House were gray), she got a feeling in the pit of her stomach. Then it all came flooding back to her. She jerked up and tried to remember everything. She did. Every last detail. Every little thing. *What have I done?*

She somehow knew she was alone in the bed, so she looked around, pressing her lips together to keep panic from tumbling out. She saw him sitting in the room's lone chair, elbows on his knees. He slowly straightened when he saw that she was awake, and, suddenly regaining her senses, she pulled the sheet up.

She risked a glance at him. He was standing now, fully dressed. She was grateful he had gotten up: she might've totally freaked out otherwise. His face was a little pale, and he opened his lips as though to speak and then closed them. She slowly met his eyes, a deep flush spreading in her cheeks.

Okay. Okay, she needed to pull it together. All of it—and she wasn't going to deny it was kind of otherworldly, what had happened between them—was overwhelming. The guilt, the total confusion this was going to bring to both of their lives— and she was supposed to be finding a *church* this morning. So, was she the kind of girl who slept with random strangers now? One might try to be all modern about it, but that didn't change how yucky it felt in the morning.

"What did we do?" she whispered, pressing her palms to her eyes.

He stood there, looking like he didn't know what to do or say. But it was obvious he knew she was freaking out. "Hey, it's okay," he said in such a soothing voice that she almost believed him. Her mind skittered from the gentleness of his voice to his hands plunging through her hair, so gentle—and back to the situation at hand.

Okay, what were the three big things that could happen: a disease, a pregnancy, a bolt of lightning. He was likely the cleanest guy she'd ever met, so mark off the first. If she'd been going to be struck by lightning, it probably would've happened last night. She moistened her lips. She couldn't think about the other possibility right now. She didn't think it was a huge likelihood, but it could still happen. "Are you going to tell me how sexual desires are normal and natural?" she asked bitterly.

"I could, but I think you already know that." He was a little more hesitant than usual, but his voice had regained its normal frustrating tone. She needed to remember that he was probably freaking out, too. However natural desires were, it didn't mean there weren't consequences in the light of day.

She expelled a breath, feeling close to tears. "Obviously, you don't have enough body fat to be able to hold your wine, but what's my excuse?"

He was looking at her like he thought she was a little crazy. Not choosing to comment on that, he said, "Look. We made a mistake. We lost self-control. I'm not the kind of person who usually loses it, and I think you aren't either. That's one of the things that's troubling you more than anything, probably. But a mistake is just that. There's no need to make it any more or less than it is. You'll deal with it, and I'll deal with it."

She bit her lip and then looked at the clock. 10:13. *Eek!* Like she wanted to lie here all day. She started to throw back the covers and then thought better of it. "Why did you let me sleep this late? We should be going!" Not that she hadn't needed the sleep. Heaven knew she'd had little enough of it last night.

He gave her a look. "After what happened, 'Pardon me, we need to hit the road, honey?'"

She met his eyes, surprised at how close she was to smiling. It would've been absurd and ungentlemanly, she would admit that. "Yeah. True." She looked around. He'd lain her clothes in a neat stack on her nightstand. It was a thoughtful gesture, and she appreciated it. It had probably taken him some time to collect them from all the different corners of the room, she thought, slipping her eyes closed.

"I'm going to go down to get some breakfast," he said. "Do you want me to bring you something?"

She shook her head. Like she could eat.

She dressed as soon as he left and then tried to make the bed look more respectable. She went into the bathroom. Great.

She looked hideous. Her heart was racing, and there was a little panic inside her. But he was right. She needed to deal with it, to move forward. She made order of her hair, pulling a bandeau out of her purse and placing it to cover some of the mess. Then she put on a little makeup. Okay. She could do this. She could ride back to Charleston with him.

She closed her eyes. She'd rather be guillotined. And she'd bet he would, too. But she didn't see that there was any other option.

Okay, she needed a plan. Life had just gotten way too complicated. She couldn't stay in his house, seeing him every day, or every other day... She needed to call the guys, tell them they were pulling out, breaking the contract. Dr. Ravenel—gah, she'd just slept with a man she'd never even called by first name—would understand. Would probably be hugely relieved.

And then, as she looked at herself in the mirror, reality, and sanity, kicked in. She might want to run for the hills, to bury herself and forget. To make the images of last night go away, as she beat herself up every day for the rest of her life. But she had men to pay. A business to build. A job to finish. This was her big break—anybody could see that. A few pictures of a Battery Street house on her website and the bid requests would come flying in. Even still, she might leave, if only her own interests were at stake. But there were people depending on her having her crap together.

She swallowed, having stood there so long that she heard the door click shut behind the bathroom. Her heart pounded and gave her a sick feeling. *Okay, open the door, Adeline, and face him like a woman.* She pressed her lips together and stepped out.

He was over at the little desk, picking up the key. He had a paper coffee cup and a little bread box in his hand. He walked toward her, handing her both. "Just in case," he said, meeting her eyes.

She held his eyes, somehow wanting him to know in the midst of her freak-out that she didn't blame him. A long moment passed, and he offered, and she accepted the breakfast, almost like an emotional truce. A strong *we will never speak of this again* rose between them. She was glad he didn't want to pretend like they had been dating, or that they would.

He cleared his throat. "Check-out is at eleven, so..."

"Yeah," she said, nodding, her voice sounding overly loud in the quiet room. "Thanks for this." She looked down, feeling incredibly awkward. A blueberry muffin and... She took a sip. Orange juice. He locked up behind them, and they walked down to the foyer. There was a long line at the desk, so he gave her the keys, and she went on out, putting her cup in the cup holder and opening the muffin. She was actually ravenous, if she admitted it to herself.

He was in there probably another fifteen minutes as she stared at the building next door, stunned. Had it really happened? She didn't even know him! It was like some sort of spell had been cast on them. But that was taking the easy way out. It had been lust, attraction. She had barely been able to control herself since she'd first seen him. She wondered if he had been feeling the same, or if she had just been an easy way to pass the time. She slipped her eyes closed, leaning her head against the headrest.

Okay, pull it together, Adeline. She did, at least not showing any emotion when he came out maybe ten minutes later.

"Ready?" he said, reaching to put his cup in and toss something into the back seat.

"Mm hmm," she said, looking out the window.

They had been riding an hour before either of them spoke. She had felt him glance at her, but she pretended not to notice. Lord knew they didn't need to be passing any more significant glances.

"I wanted to say that... Look, I know things went way out of bounds last night, crossing professional boundaries to say the least. If you want to leave—if you don't feel comfortable—just say so. I understand completely."

She moistened her lips, hesitating, before finally looking at him. There was a long pause. "I need the job," she said finally. "And the crew does, too. I have obligations to you, and I intend to honor them."

He met her eyes, and something entered his, something akin to respect. Well, thank heaven for that. "Yeah—okay." He focused on the road again. "If you're sure."

She nodded once, looking back out the windshield, the lines as they passed. "Let's just go back to the terms we were on before and move forward, like you said."

Chapter Twenty-Four

A deline wasn't sure if she was glad to see Ravenel-Thompson House, or if it loomed ahead of her like an ill omen. She still had, she thought as they walked up the steps to the back door, the rest of Sunday to kill. And she wasn't sure she should sit around and let her thoughts take over. Yet, the thought of going out was unappealing. She needed to take a shower and change clothes. Then maybe she'd go do some restoration work on one of the door facings.

They walked down the hall and heard movement, and soon Jude was running out of the kitchen and away from Jane. He was in cute little Sunday clothes, bow tie and everything, and he said, "Daddy!" with elation.

She watched as Adrian knelt to pick him up and said gently, "Hey, buddy. Have you been to church?"

He nodded. "Were you caught in a storm, Daddy?"

"I was, but I was safe," he said. "Sorry I had to spend the night away."

Adeline smiled and went to move up the stairs as Jude chatted to him about his night. She felt his eyes following her and thought he might actually be a little worried about her. Good—maybe he knew she wasn't accustomed to such behavior, though what reason she'd given him to think that, she didn't know.

She showered, changed into some comfy clothes, and went downstairs to work. The quicker things got back to normal, the better.

They made great progress on the balconies over the next two weeks, with a specially hired crew helping out. Adeline couldn't wait to get those beauties straight and secure and painted. If she accomplished nothing else, she could be proud of that.

The library fireplace was slower work. Every inch of it needed careful treatment and restoration, and she had to do most of that herself. Meanwhile, it was questionable whether they would be able to save the silk wallpaper. It had glue staining it from the paper that had been over it. She was looking for the right product with which to treat it but had been unsuccessful thus far. If it was her house, she might leave it for history's sake, but even she had to admit it looked pretty rough. Still, it would probably break her heart to remove it, so she was holding out against all odds.

She saw Adrian rarely, which was good, she thought. She heard him when he got home, helping Jude with his homework or playing with him. He seemed to be doing a good job with him: he was a quiet kid, not disruptive, and he never touched anything she kindly asked him not to.

She stayed away from the kitchen when Adrian was in there cooking or when they were eating something Jane had made. He had to notice the difference, but she thought he probably appreciated it.

Other than that, her life was pretty normal, the days flying by. She had a comfortable coze with Jane when the nanny stayed late one Thursday night while Adrian was at the university. Jude had fallen asleep against the older woman while watching a Disney movie, and Jane, unusual for the close-lipped secretary, was in a chatty mood. She talked about her family and life in Statesboro. She filled her in on the Ravenels. Adeline learned that Virginia Ravenel had been the CEO of a group of hospitals in southeastern Georgia before she had retired. No wonder she was so intimidating. Harris, Jane thought, was a good boy but needed to settle down. The Ravenels were Catholic, which Adeline had already gathered from the name of Jude's school. Jane told stories from her working days and confided that she and her husband had never been able to have children.

Adeline went to bed much in charity with the older woman. This, despite the fact that she had gotten some tight-lipped looks from Jane in the past when she'd put her feet on the coffee table or failed to rinse a bowl out when she put it in the sink. But Jane was a good one, deep down, she thought.

Adeline was in the kitchen making guacamole for supper when she heard the guests start arriving on the night of Jude's graduation. She could see a slight glimpse into the hall. Mrs. Ravenel was bending to kiss her grandson, who was sharply attired in a suit. He basked in attention from his grandparents for several minutes, and then she heard his father come down the stairs.

There were some words exchanged that she couldn't hear. All she caught was, "No, they're going to meet us there." More muffled words. "Theresa made a reservation at Husk, and I didn't argue."

She caught a glimpse of Adrian, looking impossibly good in a pair of blue pants, a brown belt and shoes, and a tan pullover over a light blue button down. He smoothed a hand over Jude's hair, which had probably gotten messed up somehow on his long journey from bedroom to foyer.

Finally, the grandpa, carrying Jude, said, as though intermediating, "Well, let's get him to school. The guest of honor can't be late."

And then they left—Jude's family, and Jane—and the house was entirely quiet. The men had already gone home, and Adeline had everything to herself. It was funny how unwelcome that was. She was soon commanding herself not to even consider driving by Husk to see who Theresa was. She took a sip of her juice. Yeah, that would be totally stalkerish, and she wasn't really the sunglasses and ballcap-pulled-low kind of gal.

She took a bite, the chip crunching, the noise from the foyer still sounding in her ears. He led such a busy life, had such a comfortable place in the world and his family, that she would bet he had pretty easily put it out of his mind. He had honored her request to go back to the status quo, but she irrationally felt herself a little put out by that. When they met in the hall, they said a polite greeting and went about their business. When Adeline was lost in work, she never gave it a moment's thought. But it would creep up on her at night when she was lying in bed, or now, when she was feeling a little lonely. That was probably all that night had been about for both of them, at bottom. Just because she was happy in her singleness and job didn't mean she didn't have a desire for something else every now and then. And just because he had a comfortable life with friends and family didn't mean that he wasn't, at the end of the day, a single dad who worked too much and confined his social life to basically Jude.

Maybe, she thought, standing there, she needed a weekend at home. But then she remembered all of her obligations for the house and all the things she had scheduled, not to mention the drive time and lost hours, and she knew it was impossible for the near future. She'd settle for a phone call to her dad.

Husk had risen before them so peacefully, the house a grand Southern beauty with gentle lights emanating from within. A live oak's limbs bent into view, eerily evoking the Old South. It was one of the best restaurants in Charleston, the food exceptional, the atmosphere calming. But Adrian was enjoying it not at all.

Lauren's brother was drinking too much, and her mom was talking too loudly. Adrian's mother sat there like a particularly prickly pinecone. About the only thing he was thankful for was that Lauren's sister and her husband made rational conversation with his dad, who was holding Jude and every now and then remembering to make him eat his shrimp and grits. Jane talked with Jude's other grandmother, Theresa, making polite conversation.

He noticed that Lauren's dad didn't seem to be able to look at Jude. Adrian would like to help, to give him a referral, but he doubted he would ever submit to therapy. And if that was hard for him, how grueling must it be to look at his other daughter, who actually looked like her sister. He had a feeling nobody found these get-togethers easy.

"I swear if she mentions The Yacht one more time…" his mother mumbled, picking up her phone to scroll through it. He wasn't going to lie: he was sick of the yacht, too. They were wanting to take Jude out on it in a couple of weeks. Not happening.

"Harris said the jury is deliberating," his mom whispered to him.

He turned his head toward her. "I bet he's pacing."

"I feel ill, and I'm not even there," she said.

He did, too, a little. "He'll do great. He always does."

"Both of my boys do—all of them," she said, looking toward Jude. "He was the valedictorian, if only they would call it what it is in kindergarten."

"There's no doubt," he said, lips twitching.

She looked at him, studying him for a long moment. The server brought their dessert, with something special for Jude. After a silence, during which they listened to the conversation at the table, she again lost interest and looked back at him. "Honey, are you okay?" she asked softly.

His brows drew together. "Of course."

She continued to make a close survey of him. "Jude is okay?"

"We're fine, Mom," he said. "What brought this on?"

"You seem distracted. I haven't seen you like this in a long time."

There was only the slightest hesitation. "I guess I have a lot going on."

"Do you need help? You know I would be willing to come stay with you as long as you need."

Seeing his peaceful life sliding away, he said, hopefully not too quickly, "Thanks. But we're doing fine." Or they would be once they got out of here.

Adeline finally took the next Saturday off. She considered taking a walk on the Battery, even though she wasn't really the athletic type. But she had topped the stairs and seen Adrian below in shorts and a T-shirt. She assumed from the earbuds in his ears and shoes that he was going for a run. And running into him was really the last thing she wanted to do. It was hard enough not to think about his calves. All of that running paid off.

Sooo... She got in her car and drove toward the Ashley River. She wanted to tour one of the homes—maybe she would find something there that would lead her toward Santarella, which she had neglected over the past few weeks. If only she could hunt down a curator and get him or her to speak with her.

In the end, she chose Middleton Place because she'd always wanted to see the grounds. And she seemed to remember some connection, maybe by marriage, between the two families. She hadn't gotten very deep into the box, but she did remember the name popping up now and then.

The fee had left her standing there, holding her wallet, dumbfounded for about ten seconds, before she remembered that she needed to respond. She did a quick analyzation in her head about how badly she wanted to see it and things, like food, that she could go without. She handed the woman her card, although not without a little bitterness.

The pamphlet was really helpful, and she had about thirty minutes to kill before her tour. So, she walked the extensive, beautiful gardens and grounds before joining the other tourists on the benches outside one of the flankers. The main structure and second flanker no longer stood.

The guide asked where everybody was from and then started telling the property's story. There were two problems with the tour, one of which was that the guide looked like her dad's contemporary yet still seemed to think he and she should be a thing. The other was that there was a British couple on the tour to whom he kept making embarrassing British references. Oh, and the guy in all black who kept creeping up behind her. But those were pretty much house tour staples, so she wasn't really thrown off.

She really enjoyed the tour and then went to the gift shop to ask if the curator was in. She really hoped he wasn't that guide. The lady at the desk said, "Oh, yes, he's in his office. Let me see if he has a minute." She slipped off down a small hall and returned with a man with a ruddy complexion and a friendly face.

"This is Adeline," the lady said. "She's one of your type, Joe."

The man laughed. "Come on back, Adeline. I hope I can help."

"Thank so much," she said, following him into his little office. They made small talk, and she explained what she was doing. Before they got into real conversation, she learned that he had a wife, two kids, and that they had recently acquired a puppy. When, finally, she was able to bring it around, she said, "You see, I'm looking for a plantation called Santarella. Have you ever heard of it? We think it's in the Sea Islands."

"Yes, I've come across it," he said. "In family letters. Would this have been John Ravenel's family you're researching—the John Ravenel who built your employer's house?"

"Yes!" she said, excited.

"Like I said, the Middleton family often mentions Santarella. I believe they even visited." He closed his eyes and pressed his temples for a minute. "Don't hold me to this, but I think that's the one that I always got the impression was a little difficult to get to. Within a day's travel, but probably not an easy day."

She nodded. "So maybe not on one of the larger islands right here in Charleston."

"Maybe not," he agreed. "And don't get discouraged and think it's not there. It could be, you know—there are lots of old houses buried on the smaller islands. I'll be happy to look into it and contact you if I find anything," he said.

"I would really appreciate it," she said, opening her purse to give him her card. It never hurt to give a person in his position a card anyway.

He did the finger-temple thing again. "I'm trying to think... There was a daughter of the house—our house, I mean, during the Civil War Era. I think she was friends with John Ravenel's daughter."

She studied his face closely, feeling that she was onto something here. "Do you... Is there any chance you remember her name? The Ravenel girl."

He closed his eyes and took a deep breath. "Shannon," he produced. "I believe it was Shannon."

Adeline stared at him. Shannon. Yes, she was familiar with Shannon. Only her last name hadn't been Ravenel.

Chapter Twenty-Five

The Haley ladies noticed that Shannon was quiet at dinner the next night. While Miriam assumed, romantically, that she was mourning the first separation from her beloved, Mrs. Haley thought something was weighing on her spirit. She studied her as Vincent and Sarah, enjoying the small dinner party which allowed them more time talking, asked if they might go to the theater once they returned to Boston.

"Vincent will board with the Whitcombs, and you shall continue your lessons, Sarah," Mrs. Haley answered, taking a sip of her soup.

"Yes, but Vincent will visit us sometimes, and perhaps Shannon and John Thomas will, too!" Sarah said.

Shannon smiled.

"I hope you are not feeling unwell, Shannon," Lizzie said.

"I *do* feel a little unwell," she answered quietly. "It began to come upon me this morning. Forgive me, I ought not to be sitting with you, I suppose."

Lizzie covered her hand, concern in her eyes. "Oh, and with John Thomas just gone away. Do you have a sore throat? Priscilla Lamb was telling me that little Amelia was unwell, and they did sit behind our pew."

"Yes," she admitted.

"I am sure it is only a trifling cold," Mrs. Haley said with a comforting lack of concern. "Shannon, my dear, it would perhaps be best if you lie down. We will send Phoebe up with a tray."

Shannon nodded, rising. "I shall, then. Goodnight to all of you."

Shannon walked to the stairs, her bones aching, and was surprised to find herself dizzy at the top of the stairs. By the time she was changed into her gown, she was exhausted. Curling on her side, she fell asleep.

Mrs. Haley awakened in the night with a pressing foreboding. She sat up in bed and, slipping on her dressing gown, thought suddenly of Shannon. She could not have said why, but her steps quickened as she approached John Thomas's door, and she opened back the door quickly.

She sucked in her breath and crossed the room to the bed, where Shannon was thrashing, though unconscious. The room was lit by the dying embers of the coal, and she could see that she was wet with sweat. Mrs. Haley lifted a hand and found her forehead singeing to the touch.

Wasting no time, she crossed quickly to the bell and pulled it. She was soon joined by Phoebe, her own maid, and Lizzie.

"Martha, have them send for Dr. Perkins immediately," she said, throwing back the covers and taking the wet cloth Phoebe was rushing to her mistress. "Elizabeth! What is wrong with Amelia Lamb?"

Lizzie, standing at the door with her hand clutching the top of her nightgown, said, "I did not like to say so to Shannon, but it is the influenza." Her mother met her eyes.

"Miss Shannon," Phoebe was saying, trying to revive her.

Breaking out of her stupor, Mrs. Haley joined her, saying, "Shannon!"

She could not be recalled, even when the doctor arrived, but instead continued her fevered thrashing.

"Influenza," he said almost immediately upon seeing her. "The fourth case I've seen today, though only children and an old man—not one in her prime. But she'd be more susceptible to our strains. Her fever must come down, or she'll start seizing," he said, ordering the bath to be brought up.

"Mrs. Haley," the doctor said sharply, trying to recall Shannon once she was again in bed.

"Call her Miss Ravenel or Shannon—she'll not recognize herself by his name," her mother-in-law said, standing nearby.

The doctor looked startled but after a moment said, "Miss Ravenel!"

Finally, her eyes began to flicker, and she looked around the room, her eyes coming to rest, heavily lidded, on the doctor before drifting shut again.

Throughout the night, her fever spiked several times. The doctor stayed and assisted. By the first light of dawn, the doctor, noting that young Miss Haley and the two maids had drifted to sleep, said to his stalwart helper, "You must send for her husband, Mrs. Haley."

The color drained from her face as she stared at him. "Merely as a precaution," he said, not quite meeting her eyes. When she still seemed stunned, he added, "Can he be reached?"

"No, not by telegram, if that's what you mean," she said. "They are in the middle of a farm in Connecticut, and they have a full day's start on any messenger. And—oh, good heavens, they will be leaving tomorrow morning for Washington City."

"Then I would send the messenger, and also send a telegram to his hotel in Washington," he said firmly.

She held his eyes another moment before looking away, quite pale. Lizzie, who had been listening, said softly from the other side of the bed, her eyes filling, "Ought we to write to her parents?"

"I... I think it would do more harm than good to send it until we know," Mrs. Haley said, rising and going to Shannon's bedside once more. "Though what I shall say to them, I cannot think."

Shannon's maid sat by her side, her expression troubled and frightened. Then, Shannon's hand in hers, she looked back down and stroked her forehead with a cloth.

Shannon's eyelids flickered open painfully, weakly. The sun seemed overly bright, but she knew instantly she was at Harmony Grove from the utter peace and stillness which reigned. Outside, a bird tweeted, and she could faintly hear the wind rustle through the small spring leaves.

Lizzie sat in the window sewing, her pale head bent over the loom, her movements intentional and quiet. She must have felt Shannon's study, for she looked up, breathing, "Oh!" and got up, coming to her. She took Shannon's hand. "Your fever broke last night," she whispered. "The doctor said you would awaken when you could, but we were so worried."

Shannon attempted to moisten her lips. She tried to speak, could not, and then tried again. "How long have I been unconscious?" she whispered.

"Three days," Lizzie said, eyes downcast, and then lifted water to Shannon's lips. Shannon studied her after she had sipped the cool water, a balm to her parched throat. After a long silence, Lizzie looked up, her eyes moist. "I won't conceal from you that we feared for your life, Shannon." She swallowed, still gripping her hand. "And I couldn't help but think," she said in a voice of forced merriment, "that there was so much we never talked about."

Shannon's eyes flickered over her face. She was unexpectedly moved. "Now we shall talk about things, Lizzie," she managed to say softly.

Lizzie looked up, smiling a bit. "John Thomas is very lucky, I think."

Shannon's smile slipped, and she held Lizzie's eyes. Lizzie opened her lips to speak, hesitated, and then said, "We sent word to him, Shannon, but we are unsure whether it has reached him. I know you must feel his absence keenly."

Shannon moistened her lips, the enormity of her ordeal still not fully comprehended. "He...He will come if he can, I imagine," she said. She pictured again his anger and wondered if the words "*John Thomas, I am ill*" would've stopped him. Reason told her it was so, but reason seemed far from her as she lay feeling so very poorly, so many miles from him.

Chapter Twenty-Six

S hannon slowly drifted awake, and she realized it was night. Her chamber was lit by the golden light of a fireplace recently stoked. That was unusual, for Mrs. Haley was not one to waste coal. Her eyes drifted across the room to her mother-in-law's accustomed chair, and she was surprised to find it empty. She had religiously kept the night vigil, while Miriam and Lizzie sat with her during the day.

She turned her head toward the two Shaker chairs where the girls usually sat and encountered instead John Thomas. Her heart jumped, but she was still too weak to move. He leapt to his feet, his face pallid and haggard.

"John Thomas," she whispered.

He bent over her, smoothing back her hair with a hand that was not quite steady as he drank in her features. He was not speaking, only crying, hot tears that occasionally fell onto her. He touched his forehead to hers and kissed her cheek, lingering there. She smoothed a hand down his arm and felt her eyes burning.

They stayed as they were a long time until, finally, he lifted his head and swept his eyes over her face. She was fully aware of how she must appear: gaunt and pale, her hair slipping out of its once-neat braids. "How are you feeling?" he whispered.

"Weak," she croaked.

He hesitated, still surveying her deeply, with raw love. "Do you need anything?" he rasped.

"Water," she said, and when she was too weak to hold the glass, he held it to her lips. When she finished, he brushed salve onto her cracked lips. The fireplace cast flickering shadows over the room, but it illuminated his face well enough that she could see his handsome features, his eyes steadily regarding her. She did not know if he was still angry. It was her last thought before drifting to sleep.

Shannon awoke the next morning to find the room full—her mother-in-law and two sisters-in-law sat sewing quietly. John Thomas was nowhere to be seen—had she only dreamed him? Lizzie, seeing that she was awake, said with a smile, "He has gone to send a telegram to your mother that you are recovering. He believed your last letter had her in Charleston, and your father still on the island?"

Shannon nodded. "Yes. Yes, that is correct."

Mrs. Haley stood, helped her drink, and then insisted that she eat a little from the tray Phoebe had brought up. She felt much stronger than the day before, well enough for Phoebe to change her nightgown and Miriam to brush out her hair and braid it neatly. Mrs. Haley was gently washing her face

when it struck her that it was Sunday, and they were all staying home for her, and John Thomas was travelling to Weymouth and back.

She felt a surge of affection and was perhaps more loving
with them than she had ever been. They were talking in the
way of females about Frederick's baby and furnishings in the
nursery at Ravenel House when there was a light knock at the
door, and Mrs. Haley called, "Come in."

John Thomas entered, looking immediately at Shannon. She
was propped against the pillows, emaciated and weak. How
could a person look so different in so little time? Then he looked
around, apprehensive about the circling of wolves around her,
metaphorically speaking, of course.

But he perceived almost immediately that there had been
a shift. Shannon had just been smiling, and his mother had a
look of peace on her face. There was no discomfort in Lizzie,
and Miriam's eyes were shining. He smiled cautiously, handing
his mother the medicine for Shannon which he had retrieved at
the apothecary's in Weymouth. He stepped hesitantly toward
Shannon, very much at a loss as to what to say.

It hadn't taken her illness to awaken him. He had not been
gone two hours when suddenly the look on her face had col-
lapsed on him. She had been trying to tell him something,
something about the night before, but he couldn't quite grasp
it. They had ridden another hour before it struck him that she
was trying to say that she had been hurt, and that her letter
was the result.

By the time they had made it to the hunting lodge, he gathered that he was not very good company from Charles, who had said those exact words. He had put on a good face for their hosts and tamped down his guilt with a reminder of her words about his family, which showed general ill-will and no desire to forge any bonds, even contempt. It had seemed so unlike her that he had been thrown into confusion, and yet just enough like her that he had felt crushed. But her temper—he ought to have known it; he *had* known it, really. It seemed unthinkable that he had acted in such a manner toward his Shannon, whose soul he knew to be sweet and gentle.

Just now, he wasn't thinking of his sisters and mother sitting about. They seemed to recede. Shannon was past the crisis, and now usual emotions returned. She would remember. Could she forgive him for that night and the next morning? He looked at her, hesitating, trying to judge what she wanted. The last thing he desired was to upset her. If she preferred him to leave, he would.

She gave him the slightest, weakest smile, and he looked at her in a way that he hoped conveyed his bitter regret and apology and love. A sheen came to her eyes, and, encouraged, he walked forward, bending to kiss the top of her head gently. "You look better," he said softly, surveying her. Her blue eyes looked up at him, so delicate. Was it all he could think to say?

"Is that your way of saying that I looked haggish last night?" she asked softly, her tone light. He was glad someone had remembered there were others in the room: he had not.

The ladies laughed, and he managed a flicker of a smile. He stroked his thumb over one of the twin spots of color on her cheeks, glancing at his mother. She smiled gently. "Her color became heightened while we ministered to her, but there is no fever."

He continued studying her, flushing for reasons he did not know when she met his eyes.

"Are all Southern girls so headstrong, John Thomas?" Miriam asked merrily as they continued to look at one another. "Shannon has been the worst invalid imaginable."

He glanced over at his sister, the tension easing from his shoulders. "Yes, they are, while seemingly so meek."

Shannon smiled at him docilely, and his mother said, "There is nothing wrong with being decided in one's mind. I am myself."

John Thomas smiled at her. "I know you are, ma'am."

She seemed surprised at his cheekiness, but his smile had won him many battles with her. "Very well, sir: you believe you may say what you choose because your wife is ill, and we will take pity."

"But she will not be ill very much longer," Lizzie said cheerfully, rising. "I think you are tiring, Shannon. We'll leave John Thomas to sit with you."

They filed out quietly, and the door closed. He waited just a moment, hesitant as to what to say. She looked up at him. The silence, the aloneness of the room, seemed to grow larger. His lips parted. "Something is different," he said gently.

"Yes. But it isn't any business of a man's, what happens between women," she said, looking very wise.

"Very well," he agreed. He sat gently beside her, content just to survey her features. "You ought to go to sleep," he said, removing her pillows until she was lying down again.

She looked up at him, and, slowly, her eyes welled up even as exhaustion threatened to claim her. He shook his head, his throat tightening. "No," he whispered. "No, please. The fault was my own. The thought of leaving you in such a way, and you ill and alone, Shannon, I..." He stopped, unable to go on, his eyes moist.

She shook her head, covering his hand, her thumb stroking lightly over it.

He held her eyes. He could think of nothing to say when she looked at him like that. His mind failed him completely.

He bit his lip and let several moments pass. "You're tired," he forced out.

"Am I?"

A smile flickered as he covered her. She met his eyes, her own growing heavy, still fragile enough to seek comfort. "I'm not going anywhere, Shannon," he whispered. "Ever."

Two nights later, all of the family had returned, fearing the worst and delighted to find their predictions wrong. Charles had brought Shannon a flower, which he said grew in a pretty little park just across from her home in Washington. Shannon, touched, had looked up at her husband. She saw such love for his brother in his expression that she tightened her hand on Charles's. "Is it very beautiful?" she asked, blinking rapidly.

"The city? Yes. You'll take it by storm. John Thomas and I have already decided."

"It is entirely unaware of its fate," John Thomas confirmed. "It will be a surprise attack, which brings it to its knees overnight." Shannon laughed, enjoying the wild flirtation, reminded of her days in Charleston, surrounded by hopeful suitors, who by now wished great ill upon John Thomas.

As for Adams, he quietly brought her a stack of books precisely to her taste, asked vaguely if she were feeling better, and departed. John Thomas, a scholar himself, distractedly handed her *Othello*, which she, picking up, dropped with a scream. That brought him out of his reverie and to his feet. "It is the Adams copy!"

"What?" he asked faintly, picking up his discarded tome.

"Look at the inscription!"

He bent over her, opening the cover. *To my darling Abigail.*

He looked down at the stack and saw Adams's own copy of *Othello*. "He would've meant to show it to you, I daresay, and forgot. It belongs to him: our grandfather willed it to him." He handed her the more modern book.

Shannon's fingers glanced over the cover of the old one. "Oh," she breathed reverently. "How kind to share it with me."

"He is very kind," John Thomas said.

Shannon looked up at him. "All of them are, John Thomas," she said, eyes cutting away. She swallowed. "So truly kind and generous."

She felt him watching her. "Shannon..." She looked back at him, and he seemed unable to speak, unsure of what to say. She swallowed, blinking rapidly, and attempted a laugh. "And here is your father, insisting to your mother that I must have *lamb*, to build my blood, and the idea makes me very nearly *ill*."

He laughed softly, covering her hand. "I'll speak with my mother."

Shannon smiled briefly before looking away. After a moment, she turned her head back toward him. "John Thomas," she said, delicate brows drawing together, "why doesn't Lizzie have a beau? She is pretty, and Mr. Richardson comes calling on every pretense imaginable."

His eyes roved her face, and he hesitated a moment. "She was engaged before," he said finally. "To an Albert Weatherford. She met him while they were in Boston, and I believe... From everything I am told, there was true affection between them. He travelled to Philadelphia for something concerning his business—shipbuilding—and was struck with cholera and died there."

Shannon moistened her lips, her hand tightening on his. He met her eyes. "Frederick and I had just arrived in London when I received word. I began a correspondence with her in hopes of alleviating her spirits. She said it helped," he said, lifting a shoulder.

"Oh, John Thomas," she said. "I had no idea."

John Thomas would not leave her while the rest of the family dined downstairs, and Shannon was coming to enjoy their quiet evenings in candlelit darkness, talking or sleeping, with John Thomas reading by the fireplace, sometimes aloud, sometimes to himself.

She watched him in the golden glow, in the rocking chair with the Bible in his hands as he leaned over, reading. His sandy hair was longer than it generally was, for he hadn't had it cut, a testament to his worry for her. The curve of his jawline, the line of his neck, were so masculine yet elegant, the length of his nose, the curve of his upper lip so appealing. She had for many months thought the most beautiful part of him were the subtle changes of his eyes, the shifts from stubbornness to kindness, from distant reserve to warmth. But there was no need to forget the rest of the visual exhibition. And, heavens, it did not end with his face, as she knew perfectly well.

She swallowed, trying to moisten her mouth, but her eyes caught on him again. He was smiling faintly, rare for him, except when he was looking at someone he loved. She found a smile tugging at her own lips. "What pleases you?" she asked.

He looked up, the smile remaining in his eyes and growing more tender as they rested on her. Then he read, "'And I pray that you, being rooted and established in love, may have power, together with all the Lord's holy people, to grasp how wide and long and high and deep is the love of Christ, and to know this love that surpasses knowledge—that you may be filled to the measure of all the fullness of God.'"

"Oh," she said softly. "How lovely."

He looked up at her. "Yes."

"Will you read to me?" she asked.

His eyes were loving. "Of course," he answered softly, and did just that until she drifted to sleep.

Chapter Twenty-Seven

A week after Shannon's fever broke, her husband began to take a more favorable view of her condition and might have let her rise from her bed had a coughing fit not awakened them both the night before and left her exhausted.

He was looking grim and contemplating sending for the doctor, not at all willing to hear Shannon's point of view, when a manservant knocked on the door. The man said, upon John Thomas opening it, "Letters, sir. There are three from South Carolina, as Mrs. Haley will be happy to know. Would you like breakfast brought to you, sir?"

"Only for Mrs. Haley. Thank you, Timms." He turned, humor in his eyes, looking through the letters. "They're all addressed to me. They must think you are too weak to read."

"Well, I'm not," she said, still defensive from their earlier conversation.

His eyes twinkled. "You frighten me when you look like that."

"Allow me to sit in the chair by the window—you may even carry me there, if you choose—and I shall do you no harm."

He gave her a stoic, unmovable look. "Shannon, there was blood in my handkerchief when I pulled it away from your mouth."

"It is perfectly normal for one who has coughed as much as I," she said. "Ask your mother."

"My mother is not a doctor."

"She may as well be! How else do you imagine she managed to keep eight children alive in such a climate?"

He laughed, acknowledging this with a nod, and sat to open her mother's letter. He looked up a few moments later, hesitancy on his face. "What?" she asked, her expression changing to one of worry and fear.

"No, no. Your mother is thinking of making the journey, that is all."

Her face underwent a transformation. "Oh, *no*, John Thomas, she will drive me to distraction!" Tears sprang to her eyes. "No, no, no, I love her, but she must not come here!"

He stood, his brows drawing together. It was unlike Shannon to cry over such a matter. He realized she was weary of being an invalid and a little low, and indeed, her mother would agitate her out of all reason, but still... He sat next to her and said softly, "There, I won't let her come. I'll tell her you are better, and that there would really be no need."

"She would bring Mammy, and they would—"

"They won't." He kissed her temple and felt her relax against him. She clung to him, and he tightened his arms around her. He gently reached to slip his arms beneath her, lifting her. Carrying her to the chair by the window, he wrapped her up in a thick blanket and looked up to find her watching him. He flushed slightly and sat down nearby. "Thank you," she whispered.

"You're welcome."

"I'm sorry I was a shrew."

"You're not a shrew," he said.

She smiled, studying him for a moment before looking out over the pasture where the sheep grazed, the growing lambs playing.

They had not been sitting thus very long when the door was thrown back loudly. Miriam crossed the threshold, a bonnet covering her fair tresses. John Thomas's brows drew together, but her eyes were shining. "Oh! I am sorry! But what do you think? Patience has come and brought all of the Whitcomb fruit which was purchased in Boston, and she has such news! She is to have a baby in January!"

There was the briefest silence.

Then John Thomas smiled. "Happy news indeed. Is she still here?"

"No, she left ages ago, and didn't come up because we told her Shannon might be asleep. Only, it is ten o'clock now, and, oh, here is your tray, Shannon," she said, turning to take it from the servant.

Shannon smiled, taking it from her. "Thank you. Yes, such happy news!"

"Mother and Father are as pleased can be! The first grandchild, on both sides, and I shall be an aunt, oh, and you shall be an uncle, John Thomas—but no! You shall already be one, by marriage. How unfair of you!"

He laughed. "Yes, very unjust. Patience is happy, then?"

"Very happy."

Shannon again smiled. "We will send her our felicitations: John Thomas has a great many letters to return, at least seven. I find myself too ill to do so."

He looked at her, eyes twinkling. "It must have come upon you quickly."

"Indeed, very suddenly. I shall write to Patience, though. Miriam, will you take John Thomas away from this room? His sacrifice is noble, but truly, he must escape me for a few minutes at least."

"Oh, yes, I shall take him away. Father was just saying this morning how much his hair needed to be cut. You may ride into Weymouth."

He laughed but made no move to rise. "I'll have my hair cut in due time. I missed Shannon's entire illness, and I'll be here during her recovery."

Miriam's breast swelled as she took a romantic breath, dark eyes moist. "Oh, no, Miriam," Shannon said. "Take him away."

John Thomas looked at her a little uncertainly. "I didn't think... If you would like to be alone, Shannon—"

"Dearest!" she exclaimed involuntarily. She reached for his hand, and he gave it, still studying her. She pressed a kiss to his hand. "I think you need some sunshine, and food, and yes, a haircut— that is all!"

He wavered. "I don't feel as though—"

"Oh, John Thomas, do!" Miriam said. "We will minister to her and tidy up, and we cannot do that if you are here, you know."

"Oh!" He flushed. "Yes, of course. I ought to have... Do

you need anything from Weymouth?" he asked, clearing his throat.

Shannon shook her head, eyes dancing.

"Yes, indeed, we do," Miriam said. "Mother will have left a list with Timms."

He smiled. "I see it was all planned." He stood and picked Shannon up, causing Miriam to heave a sigh and Shannon to laugh. He carried her to the bed, cocooned in her blanket, and kissed the top of her head. And after strictly interrogating his mother on the implications of coughing up blood, he departed with Charles for Weymouth.

Shannon, sitting on the furniture before the fireplace in one of her lovely dressing gowns much later, felt refreshed after a bath. Her hair had been brushed until it shined, and her skin was lightly scented with lavender. She sipped her tea and glanced at Lizzie, who was sitting in the chair across from her. "Patience will have been very happy," she said.

Lizzie looked up. "Oh! Yes, of course. I...I told Miriam not to... I was afraid you might be sleeping," she said, the slightest flush climbing her cheekbones, barely noticeable.

"She didn't wake me," Shannon said, sipping her tea, glancing out the window toward the growing shadows.

A silence grew, until Lizzie said, "It seems impossible to believe you are to leave us so soon."

Shannon looked back to her. "Indeed. How long and how brief is three months."

Lizzie hesitated. "I hope you know how dear you have

become to all of us, Shannon. The house will not be the same without you."

Her lips parted. "I shall miss all of you very much."

There was a long silence. "Shannon, I...want to ask your forgiveness. I was not welcoming when you arrived, even knowing how frightened you must have been." Shannon's eyes flickered over her face. Lizzie plucked at her simple gown, her eyes on the narrow wood planks of the floor. "My example of a married life had been Patience's, and Patience's life is very similar to my own. Only my own life has the benefit of no husband to exert control or...to lose. And then I met you, so very different from me, and I think you opened my mind's eye to a world of possibilities I might miss. I don't think I resented you so much as I was frightened." She swallowed. "I can't think how I came to be such a coward. I never was before. But you... You are afraid of nothing."

Tears in her eyes, Shannon moistened her lips and admitted something she never had. "I am afraid of...so many things, Lizzie."

Lizzie looked at her, lifting her brows. "Then you are all the braver."

Shannon shook her head, looking away. "I am not brave."

Lizzie shook her head and said softly, "You don't see, do you? You have so much capability, endless possibilities, and a heart that beats so strong it is like a bird taking flight. It is terrifying to other women." She paused, meeting her eyes, seeming to hesitate before saying, "And to the man who loves you."

Shannon blinked away the moisture in her eyes, stunned. "I am not worthy of John Thomas. He must know that," she whispered. "I think it every day."

"Oh, Shannon. I love you dearly for saying that. But he feels just the opposite, I believe. As though he could never fully obtain you, though he might try a hundred years. Please try to remember that, Shannon, when things are...difficult between you. He feels as though he has married very high above him. And it is not a usual marriage. He knows that, but he also wants to protect you, as though it were a usual marriage. And I feel," she said, eyes shining, "as though someday, it will all become much more natural, because I see the way you look at him, when you think no one is looking, Shannon, and that means so much more than all of the rest."

Shannon took her hand, unable to speak. She attempted a smile.

"And...And as for the other," Lizzie said with her customary reserve and delicacy, but holding her eyes, "God...has a plan for your life, Shannon." Shannon nodded, pressing her hand. "God has a plan," Lizzie said again softly, covering her hand with her other.

Chapter Twenty-Eight

Progress on the house was fast one day, and then they would run into a hitch the next. Adeline finally tracked down a treatment for the silk toward the end of May and, keeping her fingers crossed, decided to go in. She had two of the men spend a week carefully revealing all of the wallpaper, and, looking at it, she could only imagine what this room must've looked like and how the family had lived. The silk was an ice blue with just the barest hint toward green that you missed if you weren't looking carefully enough.

Adeline was super excited to get started, but she was distracted as she went down the stairs for what was supposed to be her big day. She was a few days late. Technically, it should be no big deal. She'd had a lot of stress, with working and… other things. But the thought constantly was on her mind. She couldn't focus on anything else for very long.

"Okay," she said to herself, entering the Silk Room, as she had dubbed it, and looking around. There were the cans of the treatment and the workstation Joe had set up for her. It had to be applied evenly, so she would be doing the bottom, and he, on scaffolds, would take it on up, hopefully seamlessly.

He walked into the room, faded blue jeans, construction boots, white T-shirt, and all, and said, "You ready?"

"Yeah, Joe," she said, trying to focus. She knelt down and tried to pry the lid off one of the metal cans. She looked wryly up at him, and he knelt with a flat screwdriver and took over.

She had stood up and was looking around, trying to pick the best starting point, when suddenly the smell from the multiple cans hit her. She looked around quickly. "Gosh, that stinks."

Joe looked up, brows together. "Do you think so?" He seemed a little confused.

She covered her mouth, surprised to feel nausea beginning to stir. He opened another can, and it was like the odor completely permeated the room. And suddenly, she knew she was going to be sick. Not taking time to explain, she ran from the room and to the downstairs bathroom, opening the toilet and losing her breakfast.

Rising back up and reaching for some toilet paper to dab her mouth, she noticed her hand was shaking. This was not good. Not good at all, her brain said really quietly. She didn't acknowledge the thought: she allowed other thoughts to be louder. Something she had eaten for supper really hadn't agreed with her. She'd maybe even caught food poisoning from it. Or maybe she'd caught a bug.

She cleaned up and then went upstairs to her own bathroom, feeling weak from her sick bout by the end of the second flight of stairs. She rinsed her mouth and dabbed her face with a washcloth, staring at herself in the mirror for a long moment. She needed to go to the drugstore.

She bought like ten pregnancy tests. When she got back to the house, the bag seemed alarmingly see-through, so she tucked it behind her purse under her arm, glancing both ways before she crossed the hall to the stairs. *Oh, gosh, oh, gosh, oh, gosh*, her mind said to the beat of every stair she took. *Just don't think about it. Go take the test and move on with your life.* It was probably nothing, after all.

She did the first test and then laid it on her sink. She waited, not sure what was supposed to happen since this was her first foray into the careless life. And then two red lines appeared. They were really bold lines. She had been leaning on the sink, but she rose, a slow breath leaving her body.

She picked up another and tried again. Really, those lines were audacious, almost screaming at her. She swallowed, starting to feel ill again.

She washed her hands without knowing it, staring off into nothingness. Then she walked into her tiny little room and sank down on her bed, the shock keeping her from thinking clearly. She couldn't comprehend everything, or anything. Vague thoughts rolled in and out of her mind without her attempting to make them flow. Maybe there was a mistake. She could still work, right? She *had* to work now. What would her parents say? How could she let this have happened?

It seemed she still could not fully comprehend it. She was pregnant. With Adrian Ravenel's child.

Adeline had told Joe that she was a little under the weather and that they would start on the silk in a couple of days. He was glad; he could return his attention to the balconies. She spent the next day doing light work, like sanding the fireplace in the library, although she questioned whether that was wise, given that her thoughts were in such a tangle. She didn't want to inadvertently remove an entire rosette, or anything.

She sat back, still unable to comprehend it. She had to tell Adrian; she knew that.

She had seen him sitting in the living room last night, reading a big book, underlining something now and then, and yawning from a long day at work. And then this morning in the kitchen, kissing Jude's cheek as he left and casually picking up a stack of bills to mail. He was going on about his life. And she wasn't in it. Of course she wasn't.

Her mind needed to think and plan. What did this mean? How would he react? She cast back her thoughts to any of her friends who had gotten pregnant. Rynn, in high school—her boyfriend had said, "It's not mine. You're a slut," before running for the hills. Then in college, there was Cami, whose lover had offered to pay for an abortion.

She hated men.

It wasn't long before she had whipped herself up into hating Adrian Ravenel, too. She didn't know what his reaction would be, but she thought of a thousand things it might be until telling him kind of assumed nightmarish qualities. She didn't know what it mattered, really. She would go on about her life, somehow figure this out. It wasn't like she was expecting anything of him. At least, she didn't think so.

She gave it two more days and took a couple of more tests just in case there was a mistake. There wasn't. And so, hearing him in the library one morning before work, she resolved to go in.

Adeline stepped over the threshold, arms crossed, shoulders set a little stiffly. He was standing behind the desk, white shirt tucked neatly into gray pants, his suit coat nowhere in sight. He was flipping though some folders. He looked good. Impossibly good. That hadn't changed. It would be nice if physical attraction fled when awkwardness arose. But it didn't.

He glanced toward the door and, seeing her, stopped what he was doing and stood to his full height. He studied her, seemingly waiting for her to speak. His eyes made that quick survey of her face which made her feel naked. For a moment, she thought he might have guessed. But even he couldn't be that good.

"Good morning," she said.

"Good morning," he returned, obviously thinking this was odd. But he wasn't impolite. Or she should say *detached*. He was never impolite. But he wasn't using that arm's length voice. They hadn't really talked since the car ride home, and the quietness of the house, the aloneness of the room, seemed to bring it all up. Was she a side-step, a brief detour that meant nothing? She didn't think it was that way; she thought he was probably more experienced than her but that it wasn't a lifestyle for him. It was somehow better, better for her own pride, but there was no guarantee she had meant anything. So what on earth was he going to say to this?

She met his eyes, dark and impenetrable, and then looked away, unable to say the words. She pressed her lips together. *Come on, get it together. He literally thinks you're crazy.*

"Are you all right?" he asked. There was a caring note in his voice, not patronizing. She imagined it was the way he talked to his clients. Great.

She looked back at him. "Oh... Yeah." She moistened her lips. "It's just..." She swallowed, holding his eyes for a long moment. She didn't know what she was conveying.

His lips parted slightly, his eyes fixed on her face. "Are you pregnant?" he asked in shock.

She bit her lip, still looking directly at him, and then nodded once. She thereafter made a complete survey of the carpet, pressing her lips together. She hated herself for flushing. She was a woman, not a sixteen-year-old girl.

He set down what he was holding and came around the side of the desk, stopping a few feet away from her.

She glanced up at him, her heart jumping, and said after a moment, "I took several tests... I have a doctor's appointment next Tuesday, but there's really no doubt."

He nodded slowly, as if trying to take it in, still looking at her. The silence grew between them, but then, shock had held her captive for several hours. Finally, he said in a gentle voice, "Are you all right?" It was said in a different way, more intimate, softer.

She met his eyes, smiling wryly. "Yeah, it's just... Whew, you know?" Her voice cracked just a little on the last word. She thought it had more to do with the fact that she was finally able to tell someone, and that he had acknowledged the craziness she had been going through the last couple of days.

He nodded, still apparently assessing whether she was going to snap, and then his phone started beeping. He looked toward the desk, frustration on his face. It finally stopped, and he looked back at her. Then it started up again, and he looked at it like he was about to throw it out the window. She laughed softly, glad *something* had broken the tension in the room. "You should get to work."

"Don't be ridiculous, we have to talk about this," he said as if she had lost her mind.

She looked at him. "You won't have someone upset or frightened at the change in schedule?"

His lips pressed together, and she knew he was thinking about the clients who would actually not be in good shape at all if he didn't show. Still, he looked at her as if he would reschedule all of his appointments if need be. She was grateful for that. She was also grateful that he didn't ask her for clarification that it was his. Oh gosh. It was *his*. She was carrying his child. How could they possibly be forever intertwined in this way and not know one another at all? It was so bizarre, so not something that was even on her radar when she had come here.

She gave a semi-confident smile. "You need to go. We have plenty of time to talk about this." Her hands clasped her elbows. Not that she was excited to talk about it. She couldn't even imagine what that would be like.

He sighed, seeming to accept it. "Fine." He reached for a file. "Why don't I make dinner for you tonight. We'll eat on the balcony if it's safe."

She nodded and then shook her head. "It's Thursday. Your class..."

He looked frustrated, drawing a hand through his hair. "I'll cancel," he said after a moment. "They'll love it."

She shook her head. "You need to teach it. It's not like you meet three times a week. You'll lose a lot of ground."

There was a long pause. "All right. Tomorrow then, if that's okay."

She nodded, and he shifted as though to go but stayed where he was. "When did you say your appointment was?" he asked, almost a little hesitantly. Appointments. Baby. Yep, it was real.

She lifted her brows in surprise, his question finally striking her. "Tuesday, at ten."

"I'll go with you." He halted. "That is...if you don't mind."

She blinked. "No, I...I don't mind," she somehow managed to answer.

The single nod again, and then he was close to her in the doorway. He looked back at her and said in that voice that she somehow believed, "It's going to be okay, Adeline."

She held his eyes and realized he was going to stand there until she acquiesced. She nodded, moistened her lips, and stepped back to give him more room.

Chapter Twenty-Nine

Other than not being able to go near the cans in the Silk Room, Adeline felt pretty good the next morning. She made up some excuse to Joe why they needed to postpone it, not willing to relinquish control, and set to work on the progress report with which she always supplied her customers monthly. She checked things off her notepad as she went through the rooms, trying to pretend this was a normal business relationship.

She also tried not to think about supper that night. He had reacted well, as far as it went, she thought. Then again, he hadn't really said much at all. That he had guessed before she even told him kind of threw her for a loop. He was wicked smart. It was scary when she thought that the baby had half of his genes. It would probably be outsmarting her before it was two. How would she even deal with it?

She stopped, actually smiling softly. It was the first time she had thought of it as the baby, had imagined how it would be. Shock and fear had been her primary emotions. The baby wasn't real to her—it was more a state of being than a reality. But it *was* real. Somewhere through all of that mess, a sensation of awe finally hit her. A new life. Her child.

She wondered vaguely through her emotions if it had hit him yet, or if it would. Of course, he had been through all of this before, probably in a carefully planned, responsible way, with the woman he had loved. With a wanted child. She shook her head, telling herself to stop it. She shouldn't do him the disservice of thoughts like that before she even knew where he stood.

She had worked herself up so much that his offer to go to the doctor had dumbfounded her. It sounded like he meant to take responsibility, although maybe he was just checking to make sure there was an actual pregnancy, she thought, pressing her lips together sourly. *Okay, cool it, Adeline.*

It was just that she wanted his reaction to be right. It was surprising how much. She wanted him say precisely the things he should. *Why, Adeline? Why does it matter so much?* She didn't even know if she would be staying in Charleston until it was born or where she would be later. She wasn't even sure she wanted his help. She didn't know him, after all. Help sometimes meant interference. She swallowed. *It's because you think well of him and don't want that illusion shattered, young lady. Face it.*

She took a shaky breath, pressing her lips together and exhaling slowly. Okay. Yeah, that was probably true. Half because it would speak poorly of her taste and discretion if he was a total jerk, half because she had seen just enough out of him that she was intrigued and maybe wanted to like him.

But the truth of it was, she didn't have any idea what his

feelings were. He had said so very, very little. He had probably freaked out all day the day before. She wondered how he had performed at work and his class. She couldn't imagine she would've done a very good job. It must be bizarre to him, some random woman he had slept with once getting pregnant. He had to have known it was a possibility, but he had equally known it wasn't a probability. Just one time. A fluke.

She hoped that wasn't the way he saw it. With the first picture of her child in her mind, some measure of protectiveness rose up inside of her. How could she have done this? How could she have been so careless? Didn't she owe it to her future children to offer more stability than this? She, so carefree in many aspects of her life, began to think about all of the ramifications.

Okay, calm it down. The good news was, he was a basically decent human being. They would start from there. He wasn't the sort of person she would care to leave the baby with. He was pretty much as respectable as it got. She bit her lip on a sudden small smile. She wondered if she was the sort of person *he* would want to leave the baby with. That was a bigger question. She had seen him looking at her food in the pantry. She knew what he had been thinking.

That was a much better thought to leave this on, she thought, flipping the light fixture off in the dining room. She glanced at her watch. She needed to go up and change. He must have asked Jane to take Jude with her, because she had seen them leave a little while ago. The men were already gone, and he would be getting home soon.

And, though the heavens might fall, she was going to look good at supper. She didn't know what she had to prove, but there was something. And she wanted to look like a freaking model.

So she went up the stairs, dropping her clipboard on her bed and getting into the shower.

She came down the stairs in a sleeveless black dress that nipped in at her natural waist and came a few inches above her bony knees. It had kind of an elegant yet breezy summer feeling to it. She wore diamonds at her wrist and in her ears, which her short curls teased, and nude pointed toe flats. Her makeup was exceptional after three re-dos. She carried a gray wrap over her arm, although she didn't think she would need it.

She went down to the kitchen but didn't find him there, so she went back up to the second balcony. She stepped through the door, seeing the bay twinkling in the distance and Adrian standing near the railing, hands in his pockets.

She closed the door behind her, and he turned around, looking at her and smiling slightly. "You look amazing," he said softly.

Gah, she was such a woman. All of that torture, and she'd do it again a thousand times over for those three words. She smiled, going further onto the balcony. "I figured you wouldn't change from work." He hadn't. He was wearing the blue pants which looked too good to be decent, though he had removed his tie and neatly rolled up his sleeves.

He removed his hands from his pockets and started toward a little table, where their food was sitting. She lifted her brows. The food looked appealing, and there were two glasses of sweet tea sweating on coasters. He would probably never drink wine again.

A candle, probably to keep mosquitoes away, was twinkling, along with the porch chandelier. This was cozy and nice. It had been a good idea. He pulled her chair out and then went to his own.

"*This* looks amazing," she said, surveying the white plate. There was a steak and mashed potatoes, roasted carrots, and grilled zucchini. She knew he was pretty much a vegetarian, so it was thoughtful. He was probably half-gagging over there. She also couldn't help but notice that it was all stuff that would be good for the baby. Protein and carbs with a healthy dose of vegetables. She met his eyes, wondering if she was reading too much into that.

He lifted a shoulder. "I wasn't sure what you liked."

"Pretty much everything," she said. *Great, Adeline, you sound like a Viking.*

They talked about the weather, then about Jude's summer plans. Then there was a silence in which both tried to think of safe, appropriate topics. It was difficult because they had little in their lives in common. He couldn't ask her about the progress of the house without sounding like he was pushing her. She couldn't ask him about his day at work, because he could say very little more than that it was good.

Finally, he shook his head, giving a soft laugh. "We might as well come to it."

She looked up, meeting his eyes. "Yeah." She twirled one of her curls, something she only did when she was on-edge.

There was a long silence. She bit her lip, not knowing where to start.

"How have you been feeling?" he asked. Good. That was safe.

"Pretty good. The chemical smell for the silk about undid me."

He made a face, pouring more tea for himself, glancing at her glass before he set the pitcher down. "Don't go near it. It can wait as long as it needs to.

"Well. There's plenty to do in the meantime."

He met her eyes. "So you're staying," he said quietly.

"Yeah, I... I mean, for the near future anyway... I haven't really had time to process it all. I'm not sure where I need to be, or what I have to do... But I do know I need to work."

He shook his head, almost imperceptibly. "You don't have to, Adeline," he said seriously, quietly.

She held his eyes. "Adrian, I..." She shook her head. "I didn't lie in wait for a rich man so I could float through the rest of my life."

He pressed his lips together, looking almost angry. "I didn't mean that. You *know* I didn't."

O-kay, then. She swallowed. "Sorry," she said softly.

He sighed. "No, I am." She assumed he was referring to his tone and not the whole situation. "I just meant that I don't want you to have to worry about anything. You have enough craziness coming without that."

She nodded. "Yeah, okay." She wiped her mouth and then lay down her napkin. "Thank you for supper. It was delicious."

He nodded in return and leaned up, looking over his shoulder. "There's a good view of Ft. Sumter at night from here if you know where to look," he said, getting up.

She rose, too, actually feeling a little chilly and putting on her wrap. "Don't tell me you used to come out here before we fixed them," she said.

"Yeah, on occasion," he answered, moving with her to the railing and pointing it out.

It was a magnificent view. She understood why he had taken a risk and come out here, even if it was historical negligence at best. She saw a lighthouse and the occasional boat passing and loved looking past the grand posts of the house. They framed the view ahead perfectly. She wondered what it had been like up here, alone, looking out like that, in the stillness of the night when all the tourists had gone home.

She felt his gaze on her and looked at him, not realizing she had stood this close. His face looked very serious. She was glad he had broken the tense moment, but he was obviously ready to return to the topic. And they needed to. "Adeline, I know you don't know me," he said. "If you did, I hope I wouldn't have to tell you this. But I want you to know that you're not alone in this. Not for a single second. I want to have as much of a role as you'll let me play."

She felt the prick of unshed tears and swallowed. A long silence followed, in which he seemed to be measuring whether he had said enough. "Thank you, Adrian," she said softly. And she meant it. He didn't touch her, and she was glad of that. It seemed to show respect, after the crazy things they had done. He slipped his hands into his pockets, and she suddenly wondered if it was because it was hard for him not to. She looked from there back up to his eyes. He was already looking at her.

"Adeline, I want to marry you," he said seriously, eyes not wavering from her face.

Her lips parted. She blinked—once, twice. *Not* what she had expected.

He shook his head slightly. "I know, but it's not something I've arrived at impulsively. I want to take care of you and do what's best for the baby." It was said in his clinical way, smoothing over his emotions carefully. She opened her lips to speak. "I'm not asking for an answer tonight," he said before she could speak, "and I hope you won't say no immediately, unless you find me totally repugnant, which is understandable under the circumstances." He paused. "Let's just...get you through the pregnancy and go from there. We'll see how it goes."

She bit her lip, studying him rapidly. "Adrian, I..." Crazy, it was crazy. It was a marriage, not some sleep over. How could they make it work when many people who had dated for years couldn't? How could it be good for the baby for it to go through a divorce? For her to marry a man she didn't know? She was feeling pretty protective of herself and the baby and didn't want to do anything rashly. And yet, even still, some niggling voice told her it would be better for it if its parents were married even for a short time. And who knew, maybe there was a two percent chance it could actually work. She clung to that two percent. Marriage was forever in her family and in her heart, if she were honest with herself. It wasn't something old-fashioned, out-of-touch people had thrown off on her. She believed it, too. But she was doing the best with what she had to work with here. She needed to at least consider it.

"What about Jude?" she asked, scanning his face. "I thought you said..."

He hesitated. That little boy had his heartstrings pulled good and tight. She could tell he hated himself for doing anything that would throw his little life into turmoil again. "I don't see how being with you could possibly hurt him," he said.

Her lips parted, and she somehow managed a grateful smile. "If I'm being honest, I probably won't say yes, Adrian. I mean, why start something that's almost certainly not going to work anyway. I...I don't think these are normal circumstances where it's necessarily a given that it's right to get married, like if we had been dating or..."

He nodded.

"But I'll think about it." She met his eyes. "I will."

He nodded again. "Just let me know."

Chapter Thirty

The Baltimore and Ohio Railroad steamed forward for the last leg of the journey. Shannon watched out the window with pleasure at the panoramic view of sprawling green fields. She couldn't comprehend why her mother and father had hesitated in granting their consent to her marriage: it seemed to her as though John Thomas had shown her the country in a very short time.

In this case, though, it was Adams accompanying her, since it had been necessary for her husband to report before she had been granted leave to travel. Now the family was in Boston, and it had been determined that one of the brothers should accompany Shannon for protection. She rather thought Adams had been chosen because he had not been listening, but she was glad of it; he was a peaceful person, reading the whole way, and he was absently thoughtful.

As they came into the station, she searched the platform for John Thomas. She had not seen him in two weeks, and her hands tightened on her fan, nervous and eager all at once. She was too hot in her high-necked green travel gown and gloves, and Adams, used to New England, seemed to be wilting.

He was, however, extremely capable with trains, knowing Boston, a much larger city, and the entire Northeast as he did. He stood and took Shannon by the elbow, protecting her from the jostles of the unsteady and overly eager passengers and shielding her as they climbed down the steps and stepped out onto the platform. Her eyes scanned the people, while Adams seemed to be distracted by a dog giving chase to a bird.

And then John Thomas materialized, striding toward them, his eyes upon her. Without so much as a by-your-leave, he pulled her to him and kissed her on the lips, passion in his touch. Adams's attention was recalled by the cheers of some well-meaning bystanders. Shannon, blushing, laughed, and let her eyes skitter up to John Thomas. He was flushed, too, belatedly self-conscious, but still smiling at her. His New Englander brother asked abstractedly what had overcome him, and oughtn't they to get Shannon off of the platform?

A smile entered his eyes, and he said, "Yes. Yes, we should." He put his hand on the small of her back and guided them to the hired carriage, where they waited for Phoebe. Most of Shannon's trunks would be shipped, but she had brought a small one, as well as several valises. John Thomas had arranged to have these delivered to their house.

"There she is," Adams said as Phoebe emerged from the crowd.

"We thought you had been swallowed," Shannon said.

"Oh, no, ma'am. It's like a beehive with all of this swarming."

John Thomas handed Phoebe up to sit by the driver, a courtesy which seemed to make her uncomfortable, and Shannon flushed. At least he had stopped short of insisting her servant ride in the carriage. And yet, strangely, there was something appealing about his action.

John Thomas turned to Shannon and, stroking his thumb over her gloved knuckles, handed her in. "I'll ride forward. You have been travelling."

And so, Adams got in beside her, and they travelled over the cobblestone streets for ten minutes until they drew up in front of a brick townhouse with white trim and window boxes full of yellow flowers. Shannon smiled, eyes bright, face peaceful as she looked it over. It was nothing to Santarella, or to Ravenel House or Harmony Grove, but it was the first place she would call her own.

There were three servants waiting in the small but lofty foyer as they entered, a free Negro man and woman, and a white cook in her mid-fifties. Phoebe had gone around to the servants' entrance, but the other three passengers assembled in the foyer, and John Thomas made the introductions. Learning that the manservant was from Cape Town, Adams began talking with him about the fishing there.

"Are you feeling well?" her husband whispered.

"Yes," Shannon said, looking up at him. She gave a small smile, and the smile in his eyes grew. He looked up from her, found a pause in the conversation, and said, "Adams, I am sure Mrs. Hensley will show you to your room. I will take Shannon up so that she may rest."

"Yes, do," he agreed vaguely, nodding. "I shall do very well."

He returned to his conversation.

As they went up the carpeted stairway, John Thomas whispered with a smile in his voice, "I begin to wonder at the wisdom in allowing him to escort an invalid."

"Oh, no, John Thomas," she said earnestly. "He was most attentive. And I am no invalid."

"I'm glad," he said. He was looking well, almost boyish, his heart light.

He led her to the top and left, turning the knob of a paneled door and stepping back to let her enter. She stepped in, hands clasped at her belled skirt, and turned around, taking in the room, before letting her eyes settle on him. After a slow survey of her, he walked to her and put his hands on her waist, kissing her slow and sweet. She said, "We ought to be parted more often."

He touched his forehead to hers. "No."

She kissed him, which seemed to make him ache with longing, but he said softly, "Do you like your home?"

"Very much."

His eyes roved her face. "I..."

She smiled to herself, reaching up to stroke her fingers through his hair, threading them lightly, tantalizingly. His hands gripped the fabric of her dress, and he drew her against him. The passion soon built, their lips in the perfect harmony which had been present from the first. But he broke off suddenly. "What am I thinking?" His hands stroked down her arms, and he stepped back slightly, seeming to try to collect himself.

"I am well," she said, looking up at him. She stroked her hands down his lapels, making slow work of it, holding his eyes.

He took a shaky breath. "Are you?"

"Quite well."

He drew her against him again, reaching behind him to lock the door.

Shannon awoke in her sunny bedchamber in Washington, the birds chirping in the trees on the green outside, the sounds and smells of breakfast rising to her. She was sleepy but content, remembering their difficulty in carrying on with supper, the way John Thomas's eyes had kept drifting to her as he tried to make conversation with Adams in the green sitting room after they had dined.

A smile on her lips, she looked at the clock above the mantle and saw that it was ten o'clock. John Thomas would have been long gone, and he was a dear for not waking her. She rose and put on her dressing gown, finally looking around her. It was a lovely chamber, the walls a pale blue. The room was graced with a canopy bed of thick mahogany wood, a large dresser, and a small vanity. There was an empty, feminine writing desk by the window. The floors were wooden with a patterned rug under the bed covering most of them. John Thomas's belongings looked meager in their places. But then, he had no taste for *things*, as Shannon so regrettably did. Phoebe would begin filling it up immediately with her fribbles and trappings.

She spent the morning inspecting the house—the cellar, the kitchen, the sitting room, dining room, small study, spare bedchamber, and the closets. She was a bit over-trained for the house, but she intended to be a good mistress of it. She paused in the doorway of the study, her eyes scanning the room. Here, her husband's stamp was clearly written.

Papers littered the desk, a book lay open, and an inkstand had obviously been used a great deal already. She walked forward, setting the open book aside to look at the one beneath it. *Navigational Signals and Maritime Law.* She studied the cover.

She replaced the book which he had obviously been reading instead, holding his place but turning it to look at the spine. *Othello.* A smile lifted her lips.

She went to look out the window and saw a horse and carriage clipping by on the peaceful street. Across the way on the green, a Negro nurse played with two children, a boy and a girl. The child's peach-colored dress with lace frills and pantaloons awakened memories long buried. The boy pushed the little girl, and Shannon's impulse was to fly out onto the green, her skirt already clutched in her hand. But as she watched, spellbound, the nurse scolded him and picked the little girl up. Moments passed, and the nurse collected them and headed for home.

"Shannon?"

Hearing Adams's voice, she turned, her arms still crossed. "Yes, brother-dear?"

He adjusted his spectacles. "I've just remembered: I promised my mother I would tell John Thomas that you must have fresh air. I've forgotten to do that, but should you like to go for a walk?"

She smiled. "I should, indeed."

It was nighttime, and the sitting room was lit by two oil lamps and several candles, it being too hot for a fire. A golden glow was cast on the green walls, and a gentle breeze stirred in from the two small, open windows. John Thomas sat with Adams in the wing chairs before the fireplace, and Shannon sat across the room, reading by one of the lamps. Adams would return to Boston the next day, and they discussed his travel plans.

John Thomas glanced across the room at Shannon. She caught him looking, and he smiled at her, returning his attention to Adams.

"Do you think Lincoln will indeed be elected?"

John Thomas inclined his head once. "I think—yes, there's little doubt."

Adams drew his brows together, questioning. "Why do you say that?"

"I've counted the figures. It's the Southerners' worst fear: we can take the electoral college without the vote of a single slave state. We simply have the numbers."

"Hence, the need to spread slavery to the west and make more slave states," Adams mumbled. "But that isn't going to happen."

"Not if Lincoln is elected."

Adams met his eyes. "And with their fear of abolition…"

John Thomas's eyes drifted across the room to where his wife was still reading, absorbed, a slight smile lifting her lips. A smiled tugged at his own, until the sinking feeling returned.

"Does she know?"

"The seriousness? Yes." She had known since they had attended the lecture.

"What would Frederick do? I mean, should South Carolina try to secede?"

John Thomas looked at him. "Frederick..." Why had he never thought in those terms? "He would lead the rally with the loudest voice of them all."

"But he is a man of sense. He loves this country—"

"Yes," John Thomas answered lowly, feeling a bit guilty. "But South Carolina first. Always first." His voice had lowered to a near whisper on the end.

Adams studied him, his eyes unusually focused. He glanced at Shannon and back. "Does she feel that way, too?" John Thomas flushed, his heart rate accelerating. He looked her way again, seeing her slipper poking from beneath her skirt, her eyes flying over the words. He couldn't seem to think for the blood rushing in his ears. Adams was shaking his head. "Forgive me. Such a thing to ask. It is between you and she."

Slowly, the rushing ceased, and his thoughts returned. He looked at his brother, smiled, and said, "I'll keep you apprised if I hear any news. Diversify Father's funds, will you?"

Chapter Thirty-One

Shannon, sitting at her vanity, looked at her reflection in the mirror. She had done so often in the days of her coming out and up until she had married, the need for perfection and beauty like a weight around her neck. She hadn't thought about it so very much recently, at least since they had been to Massachusetts. But looking at herself now, she realized she had lost a little weight and was still a bit pale. Her blonde eyebrows and lashes even appeared lighter.

She rose and emerged from the chamber, closing the door and going off to look for John Thomas. She knew he had the day at home, but he generally rose early even when he did. She found him in the study, sitting in a chair next to a table. His bread and fruit sat untouched, even though they were Southern biscuits, which Shannon had discussed with the cook. A book was in his hands, and he was entirely absorbed. She smiled, watching him, his eyes touching the words, the pages turning at regular intervals.

Her skirts made a noise as she took a step, and he looked up. He smiled at her. "You look lovely," he said warmly.

"Thank you," she answered, going to him and perching on the arm of his chair, looking down at the book.

"Is this a new dress? You look very fine."

She laughed. "No, merely one you haven't seen. Fair colors for the summer, you see, and nothing but the purest wool for Massachusetts."

He laughed lazily, leaning up to kiss her lips. Her hand came up briefly to touch his cheek, and she saw tenderness in his eyes as he pulled away, his face nearby. He had been less reserved about little displays of affection since her illness, and she supposed she had responded in kind. In any event, it seemed to give him pleasure.

He fingered the fabric of her sleeve. "Would you like to invite Frederick and Marie to stay with us? I don't know—would she be able to travel?"

Her eyes lit. "Oh, what a marvelous idea! I had not—but yes, I do not think it would harm her. I believe she may have been hinting at it, now I think on it. And it is summer, so Frederick could have no objection over the plantation."

"We'll send a letter. Perhaps for July? I should like to have you to myself a while longer."

She flushed, looking down. After a moment, he nudged her chin up until she was meeting his quietly smiling eyes. "Why did that embarrass you?"

She met his smile. "I can't think!"

"Just as though you had not brought dozens of men to your feet!" he said, eyes twinkling.

She laughed. "Yes, indeed, you would think… But I suppose I am still a blushing bride."

His eyes crinkled at the corners, and he reached to stroke her hair from her temple. "Come, let's find your breakfast: I want you blooming with health by August at the very latest."

"Yes, Lieutenant."

Their townhouse was rather ancient in the ways of modernity, but John Thomas had ordered a bell to be installed in their bedchamber for her while she recovered at Harmony Grove. Shannon pulled it now, summoning Phoebe.

Her maid arrived in two minutes, bringing Shannon's carefully pressed ice blue day gown with pagoda sleeves, which would be becoming at the breakfast she was attending. It was at the home of Mrs. Phillips, a leading matron of Washington society whose husband had been a senator for many years. She had a fancy to have Shannon in her home since she had met John Thomas at a dinner and learned who his wife was.

"Thank you," Shannon said as Phoebe finished her hair and handed her gloves to her. "I suppose I shall walk."

"Oh, ma'am, it's so hot."

"Very well, you may send for a carriage, then," she said.

She was stepping into the carriage ten minutes later, and she travelled down their street to nearby Second Street, where many wealthy politicians lived. And so it was that she found herself in a blue drawing room surrounded by elegant ladies who alternately talked, fanned themselves, and ate.

"Where in South Carolina is your home, my dear?" Mrs. Anderson asked, dipping her strawberry in cream.

Shannon, sitting about halfway down Mrs. Phillips' table, answered, "In Charleston, and at my family's plantation, Santarella, in the Sea Islands."

"Santarella!" Mrs. Phillips said. "How that does roll off the tongue!" She tucked some of her fading blonde hair beneath her lace cap. The ladies agreed in murmurs. "You may not know that I myself am from South Carolina, Mrs. Haley. Not the Lowcountry, of course. But I have heard of your family."

Shannon's eyes brightened. "Indeed, ma'am? I thought you haled from Delaware!"

"Mr. Phillips does—I suppose we both do now and have for the past twenty years. But yes, I remember it all so well."

Later, they adjourned to the sunny parlor which boasted bay windows. Shannon, sitting in a window seat, was looking out at Capitol Hill when an elegant lady in her late forties approached and joined her. Shannon knew her to be Mrs. Greenhow, a renowned Washington socialite who had been taken under Dolley Madison's wing in her youth and ushered into the very heart of power. She was a widow with four daughters and connections to nearly every founding family in the nation. "You are pensive, Mrs. Haley," she said softly. She was pretty, her eyes sharp and knowing.

"I suppose I am," Shannon answered, noticing that she was drawing envious stares.

"My oldest daughter, Florence, is married to a military man. They live in Ohio."

"Indeed?"

"Yes. I gather it is a lonely life."

Shannon's lips parted. She said, after a hesitation, "Do you hail from Washington, Mrs. Greenhow?"

"From Maryland, though Maryland seems a lifetime away now."

"Your husband brought you to Washington, then?"

She shook her head. "My aunt." She said no more and changed the subject, inviting Shannon to her house for tea the next day, which would ensure Shannon's place in society. For one brief moment, Shannon considered declining, almost having enjoyed the obscurity of her life in Massachusetts. But she was in Massachusetts no longer.

The invitation to Frederick and Marie was sent and accepted, both assuring Shannon and John Thomas of their delight in the idea. Shannon made plans with Mrs. Hensley for their arrival on the twelfth of July and went to stand in the spare bedchamber and look around. It was large and furnished with good furniture, but it was rather sparse, and she wanted Marie to be perfectly comfortable and at home.

This led to a meeting in the dining room with the draper. When the precise bed hangings and curtains could not be found in his catalogue, Shannon dictated, and his hand worked rapidly on a pattern. She also sallied forth to a furniture maker, Phoebe a step behind her, and ordered a little writing table and a bed stool.

"Can you think of anything else, Phoebe?" she asked as they walked down the walkway along the street. "We must order it now if we wish to have it ready by the time of their arrival." She fanned herself when a gust of wind brought a dry heat upon them.

"Well, yes, ma'am. We'll need a cot for Mrs. Ravenel's maid."

"Oh, yes! And Mr. Frederick is bringing his valet. I shall send the order tomorrow. Do you think I have bankrupted Lieutenant Haley this morning?"

Phoebe considered this, too, even though Shannon had meant it jokingly. "Things will be tight, ma'am, I think, until he's been here a while."

Shannon blinked. "Oh, dear. Yes, I hadn't thought."

"I don't think he'd want to deny you anything, ma'am."

Shannon looked toward the Capitol, near where the Naval Headquarters were. "That is why I must be careful, Phoebe. Come, I must be ready by seven o'clock for that silly dinner I agreed to attend."

It was eleven o'clock by the time Shannon was finally let down in front of her own house, and she was fatigued, tired of her corset and her shoes, and dreading the conversation to come. But perhaps John Thomas would have gone to bed already. The door opened, and Saul opened the door for her. "There's a candle there for you, ma'am," he said.

Shannon glanced at it and then felt her hopes dash as she saw a warm glow coming from the door of the study. She sighed, declining the candle and walking that way. She paused in the door, seeing him sitting there, head bent over his writing, hair golden in the candlelight.

She watched him for a moment and then said, "I thought you might be in bed."

He looked up. After a moment, he said, "I wanted to make sure you returned safely."

She stepped into the room, conscious of her elegant green skirt as she navigated the furniture. "I'm sorry it was so late."

He lifted a shoulder, looking at her. "It makes no difference. Did you enjoy yourself?"

"Oh...I suppose." She pressed her lips together. After a long moment, she said, "John Thomas, I must tell you that I have spent a great deal of money today."

Surprise flickered. "Have you? You needed some things for the house, I daresay."

Her shoulders eased. "Yes. I did."

He smiled and started to go back to his writing. "It makes no difference, Shannon."

She swallowed, letting the silence draw out. He seemed concentrated on his work. "John Thomas..."

He looked up, and, after coming to himself, looked penitent, setting his books aside. "Forgive me. Yes?"

"Suppose I should want a dress..."

"Purchase the dress," he said. His brows drew together. "I should've thought... What do other husbands do—pin money?"

She nodded. "My father gives my mother a quarterly allowance." He started to nod, and she said, "And she pays no mind to it at all." He smiled, and she met it. "Do you mean that I may buy what I choose?"

"Yes. Well, within reason."

"What do you consider within reason?" she asked.

"Shannon, I don't like talking money with you," he said.

She smiled. "I know. But I must have some idea. My father once tallied my wardrobe expenses in a year for my edification." She paused a beat, suddenly thinking of his family, and wondering if he would think less of her. "It came to nearly five-thousand dollars."

His lips parted slightly, and he merely continued to look up at her, frozen. After a moment, he almost whispered, "I won't earn that in three years, Shannon."

"That is why I asked," she said, shoulders again tense.

There was a very long silence. He looked away, running a hand through his hair. He looked at the bookshelves, but he didn't appear to be seeing anything.

"What?" she asked softly, finally.

"This is what your father meant, I suppose."

"What do you mean?"

"Shannon, I cannot support you in such a lifestyle. I had no idea..." He seemed dazed.

Shannon put her hand on the back of a chair, gripping it. "If you had taken a wife from Weymouth, she would not shock you thus, I suppose."

He looked up suddenly and, seeing her paleness and the fragility in her eyes, came to his feet. "No, that wasn't what I meant!" He searched her rapidly and finally came toward her.

Shannon looked away.

He lifted his hand to touch her forearm. "It must have been naivete that kept me from realizing the vast gulf between us. Or perhaps willful blindness because I wanted you so much." He dragged a hand through his hair. "It isn't only the money, but an entire way of life. I have cut you off from it through selfish stupidity. I..." He looked away.

She looked at him, moistening her lips. "Yes?" she asked breathlessly.

"I cannot bear the thought of not providing for you as you were meant to be."

"It is a little late to be rid of me, I am afraid. I don't suppose anyone else would have me at this late date."

His face drained of all color. He whispered, "Shannon... Don't speak of such things."

"Well, do not speak to me of your regret if you do not wish me to misconstrue your words," she snapped.

"You *know* what I meant."

"Yes." She pressed her lips together. After a long silence, the clock ticking off fourteen seconds, she said evenly, "And you insult me." She stepped away from him. "You do me such an injustice. Am I not wise enough to know what I want? Do you know how many men richer than my father proposed to me? And I said no every time. Do you have any idea how many times my mother and father arranged a marriage for me with such a man? And I, without fail, said no. And then you came." She swallowed, feeling as though she were baring her soul. Her eyes burned. "And I knew the man I wanted to marry. And not to spite my parents, or because you were handsome, or because I was lonely, and it was romantic. Simply because I saw you and thought: yes. Him." She took another deep breath. His face was twisted, and his hand reached out, but she turned and went quietly from the room.

Shannon lay in bed hours later, sleep far from her, wondering whether John Thomas would come to bed, and thinking on Lizzie's words.

It was becoming plainer by day that Shannon's éclat had spilled over from Charleston. She had known the ease with which she had been accepted into Washington society had disturbed her husband, and she wondered to what extent that weighed with him tonight. She did not think he liked such society or the fact that she was a product of it, even if he said tonight that he didn't wish to keep her from it.

She was known as the Rice King's Daughter, and the knocker on her door was never left alone. Among her callers were highly regarded matrons, who were wives of dignitaries, and young matrons who had begun to copy her fashions with swift readiness. There were friends of her husband who were charming, missing their mothers and sweethearts and entirely inoffensive, and other, less harmless gentlemen admirers.

Her head had not been turned, but he might think it had. He had opened his lips once, she thought, to speak on the subject, but something in her posture must have held him back.

He never did come to bed, and he was gone by the time she awoke to a sunny morning, her eyes flitting open reluctantly, for she had not slept well. And then she caught sight of something on John Thomas's pillow and sat up slowly, reaching for it. It was paper, folded in the shape of a bird.

Frowning, she unfolded it and saw words written in his hand.

'Tis not to make me jealous
to say my wife is fair, feeds well, loves company,
Is free of speech, sings, plays, and dances.
Where virtue is, these are more virtuous.
Nor from mine own weak merits will I draw
The smallest fear or doubt of her revolt,
For she had eyes and chose me.

Shannon wiped moisture from her eyes. *Othello*. A sweet smile touched her lips, and she took the paper in her hand, getting up and trying to think of somewhere to keep it where the servants would not throw it away. She opened her armoire and, seeing her valise in the bottom, tucked it away there.

She dressed and went about her day, going to watch Congressional debates with the wife of another officer and leaving for a drive in the park during the promenade hour.

Then she dined on supper alone and was sitting in the parlor, knitting for reasons she did not know, when she looked up and saw him standing in the door. He looked anxious and tentative. She was still for a moment and then smiled very slightly, and that seemed to give him courage.

He walked forward and, before she knew it, was kneeling at her feet and taking her hands. "It was the same for me," he said, looking up at her emotionally. She cast her mind back, and, when she realized to what he was referring, she smiled softly. He kissed her hands, lingering there for a moment before looking up. "You do know how dearly I love you."

"I know," she said gently.

"I didn't doubt you. It is only pride and fear," he said, his look an apology.

"You think that I am above you," she said.

"I know that you are." She shook her head, but he shook his, too, smiling. "It is true. When we attend parties, people think: what on earth was she thinking?"

She laughed. "That is not true. You are already making a name for yourself, as I knew you would in anything you undertake, or ever will undertake."

"You will always be above me, even should I be president."

"I am above you in this chair. I rather fancy it," she said flippantly.

He rose slowly and sat next to her, casually drawing her into his lap, to her laughter, and stealing a kiss. "Are you afraid of me?" she asked between kisses.

"Yes, of *course* I'm afraid of you," he responded, kissing her until neither remembered his or her name, much less any argument.

Chapter Thirty-Two

Smoke filled the air, and the train gave a final whistle. Shannon stood next to John Thomas, her arm tucked in his. He looked down at her. She was beautiful in a green walking gown. He covered her gloved hand, pride filling him. She looked up at him. "Do you suppose they are in this car?"

He smiled. "I have no idea."

"Well, it is taking an enormous amount of time. They will be very warm."

"I suppose that is why the windows are open."

"Do not try to put a damper on my wrath. I shall be wrathful if I choose."

He smiled down at her.

After what seemed a lifetime, passengers began making their way down, making her tighten her hand on his arm and tip up on her toes. About halfway through them, Frederick emerged, followed by Marie.

"I do not think they see us," Shannon said, "and indeed, how could they in this chaos?"

John Thomas, one of the taller men, waved, but they seemed to be swallowed up. Then, much against his inclination, he whistled and called, "Ravenel!"

That did the trick, both smiling as they caught sight of them. They began to walk toward them. Marie wore a blue travelling gown which bespoke their wealth, and Frederick wore a blue coat and a patterned waistcoat, his hair neat, for once, beneath his hat. Although the general din made it almost impossible to hear one another, the women gave exclamations of joy, and John Thomas and Frederick shook hands and embraced alternately.

"Such a place you have chosen to live, Haley!" Frederick exclaimed. "We were lucky to escape with our lives!"

"You ought to leave Santarella occasionally!"

"I think it is beautiful!" Marie said, eyes shining. She took Shannon's hands, adding, "And you! How very smart the two of you look!"

Shannon tried to say something, but it was swallowed up in the air.

"Let's get the ladies off of the platform, Frederick," John Thomas suggested, putting a protective hand at Shannon's back as they pushed their way through the crowd.

They persisted, no small amount of maneuvering required, and the ladies were handed into the carriage, Shannon and John Thomas taking the forward seat. "Thank heavens!" Shannon said, sitting close to him. "I have no notion how to shout!"

John Thomas looked down at her, eyes twinkling. "Don't you?"

The others laughed, and Shannon gave him a scathing look. He brought their hands onto his leg, squeezing hers.

"Shannon, how well you look!" Marie said, eyes bright, glancing briefly at their hands. "Are you quite recovered, then?"

"Of course she is," Frederick said. "It was only ever her dramatics." He smiled winningly, and Shannon's chest ached with missing him.

"Oh, Frederick, do not tease her about such a thing, especially not in front of John Thomas!"

"Why not?" John Thomas said. "I agree completely!"

"Marie, do you happen to know of a decent burial ground in Washington?" Shannon inquired, making her cousin laugh.

"We shall never stay ahead of them, now they are together," Marie commiserated.

Shannon kept an eye on Marie since it was so warm, and indeed, she was quite flushed. She soon realized Frederick was doing the same, which pleased her. He was still watching her when they reached home and, after proper exclamations on the size, location, and quaintness of the house, Frederick said quietly to Marie, "You ought to go up and rest before supper."

Marie touched his arm. "I am quite well."

He was looking uncertain, and Shannon said, "Of course you shall rest. Come, I wish to show you the upstairs, in any event."

"Very well, if you insist," Marie answered in her calm manner. She started up the stairs, and Shannon began to follow her.

Frederick caught her arm, and she turned back. He studied her for a moment, his eyes unusually gentle and earnest. "We were so very relieved to hear of your recovery, Shannon."

She covered his hand, surprised, but touched. "Thank you, brother-mine. And thank you for holding Mother and Papa off from coming to Massachusetts."

"John Thomas told me how much you didn't want it. I supposed it was the least I could do."

She pressed his hand and started up the stairs. She showed Marie the critical points and then took her into the guest chamber. Looking at her, she saw evidence of fullness beneath her skirts and noticed that she was generally plumper. "You look very well," Shannon said.

Marie flushed, apparently embarrassed, and said, "Oh, I wouldn't say that. Certainly, I have looked better. But you never have. John Thomas must have been taking very good care of you to nurse you back to health so soon."

"Yes, he is relentless. I feel for his men, should he ever captain a ship. Let me help you undress; it may be a little while before your servants and baggage arrive."

"All right," she said, turning, and Shannon started to unfasten her buttons.

"Are you quite exhausted?"

"Only a little tired."

She lay Marie's dress aside and said, "Come now, into bed."

"No, Shannon," she said calmly, as Shannon tucked her own dressing gown over Marie's undergarments, though it didn't quite meet. "I shall lie down in due time but not when I am told, like a child. I want to talk to you."

Shannon smiled. "Very well, but I shall very likely tell Frederick, and then you *shall* be in disgrace."

Marie smiled, retaining her hand. Shannon led her to the bench by the window, and Marie's eyes scanned her face. "Shannon, this is a lovely house. And it is truly yours, and your husband's." Her eyes flitted away. She looked out the window and then back. There was a slight silence. She smiled. "John Thomas is still very attentive."

Shannon smiled. "He is a complete gentleman. But l do not wish to talk about me. Marie, I can scarcely believe you and Frederick are to be parents," she said softly, smiling.

Marie smiled. "Neither can I, sometimes."

"Is Frederick pleased?"

"Yes."

Shannon squeezed her hand. "Does he want a son?"

"I suppose so," Marie said.

"All men want a son, don't they?"

"Yes, I suppose so," she answered, studying Shannon, looking as though she wished to say something. But Shannon looked away, saying merrily, "I suppose my mother and father are pleased."

"Yes, very pleased," Marie said softly, studying her with hesitation in her demeanor.

Shannon paused for a moment. "Papa will have joined Mother at Ravenel House now, I believe."

"Yes, and they are well, though the talk is all of this political battle." Marie searched her face. "Shannon, does John Thomas ever speak of it?"

She hesitated. "Yes. But we...try *not* to speak of it as much as we can."

Marie studied her gravely. "You...disagree, then?"

Shannon flushed. "He is an abolitionist, Marie. My father is one of the largest slaveholders in South Carolina."

"I'm sorry," Marie said penitently, pressing her hand. "It is not my concern. Only I...sometimes think about your position, should there be war."

Shannon swallowed. It didn't bear thinking of. She attempted a smile. "Well. John Thomas puts a great deal of stock into his precious Mr. Lincoln."

Marie paled. "Oh, good heavens. I ought to warn Frederick not to bring it up. He despises him so. I hadn't realized..."

"That my husband was indeed an abolitionist? Yes, I seemed to have suffered from the same misimpression. He set me to rights on that point, however."

Marie was not blinded by her flippant, worldly tone. She took her hand. "Shannon, you mustn't let it come between you," she said urgently.

"It seems almost impossible to believe sometimes that I am married to precisely the sort of man all of our neighbors would scorn and ridicule." She swallowed. "That I myself once did."

"Shannon, you *must* learn that we can disagree, even on the material things, and maintain our respect. It is the very core of humanity."

"Tell that to the Congress."

Marie's brows drew together. "You mustn't speak so. Why, Shannon, he loves you to distraction."

Tears rose to Shannon's eyes. She moistened her lips and then closed them, sitting silently for a time. "You make me feel like a spoiled child. I can't think what overcame me, only I...

It has been so long since I have been able to voice such things or my own beliefs…"

Marie looked at her sympathetically. "John Thomas does not tell you not to speak your beliefs?"

"No, but I cannot." She swallowed. "Sometimes I felt, in Massachusetts, such a traitor. Carrying on at their supper table when any proper Southerner would've walked out in outrage. And if they knew how John Thomas truly felt—my family, I mean…"

Marie studied her for a long time, finally saying, "But you have not been unhappy?"

Shannon was silent for a moment, her blue eyes tragic. "He… He makes be so happy, Marie. He is so gentle and kind… My best and dearest friend."

"Oh, my dearest," Marie said, embracing her. "Such torment you have been in. Indeed, he is a good man, and you must never forget it." She held her for a long moment before Shannon finally pulled away, discreetly wiping her eyes. "I…didn't ask about your mother and father," she said. "I suppose they are well?"

Marie, taking her cue, knew that conversation was at an end, and said with a sigh, "Yes. They want to wrap me in wool, my mother and grandmother. They were discussing all of the merits and disadvantages of my travelling here, as though they had any say, until I was forced to tell them that Frederick was my husband, and if he had no objection, that was an end to the matter."

Shannon's eyes lit. "Marie! Well, done, Cousin! Well done, indeed." She sobered. "But it hasn't done you any harm, has it?"

"No, I am quite well."

Shannon pressed her hand. "Have you decided it between you whether my niece or nephew will be Catholic?"

"Frederick...does not want it," she said, nodding. "And I...will be guided by him. He must be the master of his household."

"Marie!" Shannon exclaimed. "But it means so much to you!"

"Yes. But I won't defy him in this, Shannon. This is something I feel strongly, too."

Shannon was inclined to argue, but, seeing the stubborn set to her cousin's chin, something she knew very well from childhood, she decided against it.

She turned the subject and asked whether Seymour Christian had yet chosen a bride.

"No, indeed, I believe he mourns you most sincerely," Marie answered.

"I trust he will overcome it yet," Shannon returned heartlessly, making her cousin laugh.

After a time, though, her smile fell, and she studied Shannon. "Shannon...we were so worried, all of us, that when you were ill... That is, John Thomas's tone was so grave that we feared... But, of course, he would not say so in a letter, and..."

Shannon studied her before realization dawned. "Oh," she said, numbly. "No. I..." She looked away. "His tone was distracted because...I nearly died. We...agreed not to say so in the letters because it would do no good and only cause all of you pain. But there was a time when they did not know..."

Marie's eyes welled with tears. "Oh, Shannon!" she whispered.

Shannon pressed her hand. "And the Haleys...they were so wonderful..."

Marie beamed. "I am so glad to hear it. I am sure they could not help but love you."

Shannon smiled wryly and hesitated before saying very quietly, "It would seem…" She swallowed, uncertain she wished to delve into those depths. "That is, I have been married long enough that by now I…"

Marie pressed her lips together. "Dearest," she said softly, looking stricken.

She shook her head, standing. "Forgive me. I hadn't meant to speak of such things. There, sleep well. I will see you at supper." And then she fled.

Chapter Thirty-Three

S hannon had barely closed Marie's door when she was met by Frederick in the hall, his brows drawn together. "Is something the matter? Why were you with her so long?"

Shannon, setting aside her disordered spirit, said, "You are becoming a mother hen!"

"What?" He shook his head, as though clearing it of her remark. "Answer my question."

"She is quite well and resting now, Your Serene Highness. We were talking of home. May I not speak with my cousin if I choose?"

He sighed. "Yes. I don't know how Haley bears with you, truly I don't."

Shannon smiled, tucking her hand through his arm and leading him toward the stairs. "You have always had excessively poor taste, except in choosing Marie. There, I shall forget the note of truth in your voice and take you to my husband, who shall pour you some wine."

He glanced once more over his shoulder and then allowed himself to be led. John Thomas, sitting at the desk in the study, smiled at them as they entered, extending his hand toward Shannon. She gave hers, and he kissed her fingers, saying, "You do not favor very much, you know, to my eternal joy."

Shannon smiled, and Frederick, sitting down and looking disgusted by this display, said "Stow it, and pour me this wine I was promised."

"Did Shannon promise you that? Oh, but I have banned alcohol, in all of its forms, from this house." Frederick's eyes widened as he studied his friend, and he paled slightly just before John Thomas started smiling.

"*Much* too gullible," Shannon said.

"Oh, to the devil with you!" Frederick exclaimed, blushing slightly, which made John Thomas laugh.

"Much too easy to believe, I should say," John Thomas said, getting up and pulling a decanter from a cabinet.

"No, no, I don't think you're a prude," Frederick rushed to assure him. "That was Shannon!"

"This is excellent news," he said, uncorking the bottle and pouring.

Shannon shot her brother a heated look and said, "It is untrue! When have I ever said such a thing? When?"

"I can't recall," Frederick said, feeling closed in. "Perhaps... Yes, it must have been when he very first came to Santarella— before...before you knew him, of course!"

"Indeed?" John Thomas said, handing Shannon her glass first.

"No! Take it back!" she demanded hotly. "*You* said he swam

the Thames when you were both drunk—"

"*I* was not drunk," John Thomas protested mildly, apparently following the thread.

"—just after I asked what a Congregationalist was, and you said you couldn't work it out but that he was not a stick."

"Didn't you know?" John Thomas asked her with mild interest, handing Frederick his glass.

"No, and of all of the most abominable things in the world, I despise, and loathe, and spurn a snitch!"

"A snitch!" her brother demanded.

"Yes, especially an *untruthful* one!"

"I question the advisability," John Thomas said philosophically, resuming his seat, "of having a house full of Ravenels. It makes me almost glad I shall have to leave you to work."

"Well, perhaps Shannon didn't say that. I don't remember," Frederick said, shifting uncomfortably. "There, don't eat me! And John, you won't be angry with her, will you?"

"I am fuming. The situation is past repair."

Frederick smiled. "There. I knew he would not take offense, Shannon."

"Through no fault of your own!"

"No. You haven't the ability to anger him, I think," Frederick said, sipping his wine.

Shannon started for the door, smiling over her shoulder at John Thomas. "Don't I?" she asked her husband.

He flushed, and she laughed. "I thought not. I regularly enrage him, Frederick, if only you could believe it."

"Well, I don't believe it. John Thomas is never angry."

Shannon tossed her husband another arch look, and he

appeared at a loss for words, sending her a slightly penitent look. "Indeed," she said, laughing and departing.

"What was that?" Frederick demanded as soon as the door had closed, leaning forward to look at the door with brows drawn. "If I've caused an argument between you, I'll leave this instant!"

John Thomas leaned against the desk, crossing his arms and holding his glass in one hand. "Of course you have not. Shannon was only teasing me."

"I know, but you would not lie and say she never makes you angry. I'm shocked, Haley. I thought you had her firmly on a golden pedestal."

John Thomas looked at his wine. "That wouldn't be fair to Shannon. I try not to do that, though I grant you, it is difficult sometimes."

"*I* didn't say keeping her off a pedestal would be difficult: don't accuse *me* of such a thing."

John Thomas smiled. "I know you'd knock out the teeth of anyone less devoted to her who said she was less than perfect."

Frederick grinned, sitting back. "Well, that's true, I suppose. How is the old girl?"

"Frederick, I am going to have to knock *your* teeth out!"

Shannon's brother laughed. "All right, how is my dear sister?" His features sobered as he looked up at him. "We were so worried."

"You have nothing to fear now. She's fully restored. I wouldn't let her go out to parties if I thought differently."

"Taking Washington by storm, is she?"

John Thomas set his glass aside, getting up. "Indeed." He

said no more, causing Frederick to take a second look at him. "Come, would you like to see our defenses on the Potomac? I'll ask Shannon, but I think we have time before we dine."

"By Jove, *yes!*" Frederick said enthusiastically.

John Thomas smiled. "You shan't abandon Santarella and join, will you? I can't afford to have your father as my enemy."

"No, that is behind me now. But, my God, I still love ships!"

Shannon had already been asleep when John Thomas came to bed, he having lingered, talking with Frederick until late in the night. They usually attended the Trinity Congregationalist Church, and morning dawned on a pretty Sunday, but they had agreed before their guests arrived not to attend since the travelers would need rest.

She rose while the house was still quiet and went down to the kitchen to talk to the cook and Mrs. Hensley about breakfast, before overseeing its placement on the board in the dining room. The meal consisted primarily of cold cuts, fruit, and bread, so it would keep.

That finished, she went to stand at the window, looking out onto the street. The occasional carriage trotted sedately past, carrying women in bonnets and men in ironed shirts, bound for their various houses of worship. She crossed her arms, staring into nothingness, thinking on her conversation with Marie and her increasingly conflicting emotions about John Thomas's politics. She felt such a traitor to her home and family by not arguing with him when he attended abolitionist meetings or donated money to such causes. And yet, she had felt such a traitor to *him* yesterday, talking to Marie, that she had avoided him; it had been easy enough to do so with guests in the house. Guilt consumed her again as she pictured him sleeping above stairs, innocent of the knowledge that she had betrayed their bond in her unguarded language. He would never do so to her.

She looked out the window close to thirty minutes before she heard a stirring at the doorway. She recognized his walk and looked over her shoulder. He smiled gently at her. "You are awake early," he said.

"Yes. And you slept into the morning." He smiled in that gentle, distracted way. She said softly, "I'm glad you did. Sometimes I think you never sleep."

"You look beautiful," he said, eyes soaking in her features.

"I shall not dispute the statement," she answered, "though I question whether you were listening to me."

"I always listen to you." She could not deny the truth of the statement. Guilt consumed her, and affection surged. She closed the slight distance between them, touched his jaw, and turned his head to kiss him, which caused him utterly to lose his senses. He kissed her, his touch gentle and reverent. She would have enjoyed it merely because it was him, but he had always had a way with such matters. He drew her against him slowly, hands moving from her waist to her hips as her hands slowly moved up his chest. Shannon heard a noise, which gradually entered her consciousness, and she broke away.

At the doorway stood Frederick and Marie, both averting their eyes.

Shannon flushed, clearing her throat, reaching up self-consciously to touch a loose curl. There was the faintest tinge of color at John Thomas's cheekbones.

Marie cleared her throat, saying, eyes twinkling slightly, "Something smelled so delightful that we were drawn from our chamber. It must be the bread, I think. Shannon, does it have blueberries in it?"

Shannon cleared her throat, moving forward to the sideboard, her skirts rustling. "Yes, indeed. I shall send the recipe home with you. It is Mrs. Haley's."

"How delightful!" she said, asking about New England breads, while Frederick continued to look flustered. John Thomas could not quite meet his eyes yet. He received his plate to fill from Shannon, giving her an apologetic smile.

John Thomas said to Marie once they were seated, "Is there anything in particular you would like to do today? We are at your service."

"I should dearly love to go rowing on the Potomac," she answered, smiling, in perfect harmony with him.

"It will be too hot for that, I think," Frederick said, looking at her.

"I shall be all right," she said softly.

"I'm afraid I will have to agree," Shannon said. "A handsome lieutenant rowed me last week, and I thought I should perish, to say nothing of him." A smile touched John Thomas's lips.

"Indeed?" Marie asked.

"Yes," John Thomas answered. "Unless it rains this morning. Then it might be cool enough this evening, although the waters might be choppy."

It did indeed rain, which led to a series of merry parlor games, some fierce competition between brother and sister, and the development that being raised in a houseful of children gave Lieutenant Haley the upper hand in most every game.

"Oh, I cry foul!" Shannon said, leaning back in her chair when he once again soundly triumphed. "And he comes from such a quiet household!"

He smiled, collecting the jackstraws, and Marie said, "Were you the best of your brothers and sisters, John Thomas?"

"Charles and I could always beat poor Adams, and Patience was very good, too. We taught all of the younger ones to play, and Miriam was soon beating all of us."

"Miriam! Yes, of course!" Shannon said, laughing. She turned her head to Marie, who was sitting on the sofa. "She is the sharpest little minx! And she will be quite beautiful, too, when she is grown."

"She haunted Shannon's every step while we were in Massachusetts," John Thomas said. "I daresay she has now copied every style she ever wore."

Shannon said, eyes downcast, "Not every style, I hope."

When she looked up, John Thomas was giving her a look, his jaw hard, eyes narrowly focused. She flushed, hoping her guests hadn't caught the note of challenge in her voice.

"But Boston must be a very fashionable society, I have always thought," Marie said, apparently unaware, turning the conversation in that direction.

When the afternoon came, the rains cleared away, and the men rode out to judge the safety of the river. When they returned, the ladies were waiting in the foyer, dressed in light-colored day gowns, Marie's with a tiny floral print and Shannon's a soft blue. Straw bonnets sat atop their hair, one a deep auburn, the other a fiery rust.

Shannon could feel John Thomas looking at her, but she did not meet his eyes, nor did she do so when she and Marie were sitting together on one of the carriage benches.

When they made it to one of the boats for hire, John Thomas paid its caretaker, and the men climbed aboard. "I shall go first," Shannon said. "Better I fall than Marie, if it is unsteady."

"You shan't fall," John Thomas said softly, reaching for her hands. Shannon crossed onto the boat, glad she hadn't worn her hoops. She felt him studying her as he held her hands for her to steady herself, but she still did not look up. When he released her, he helped Marie aboard while Frederick steadied the craft, and soon the ladies were seated together, allowing themselves to be rowed, although there wasn't much of that involved since they were floating with the current. Marie gripped Shannon's hand in a little fear at first, but she soon began to enjoy herself, her hand coming to rest without knowing against her middle. Shannon studied her for a moment, and then, moistening her lips, redirected her attention to the gentlemen.

They were very handsome as they rowed, both in blue coats and tan trousers, John Thomas with a plain necktie, Frederick with a patterned one. Each had removed their brown bowlers and placed them on the seat beside them. "You shall not offend our sensibilities if you wish to remove your coats," Shannon said. "It must be very warm for you."

Frederick needed no further encouragement, and after a hesitation, John Thomas removed his as well. They floated along peacefully, waving at another party out for a leisurely Sunday. Frederick exclaimed, looking at the wide river and green embankments, "It is magnificent!"

John Thomas said, nodding to the east, "Look there."

They turned their attention that way to see a beautiful Greek Revival manor, where children in pastels were playing on the lawn. "There must be ten of them!" Marie exclaimed.

John Thomas laughed. "The words of any passersby at Harmony Grove once upon a time."

They all laughed, Marie saying, "I envy you. If I hadn't had Frederick and Shannon, I should've been so lonely."

Frederick smiled at her, while Shannon said, "Yes, and you had that little Negro girl as your companion. What became of her?"

"Sarah." She looked across the river. "She was sold. My mother...did not like her."

Shannon sat, startled, and a silence descended. No more was said on the subject.

They found a likely embankment, where they, some three miles away from their beginning point, tied off and got out to picnic. Shannon and John Thomas spread the blanket. She felt his gaze again, but she kept her eyes on her tasks, first anchoring the blanket and then removing the food from the basket.

They dined with little speech until their hunger was sated, and then Marie and Frederick got up to walk toward the river, hoping to espy some of the mansions through the trees.

John Thomas was leaning back on his hands, his fingers close to hers on the blanket since she was doing the same to accommodate her corset. He looked at her, his eyes gentle and pinched at the corners. "I'm sorry," he said softly. "I thought you were referring to… But you could not have been if I hurt you so."

Shannon pressed her lips together, staring at the stripe down the side of his trousers, toying with the idea of allowing him to believe he had been mistaken. No profit could come of disillusioning him, for it was as though some demon had possessed her to make her say such a thing anyway. She felt him touch her chin gently and lift her face up. He subjected her to a searching look, and she met his eyes. "You weren't mistaken," she said quietly.

He studied her for a moment as though he did not at first grasp her meaning. Then he did, and he didn't speak, his fair brows drawing together. She swallowed, looking away.

"Why?" he asked very quietly after a time, looking into the distance. "I thought it was behind us."

She moistened her lips and looked away, toward the river. "I sometimes think you don't know me at all, John Thomas."

He touched her face gently and brought it back toward him, his forehead wrinkling. She was startled at the pain in his eyes. "That is…a terrible thing for any husband to hear. Have I been so obtuse?"

She swallowed, her throat burning, tears threatening. "Do you know, John Thomas, I don't know why I said what I did," she said, an edge to her voice. "I suppose you never knew that I am spoiled, and petty, and that I… I quarrel for reasons even I do not understand—"

His face had been growing more aggrieved during this speech, and he interrupted, "I know your soul, Shannon. I see…"

He hesitated, emotion in his face. "I... Forgive me, but yes, I see all of those things. But I see more, my darling love, and I'm not sure there is anything you can say to convince me otherwise. I see a sweet spirit and a gentle soul, and I won't pretend to understand you, but I am in love with all of you, and it's no use sitting there thinking I haven't already forgiven you, as I can see you're doing, for I have."

Her lips parted, and she let the silence draw out. Then she moistened her lips looked away, surreptitiously swiping at her eye. She glanced toward Frederick and Marie, glad to see they were still walking and talking.

She bit her lip and finally looked back, her blue eyes full, her expression penitent. "I am sorry, John Thomas!" she said softly. "I can't think what possessed me!"

His face softening, he reached for her hand, gripping it and kissing it. "Well, you could have let me believe I was mistaken."

She gave a difficult laugh, wiping at her eye again. "You wouldn't have believed me. But you would have swallowed it."

His brows lifted slightly, and a delighted smile entered his blue eyes. "Yes. That is precisely true." His eyes grew more serious, and he reached up, cradling her face, stroking the soft skin with his thumb. "You would tell me if something was troubling you."

Her lips parted slightly. "Oh, yes," she said. "Yes."

He sat back, letting some time pass. His fingers touched hers on the blanket, toying with them. She knew he was trying to make her smile, so she did. After some time had passed, the contention fading, she looked up at him. Tentatively, she reached to cover his hand. "It seems we have scarcely seen one another these past few days."

"I was just thinking the same." His brows drew together. "And I have an uneasy feeling that it is my fault."

"Merely the circumstances."

"Yes, but I happened to think last night, as I sat up with Frederick, 'Now, why am I here with this fellow when there is such a creature lying in my bed?' I assure you, I could think of no reason whatever."

Shannon flushed, smiling and averting her face. His thumb caressed hers, and she looked back at him. "How shall I redeem myself?" he asked with gentle amusement. "An increase in pin money? Some biscuits made by my mother's cook?"

She smiled, lips tucking at the corners, and said with an attempt at airiness, "I should like a new piece of jewelry. Something simple, mind you, and I wouldn't want you to spend above four-hundred dollars." He smiled, glancing toward the shore and then tilting her chin toward him for a quick, chaste kiss.

They settled back, watching Frederick and Marie as they stood at the shore. "Are they happy, do you think?" John Thomas asked softly.

Shannon let a few seconds pass. "They seem content, at peace."

John Thomas looked at her, and then back at them.

"I am glad to see Frederick so attentive to her," she said as he helped Marie over a rock. "I was rather afraid he would forget she is not merely his cousin."

"Do you forget it?"

"Yes," she confided, laughing. "It is so strange!"

"I thought it must be," he said. "I try to imagine Patience married to my cousin Oswald, and—"

"No, not *Oswald!*" she protested, making him smile. "Has Jonathan written to you? Is she well?"

"I am informed that he is too busy with his parish to write," he answered, smiling. "But yes, Lizzie tells me she is very well."

Shannon's eyes brightened as though remembering something, and she bit her lip.

"What?" he demanded.

She shook her head.

"You know something. Gossip, I imagine, but my interest is piqued."

She shook her head again, making one of the curls from her twist bob. "I shan't tell."

"Oh, won't you? Do you think I could not hurl you into the Potomac?"

"The words of a lover, indeed! I protest, there is no one like you New Englanders for romantic language—"

He laughed, interrupting her. "Shannon!"

"Oh, very well." She waited a moment for effect. "Lizzie has a beau."

His brows lifted instantly. He stared at her enquiringly.

"Well, not a beau, precisely," she conceded, "but Miriam writes me that she has allowed a Mr. Winthrop to call on her a few times and even consented to go driving with him in Boston."

His eyes widened. "Good heavens. Tell me about him. I am certain you can, if I know Miriam."

She laughed. "He is a little older than she, perhaps thirty-four, very handsome, a Brahmin—"

"Forgive me, what is a Brahmin?" he interrupted.

She sighed. "Do you read nothing Oliver Wendell Holmes writes?"

"I have been a little occupied," he explained.

"*You* are a Brahmin, my dear."

"Am I?"

"Yes. It is the very highest caste of Indian society, and he has used it to refer to a certain set of Bostonians. Descended from old families of England, highly moral, Harvard people, Protestant, the caretakers of society, exclusive, Unitarians or Congregationalists..." John Thomas began to flush.

He looked off into the distance peacefully, seemingly. "I have always been more comfortable in Weymouth than Boston. I don't think we were from an old family in England. Well, the Haleys might be, though they've never cared to know. Certainly, the Adamses were not."

"The Adamses were something else entirely. And you were to marry an heiress with strong family ties in that same set, Mr. Holmes tells me."

He smiled at her, his eyes warm. "Well. I married an heiress."

She smiled, but at length it faded. "I did not realize the pressure was as strong on your side," she said. "I wish I had. Perhaps it would've helped me to understand their feelings."

"There was no pressure at all. Not once I saw you. But this Winthrop: you don't mean Isaac Winthrop?"

Shannon's brows rose. "Yes, I do. What? Do you know something? Has he a house full of illegitimates? A wife in the attics?"

He laughed. "Not to my knowledge. He has three railroads, though. What do you say to that?"

Shannon beamed. "I say *brava*, Lizzie!"

He shook his head. "He'll have to win her first."

Chapter Thirty-Four

The young couples always dined as soon as John Thomas arrived home and changed from his uniform into formal dining clothes. With not very long left in the Ravenels' stay, they discussed how they would spend the remaining Saturday, when John Thomas would be excused from reporting.

The ladies looked elegant, Marie in an exquisite green gown and Shannon very fine in deep blue. They were laughing over something when Mrs. Hensley, the Negro housekeeper, entered and waited at the door. John Thomas looked up and said, "Yes, Mrs. Hensley?"

She hesitated and then took a few more steps in the room. Shannon watched her with curiosity. "You wanted news, Lieutenant, if we heard anything?"

John Thomas waited a beat. "Yes, I suppose I did."

"The Southerners... The Democrats, I mean. They've nominated Mr. Breckinridge."

Shannon watched the two men after Mrs. Hensley departed.

John Thomas did not move or show any emotion, while the faintest smile grew on Frederick's lips. Shannon's husband said nothing for several seconds, and she was surprised when the first thing he did was meet her eyes. She swallowed.

"But... With Northern Democrats nominating Mr. Douglas, they cannot possibly prevail against Mr. Lincoln!" Marie said faintly.

Shannon stared at her plate, thinking they were lucky to have avoided the subject thus far.

"I fear not," Frederick said.

"But...South Carolina will secede if a Democrat is not elected," she said, looking at Shannon, who studiously regarded her food. Marie looked around the room when no answer was forthcoming, meeting John Thomas's eyes.

"I'm afraid so," he answered. "Indeed, sometimes I think that was the sole object of the separate conventions."

Frederick's head reared back. "You can say this?" he demanded. "John Breckinridge is the Vice President of the United States. Is his nomination an act of aggression? There was not even one concession to the South at the convention in Charleston!"

"There have been plenty of concessions, Frederick. For far too long," John Thomas said softly.

Frederick flushed with anger. "What concessions?"

John Thomas looked outraged. "Oh, come! We are required to return fugitive slaves when they can make it to freedom in the North. Lincoln—"

"Lincoln! Do you support that fellow?"

There was a long silence. Finally, John Thomas said, "You

have long known my beliefs, Frederick."

Frederick was so outraged, he could not speak. At least, he could not speak for a few seconds. "You intend to vote for that abolitionist? A man who would rip away our holdings, our way of life, everything we hold dear? Who can no more understand Southern society than he could that of Egypt? I cannot believe it of you!"

"He does not want to touch slavery where it exists," John Thomas said, jaw flexing. Shannon's eyes glanced between them, fearful.

"Oh, he appeases, and appeases, but if you read anything he ever wrote before he thought of running for president, it is all there before your very eyes! He loathes slavery!"

"And so do I loathe slavery!" John Thomas said, for the first time raising his voice. "I cannot hear you sit there talking as though you have the right of it without telling you that: I think it is wrong, and demoralizing, and cancerous. I am sorry if that offends you, but it is the way I was raised to feel, just as you were raised to feel the opposite. Now, I have no wish to argue with you. The ladies are present, and the bonds between our families are too deep to allow this to divide us."

Frederick shook his head. "You cannot say your piece and then tell me you have no wish to argue with me! I knew you did not like slavery, but I did *not* know you were a radical. An Immediatist! Do you think I would've stood in front of my mother and father and argued on your behalf, if I had?"

John Thomas looked as though he had been slapped. He had no rejoinder to offer; he just sat looking at Frederick.

But Frederick was in a rage. His jaw clenched and

unclenched. "And what of my sister? If Washington should turn dangerous, will you keep her here, despite it, so that you may advance your glorious cause?"

A pin could've been heard dropping. John Thomas stood, as though he would leave. He said, however, before he did, "Your sister is all I ever think of. *That* is why you advocated on my behalf, if you would only remember it."

Shannon sat in their bedchamber by candlelight in her white dressing gown, her long hair around her shoulders, drying. She was sitting, her legs crossed, in one of the chairs by the fireplace, staring into the abyss. She rather thought John Thomas had gone for a walk, which was for the best, but he had been gone for some time when the door finally cracked open. He looked in, meeting her eyes, and came in fully, closing the door behind him.

He did not say anything, only drew his hand through his hair and leaned against the bedpost, still looking at her. She had been quite angry with him, but the wind had been taken from her sails by his parting speech.

"I am very sorry that your name was tossed about in an argument," he said stiffly.

"I am, too," she said.

He met her eyes, looking strangely unsure. "Are you angry with me, too, then?"

"I don't know." She shook her head. "It seems I never know how to feel, what to think anymore."

"Think what you will. I might wish we felt the same, but

I have never tried to force my beliefs upon you." She knew his cold tone was evidence of how much Frederick had hurt him. But still she swallowed and looked down, stung.

At length, she looked up. She watched him for a few moments. "Could you not have sat silently?" she asked in a passionate whisper.

"It seems all I ever do is sit silently."

"But this…may have caused a rift with my family, John Thomas! You may have done irreparable damage, the two of you, and *I* will be the one to pay for it and pay dearly!"

He sighed, shaking his head softly.

"Are you indeed as radical as Frederick believes?" she asked, studying his profile.

"I have no notion of what Frederick believes anymore. If we are to speak of radicals, you may look no further than your precious South Carolina. To talk of a state having the power to break away from the union as though it is not treason! To speak of men having the right to own other men as though we were speaking of cattle!"

"Are you an Immediatist?" she asked faintly, aghast.

He stopped, looking at her. "No," he said finally, voice hoarse.

She softly released a relieved sigh.

"But only because it is unwise, Shannon. Not because it is not right," he said firmly, his jaw hard. "When will you believe me when I tell you that *I am an abolitionist!* To the fullest extent, to the furthest edges of what you term radical."

"I believed you," she said, looking down her nose at him and coming to her feet. "Has it not brought me hours of pain?" she asked, emotion in her voice.

"Pain?" he asked, his voice lowered now but emotion still on his face. "How, when you knew it when we married? How, unless you refuse to believe it?"

"Do not presume to tell me what I believe or what I ought to feel! I tell you, it has not always been easy to be your wife!"

His eyes pinched at the corners. "How?" he demanded. "Tell me what I have done! What, besides hold to my own beliefs? If we are to speak in such terms, there have been ways in which you have not been satisfactory as a wife, Shannon!" he said harshly.

Shannon blinked, letting the room go silent, stunned. She opened her lips as though to speak but could not. Her chest ached from a pain which started there. The silence drew out between them, and his accusation boiled down into one charge which she could not overcome, for which she knew she had failed him, and blamed herself without mercy. She could hear herself swallow as time stretched out.

"You...refer to the fact that...I...have not conceived..." Her voice failed her, and she watched remotely as his expression changed to one of horror.

He mouthed her name, his face altered. "No," he whispered. "No," he said urgently, going to her and gripping her upper arms. "Of course that is not what I meant!" His eyes seemed to fill as tears rolled down her cheeks. "You must believe me: it wasn't what I meant! It doesn't matter to me. Shannon!"

"It matters to me," she whispered shakily.

"I'm so sorry, my darling," he whispered, searching her face in agony. "Oh, Shannon."

"I know it is a failure. We...have not spoken of it, but..."

Expression broken, he held her for an emotional moment before pressing her gently into the chair. He went down on his knee in front of her, retaining her hands, looking up at her. "I have not spoken of it because I know it must give you pain," he said softly. "How could you think you have failed me?"

She looked down. "I cannot help thinking that if I were like Marie..." She paused. "I might have given you a child soon," she whispered.

He kissed her hands poignantly. "You are the only woman I would wish to bear my children, but I did not marry you for that reason, Shannon."

She breathed shakily, studying him, seeing only truth in his eyes. But it didn't make her feel any easier. It was her only role to play, the only thing for which she had been trained. The only purpose she had been told she was to serve.

She swallowed, then took a steadying breath. "Yes," she whispered. She looked at him hesitantly. "You said...there were...ways in which I had not been satisfactory as a wife?" she asked, swallowing. "Please. Tell me."

His eyes filled with tears. "No! The ravings of a mad man, Shannon. Forgive me for putting such a thought into your head." He lay his head against her lap, and she felt his deep turmoil. She stroked his hair. After some time had passed, he said, "I have never argued with Frederick before." She continued to stroke him, looking into the distance. "All I could think was that his words were *your* words that you have never spoken, and I..." His voice faded off, lost in the night.

She touched his chin, tipping his head up until he looked at her. "Not those on the end," she said. "You know that is not true."

She saw his weary eyes, and her heart seized. "I don't know what to do, Shannon," he said. "He is like a brother to me."

She reached up, smoothing his hair. "Then make it right," she said. "For my sake and your own."

John Thomas had been thinking, almost all night, about what Shannon had said, that she would be the one to suffer should there be any breach. He knew it for the truth, and he went downstairs, determined to appease like his precious Mr. Lincoln, if only Frederick had not left on the night train.

He was walking through the door of the study when Ravenel also appeared in the doorway, looking haggard and ill, much like Shannon after her bout with influenza. "John." He looked surprised to see John Thomas and did not meet his eyes fully until he came into the room. John Thomas stood a few feet away from him. "I was coming to see you!"

"I was coming to see you," John Thomas answered.

"We heard you and Shannon arguing," he said, looking up, face tight in pain. "Not what you said, but...that you were. If I had thought I would create a rift between you, I..."

John Thomas was surprised they had been overheard, and he did not know how to answer him. He finally said stiffly, "I... yes. But we settled it between us."

"What, that she will live in Massachusetts, and you in Washington? Because that is the way it sounded from our side of the wall."

John Thomas almost smiled. "You are frightened because you and Marie never argue."

Frederick looked away, crossing his arms and holding one hand at his temple. "Shannon...did not have a happy childhood. She has told me little, and my parents nothing, but I know it all the same. I wanted her marriage to be different. I didn't want her trapped in a highbred, loveless arrangement in which she had to look upon her husband's image in every mulatto on her plantation. When you made your feelings known, I knew her best chance for happiness was with you, all of the foolish words I spoke last night to that regard aside. You are the best man alive, as I have always said, and if you say slavery is wrong, well, I am almost convinced," he said, giving a small, pained smile.

John Thomas's lips parted. He had expected all of the apology to be on his side, but Marie had done her miraculous work. "Frederick, I'm sorry I provoked you," he said softly, earnestly.

"All of the provocation was on my side," Frederick answered manfully, shaking his head, looking truly worried that he had injured his (as he thought it) gentler friend. "We agreed to leave that subject years ago, and it would appear age has not given us wisdom."

"No." John Thomas sank down onto the edge of his desk. "But it is because we are forced to it now. We are being closed in by the times in which we live. I sometimes think that if Shannon and I had married in any other year..." He let the sentence fade, and Frederick looked at him painfully.

"I still think it is possible that we can throw the election into the House. And Jefferson Davis—you know, the fellow from Mississippi?"

"Yes, the Senator. I have met him."

"He has been proposing a plan to reunify the Democratic

Party, and to consolidate it to one candidate. They say Breck-inridge is more than willing to step aside. At least if we lost then, it will not have felt so hopeless, as though the South had lost any voice it may have."

John Thomas hesitated, feeling as though it were wish-ful thinking on Frederick's part but not willing to say so. He hesitated for a long moment and then felt as though he must add: "But…if there should be any threat of danger," he said, not wishing to raise the prospect of war, "I should send Shannon north to my family. They will take care of her. That is, I am convinced Shannon could take care of herself. But I do not wish her to have to."

The ladies were justifiably surprised when they came down to find their husbands in perfect harmony with one another. Things were strained between Shannon and John Thomas, though he was gentle with her. They set it aside for the remaining days and saw their guests off with regret.

As they waited at the train station, the gentlemen talking, Shannon stood with Marie, clasping her hands, close to tears. "My dearest cousin," she said, looking into Marie's sweet, genteel face. The moment was poignant, and both knew the reasons. She bit her lip.

"Be strong and courageous, Shannon," Marie said softly. She was able to do so, for the station was not crushed with people, it being a Sunday. "You have everything you need within you to see you through any trial which besets you."

Shannon pressed her lips together, trying not to allow

her emotions to overflow. "Give my love to my mother and father," she said.

"Yes. I will."

"And write to me when you make it home safely," she said. "And when you have the joy of holding your little one in your arms. I hope it will know how much I love it, though we are far apart."

They embraced, Marie whispering in her ear, "Even if there is war, it will be short, and you will be restored to us soon."

Shannon nodded, stroking Marie's arm.

As they boarded, John Thomas looked at her. She swallowed, standing next to him. The train slowly rolled away, puffing its smoke into the air and gathering speed until it disappeared in the distance.

Chapter Thirty-Five

Adrian sat in the library at his desk, which had been moved beside the windows and away from the fireplace. It was a beautiful Saturday morning, and he simply stared into the distance. He had left Jude upstairs cleaning his room after breakfast and had come down to get caught up on work. But papers lay in front of him, unheeded.

He had seen Adeline pouring her cereal this morning in the kitchen. She was wearing blue shorts and a T-shirt from some concert with a peace sign on the back, her hair caught up in a multi-colored band. He had offered what they were having. But she had touched her middle at the word "eggs" and shaken her head, giving a polite "no thanks" and taking her cereal off, presumably to the living room. It was probably a good thing: Jude was onto them, his eyes cutting between them. The boy had noticed the awkwardness, the change in behavior. But luckily, he was too young to put his feelings into solid theories or to think there was any justification for them.

It would be the hardest to keep Jane from being suspicious. And from Jane it was just one step to his mother. He put his elbows on his desk and touched his temples, the thought of either of them breathing down his neck making him want to rip his hair out.

The door opened, and he looked up, seeing his brother. He lifted his brows, straightening, and said with surprise, "Harris."

Frowning, Harris advanced. "Adrian? What's wrong?"

"Wrong? Nothing. Why?"

Harris sat down across from him, making a study of him. "You looked like you had a migraine, or something."

"No," he said, surveying his brother. He was wearing shorts and a light blue polo and looking refreshed, like he had slept in that morning. "I didn't know you were coming to Charleston."

"Mom was freaking out—"

"Mom doesn't freak out."

"Okay, whatever the equivalent for her is. She was talking about you on Sunday. She said something wasn't right with you at the graduation. Dad told her he hadn't noticed. She told him it was no surprise."

"Sounds like a fun dinner."

"You have no idea. She commanded me to come." He made a survey of him, eyes narrowed. "I wasn't going to, but when we talked—Thursday?—you sounded really distracted."

"I don't think so," he said, protesting.

"Adrian, you sounded like you did after the wreck," he said seriously, and forcefully. "Vague and...distracted."

"I don't know what you're talking about."

"Have all your stocks plummeted?" he pressed.

"Not to my knowledge. I haven't talked to my financial advisor lately."

"Adrian, something's wrong," he said, slapping the desk. "Mom's got you being brought up on ethics charges, or Jude diagnosed with cancer—that's just two of the theories she's come up with."

He sighed, touching his forehead again. "Oh, my God."

Harris gave a slight laugh suddenly. "I know. But she has a point. You're always the same, Adrian, and it flips people out when you act differently."

His mind went back to that night at Husk. That was before Adeline had told him about the baby. Strange. But that Harris had noticed distraction on Thursday was no shock at all.

He studied his brother, hesitating. Harris watched him intently. A minute dragged out, and he regretted nearly giving in. Having come this close, Harris obviously had the scent of the kill. He had that keen look: he'd drag it out of him through sheer persistence. "Adeline's pregnant," he said finally.

Harris nodded, pulling his mouth down at the corners as though surprised. "I didn't know she was dating anyone."

"She's not."

There was a pause. Harris met his eyes, drawing his brows together. "Well, it's not mine, if that's where you're going," he said defensively.

He held his eyes for a long moment, blinking pensively, considering, before saying, "It's mine."

For five full seconds, there was no reaction. Then Harris jumped up, saying, "*What?!*" The look on his face was a good mixture of horror and disgust.

"Lower your voice," he said.

"What the *hell*, Adrian?"

He sat back, pressing his lips together, crossing his arms.

"What, have the two of you been having an affair? *Obviously*—what am I thinking?" He still wore that lip-curled look of shock.

"No," Adrian said.

"No?" his brother demanded ironically.

"It's none of your business, but if you must know, we lost our heads the night of that storm. We had to stay in the same room, and..." For the love of everything, he was *not* talking to anyone about this.

"Something *is* wrong with you. Since when do you sleep with random strangers?"

Adrian narrowed his eyes, jaw clenching and unclenching. Harris took his head back an inch, an automatic reaction from the days Adrian could still beat him in a physical match. "Are you without sin, Harris?" he asked mockingly. "If you are, by all means, throw that stone."

Harris held his eyes, slowly loosening his shoulders, sighing. "Yeah, all right. It's not that: I'm worried about you." He trailed a hand through his hair, then replaced his hat.

Adrian sighed. "I'm not a monk, Harris," he said softly, as though he were talking to a child. "There's no need for you to freak out because—"

"Well, that does freak me out. Just when I think you're a sciency nerd—"

"Thanks."

"—I remember you're actually hotter than me."

"Who said that?"

"That woman in Nantucket!"

"Is that still bothering you?"

"You are straying from the point. So yes, when I remember that you're...you know, passionate, it does throw me off for a minute."

"For the love of God, I'm not your sixty-year-old widowed mother."

Harris held up his hand. "Fine. Sorry. But, no, Adrian, it's about Adeline, too. Do you know she could have an abortion without even telling you?"

Adrian sat back, crossing his arms, looking into the distance. "She's keeping it."

A pause. "Oh." There was a long, awkward silence. Finally, he resumed, "Do you know how many rights nonmarital fathers have? Like zero. She could literally take it to another state, and if you don't do everything perfectly, you could never see it again."

"Damn it, Harris, do you think I don't know that? But I'm not *worried* about *me*." His voice trailed off. "I'm worried about her." He fingered the pencil in his hand and said quietly, haltingly, "She feels...loose or something, I can tell. And she's not. But if I'm not mistaken, she comes from a pretty strait-laced family. This is going to go over badly with them, or at least awkwardly. And she's scared."

Harris's lips parted. Slowly, he sank back into his chair, cooling it a little. He thought for a while, forehead wrinkling. "Has she told you all of this?" he asked.

"No, she hasn't even cried," he said, laughing non-humorously.

"She's handling it amazingly well, under the circumstances."

Harris's brows drew together. "But she knows you're going to be there, right?"

He met his eyes and hesitated again. "Yeah, if she believes me. I think she does. I asked her to marry me, Harris," he said quietly.

His brows lifted. "Oh." He didn't seem to be able to think of anything else to say.

"She hasn't answered yet."

"Well, I... I probably would've done the same thing," his brother answered quietly.

"I know."

"I didn't mean... I mean, if I said anything disparaging about her, it's only because we don't know her. I actually liked her."

He laughed. "I know."

Harris shook his head, still in shock. "Good God, Adrian. What a freak thing. I can't believe you're not more than merely distracted."

"Adeline doesn't deserve that," he said. "The baby doesn't deserve it. The problem existed whether there was a baby or not. This doesn't really change that."

He nodded. "I probably should've said congratulations. You never know what to do, though, when it's a mistake—"

"*We* made a mistake; the baby's not a mistake," he said firmly.

Harris smiled slowly. "All right, then. Sorry I yelled."

Adrian waved a hand. "I just didn't want Jude to hear. You're something of a mother figure to him, and—"

"*What?*" Harris said, scowling horribly.

Adrian lifted his brows. "It's perfectly normal."

"It doesn't *sound* normal. Oh, my God, have I messed him up? I *told* you I should never have children."

Adrian tried to suppress a smile, but when Harris looked at him suspiciously, his shoulders started shaking.

Grinding his jaw, Harris slung his cap at him before forcefully slamming out of the room.

Adrian turned off the blender, handing Jude one of the glasses with a banana smoothie in it and saying softly, "Take this to Ms. Miller."

Jude smiled conspiratorially and held it with both hands.

He watched him go, leaning against the counter. He had heard the Masterpiece Theater trumpet on the TV, something that seemed to be a Sunday night ritual for her. At least it wasn't football season yet. He wasn't really sure how this would go down then.

He walked down the little hall and stopped to watch, smiling as she leaned up and took it from him. "Aw, Jude, thank you!" she said sweetly. "Did you make this?"

He shook his head, smiling, shy. He got that from Adrian. Adulthood would take the edge off, though.

"Your daddy did?"

Jude nodded.

"*Mmm*, it's delicious," she said, looking up and meeting Adrian's eyes as he came into the room. "Thanks!" she said with a smile.

"You're welcome," he answered, handing Jude his smoothie. He and Jude sat on the couch, and it wasn't long before his traitor son was absorbed in the show.

"Can we turn it up, Ms. Miller?" he asked, sucking his straw vigorously.

"Yeah," she said, looking like she had been waiting for the opportunity. "I have trouble understanding them, too."

Great. Nothing more was said until it went off, and both, having been glued to the TV until the scenes from next week played, finally looked up. He tapped his phone on the coffee table and saw that it was ten o'clock.

"Up to bed with you," he said to Jude, kissing his hair. "Brush your teeth. For real this time."

"You tuck me in?" he said sweetly, arms around his neck.

"Yeah, I'll be up in a little while."

"Okay," he said, going toward the door in his little blue pajamas.

"Night, Jude," Adeline said, smiling like she thought he was cute. Which he was.

"Night," he said, moving along.

Adrian waited until he heard him running up the stairs before he looked at Adeline. "I want some pajamas like his," she said when he met her eyes. "Very 1920s posh."

"My mom," he said. He glanced at her empty glass. "Does milk bother you?"

"No, not yet," she said. Her bare feet were on the coffee table, putting her impossibly beautiful legs on display. "Only really pungent smells, so far." No more fish or eggs for them. He cast his mind back over what they had eaten this week, surprised at the number of things which were kind of strong.

He studied her for a long minute. "You know I feel like a real jerk about your room, right?"

She laughed suddenly, seeming to be very amused. "It's no more than you deserve. You thought you would show me, didn't you?"

He shifted uncomfortably. "Let me move your stuff down to the second floor."

"No," she said firmly. "We're starting on the guest bedrooms *very* soon."

"Then take mine." She met his eyes. "I'll move up there," he hastened to add.

"How is that going to look?" she said, raising her brows. "Are you prepared for your whole family to know about this yet?"

He hesitated. "I told Harris."

She flushed, reaching up to do that hair-twirly thing with her finger. "Oh!"

He studied her. "Sorry if—"

"No, that's perfectly fine," she said. "What did he say?"

A moment's pause. "He said congratulations."

She lifted her brows, looking relieved. "Oh. That's good, then."

"He won't tell anyone. We can wait as long as you like."

"Yeah, okay, that's good."

He sat back, noticing that her hair was pinned up, all of her makeup off. "Who is your doctor?" he asked, trying to sound off-hand, like he wasn't trying to interfere.

"It's Women's Health Group—I think it's Dr. Jay. Do you know anything about him?"

"I've heard good things," he said, narrowing his eyes in the distance in thought.

"They got good reviews, so I'm hoping I like them."

"Well, if you don't, you can change," he said.

"Yeah." She studied him. "Do you have any idea when I might be due? I did one of those online calculator things, but I don't trust it."

"Oh." He sat back, calculating. "I would imagine around the second week in January," he said. "Maybe the tenth?"

She lifted her brows. "That's exactly what the calculator said. How did you remember how to do that?"

He lifted a shoulder. "We studied it—it's been awhile, but I remember the basic calculations."

She looked like she was a little scared of him, which made no sense to him. But women weren't always easy to understand. He glanced out the door, thinking Jude should be finished. He looked back at her, almost hesitating. "So if I don't see you tomorrow, I guess I'll meet you over there at ten on Tuesday?"

She nodded, looking a little nervous. "That sounds good."

He nodded in return, getting up. "Goodnight, then."

Chapter Thirty-Six

Shannon immersed herself ever more into Washington society until there was not a senator, senator's wife, secretary, or famous congressman to whom she had not been introduced. She had met President Buchanan and been unimpressed, as well as Vice-President Breckinridge, whom she liked and privately supported. She attended ladies' teas and brunches, called upon the reigning dames, and was called upon in her turn.

Today, she lay in bed, however, having endured a humiliating examination which Dr. Smith did little to alleviate. The sun was shining outside, and her chamber, with all of its blues, was lovely. She tried to think of those things, or of the man's brown coat, of his tightly clipped gray beard, anything to occupy her.

"You say the pain is not constant?" he asked as she covered herself.

"No."

"And it is only during intercourse?"

She moistened her lips, unable to meet his eyes. "Yes."

He was an older man, perhaps sixty, and, while he was reportedly a good doctor, he was abrupt and direct.

"Is your husband rough with you?"

Shannon took a shaky breath. "No, he...he is very gentle," she whispered, mortified.

His white brows drew together as he seemed to be thinking, perhaps at a loss. "You have been married how long?"

"Since December. Ten months."

"No miscarriages?"

"None."

"Has the pain been present from the beginning?"

"No. Only the past two months, and intermittently. That is, not always."

"Are your courses regular?"

"Yes. Very."

He sighed. "I confess myself at a loss, ma'am. I have heard of such ailments, but usually they are more persistent, with other symptoms present. Sometimes these things have no real cause, and pass. We shall hope that is the case with you. I would recommend abstinence for at least two months."

She nodded, keeping her head down. "Please send your bill to my name. I would prefer my husband not know."

He shrugged, gathering his bag. "As you wish. Send for me if the problem worsens."

"Yes," she said, sinking back against her pillows with a sigh once he had left, lifting her hands to her burning cheeks.

The teacup clinked as it was placed back in its saucer. Shannon was returning Mrs. Greenhow's call at her home. The parlor was large and elegant, the wallpaper beige and heavily patterned, the carpets rich. "Well, you have become quite popular, my dear," Mrs. Greenhow said in her soft, elegant voice.

"Yes, I suppose, through your support, ma'am."

"Do you find the young gentlemen difficult to fend off?"

A few circumstances came to mind. Shannon smiled, however, and said, "You are forgetting that I am from Charleston, ma'am." Seymour Christian fluttered into her consciousness.

"Who is the belle of Charleston now that you are not there?"

"I suppose my dear friend, Miss Middleton. She evades marriage more heartily than I did. I have no doubt she will make a splendid match. She writes me of her suitors and keeps me vastly entertained.

Mrs. Greenhow smiled. "I daresay she does take very well, with her wealth and family name. I am glad to have Florence settled. I worry for Gertrude and Leila. To say nothing of Little Rose."

"Little Rose has a few years yet before her coming out, ma'am," Shannons said, smiling. She had met the delightful imp, who had all of seven summers behind her and sharp eyes, like her mother.

Mrs. Greenhow smiled. "What is the political climate in Charleston, my dear? Does your mother say?"

"Tumultuous. It is as though they are collectively holding their breath until the election."

"My dear, what will your situation be, should there be a secession?"

"I must follow my husband. I believe my family knows that, but we don't speak of it. And perhaps once things settle down, the government will accept that there must be two countries, or more. Sometimes I think it will be for the best anyway." She thought suddenly of John Adams and almost teared up.

"My dear..." Mrs. Greenhow pressed her lips together. "I believe our sympathies are as one. But you and I know what they do not in the South: these people will never accept the secession of any state. They believe states lack that authority and that it is tantamount to treason." She dusted the crumbs from her biscuit into her plate. "Mr. Lincoln will be elected. Some of the states will secede. And our best hope, therefore, is for a short war."

Shannon moistened her lips, trying not to show the disturbance of her mind. "It would...seem so odd to be cut off from the South. To...to not have access should I need it. It makes me feel as though I cannot breathe."

Mrs. Greenhow looked sympathetically at her, reaching for her hand and pressing it, saying nothing.

After some time had passed and Shannon had been staring out the window, her thoughts lost in a tangle, Mrs. Greenhow said in her soft voice, "What do you miss most about being down there?"

Shannon looked at her. "My family, of course," she said softly. "John Thomas thinks I miss the way of life, and I suppose I do—being waited upon hand and foot, the richness, the society, our friends. But I... There are other things, too." She looked at Mrs. Greenhow, her eyes suddenly wistful. "The moss, and the trees... They feel like home to me. And just before it rains, there is a smell in the air, sweet and earthy." She pressed her lips together. "I miss that, too."

Shannon sat on the sofa in the study with John Thomas on the first night it was cool enough to light a fire. It crackled and cast shadows, and it reminded her of cool nights at Harmony Grove. They had planned to go to the opulent National Theatre but had decided against it when rain had threatened.

John Thomas had begun teaching her Naval signs and commands, and they spent some forty-five minutes thus engaged before Shannon began to grow restive. "What is this knot?" she asked, pointing to the drawing in the book he held in his lap. His arm was around her waist, hand playing with her sash occasionally.

He studied it for a moment. "That is a Fisherman's Bend."

"Can you do it?"

"I think so."

"I wish to try it with my hair."

He laughed. "I thought you were serious!"

Her eyes danced. She smiled, tucking her feet up and leaning against his shoulder. "I am, naturally. Enough for tonight."

"Very well," he said, laying the book aside, a smile in his voice. "Do you wish to go into the sitting room?"

"No, I like it here," she said.

He looked down at her, love stirring in his expression, and their lips touched. "I do, too," he whispered. He kissed her again, and she turned so that she might reach him better. His movements were slow and gentle and agonizing. Her hand trembled as it explored his jawline. The kiss deepened, and, just when she knew the next thing to happen would be for him to sweep her into his arms and hope none of the servants saw as he carried her up the stairs, she pulled away. His arms were still around her but loosened as he met her eyes. He looked surprised, justifiably so, given her ardor.

She touched his chest. "Do you mind if...we just...stay and talk? I am a little tired tonight."

His brows lifted. "Yes, of course," he said, barely above a whisper. "You are not ill?" His eyes searched her face closely.

"No." She shook her head. "No, I am well." She settled against him, staring into the fire.

The election was two weeks away when Shannon heard the knocker on the door. Thinking it would be a caller, she set her book aside. She had already had four that morning, one set consisting of Mrs. Greenhow and Mrs. Phillips. The other two bore only the slimmest of pretexts, obviously hoping for friendship and entre into Washington society, which amused her, queen of her townhouse as she was.

Mrs. Hensley appeared in the sitting room doorway. "Excuse me, ma'am. There is a caller at the door, but she won't give her name."

Shannon lifted her brows. "Good heavens, a mystery! Do you think she intends to assassinate me?"

"No, ma'am. She's tall and pretty. She speaks like you do."

Shannon's brows drew together, and she stood. She crossed the room and walked down the little hall until she was in the foyer. And when she saw the elegant stranger in travel clothes, she gasped. "Elizabeth!" she exclaimed, going forward. "I *hoped* it was you." She extended her hands, and Miss Middleton took them, eyes twinkling. "Oh, but what are you doing here? Tell me nothing is wrong at home!"

She smiled in her calm, elegant way. "Nothing is the matter. Won't you invite me into your parlor? I declare, you've forgotten all of your manners, Shannon!"

"Yes, indeed, come," she answered, taking her hand and leading the way, her brows pinched. She was still feeling a little shaken as she ordered the housekeeper to bring refreshments.

"Now, you *must* tell me," Shannon said as soon as the tea-cakes and lemonade had arrived. "What on earth brings you to Washington? And alone!"

"I am not alone. I accompanied Papa. He has gone to the Capitol and instructed me most severely to take my maid with me if I went out." Her blue eyes twinkled.

"Oh, Elizabeth," Shannon said, laughing. "Is it something about the election?"

"Yes. Papa was a delegate to the conventions, you know. The Legislature sent him to gather what information he could and report back on the general feeling and such, in case..." She bit her lip.

Shannon knew Elizabeth meant *in case he needed to give a speech at a secession convention.* She did not speak for a moment, for she was at a loss for words. Elizabeth, regal as ever, calmly withdrew her hand. "Oh, Shannon," she said softly. "What was I thinking? It can do you no good to have ties with me. Lieutenant Haley may not even wish for me to enter the house."

Shannon took her hand as she started to stand, saying, "No, my dear friend. My ties with you are old and deep, as anyone may know. And my husband would never scorn any friend of mine."

"Still, I ought to have thought of it. I know you will be scrutinized very much should there be any breach."

"I may withstand a little scrutiny. And you mustn't think I do not support the cause of the South Carolina legislature and your father. I do. Most heartily."

Elizabeth pressed her lips together, turning her head away. Not a hair of her elegant brown coiffure was loose, and her posture was perfect. "Shannon, I've been thinking... Your letters proclaim your love for your home and...all of our ways. But Lieutenant Haley will hardly feel the same." She pressed her hand, meeting her eyes. "I do not think you should feel guilty for supporting him in whatever he does."

Shannon withdrew her hand. "Perhaps some girls are so spiritless. But I? No, to think of such a thing is unbearable, Elizabeth. If there should be war, I must remain in Washington, and I could never wish for *his* ill, but...support a Northern victory I will not."

Elizabeth studied her calmly for several moments. "I think it will cause a breach in your marriage," she said bluntly.

Shannon looked away, taking a breath and pressing her lips together. "Elizabeth, should you ever be married—"

"Yes, I know. I shall tell you that I will ask if I ever desire your advice. Meddlesome of me, wasn't it?"

Shannon smiled, releasing her breath. "Very meddlesome." Her eyes lit. "You and Mr. Middleton shall dine here tonight."

"Papa means utterly to neglect me and have dinner with some senators. But certainly, I will be delighted to come. Will Lieutenant Haley be joining us?"

"Yes, if they release him soon enough. That has rather been in question lately, however, for they seem to need him more and more."

Elizabeth lifted her brows but did not respond. "We shall see if he recognizes me. I daresay he shan't." Her blue eyes twinkled.

Shannon laughed. "Of course he will recognize you. You were a bridesmaid for our wedding."

"We shall see!"

On the day of the election, John Thomas was on duty until midnight, for reasons he could not, apparently, divulge, and so Shannon spent the day with the Middletons at the hotel. She knew her husband would go and cast his vote, and the thought of his choice made her ill. Mr. Middleton, always kind and fatherly, kept her distracted with cards in the elegant sitting room of their suite.

It had just turned dark when fights began to break out in the streets, and, going to the window, Shannon looked out and saw such a scene of confusion that she felt herself to be in California rather than the nation's capital. Men were drunken, tossing their beers and screaming, shouting at one another from across the street and ending up in brawls with no concern for the hazard of carriages rolling through the streetways.

Shannon heard a movement and saw Elizabeth coming to stand beside her. She reached to take Shannon's hand, the dread in her eyes matching that in the pit of Shannon's stomach.

"Do you think Lieutenant Haley is in danger?" Elizabeth asked kindly. John Thomas, having, of course, recognized her, had gone out of his way to make her feel welcome, not batting an eye when she had told him her reasons for being in Washington.

"Yes," Shannon said faintly. "I presumed the military to be plotting, but they must have anticipated this...this lawless riot." She watched the scene below her unseeingly. "I asked if I might come here, and he said yes, that he would be grateful to Mr. Middleton. Now I understand what he meant."

Elizabeth pressed her hand. "I think we will hear nothing tonight. You will stay here. He knew you might do so, I suppose. I do not want you to set foot out of the door."

Shannon did not respond, barely hearing.

"Come, Shannon, you mustn't worry. It will do no good."

"Not only that. The election."

Elizabeth glanced at her father.

"You mustn't worry, my dear," he said, looking the epitome of the Southern gentleman as he sat, legs crossed, with his glass in hand. "I am sure some peaceful resolution can be reached. Come now, your father wouldn't wish to see you looking like that. It isn't for you to trouble yourself with."

Shannon turned her rings on her slim fingers. "I only wish the ones who *can* trouble themselves instilled more faith in me."

"Well, you are certainly in a unique situation, and naturally, you are worried for your husband should there be a conflict. Indeed, any devoted wife must be, I imagine. But he is a commissioned officer and unlikely to be deeply involved in any short unpleasantness there might be."

"There, you see?" Elizabeth said. "Come, Shannon, I will show you to my room." She looked over her shoulder. "Goodnight, Papa."

"Goodnight, my dear. We will have news in the morning, I imagine."

And they did. Abraham Lincoln was elected without a single vote from a Southern state. And South Carolina was calling a secession convention.

Chapter Thirty-Seven

John Thomas climbed the stairs at his house, the hallways darkened. He had hoped to be released early and spend the evening with Shannon. Her nerves were tense since the election, her eyes troubled, and he wanted to be with her as much as possible. But instead, he would be lucky if she weren't already asleep. He didn't knock for fear of waking her but instead opened the door softly. He saw her in their bedchamber, sitting on the hearth by the fireplace in her dressing gown. Her hair was almost dry, and perhaps she sat there because of the chill in the air.

He met her eyes, and she smiled. He went forward, sitting down beside her. He touched her cheek and kissed her lips.

"I missed you tonight," she whispered.

"I missed *you*." Eyes closed, he kissed her cheek, her temple. "You look weary."

"Not too much." He lifted his head, forcing himself to tamp down his passion. He had only said six words to her. "Your day?"

"Pleasant enough. I have been hatching a plan to have Lieutenants Hughes and Jay to supper. And then, before they know it, I shall have taken them under my wing and found wives for them."

He laughed softly. "Invite them if you wish, but must you play matchmaker?"

"Yes, you cannot think how fatiguing it is always to be the only female in the room whenever we are with your friends. If they are not single, they seemed to have left their wives at home, and I do *not* count that vulgar Milner woman as a contemporary."

"That is because you are uppity, love," he said, sitting back on his hands.

"If it is uppity to disdain garish plaids and a voice booming across the dining table asking where the hostess came by her pig, I claim the moniker with pride."

She had him laughing halfway into this speech, and he looked at her with challenge as her eyes sparkled with something else. "Don't say it."

"Well I *wasn't* going to mention that she is a Northerner, but—" She laughed as he reached for her and drew her into his lap. "There, you have quite overpowered me, you brute."

His eyes shone. "You are beautiful," he said softly.

The touch on his shoulders changed from light to longing in seconds, her hands smoothing down them.

He began kissing her again, and she soon was lost in passion, too, and he thought that maybe tonight... Her hands mussed his hair, her back arching as he brought her closer, lengthening the column of his throat to reach her. He reached for the ribbons on her dressing gown, edging away from the fire. But then he felt her hands against his chest and broke off, pain tightening his lungs.

She smiled gently, stroking his arm. "It is so late, and...I am tired."

"Tell me the truth, Shannon," he said softly, holding her eyes. "No matter how unpleasant, I'll bear it easier than knowing you are lying to me."

She paled. He waited, his eyes never leaving hers.

She pressed her lips together, looking away, and then finally met his eyes again. After another moment passed, she said softly, "Sometimes..." Her cheeks bloomed with color. "Sometimes I have pain," she said haltingly.

She watched his brows draw together, and then, when understanding dawned, his lips parted, his face paling. His lips moved, but it seemed he could not speak. He gripped her hand. "Shannon..." It was a mere whisper. She had never seen him look thus. "I have been taking pleasure, and causing you pain?" he whispered, barely audibly.

"No," she shook her head. "No, it has only happened a few times, and—"

"Why didn't you tell me?" he demanded, anguish in the lines of his mouth.

"I didn't wish to upset you. I...I spoke with a doctor." He looked shocked anew. She rushed to add, "He said that he cannot reason as to the cause, and that...that it might be better to wait two months... And then to see."

He set her gently aside and got up distractedly, pacing a few steps away in the glow of the fire as she watched him. He dragged a hand through his hair and said nothing, seemingly in great turmoil.

Shannon tucked her dressing gown about her, feeling the absence of his warmth. She moistened her lips. "You...You must not feel it so," she said very softly.

He finally looked at her. "How many times?" he whispered.

"Not...not many."

"How many?"

She swallowed. "Three."

His eyes closed, and he turned, to hide his emotion, she knew. She got up and went to him, touching his arm, looking up into his face. "Why didn't you stop me?" he whispered.

She looked at him, a tear rolling down her cheek, at a loss. "I..."

He turned, as though he had thought of something else. He touched her upper arms. "What if something is wrong? Which doctor saw you?"

She thought for a moment, summoning his name. "Smith."

"What did you say that he said?"

"That he has heard of such things, but usually with more symptoms—"

"What symptoms?" His eyes scanned her face.

"Please, I cannot... And I do not have them. He says that sometimes there is no cause, and it will cease, given the proper time. And indeed, I am very sorry that I...lied. But I hoped not to trouble you."

He cupped her cheek, stroking it. "Please. Trouble me in the future."

She moistened her lips. "Very well," she whispered.

He held her eyes. "I'm so sorry," he whispered.

Her eyes misted at his gentility, his goodness. She shook her head, bringing his hand to her lips for a kiss.

He swallowed. "It is late."

"Yes."

"You ought to go to bed."

"Yes, Mammy."

Finally, he smiled. He touched the small of her back, leading her and then lifting her so that she did not have to use the stool. He kissed her forehead as she lay back. "I...miss you," she whispered. She kissed his cheek, whispering in his ear, "And it is only for another week."

He covered her with the sheet, cupping her cheek briefly. "It can wait," he said simply, seemingly distracted. His fingers grazed her cheek in an absent caress.

She smiled, but it slipped as she watched him walk away, presumably down to his study to read, or perhaps collect himself. She had put a distance between them, as palpable as the empty place next to her in the bed. How differently tonight might have been if not for her.

Determined to put aside the gloom of politics, Shannon did indeed invite Lieutenants Shalto Hughes and Richard Jay to dinner, and they were delighted to attend. They were invited often enough to parties but rarely to intimate ones with a charming hostess who made everything so comfortable they felt themselves to be at home.

Shannon stood to greet them when John Thomas brought

them into the parlor, extending her hands and looking exquisitely feminine. Both were extremely gallant, and she was lavished with so much attention that her mood was set for the evening. "Which of you is the elder? You may take me in to dinner. John Thomas has given me permission to flirt with you tonight, you see," she said, tossing a roguish look over her shoulder.

"Have I?"

"You have, indeed. Well?"

"Hughes, by three months," Jay sighed.

Shannon gave the Georgian her hand, saying, "I should've preferred to be walked in by a Southerner, in any event." He grinned, eyes twinkling. His hair was golden, his face passably good-looking.

"Oho!" Lieutenant Jay said. "*That* is meant as my punishment for bad flirtation over the course of these last weeks, I daresay, but what are *you* being punished for, Haley?"

"The dog, I imagine. My wife fancies a lapdog, and believes it should keep her good company," he said, touching her back briefly as he helped her into her chair, allowing her to arrange her skirts before pushing the chair in. "I say she would soon grow tired of an overfed pug and wish me to dispose of it."

"Not *dispose!* What a terrible word!"

"I shouldn't think you would like it, Mrs. Haley," Lieutenant Jay said. "Perhaps an Italian Greyhound, but not a pug."

"Oh, very well, I am overborne. You may purchase me an Italian Greyhound, John Thomas." He looked at her, shaking his head indulgently, and said, "Witness my wife's meekness, sirs."

"Mrs. Haley is the greatest lady in Washington," Lieutenant

Jay said, to which Lieutenant Hughes added, "Here, here!" raising his glass.

"It is unanimous, then," John Thomas said, smiling lovingly, raising his glass also. Shannon, quite merry, set the conversation in pleasing courses, as she had been trained to do from an early age.

Lieutenant Hughes was an only son of a widower father of moderate means who owned a charming house in Savannah and some five or six slaves. Lieutenant Jay was of a large Philadelphia family. His father had served as a magistrate for a few terms after many years as a solicitor.

"Did you say that he is in his retirement, Jay?" John Thomas asked during the course of the meal.

"My father? Good heavens, no. With twelve children, and the girls likely to be expensive, he must work himself to the grave."

"Now, I consider that most unjust, Lieutenant," Shannon said, sipping from her glass. "Sons are far more expensive than daughters, with their grand tours, university fees, and horses, and such."

"No, no, no! Ballgowns, and bonnets, and dowries... And there were no grand tours or horses for me. We were rather more modestly situated than Ravenel or Haley, the two wealthiest fellows in our class, as we all knew," he said, eyes twinkling.

A slight flush tinged John Thomas's cheekbones, and he looked up, shaking his head long-sufferingly.

"Yes, very true," Lieutenant Hughes chimed in. "Ravenel with his Negro valet and Haley with his charity. I wish I might've been one of his charities!"

Shannon laughed. "I doubt he should've improved upon you, although if anyone could..." she said, extending a hand lovingly toward her husband. He smiled, kissing her fingers dutifully.

Lieutenant Jay, his dark locks glowing under the gas lighting, said, "A romantic ideal, wouldn't you say, Hughes?"

Shannon flushed as Lieutenant Hughes said, "Yes, it makes one almost ill, the love and harmony around one."

"That is why Shannon has brought you here," John Thomas said. "She intends to find wives for the both of you, purely for selfish purposes."

"No, not *purely* for selfish purposes. I should like to see the both of you happily settled. Men were not really meant for bachelordom, you know. Now Lieutenant Jay, I believe I have someone in mind for you: she is a lively girl with a very pretty face, an excellent figure, and very moral—of good quality, you see."

"My dear Mrs. Haley, I shall take your word for it and marry her tomorrow, if such a lady does indeed exist—other than yourself, I mean."

Her eyes twinkled, but she said dampeningly, "Certainly you shall not be trusted to choose for *yourself*. But I confess myself rather at a loss as to what to do with Lieutenant Hughes. He is a quieter sort, and I do not think he would match well with a lively girl. I think she would agitate him."

"Yes, that is probably true," he responded, joining handsomely into the spirit of things.

"Tell me, do you like red-heads, like Lieutenant Haley, or dark beauties or fair?"

"Do I prefer red-heads?" Lieutenant Haley asked.

"Indeed, you do. Well?"

"I suppose..." It was a terrible quandary for a Southern gentleman. "Naturally red hair is beautiful—"

"Careful, Shalto," John Thomas warned.

"I said it was beautiful!"

"But, sadly, he prefers blondes," Jay said.

"Oh, do you? No, I am not offended, for there is no accounting for tastes. I shall think on it and hopefully have someone in mind by Christmas."

It was not long before they moved into the parlor, Shannon sitting near Lieutenant Hughes by the fireplace and the other men taking the chairs across the room. Shannon had watched them, pleased to find that they had a great affection for her husband, even seemed to defer to him sometimes, as though he were their natural leader or superior in rank. They treated her with gallant flirtation but never passed the line, and she felt herself to be safe with them.

She was just imagining inviting them to dine often during the winter when she saw Lieutenant Hughes staring into the fire, and the enormity of the situation crashed around her again.

She moistened her lips and said softly, "Will you...stay if..."

He glanced at her, silent for a moment, and then answered almost in a whisper, glancing at the other two, "I cannot... I hope Georgia remains. But I cannot cut myself off from my father, fight against him... I am all he has."

Shannon swallowed.

"Please," he said. "Don't...I ought not to have said that, only you..."

"I shan't reveal your confidences. And of course, I...under-stand..." She only then realized the gravity of what it would mean for a man like Shalto Hughes to decamp, how his life might be at stake, any chance of a career, at least with the United States military, at an end. "Might you not...bring your father north?"

"I shouldn't ask it of him," he said simply.

Lieutenant Jay said something then about the need to allow Mrs. Haley her beauty rest, and they both got up soon. Their hosts bid them goodnight.

When John Thomas came back into the room, his brows were drawn together.

Shannon watched him for a moment as she snuffed out a candle. "You did not mind my flirtation?"

"What? Oh. No," he said, smiling fleetingly. "I'm worried about Hughes."

Shannon met his eyes in the gentle glow of the darkened room. After a tick of the clock, she said, "I believe he does feel it very deeply."

"Yes." She watched John Thomas. He had been reticent, abstracted since that night. She might have continued a lie if she had known how deeply it would affect him. He had not touched her, and she did not think he would, perhaps, ever until she came to him.

Seeming to remember his audience, he walked toward her, putting his hands on her waist softly, her skirt belling over his shoes. "You are an excellent hostess," he said, kissing her cheek.

Moving her hands from his arms, Shannon touched his cheek and boldly kissed his lips. He pulled her a little nearer, his lips touching hers again. He stopped a few moments later, however. "You must be tired," he said, releasing her and looking away.

"No," she said softly. "I am not."

He looked up at her, holding her eyes for a long moment. He shook his head.

"Why?" she croaked.

There was emotion in his face and in his voice when he spoke. "Shannon, I cannot..." She swallowed, a tear rolling down her cheek. He went forward immediately, face breaking. "The thought of hurting you, I..."

She pressed her lips together, finding the courage to whisper, "I will tell you."

"Will you?" he asked hoarsely. "You—"

"Yes," she whispered.

He seemed to waver, looking away, swallowing.

She bit her lip. "I wish I had not told you," she whispered. "I did not mean to ruin..." What had been a delight to them both, what had connected them, reconciled them, strengthened them.

"You have ruined nothing," he said, emotion in his voice, before kissing her again, their lips touching softly, lingering. She realized he was almost trembling with passion, but he broke off. "Forgive me," he mumbled, releasing her and walking away. He strode through the door, leaving her to wonder at his thoughts, and a tear to roll down her cheek.

Through all of the beginning of December, the news was about South Carolina's convention to draw up an ordinance of secession, which was taking place in the Baptist Church in Columbia.

Shannon received a letter from her mother when she and John Thomas were having breakfast one icy morning. Her hand shook as she opened it at the table. "It will be about the baby."

He laid a hand on her arm, and she unfurled the pages. She breathed deeply and exhaled. "I shall read it to you. 'My dears, you will forgive my lack of interest in the current Crisis when you learn that I am now a grandmother.'" Here, she broke off as both exclaimed with joy. "'Marie was brought to bed three days ago and delivered yesterday...'" Shannon paused, her brows drawing together as she met John Thomas's eyes. "'—Delivered yesterday of a daughter. It was a very difficult labor, and she is quite exhausted. I would not write to you, though, if we still feared for her life. Dr. Travers believes she will mend in time.'" She broke off, looking at John Thomas. "It must have been very serious!"

"It sounds so," he agreed softly.

"Do you think... Good heavens, ought I to go to them?"

"Read on," he said with comforting calm.

"'Indeed, she does grow stronger by day and is in raptures over her little daughter. They have named her Rose Marie but intend to call her Rose. *She* is excessively healthy with a head full of curling dark hair, porcelain skin, and a double chin.'" They laughed. "'I believe she favors *you*, Shannon, as a baby, for I seem to remember that your hair was dark at first. Indeed, though, there is no doubting that she has her father's chin. Frederick is relieved and yet still nervous. He does not like to hold the baby for fear of breaking her, but he does watch her sleep in her cradle while he sits at Marie's side.'" Shannon made a noise of sweetness, and John Thomas chuckled softly.

"'I hope I have not alarmed you unduly. There is no cause for worry at present, and we should alert you if ever there were. We send you our best love and hope to dispatch to you a sketch of your niece soon.'"

Shannon breathed a sigh of relief. "It sounds as though she is mending."

He nodded.

"I cannot imagine the scene at Santarella during those few days. It must have been hellish."

"It sounds as though it must. Do you feel you ought to go to her?"

"No, not with Mother's parting words. I shouldn't like to leave you just now, in any event. And at Christmas, too."

He reached into his coat and brought forth a small box. "And on our anniversary."

She gasped, covering her mouth. "Forgive me! With the letter, and everything..." She held his eyes, her own wide with guilt.

He laughed. "And you say *I* am unromantic."

She reached to take the box from him. "It seems impossible that it has been a year," she said.

He smiled.

"You are thinking it was a very long year, no doubt," she said.

"I was thinking of how wonderful it was." It was said softly, with simple truth. Shannon bit her lip. She swallowed and then opened the box, finding inside a pretty necklace, its pendant in the shape of the North Star. She thought of all of the signals they had been studying and the importance of this one, and her eyes misted. She could not speak. She studied it for the longest time.

"I want you to know that I did not spend above four-hundred dollars," he said with soft amusement. "And even you must admit it is quite simple."

She choked on a laugh, overwhelmed. "Yes. It is perfect."

Chapter Thirty-Eight

S hannon would remember, perhaps forever, where she was when she learned that South Carolina had seceded from the union. It had snowed for the first time, and Washington was blanketed in white. She had just returned to the house after walking in the park and was met by Mrs. Hensley and Phoebe at the door. They were both carrying boughs of greens, and Shannon said, "Oh, they have been delivered!"

"Yes, ma'am, just now," the housekeeper said. "We were thinking of wrapping the banister."

"Oh, yes, and perhaps the doorways. I will help. Phoebe, you must wear gloves. It will bite at your hands," she said, knowing her maid had never performed such tasks at Ravenel House. "I will bring some down," she said, starting for the stairs.

"Oh, no, ma'am, I'll—"

"It is nothing. You are already covered in sap." She climbed the stairs and located two pairs of driving gloves, thinking that

Mrs. Hensley had no need of them; her hands were calloused from years of labor.

She was just returning down the stairs when the door opened and John Thomas entered, his back to her as he dusted off his shoes. It was the middle of the day, and worry rose, halting her midway through the flight. "You are early," she said, hand still clasping her skirt.

He turned, looking at her, not speaking for a few moments. He took in the others and then met her eyes. "May I speak with you?"

"Yes," she said, going down, eyes not leaving his as she lay the gloves aside. She led the way into the parlor, and he closed the door behind them, studying her for another moment.

"You are frightening me," she said, wondering if he was angry with her. But that was irrational, for there had been no words spoken between them. She quickly checked her conscience, however: she had flirted with no one who meant anything by it, she had not let her tongue run away with her in at least two weeks, and she had faithfully attended the Congregational Church every Sunday for the past month.

"I'm sorry. I don't know how to tell you. South Carolina has seceded."

She blinked, raising the backs of her fingers to her mouth. A long silence passed, and then she said, "I see." She saw that he was looking at her a certain way, and she said, "Do you think I shall go insane? You needn't look at me in that way. I can bear it."

"Do not lash out at me, Shannon," he said very softly.

She swiped at her eyes, looking away. She was not feeling

very broad-minded in that moment. Her home—her beloved home—had been forced to sever ties with its country, and her husband, as much as anybody, had brought it to fruition. She swallowed, not meeting his eyes. "Thank you for telling me. I do mean what I said: I shall bear it. Only perhaps I ought to be alone for a little while, so that I do not say things which I later regret."

He nodded his acquiescence, looking down at the carpet, and let her pass, not attempting to touch her as she swept by.

Christmas passed in a haze, and the month of January saw tensions escalating almost every day. Shannon watched in muted horror as states dropped away: Mississippi, Florida, Alabama, Georgia, Louisiana, Texas. She felt as though she walked about in numbness, waiting to see how the government would react, waiting, really, for Lincoln's inauguration in March. But when she read the news early one cold February morning that the Southern states were holding a convention in Montgomery, drawing up a Constitution, and electing a president, she began a flurry of letters to her family, seeking their take, knowing that she could not trust everything she read in Washington or in the Boston newspaper they subscribed to. The same editors had allowed stories to be published after the election that the radical Southerners had been silenced and that the situation had now passed.

Her father advised her that South Carolina was indeed serious and that there was very little chance of its returning to the union, whatever appeasements Lincoln offered.

"My advice to you, Shannon, is to wait and see. You may think it odd coming from your father, a committed South Carolinian, but I cannot advise you to go against your husband's wishes. I could blame him for having those wishes, as I am sure, sometimes, you do, but it does as much good as whistling in the wind. He has his beliefs. He is a Northerner. I am sorry for it, but it was his raising. I will not say you have married a dishonorable man. Therefore, I believe you should abide in silence, whatever is to come, and hope for a better day. You are not the only young lady in such a situation. If there is to be a separation between you and our family, we must pray that it is a short one. You must be guided by your husband, for he knows his world. Endure it, tolerate it, and do not let it cause a breach between you. Do not fear that we, your family, should ever blame you. We wish only for your happiness, health, and safety."

"He is speaking as though I am a woman!" Shannon said, having read it to Phoebe in her bedchamber, her blue slippers peeking beneath her hem as she sat on the bed, letter in hand.

Phoebe, standing nearby, said gently, "He only wants what is best for you ma'am."

"Do you think he is *right*?"

Phoebe hesitated. "Well, I... If you really want me to say, Miss Shannon..."

"I do!"

"It seems to me this...conflict may be short, and it may be long. You'll be here either way. You can either resist in your heart, making a distance between you and your husband and making your life a living misery. Or you can support your husband, loving your home in your heart, and..."

"And living with myself the rest of my life as I am false to myself and my family?"

"Lieutenant Haley is your family, ma'am," Phoebe said softly, looking at the ground. "You would have something to live with the rest of your life if you thought yourself false to him, too."

Shannon swallowed, looking away as tears welled in her eyes. She stared out the window a long while until she whispered passionately, "It is impossible!"

"You'll be late for Mrs. Hartwell's tea if we don't dress you, ma'am," Phoebe said gently.

Shannon swiped at her eyes, sniffing and saying after a moment, "Yes."

Phoebe dressed her in a green walking gown of wool with tassels and pagoda sleeves and sent her outside. A hired carriage was waiting, courtesy of their manservant. They clopped along down the avenue until a brick mansion with blue shutters was reached.

Shannon was taken to a formal parlor with mirrors above the mantles on either end of the long room. Ornate gilded trim near the ceilings framed an egg and dart pattern. The hostess, a gently rounded woman in her late thirties with dark hair, rose, saying, "My dear Mrs. Haley. How lovely to see you." She extended her hands and then led Shannon to a sofa with some other young matrons. Mrs. Hartwell was from Virginia, and her husband was a senator. She had the same look of quiet unrest that Shannon had known since December. Virginia, however, had not seceded and might not yet. Mrs. Hartwell decided to join them, leaving the older ladies across the room to their conversation on quilting, perhaps seeing the need for diffusion.

"I trust your family is well?" Mrs. Franklin, a lady from Ohio asked, sipping her tea and looking innocent.

Mrs. Hartwell handed Shannon a tray of sweets, looking at her apologetically. Shannon smiled wryly as she took them. Shannon passed the plate to the other woman sitting nearby, the young Mrs. Pepper, a sweet but quiet woman with limp brown hair and large eyes.

"Indeed, they are quite well," Shannon said. "Have I told you that I have a niece?"

The ladies made noises of sweet pleasure.

"Your brother's child?" Mrs. Hartwell asked.

"Indeed, one Miss Rose Marie Ravenel, all of two months old, and reigning, I am told, in my father's household."

The other ladies laughed, and conversation continued pleasantly.

Mrs. Hartwell took Shannon aside before she left, saying, hand on her arm in a motherly fashion, "You have heard from your family, then?"

Shannon nodded. "My father advises me to wait and see."

Her dark eyes studied her. "Good advice, I should imagine. I am on tenterhooks. I believe even my children feel my distraction, from our dear Rebekah, at sixteen, to the baby. Does your husband, the Lieutenant, foresee calamity ahead, or are we all being quite dramatic?"

"I cannot say. If they will just *let them secede*," Shannon whispered.

"I *know*," her hostess whispered back, in perfect harmony, closing her lips when a Pennsylvania dame walked by. When she was gone, she patted Shannon's arm. "Let me know if you hear of anything. My good friend, Mrs. Greenhow, was asking. I believe she worries for her daughters' futures."

Chapter Thirty-Nine

The fiddlers struck up the first cheerful notes of the Cally Polka. Shannon, in a sea of belled skirts and glittering jewels, danced rapidly in the arms of a handsome captain. His eyes twinkled roguishly, and his lips held invitation. He was a charming rake, even if he was past fifty. They were at the home of the Secretary of the Navy, dancing in his expansive ballroom with dignitaries and military men.

She glanced across the room to where John Thomas was talking with several other young officers. She hadn't seen him show his reserved face in so long that she had almost forgotten it, forgotten how long it had taken to win little smiles from him whenever she chose.

She looked back at the Captain, who told her that he had fancied a red-haired beauty once upon a time, and they passed the rest of the dance talking about his youthful exploits. The song ended, and Shannon curtsied while he bowed. Before there was even time for refreshment, she had been claimed for the next dance, a reel, by Lieutenant Hughes.

"Were you on my card, Lieutenant? I specifically remember leaving this dance open so that I might rest," she said, allowing him to lead her nonetheless.

"No, of course I was not on your card: I didn't have the forethought to sign it six months ago!"

"Dear me, what a lapse of memory on your part," she smiled. "What do you think of Emily Lennox?"

He lifted his brows. "I'm afraid…"

"The accent?" she asked.

He would not admit it, of course, but he smiled. Shannon sighed. "I shall keep looking."

She glanced at her husband again to find him watching her, expression unreadable. He looked away after a moment, and Shannon returned her attention to her partner.

She danced with a Congressman after that. She had left the last two dances open so they would not stay unfashionably late, and when she was finished, she scanned the floor for John Thomas. He was talking with other gentlemen in a bright corner of the room. He looked very handsome in his dress uniform. He was tall and elegant, and she felt great pride in him and his accomplishments. She had not realized how well he had performed at the Academy until some of his schoolmates had begun talking about those days in her presence. And even now, it seemed he was becoming indispensable at the offices. Perhaps especially now.

He saw her and gave a very slight smile, his eyes a little reserved, perhaps a dash unsettled. She extended her gloved hand, and he took it, drawing her forward into the talking group and introducing her. "Gentlemen, my wife, the former Miss Ravenel, of Charleston.

"Your wife is an excellent dancer, Lieutenant!" a cheerful corporal said. "Very merry and gay."

"Yes, indeed," he said softly.

"I am sure Washington is nothing to Charleston, ma'am," another man said, "but I believe you will acknowledge that it has its own appeal. So charming, Haley, to have chosen a Southern wife. Southerners are the greatest ladies, I believe, present hostilities notwithstanding. A dash of something extra, wouldn't you say, Simmons?"

"Yes, indeed, I was just telling Haley so."

She felt John Thomas's hand close on her arm. He smiled. "If you will excuse us, I believe my wife is tired."

Farewells were said, and John Thomas led her through the throng and out to the carriage, where he assisted her in climbing the step, waiting while she arranged her skirts. She peeped at him warily, but he merely got in across from her.

The carriage began its journey toward home. Shannon watched him as he lay his head back against the seat. Folding her gloved hands over her reticule, she studied him for a moment and then hesitantly reached across, touching his knee. "You are worn to the bone," she said softly, sweetly.

He looked at her, studying her face.

"Can you not...take some time away?"

His expression gentled, and he took her hand in his and studied her for a time before shaking his head infinitesimally. "We are so unprepared in the event of war," he said softly, suddenly confiding in her. "We haven't proper Naval ranks so that we may have authority as a branch—no admirals, I mean, only captains, so that we must always bend our will to the army generals. Our ships—what few we have—are in terrible disrepair, and as a branch we are so small... There are so few men... I believe we must rely on volunteers among the immigrants, and how we shall manage when they speak various languages, I..."

"John Thomas, how much are they relying on you?" she questioned, knowing well that bright minds were few and far between, especially highly trained ones. He met her eyes, and she felt she had a pretty firm grasp of the truth. "What are they having you to do?"

"We are redesigning our ships." He looked out the window. "I ought not to tell you that, but they'll be seen being built soon enough."

"*You* are designing them?"

He looked back at her. "Lending my assistance. A sad state, is it not?"

"No, of course not. I merely hope you are given your due."

He pressed her hand, gently tugging her across the seat and slipping his arm around her. He pressed a kiss to her temple. "You are a darling. Likely I am not being paid enough, but who is? We are all doing what we must just now."

She settled into his side, grateful for his warmth. "You are speaking of war as though it is certain, despite the new President's claims to the contrary." She lifted her head, searching his profile. "What do you know that I do not?"

He looked at her and then back out the front window, where the driver was dimly visible. "Once we are inside," he said, squeezing her hand.

Shannon swallowed as the driver pulled up before the house. He got down and helped her, and she looked over her shoulder in the general direction of the President's House, thinking that the Lincolns were there now, perhaps hosting tonight, or perhaps, like them, on the point of turning down the lamps and going to bed.

John Thomas peered down at her and then touched her arm, looking toward the house and waiting. She turned, walking with him up the footpath and waiting while he unlocked the door. She moved past him once it was open, her skirts gently brushing this and that, and waited in the foyer while he bolted the door.

Once they had stepped across the threshold into their bedchamber, he closed the door, and she stood waiting, eyes fixed upon him. He turned back toward her, looking grim, but hesitating.

"Tell me."

"The Confederates have fired upon Fort Sumter for thirty-four hours and been met with return fire. The United States Army has surrendered the fort, and it is now in the possession of South Carolina."

Shannon did not move; she merely stood in the middle of the room, her color draining. "But you can *see* Fort Sumter from Ravenel House!" she exclaimed, feeling an inward tremble. Hostilities, gunfire, war... Perhaps they happened in Europe or Africa, but not mere miles from one's home.

He touched her arm. "I didn't mean to frighten you. I have not heard that any civilians were injured, or that the houses were touched. And your family is in the Sea Islands presently, are they not?"

"Yes, but..." She could not seem to string two thoughts together. She could not process it. "But hostilities have begun, then," she said softly, looking up, meeting his eyes. "Truly, this is war."

He nodded, and her eyes filled. He took another step forward, his other hand coming up to her elbow. He looked at her as though he didn't know what to do.

She turned her head away, closing her eyes. "Please, I..." She needed to sit, was afraid her legs would give way soon if she did not. She walked toward the bed and sank down, her skirts pluming around her. She hugged her arms around herself, and he sat down next to her, wrapping an arm about her, drawing her in to him. "I'm sorry," he whispered, kissing her temple. She began weeping, and he drew both arms around her tightly, his voice rasping as he whispered to her.

"How shall I survive it?" she mourned, emotion giving her voice an edge.

He held her against his chest for perhaps an hour. When her emotion was spent, and they both stared into the fireplace, he said softly, his voice not quite his own, "I *am* sorry. It was not what you bargained for when you married me and left your family."

She looked up at his defeated tone, her lips parting. She had not realized that he had been thinking in such a way. She thought now of Lizzie's words. "No," she said earnestly, reaching up and taking his face in her hands. "No, my dear man. You are worth it to me, don't you see? I'm sorry if I do not say it, but..." Her eyes swept his beloved face. "Sorry if I am a shrew—"

"Shannon," he whispered passionately, apparently overcome. "You are my life. And whatever is to come, we will face it together."

"Yes." Her eyes closed, and she whispered, "Yes, we shall." Their lips touched, and danced, giving, deepening, until time was lost. Shannon felt his hands come on either side of her, and his body gently nudge hers down, and she pulled him closer.

Shannon was awakened in the stillness of the early morning. Her eyes fluttered open, and she saw John Thomas lying beside her, his cheek on the pillow. His blue eyes were upon her face, and she met them. He had laid waste last night to any misguided notions that he no longer desired her.

His hand came up and gently smoothed her hair before tucking it behind her ear. "You were sleeping so peacefully," he said softly.

In general, she didn't see him in the mornings. She contemplated it and studied him leisurely.

His eyes roved her face. "Are you well?" he asked softly.

"Yes," she said. "I told you I should be."

He continued to regard her steadily, his expression losing some of its worry. His hand covered her cheek, and he pressed a kiss to her forehead, as though savoring her. She knew he could not say that he had desired her during those months, but his trembling passion the night before had told her. He could not just now find the words to say what she meant to him, but the way he looked at her, serious, contemplative, and gentle, said more. She remembered standing with him on the balcony at

Santarella when they'd first kissed and feeling terror in the marrow of her bones. And she felt it again now, fear that her life was beyond her control.

Chapter Forty

S hannon watched in muted horror as the war opened before her eyes, as the ladies of her circle began sewing for the soldiers, as mail routes were closed between Richmond and Washington with the occupation of Alexandria. As the army seemed to take over Washington and one could not take a single step without seeing ten men in blue. Hospitals were set up, medical units prepared, nursing staffs gathered, munitions counted, defenses bolstered. The Union high command was stunned, could not seem to act or gather together a solid plan. John Thomas called it embarrassing.

They would soon have one alleviation in the form of Adams, who was coming to Washington to lend his aid to the Treasury Department. Apparently, the Secretary was an old friend of the family and desired a young genius at his side as preparations for war were made.

Lizzie, having stunned her family by refusing Mr. Winthrop's offer of marriage, had suffered an interview with Miss

Dix and was found to be unsatisfactory to join the Nursing Commission, as she was neither past thirty nor ugly. "Who cares for *that* when men are suffering and dying!" John Thomas had exclaimed during a rare moment at home.

"Indeed, I do not know," Shannon responded, her head bent over her sewing. "I daresay she fears younger ladies will be exploited by men, both the doctors and the soldiers." She was a little surprised he should want his sister in such a situation, but the Congregationalists never failed to shock her with their radical ways.

Jonathan Whitcomb had been commissioned in the army as a chaplain and was being sent to Kentucky, a wrench for Patience and dear little James. Still, she had the support of her family and his. Although the young Whitcombs had moved to a cottage of their own shortly after little James's birth, she was returning to the parsonage for the duration of Jonathan's time away.

Charles had announced his intention to join the army, which naturally left his parents apprehensive, but they did not attempt to turn him from what he felt to be his duty. He was now under McClellan's command in the Army of the Potomac, which was making plans to drive toward Richmond. If McClellan could ever gather the courage up, Shannon thought with a curl to her lip.

But she had little time these days for thinking of her loyalties. She kept her thoughts to herself, knowing it would be dangerous otherwise. She could not overtly support the war effort, but human suffering and need was something different altogether, as she had learned from her brief time as a Haley.

Her mother-in-law wrote to her, asking what could be done for the effort. Shannon could never see soldiers in their tents looking chilled to the bone without thinking of the men she loved, and so she requested scarves, gloves, and stockings. She soon had more boxes of those than she could give out in Washington, thanks to the industrious ladies of Massachusetts, and she and Phoebe began searching about for places in the most need. John Thomas, looking at her tenderly while she stood amidst the piles of crates in their foyer with her notepad, promised his aid, and she soon had addresses of likely regiments.

When she was alone, she wondered often about her family. What had become of them? Was Frederick involved in military action? Had he been one of the many to be taken by disease in camp before he even had a chance to fight? These thoughts disturbed her mind more than she ever let her husband know, sometimes bringing her within an inch of hysterics.

She did receive one answer in November when they heard that a Confederate ironclad sank two wooden Union ships. It was a horrid blow to the Union, confirming all that John Thomas had been confiding to her about the state of the Navy. In the reports from the massive battle, which began to come to them in the following days, even Northern propaganda could not hide the impressive Confederate Naval efforts. The victories were headed by three captains, one of them named Frederick Ravenel.

Shannon, having been handed the paper by a mute John Thomas, looked up, thunderstruck. "I cannot believe it," she breathed, lifting her fingers to her lips.

"Can't you?" He looked away. "I can."

She studied him, seeing suddenly that he missed Frederick. She was thankful she had noticed. She reached to cover his hand, and his eyes met hers. Pressing her lips together, she admitted, "I am sorry if it angers you, but I am very proud of him."

"How could you not be?" he said shortly. He got up, brushing his fingers through his hair. "I am myself." He walked toward the door, only to be met by the manservant, who stepped through the door, making John Thomas stop.

He looked startled and said softly, "Yes? You needed something?"

"Forgive me, sir, but this arrived by special messenger."

John Thomas's brows drew together, and he took a letter from him, murmuring, "Thank you," as he looked at the direction. He continued to stare at it a moment overlong. He looked up at Shannon. "From South Carolina," he said.

Her heart quickened. "Impossible."

He studied it, brushing his thumb over the direction. "It seems..." He considered pensively. "A flag of truce, perhaps."

"Addressed to me?"

"To me," he said, in more confusion still.

She swallowed and waited, her hand at her high collar, as he broke the seal. He read for a few moments, before finally looking up, his face pale, his eyes upon her face.

"What is it?" she demanded, gripping the handkerchief which was in her hand.

He hesitated before bringing her the letter, kneeling next to her, and putting one hand on her shoulder. Her heart hammered against her ribcage, a sickening feeling unfurling in her stomach, heat spreading to her veins.

She hesitated and then read to the bottom and saw her father's signature.

My Children,

I address this letter to you, John Thomas, because I want you to be near to comfort her when she reads it. I have no notion of whether this will make it to you, of whether you are still with her at home or off in battle, but I knew I must try. I have been reliably informed that there is a chance such mail might not be denied.

In short, Shannon, your mother, found, some weeks ago, a mass in her breast, which we have since learned is cancerous. We have seen four physicians, all of whom tell us the same: her time is short.

There is no easy way to tell you this: I pray your husband is with you. I pray for your comfort.

There is so much to say, but I refrain in hopes that this letter will find you, that the Federals feel it is unnecessary to deny or censor it. Know that you are in our thoughts every moment, in our prayers constantly.

Your Father

Shannon awakened, feeling the heaviness of her eyes and a weakness in her spirit. The room was darkened, a fire glowing in the hearth. She blinked, attempting to see the clock above the mantle. Past ten o'clock. She had been asleep since the afternoon.

She felt a hand run over her hair and turned her head, seeing John Thomas sitting beside her, for once not in his uniform, but instead in his shirtsleeves. Her eyes flitted over him. "You are still here," she said weakly. She had seen him only two hours in the last week combined. She had long since ceased wondering when he slept: he didn't.

He reached for her hand, holding it tightly, eyes gentle on her face. She thought of how tenderly he had held her earlier, how much she had missed his embrace. Her eyes welled now, meeting his, and she realized that his also were misting.

"I cannot fathom it," she whispered.

He fingered the white cuff on her nightgown, looking down at it. "She is...such a great lady."

Shannon bit her lip, tears running freely down her face. "It seems impossible that I cannot go to them."

He touched her cheek. He swallowed. "What can I do?"

She covered his hand, turned her head, and kissed his palm. His thumb stroked her temple, while his worried eyes continued to search her. "Nothing, John Thomas. You are here."

The look in his eyes deepened further still. "I do love you so," he said.

She studied his face, memorizing every curve and dip, every little perfection and flaw. Her brother's friend. She still thought of that, occasionally. Of meeting him two years ago, and lying in bed with him now.

She held his eyes, and she could see it, how deeply he felt. It frightened her, the way he looked at her. "You are going to leave me, aren't you?" she said softly.

He swallowed, holding her eyes. She bit her lip. "How long have you known?"

"Since last night," he said softly. "It is why this morning I..." He swallowed. "I didn't know how to tell you. How to part from you."

"You...will captain a ship?"

"Yes."

"And enforce the blockade?" she asked softly.

He held her eyes for a beat. "I must, Shannon," he said at length. "You know I must." His voice was soft, gentle.

She turned her head away. "When?" she asked, the word sounding scratchy, forced from her throat.

"Next month." A long silence passed. "I oughtn't to discuss it now, but...time seems so short. I have to provide for your care and safety before I leave."

She closed her eyes, promising herself that she would not again dissolve. "You have always provided for me, John Thomas."

He leaned forward, kissing her forehead tenderly. After a moment, he said, "As to money for you, I will execute a power of attorney."

"To Adams?"

"To you."

She lifted her brows slightly.

"But it isn't money I wish to speak of," he said. He studied her as if memorizing her now. He hesitated. "I would prefer that you pass the war in Boston, Shannon."

Her brows drew together. "But Washington is our home."

"I know," he said softly. "But you would have the support of my family, an entire community. You would be safer, farther away from the action, and...it would give me peace of mind."

She blinked. It was all too much. Her mother, him, her home. "Do you know how I shall be treated there?" she said, sitting up. "With scorn and suspicion, and I... At least here there are those who are sympathetic. But even so they gaze at me with a look in their eyes that says *rebel*. And I have done nothing but support this cause. It is merely for my birth, my accent, my history. In Boston I shall be a pariah!"

He looked at her in disbelief. "You are the wife of a Naval captain. You shall have the protection of my entire family. Tell me who will close his door to you in such a circumstance? You have...built up an illusion—"

She stiffened. A silence grew and thickened the air. She turned and got up, walking over to the fireplace. She felt his eyes following her. She supposed she had *imagined* she was the only officer's wife not invited to Mrs. Hempstead's charity circle. Or that Mary Linwood whispered behind her fan to her daughter when she passed her in the street. Setting aside how disastrous it could be to John Thomas, she was unaccustomed to social scorn entirely.

She stood looking into the fire. She heard him get up and, slowly, she felt his arms come around her. "I'm sorry," he whispered. "I didn't mean to upset you, tonight of all nights."

"Oh, what does it matter?" she said bitterly. "How can I be so selfish?"

"You are not selfish."

"No?" She laughed once with self-derision. A long silence passed. "I will go to Boston," she said finally, softly. "If it will give you peace."

"It will," he murmured sadly, turning her in his arms. He kissed her temple, lingering there. She stared into the distance.

Chapter Forty-One

It was not to be that Shannon could mourn her mother, or that she would have time with her own thoughts. John Thomas received an invitation two days later to dine at the President's House in a week's time, an honor that several of his circle were to receive as commemoration of their recent efforts to make the Navy competitive with the Confederate Navy.

Shannon had been very quiet, and when John Thomas had asked, a little remotely, whether she would be able to bear it, she had said, "I shan't embarrass you." His slight flush and remorseful eyes had spoken the truth of his concerns. He had, thereafter, been extremely accommodating.

As fate would have it, Shannon was not thinking about the war when she was greeted by President and Mrs. Lincoln at the White House. They had gone in front of one of John Thomas's fellow Naval men, whom she had never met, and his wife, who was with child. They had stood talking to them as they waited in the receiving line. Shannon could never see another woman in such a condition without feeling a pang.

She had watched John Thomas carefully as he had, months back, read the news that Patience had safely delivered a child. Jonathan, not thinking, had waxed eloquent on the delight of both families in welcoming the first grandchild. Yet, Shannon had seen only relief for his sister's safety, and perhaps a slight hesitance to meet her eyes. They had not spoken of it since that awful night when Frederick and Marie had stayed with them, but he must know by now that she would never bear him a child. Her only signal that it had even crossed his mind was how carefully he, when reading to her from the Bible, left off the passages on the matriarchs' barrenness, and picked up, almost seamlessly, somewhere else.

"Captain Haley—John Haley, is it not?"

Shannon looked up to find Mr. Lincoln speaking to her husband. She craned her neck up to look into his face. He had slightly curling dark hair and gaunt cheeks.

"Yes, sir," he answered with his customary calm and peace.

"Thomas," Shannon said, and afterwards couldn't think why she had. "He prefers John Thomas."

A twinkle entered the President's deep-set eyes. "Does he? Well, now, thank you for that, Mrs. Haley. A man never likes to be made a fool of, and I am a fool often enough as it stands, I'm afraid."

Shannon feared John Thomas would think she was not keeping her word. He did glance down at her. But when Mrs. Lincoln agreed, they all laughed.

"I liked your idea for twin gunports, Captain Haley," the President said, revealing a stunning memory. "I should not be surprised at your intuition, however: it seems you have chosen well in your wife. Your discretion is never at fault."

John Thomas flushed slightly. He did not like the praise, but Shannon felt immense pride in him. She found that he was looking down at her with the same feelings reflected for her. She was already holding his arm, but she covered it with her other hand. "As it relates to my wife, I must agree with you entirely, sir."

"A wise man, I'd say," Lincoln said in his humorous, homely way which Shannon found peculiar.

As they were moved along by footmen, most of them Negros, Shannon kept both hands on John Thomas's arm, feeling a little lightheaded, and in a fog. She had pictured this evening perhaps a hundred times, but she ought to have known better. One could never precisely plan for anything, where humans and their peculiarities were concerned. The gas lights were cast at a certain warm glow, and she knew she ought to look around her, at the regal walls, their elegant hangings, the famous portraits.

She was not able to collect herself, however, until she was led to her chair, which seemed miles away from John Thomas's. He was seated, poor man, between the vulgar Milner woman and a positive child who flirted with him mercilessly. Shannon looked around her, finding herself at the chair to the right of the head, directly across from the wife of the Secretary of War. It was a place of eminence and, looking around, her lips parted with the surprise of it. Someone, in his wisdom, had decided that she was one of the highest-ranking ladies present, despite the fact that there were several wives of other captains of much longer standing. She swallowed. It also meant she was next to the President. The fates simply were not in her favor tonight.

The handsome, old Captain who had danced with her and charmed her with tales of his redhead winked at her from midway down the table. That amused her, so that she was able to regain her equanimity before the President came in.

When he did enter, he sat rather ungracefully, all arms and legs, and he turned to Mrs. Cameron and said, "I always liked a good ham. This one has been cooking all day: we have not been able to keep the boys out of the kitchen."

She laughed. "Boys will be boys, Mr. Lincoln. Best to let them be."

"I'd say you're right, ma'am, except mine would kill themselves if we didn't stop them."

"Not your eldest, surely. I hear tell he is a great scholar."

"Bobby had his day," he said in his strange voice. He turned next to Shannon. She was surprised anew at how massive his frame was, and that he did not seem to be full of talk of the war. He seemed to fixate on the smallest trivialities, just as though he had not plunged them into a crisis. "It seems you're not nervous, Mrs. Haley, as most are when they're told they are to sit next to me. Mayhap rumors have been passed that I am a bully, or that my odor is unpleasant, but it always seems to be the case. I pity you, ma'am."

She could not help a small smile growing. "I am rarely nervous, President."

"You'd be well-born, then. You must be, or they would not have placed you here, as I'm learning."

She studied him for a moment, glancing up to find John

Thomas watching her with interest. He could not hear them, however, as all of the guests at the long table were confining themselves to their near neighbors. "I am a Ravenel, sir. Of South Carolina," she added.

"You wouldn't be Old Willie's granddaughter, would you?"

She lifted her brows. "Yes, indeed, I am. Did you know him?"

"I had that honor. I'm sorry you should be estranged from your family just now, ma'am."

"Thank you," she said, eyes downcast.

"My surmise was correct, then. I imagine my family would've been chimney sweeps for yours in the old days, or perhaps taken their chamber pots out," he said, with humorous modesty. "Truly, we ought to switch seats, ma'am."

"I wish we might," she said boldly.

He laughed. "Are you a Democrat, then? I've been told that your husband is a staunch Republican."

"And an abolitionist," she said, suddenly ashamed of her outburst. "He has been your admirer since long before the election."

"I appreciate that. He seems to be a talented young man, and we need those." His eyes clouded in the distance. "We need them desperately."

"And yet you have not spoken of him with hatred, my dear," Mrs. Greenhow said as she and Shannon sipped tea in the elder lady's parlor. Miss Baldwin, a charge she was chaperoning for a gentleman, a Republican senator from Indiana, played the piano by the windows. Little Rose played nearby, occasionally remembering to turn the pages, usually not before she was asked.

Shannon hesitated.

"I am not suggesting that you *should* hate him," Mrs. Greenhow said. "Only that I thought you did."

"He..." She faltered again. "He was funny," she explained, almost defensively, lifting a shoulder. "And odd. He said he knew my grandfather." She took a sip of tea.

Mrs. Greenhow smiled. "You must miss your family very much, especially after this news."

"My grandfather is deceased, but yes. I do." She sipped the tea again, realized she was using it as a nervous habit, and set her glass down with a clank. She looked at the older woman. "Sometimes I feel as though they don't exist, for they may as well not."

"Oh, my dear," her friend said. She covered her hand. "I do not doubt the President wants capable young men around him, with the debacle they are making of this war. Your husband must feel it deeply, the mismanagement."

Shannon shook her head, saying softly, "He feels they are deeply unprepared. He..."

"Yes, dear?"

Shannon couldn't think why she had stopped. Only, there was something in the other lady's demeanor that made her glad she had. She gave a wan smile. "He is worn to the bone."

Mrs. Greenhow glanced toward the piano and then back at her, her pretty face hesitant. Finally, she opened her lips to speak, though quietly. "You...are in a position to be of great help to your people, my dear child," she said, holding Shannon's eyes for an overlong moment.

Warmth rushed in Shannon's veins, hot and a little unpleasant, as she contemplated the other woman's words. Mrs. Greenhow looked at her for another long while. "You and I...have certain loyalties. And we are in such a circumstance that we know people...important people. People who can give us information which can be used by...people who are dear to us."

Shannon felt the blood rushing in her ears.

Mrs. Greenhow patted her hand. "Think on it, my dear."

Chapter Forty-Two

The day was peaceful, the sky bleak. Another week had passed, and by now, the Haleys had heard the news from South Carolina. Kind letters poured in from them. Shannon was grateful, but they were difficult to read, and she passed a morose morning doing so. Mrs. Haley especially knew just what ought to be said. She spoke with more generosity than Shannon felt she could have in reversed circumstances, not only about the news but also about Shannon's separation from her family. Mrs. Haley knew they could not fill the place in her heart that only her natural family could but asked her to allow them to meet the need until a better day. They had also just learned of John Thomas's promotion and of his deployment, and she could sense through their cheerful words that they had tried to be brave for her sake. They entreated her to come to them as soon as possible after his departure and wished to discuss arrangements for her travels.

Shannon looked up from her little writing desk in her

chamber and out the many-paned window down onto the green, where men in blue were drilling and marching. She could hear it only faintly through the thick glass. She could not help thinking that they must be very cold. She was a little chilled herself in her dark gray woolen dress, even with the white undersleeves beneath the wide outer sleeves.

Behind her, she heard Phoebe come in and remove the things from her tea. She looked over her shoulder, suddenly thinking that her maid also had been separated from her world as never before. Shannon's mother would often pass along tidbits from the slaves, give Phoebe news of her aunt, the cook at Ravenel House, and give her instructions regarding Shannon's wardrobe and health.

She pressed her lips together and thought about mentioning the separation but could not. The old ways were too strong to be forsaken.

Looking at her, Phoebe asked softly, "Do you need your rags, ma'am?"

Perhaps she had thought her hesitation was for that reason. "No," she said softly. Her brows drew together. Their courses seemed to run more or less together, and she had noticed Phoebe, who suffered silently in pain, wrapping her arms around her middle three days ago. She met Phoebe's eyes and, seeing that she was looking at her, with no expression, except something in her eyes, looked away. She moistened her lips and sought about for something to say. "Phoebe, did you tell me that they confiscated Lieutenant Hughes's house once he left?"

The Lieutenant had resigned his commission in the Navy months ago, the day after the Virginian Lee had his in the

Army. He had taken time to say goodbye to the Haleys, emotion evident in the redness of his eyes, in the way he repeatedly smoothed his hand over his mouth. John Thomas was kindness itself; other fellow officers had not been so disposed. Shannon had wiped tears by the window while they talked, discussing the future. He had been advised by his commanding officer not to tarry in Washington if he valued his own liberty, and so he did not tarry.

"Yes, ma'am."

"I don't know why I didn't think... I ought to go to them, ask for his belongings, at least a few things that might be important to him. He wouldn't have been able to take much with him on the train."

"There were so many confiscations after the exodus, ma'am, that I imagine they don't know what to do with all of it."

The exodus was what they were calling the flight of Southern senators, congressmen, residents, and military personnel before the borders had closed. Her friend, Mrs. Hartwell, had left with their children in good time, her husband following once there was no hope of reconciliation. Even they had left a house sitting full of furniture, family portraits, and belongings.

"They'll know precisely what to do with it," she said. "Sell it or burn it." She pressed her lips together, supposing she ought not to have said that. They were not allowed to think and speak as they felt, only as Mr. Lincoln did. Every thought that entered her head was technically, under the law, treasonous, and it made bitterness rise within her. But she realized that such speech was unbecoming in front of a servant. "Forgive me, I...spoke out of turn," she said finally.

A cold, rainy day turned into an even more miserable night. It was too warm to snow, and so a hard, soaking rain chilled the houses and, inevitably, the soldiers in the many camps. Shannon was reading by the light of the fireplace, still in her gown because it was warmer than her nightgown. She could not concentrate, could think of nothing but John Thomas's imminent departure.

There was a stirring at the door, and she looked up to see him standing there, his cap gone, his hair looking as though he had run his hands through it multiple times. She stood. "You are home." She started to go to him, but something held her back.

He just stood there on the edge of the carpet, in the flesh as always, but different, looking at her, a haunted expression in his blue eyes.

Her brows drew together. "What is it?"

"Mrs. Greenhow has been placed under house arrest for spying." His eyes were fixed on her face.

Shannon felt her color draining. The crackles of the fireplace sounded distant. Her heart thrummed. "What?" she breathed.

He stepped into the room. "Apparently the Rebels owe their victory at Bull Run almost entirely to her information."

Her trembling fingers touched her lips, and she turned her face away. She did not say anything. She felt his deep study of her and finally heard him say in disbelief, voice shaking, "You knew."

She looked back at him quickly. She made a rapid study of his eyes, her lips parting, but no words came forth. He cursed, turning away and running a hand over his face. Her blood ran cold, and fear clutched at her heart. "How deeply are you in?"

She gasped, thunderstruck. "How dare you!"

He looked back at her, sneering. "How dare I?" he repeated, as though her words were unfathomable.

"You have the audacity to accuse me of spying?" she asked, trembling.

"You have just admitted to knowing she was a spy!"

"There is a difference between not voicing something told to one in confidence and actively helping. I did not know any particulars. She recruited me; I never went to her house again. I could not reveal what was not mine to tell: she trusted me. I could not put her in that position; I could not put *you* in that position. You are a gentleman: would you have informed on a lady, putting her life at risk? What would have had me do?"

"I would have had you choose, once and for all, Shannon! Hundreds of men died because of her!"

"Or were saved," she said. "It is all a matter of perception."

He blinked. There was a long pause. "I, apparently, have none."

Her lips parted. "You do not believe me," she whispered in utter disbelief.

"How can I, when you so obviously support what she has done?"

She hardened herself to the pain she saw in his eyes. "I have supported *you*," she seethed. "It was a difficult choice for me to make, but I made it. She wanted me to use you, to tell her the things you tell me, presumably when you tell me the most: after we have made love. I found such an idea repugnant—*grossly* repugnant. I have forsaken my family, my beliefs, my birth, and this is my reward!"

She expected a rejoinder, but he was arrested, looking at her with parted lips. The rage had dissipated slightly, and he seemed, for the first time, to doubt himself. "Shannon," he whispered.

"Have I convinced you of something I should never have had to say at all?" she demanded, still trembling. She turned, looking toward the window where rain was slicing against the panes. "Did you remember that I have been a good Yankee? If you are feeling guilty, allow me to assuage your conscience. I *despise* your precious blockade, which has no other hope than that of starving my people into submission. I *loathe* your Republicans and your president, who have authorized the raising of a half million men to bring violence upon my family. And I cannot abide *your* hypocritical Northern morality!"

"Shannon," he said lowly, lifting a hand to his mouth and wiping it, turning away as though shaken.

"Have I hurt you?" she demanded, hot, angry tears rising to her eyes. "Good. It cannot amount to the half of what I have been forced to endure from you over the course of our marriage."

He pressed his fist against his mouth, not speaking.

Shannon wrapped her arms around herself, feeling quite ill and still shaking. "Say something," she commanded after a moment.

He shook his head. "I never thought to hear such things from you."

"A testament to my long-suffering nature!" she snapped.

His eyes pinched at the corners. "How?" he demanded,

voice rasping. "What have I ever denied you? When have I shown you anything but respect?"

"When..." She shook her head, unable to speak, the anger and hurt was so deep.

"Shannon, I cannot bear it," he said pressing his palm to his forehead and dragging his hand back through his hair. "To leave like this. But I must return to the training grounds, and I... They have told us to hold ourselves in readiness—we might leave at any moment."

She looked at him, her mouth going slack. "What?" she breathed.

He met her eyes, nodding once, and then lowered his eyes to the ground. "We will...discuss it in letters. I..." He broke off, as though his voice were suspended. "I am sorry that I hurt you."

A long silence ensued. Her lip trembled. "I want my mother," she whimpered in a whisper, feeling remote.

His eyes pinched at the corners in compassion, his lips pressing together painfully. "I'm sorry."

She swallowed, feeling an inward trembling that couldn't be stopped. "I want to go home." He met her eyes. "To South Carolina," she said.

His brows drew together. "You couldn't."

She stiffened, lifting her chin.

He amended, "You wouldn't."

He sighed, turning and opening the armoire, removing his valise and stowing several items in it. Shannon watched in muted shock, unable to move. The shaking had not ceased.

He turned, looking at her, coming to her, hesitating before kissing her cheek. "I did not mean to part on these terms," he said, his voice scraping. "Please let me know when you are safely in Massachusetts." He paused, looking at her, looking as though he wished to say something else, as though he wished she would speak. He took a shaky breath. "I must go." He looked around the room once more, as though wishing to memorize it, and turned to go.

She watched him disappear through the door, feeling as though the ground beneath her were shifting. She stood there, breathing hectic breaths, wrapping her arms around her waist, too ill in her heart to cry. She suddenly remembered him, his eyes, as he lifted her and spun her beneath the live oak tree at Santarella, around and around, her green skirts belling. She closed her eyes tightly.

She did not know how long she stood there. The next thing she remembered was Phoebe coming in, looking worried, saying, "This fire's gone out, ma'am," and bending to stoke it.

Shannon turned from her, as one awakening from a dream. She went to the screen and numbly began removing her dress—skirt, shirtwaist, shift, corset, undergarments. She paused, looking at them. She closed her eyes. She waited a long moment. "Phoebe, my rags," she said tiredly, weary, so weary of the ritual.

"Yes, ma'am," came the quiet voice from the other side of the screen.

A tear escaped the corner on each of her eyes. She closed them and lifted her face upwards, toward the ceiling. She knew she must collect herself, and she had done so by the time Phoebe brought her all that she required.

"Phoebe," she said, catching her arm.

Phoebe met her eyes. Shannon's mind spun. It was a sign,

was it not? No fruit could ever come from them. "I am going—somehow—to go to South Carolina."

"What?" the maid breathed. "The borders are closed—you..."

"Do not underestimate me. I shall do it if I wish. You may come if you choose—I will not force you. You must make your own decision. You know very well what it would mean to you. I should try to ensure you would not be enslaved again, but I could make no promises. I am sure Captain Haley would see that you are provided for if you remain here. I shan't return."

Her maid looked frightened. "But Captain Haley—"

"Yes." Phoebe searched her eyes. No more needed to be said.

Phoebe took an emotional breath, her dark eyes searching about as though for the answer. "I...I can't let you face those men, the soldiers, alone."

"Then pack our things." She turned, calmly, rationally, to sit and compose a letter. "I am going home."

Chapter Forty-Three

On Tuesday morning, Adeline told the guys that she had to make a supply run, not wanting them to be suspicious. She was going to lose a ton of respect when this got out anyway. No use in hurrying it. Since the appointment wasn't until ten o'clock, she drove through some of the Sea Islands. She was swept away by their beauty and wished she had longer to take a detour and sniff out clues for Santarella.

She had read a letter from the Ravenel daughter to someone who must have been an old beau during the war, telling him that he ought to come out and look at their rice trunks and see if they were in any better shape than his. So, rice. She would bet that could narrow down some of the islands.

It was as she was crossing back into Charleston that the doctor's office called. She hung up two minutes later, frustrated, and then, trying to keep an eye on the road, scrolled through her phone for Adrian's number. She knew he had set aside, probably with great difficulty, two hours that morning.

She winced. She still had him in her phone as "Mr. Ravenel."

She dialed, and he picked up on the third ring. "Hello?"

"Adrian?"

"Adeline? Are you okay?"

She laugh-sighed. "Yeah. I don't know why I said your name like that. They called from the doctor's office. They overbooked this morning, if I want an ultrasound, and had to reschedule for four this afternoon. I do want an ultrasound, don't I?"

"Yeah," he said, as though he were thinking.

"Sorry. I know this totally messes with your schedule, and that you probably won't be able to go. Are you with a client right now? Sorry if I'm bothering you."

"Yeah—that's okay, though. It's not your fault." A pause. "I'll do some rescheduling. This is actually better: I can pick you up before."

"Adrian, you really don't have to do that."

"I'm going, Adeline," he said firmly.

She blinked. Her heart fluttered a little. "Okay. I'll, like, be on the sidewalk at 3:45, or something," she said with a little laugh.

She could feel him smiling. "Don't get hit by a tourist."

"Good point. I'll let you go." She hung up and drove toward the house. She'd just have to make up some excuse when she had to leave before they usually stopped work.

Adeline surveyed her handiwork on the library fireplace. One fully restored rosette. She could fix all of the delicate wood herself, there was no trouble in that. Except that it would probably take two months of eight-hour days. But the inner workings eluded her. She had been on the phone with someone from Williamsburg about the possibility of flying an expert down to look at it. They were happy to oblige, for a price. She scheduled the meeting two weeks out and hoped time hadn't damaged it structurally too much.

They had asked her a question about whether some piece inside was sagging that had seemed really crucial, but she hadn't known. Now, she surveyed it, contemplating sending for Joe. She didn't want to get dirty, and who knew what lived in there? But Joe and three of the others were working on the balconies with a crew of ten locally hired men. It was a big day for them structurally.

So, wryly, she knelt down and looked into it. Unlike the fireplace which had covered it, this one had been wood-burning. There was still black charring which wiped onto her skin and, being so old, it refused to come off without soap. She reached her arm up, feeling. It was almost as if someone had nailed a piece of wood up there.

She sat back, brows drawing together. No one would ever put wood up into the flue or smoke shelf of a fireplace which they intended to use. What on earth? She reached her hand up again, feeling. It was quite definitely wood; it would have left splinters if she hadn't touched it so gently.

She stood, brushing her hands off as best she could, and went into the next room, where she found Jose. "Jose," she said, "will you come here?"

He looked up from his careful restoration of the baseboards and said, "Sure," getting up and following her. She showed him, and he was equally confused.

"Do you think it was about to crumble, and they put it in there for structural support?" she asked.

He shook his head. "I don't think one piece of wood would support all of that brick." He was watching her. "What do *you* think?"

She shook her head. "It's a crazy theory... But I think maybe they hid stuff in there during the war."

His brows drew together. "And then covered it—the whole thing—to really seal the deal?"

She bit her lip, forehead crinkled, and then realization dawned on her. She took a step back, cast her eyes over the masterful piece of work, and then added to that what it must've looked like in its heyday. Then she imagined herself a Federal soldier, very angry at Charleston for starting the war, especially at its wealthiest residents. What would she have done upon entering this house? Well, she would've wanted to explore every room, but she drew on her inner vengeance-seeker. She would've torn this down, this symbol of power and wealth and history. And the Ravenels who had lived here had to have known that. "I think they did it to save it," she said. "Probably once things started to turn rough, but they still had the money. And bonus: where better to hide your valuables than in a fireplace that doesn't exist?"

He nodded slowly. "I think you're right about the covering. I've racked my brains for why anyone in his right mind would cover that. And I bet it was famous in its day. But why leave it like that after the war?"

"No money," she said. "They probably told succeeding generations to fix it once there was, but I bet the children didn't believe how beautiful and special it was and thought the one that was there was good enough. Remember, it was really pretty. And it worked, too, channeling back to the chimney toward the top."

"All right, that works, but why literally bury your valuables where you couldn't get to them without ripping down a wall?" He glanced toward it, a flicker of something lighting his features. "Do you think they're still there?"

She laughed. "If they are, they're Dr. Ravenel's now. But..." He had a point. That made no sense. She started thinking of routes of alternate access. They could've gone through the wall behind the fireplace and broken the bricks out. If so, Williamsburg would be disgusted. But they'd found no evidence of that in the structure during their inspection.

Then she lifted her eyes up slowly, another thought forming. Jose's eyes had followed hers there, and he said, "The chimney."

She nodded slowly, excitement taking her mind off of all the craziness for the first time in days. "Jose, knock that shelf out," she said.

He was happy to oblige. He was petite, so she let him stand up in there. He said, his voice echoing, "There are pegs all the way up. I bet they lined it with shelves full of stuff."

Adeline blinked away tears. "Yes, and then accessed them later from the roof with something to pull the stuff up, pulling the shelves up as they went."

"Until they got to the last," he said.

"Until they got to the last," she affirmed. Which remained.

Chapter Forty-Four

Adeline didn't bring up their discoveries to Adrian. It seemed a little trite in comparison with their crazy personal lives, and she didn't want mix work into this. *Oh, I know you're still waiting on an answer to your proposal, but did you know your fireplace served a really cool purpose during the Civil War?* Although, she was willing to do just about anything to put off talking about the proposal. She couldn't seem to make any reason of her thoughts about it.

He picked her up at the appointed hour, and they headed toward downtown. Michael Bublé (or was it someone he had done a remake of?) played in the background softly. She glanced at him now and then, and, unfortunately, he must have finally noticed it.

"You okay?" he asked, glancing at her.

"Yeah."

"Nervous?"

"A little," she admitted.

"I knew I should've brought you a milkshake," he said.

She laughed, looking over at him. "Where would you have gotten a milkshake?"

"The hospital." When she gave him a look, he defended, "Jude could live on those things. You should come have lunch sometime."

"That's so romantic," she said, eyes twinkling.

His lips twitched, but he shook his head. She saw a bunch of sleek medical buildings start to pass and then one with palm trees in the large parking lot. "I think that's it," she said, basing it off what she'd seen on Google images.

"It's this parking garage," he said decisively. "I looked it up."

Okay, then. She was glad someone knew where they were going. They parked and walked into a nice waiting room where super-married women sat looking calmer than she felt. She glanced at him, and he nodded encouragingly, going to sit down. She walked up to the desk and signed her name. Then she turned to find him and saw him sitting by one of the wide windows which made the room sunny.

They talked softly while they waited, and she made a scant glance around the room, taking in all of the people. She had the hottest baby daddy, there was no question. Never mind that was what had gotten her into this mess; that woman who had made a careful study of their ring fingers knew it.

"Miller," a woman in scrubs called from the door.

Adeline looked up, heart in her throat, and stood, not sure whether having him here made this better or worse. She didn't want to do it alone, but it was embarrassing to think about the things he might hear about. *Okay, pull it together, honey.*

He held the door for her, and they followed the nurse back

to a room. Adeline took her seat on the patient's chair, and he took the other. In five minutes, a woman entered, giving her name (which Adeline couldn't afterwards remember) and saying that she was her ultrasound tech.

"Great," Adeline said.

"How far along do you think you are?" she asked chipperly.

"Um, six weeks," she said, lying back as the tech nudged her that way. She had beautiful ebony skin. Adeline tried to focus on that rather than her shirt being lifted. She was pretty sure that at the point you were having a baby with a guy you weren't supposed to be embarrassed by an exposed tummy. Or by the fact that it was really cold in the room. Note to self: wear padded bra to next appointment.

She looked up at the screen as the woman put the lotion on her and waited.

"Aww. Yeah!" the woman said a few seconds in. "There it is. Sweet little thing."

Adeline caught a glimpse of Adrian. His focus was intense on the monitor, scanning over it, and his eyes were different— she finally realized it was moisture. He was clearly in love with their little pea, and she couldn't even find it on the monitor. She looked back at the monitor, swiping at her eye surreptitiously. "I'm afraid I don't know where it is," she said. Her voice didn't sound like her own.

"Dad knows, doesn't he?" the tech said, smiling at Adrian.

He nodded, leaning up and pointing. Adeline bit her lip. "Oh, I see," she breathed. A little tadpole-like, and teeny tiny, but in the general shape of a body. She blinked away tears and stared forever.

"It's just sitting there, comfy and waiting," the woman said.

Adeline swallowed and then bit her lip. "Everything looks okay?"

"Fine and dandy!" she said. "I'll show Dr. Jay the pictures and send him in. You'll talk about what will happen going forward and ask him any questions you have."

Adeline nodded, still swiping at her eyes. The doctor came in, all business, but she formed a good opinion of him. A few awkward questions were thrown in, but Adeline responded like an adult, and they left fifteen minutes later.

Then they went out into the sunshine briefly before entering the parking garage again and getting into the car, Adeline's thoughts more in a whirl than ever, her heart pounding. She glanced at Adrian when they got in, but neither seemed to know what to say. And though he started the car, he didn't leave; it was almost as though he could feel that she had something weighing on her. The air seemed especially thick in the Land Rover.

She looked at him, getting a lump in her throat. She'd been totally taken off guard back there by his reaction. But that was the way everything seemed to be with him. She'd never seen something so sexy in her life. She swallowed, tearing up, feeling a strange ache of affection for him. She bit her lip, holding his eyes, and said, "Pretty amazing, huh?"

He smiled softly, nodding.

Nothing else could really be said. Nothing could adequately capture what they were both feeling, this heady, strange sense of awe. His hand slowly found hers on the console, and he pressed it. She looked from there back up to his eyes and swallowed.

There was a long silence as the seconds ticked by, the moment expanding and holding. "Does your...offer still stand?" she asked, trying to smile just a little.

"Always," he said, eyes never straying an inch from hers.

She moistened her lips, feeling her throat tighten. Her thumb trailed lightly over his hand. "Then, yes. I'll marry you, Adrian."

THE END

Author's Note

DEAR READER,

Halt! Don't be alarmed! This journey is far from over. There are two more books in the *Torn Asunder Series*. I certainly hope the journey has been enjoyable thus far and that you will be interested to see what happens next to Shannon (a great deal!) and Adeline (a bunch!).

One thing I must note is that I took historical license with the date of Rose O'Neal Greenhow's arrest to suit my own timeline. I have her placed on house arrest in November of 1861, while, in real life, those events took place in August of that year. Another thing to note is that while some of the characters were real people, most actions or words portrayed are of my own devising. However, the speeches portrayed by William Lloyd Garrison and Frederick Douglass are composed mostly of their own words.

I would like to thank my sister, Hannah, for being my first

reader always and for brutally scenting out my literary weaknesses and knowing just how to fix them. I am thankful we are sympatico. We have been on this journey together since you were eleven years old, and you know this would not be possible without you.

Thank you also to my brother, Matt, for whose support and encouragement through the considerable ordeals of law school and the Bar Exam I cannot sufficiently express my gratitude. Thank you, in addition, for marrying Beth and giving us a wonderful addition to our family, and for having Catherine, the light of our lives.

Thanks to my mom for her skillful editing and sharp eye for anything remotely smacking of the wrong era. And thank you to both my mom and dad for always encouraging, supporting, and loving me selflessly. Your sacrifice through the years has been boundless.

Thank you to my Lord and Savior, my stronghold, who has shown me what freedom looks like. All I am and all I ever hope to be is because of Your transforming love.

And I would like to thank you, Dear Reader, for taking the time to read my book. You have given me an honor that I do not take lightly, and never will, as I continue writing tales which I hope you will enjoy.

TARA

Books by Tara Cowan

THE TORN ASUNDER SERIES

Southern Rain

Northern Fire

Charleston Tides

About the Author

TARA COWAN is the author of the *Torn Asunder Series*. A huge lover of all things history, she loves to travel, watch British dramas, read good fiction, and spend time with her family. An attorney, Tara lives in Tennessee and is busy writing her next novel.

Tara holds a Bachelor of Science Degree in Political Science, with minors in English and History, from Tennessee Tech University and a Doctor of Jurisprudence from the University of Tennessee College of Law.

To connect with Tara, visit her blog at
www.TeaAndRebellion.com,
follow her on Instagram @teaandrebellion_,
or find her on Facebook or Twitter.